ILLYRIAN SPRING

ALSO BY ANN BRIDGE

NOVELS

Peking Picnic
The Ginger Griffin
Enchanter's Nightshade
Four-Part Setting
A Place to Stand
Frontier Passage
Singing Waters
And Then You Came
The House at Kilmartin
The Dark Moment
The Tightening String
Permission to Resign

JULIA PROBYN SERIES

The Lighthearted Quest
The Portuguese Escape
Julia Involved
The Numbered Account
The Dangerous Islands
Emergency in the Pyrenees
The Episode at Toledo
The Malady in Madeira
Julia in Ireland

NON-FICTION

Portrait of My Mother
The Selective Traveller in Portugal
Facts and Fictions: Some Literary Recollections
Moments of Knowing

Illyrian Spring

ANN BRIDGE

DAUNT BOOKS

This edition first published in 2012 by
Daunt Books
83 Marylebone High Street
London W1U 4QW

First published in Great Britain in 1935
by Chatto & Windus

A CIP catalogue record for this title is available from the British Library.

ISBN 978 1 907970 07 8

Typeset by Antony Gray
Printed and bound by T J International Ltd,
Padstow, Cornwall

www.dauntbooks.co.uk

To all the Linnets
To one Nicholas
and to Frances and Patrick

AUTHOR'S NOTE

The spelling of the name Komolac has presented something of a problem. On the spot it is called 'Komolatch'; this pronunciation would properly demand an accent on the final c. The best Yugo-Slav authorities, however, leave the c unaccented, and I have followed their usage.

A.B.

Place names in Illyrian Spring

Pola	Pula
Spalato	Split
Traü or Trogir	Trogir
Ragusa	Dubrovnik
Salona	Solin
Clissa	Klis
River Giadro	Rijeka (river) Jadro
Mount Mossor	Brdo (mountain) Mossor
The Stradone	Stradun
Monte Sergio	Monte Srdo
Mont Peline	Peline
Porta Ploce	Luka (gate) Ploce
Porta Pile	Luka Pile
River Ombla	Rjeka Ombla
The Borgo	Tro
Piazza delle Erbe	(marketplace) Gunduliceva Poljana
Bocche di Cattaro	Boka Kotorska
Cannosa	Trsteno
San Biagio	(St Blaise) Sveti Vlano
Duomo	Dom or Katedrala
San Salvatore	Sveti Spa
Dance Chapel	Dance

ONE

Lady Kilmichael took her seat in the boat train at Victoria hurriedly, opened *The Times*, and hid behind it. When another passenger got into the carriage, she peeped out furtively to see who it was – but it was only an archidiaconal-looking clergyman, a total stranger, and she relapsed behind *The Times* again, with a sense of guilt. Women in the early forties who have been wives and mothers for over twenty years are liable to suffer from a slight sense of guilt whenever they embark on any purely self-regarding activity; but Lady Kilmichael had better reasons than this for her desire to avoid the eyes of acquaintances on her journey. She was leaving her home, her husband and her family – possibly for good. In a way it is rather a mistake, in such circumstances, to travel by the Simplon Orient Express; but Lady Kilmichael was going to Venice, and she lived in a world which knew no other way of getting to Venice than to travel by the Simplon Orient Express. The King's Messenger, she had observed with relief, was one of the ones she didn't know.

When the train pulled out and began to lurch through the south-eastern suburbs of London, she put her paper down with a slightly increased sense of safety, and sat staring out over the chimney-pots of the poor. It was right to have come away, she told herself; there was really nothing else to do, in the circumstances. And no one really needed her any more. The boys were both at Cambridge; Nigel had his fellowship practically secure; and when Teddy had finished with college, Walter had only to lift his little finger to get him into a job. The best of being an economist, and a rich one, was that you had the commercial kings in your pocket. As for Linnet – Gina was going to chaperon Linnet this season – for what that was worth! Linnet would get on as well, or really better, without her mother. A delicate contraction emphasised Lady Kilmichael's fine clear brows at the thought of her daughter. Why, oh why, had she and Linnet got so hopelessly across one another? She loved the child, she admired and even respected her; up till a year ago she had thought Linnet very nearly perfect. And Linnet, most comfortingly, had seemed to think the same about her mother; absurdly, touchingly, undeservedly fond of her, the child had been. But for the last year, hopeless! She had tried so hard not to ask, not to grasp, not to criticise; she hardly ever did anything but praise and agree. But even that was wrong; whatever she said or did was wrong. Linnet's criticisms, Linnet's neat derision, were really what she minded most, though she hesitated to admit so much, even to herself. The fact was that Lady Kilmichael was not very good at thinking clearly. As, the suburbs left behind, the train ran smoothly and steadily across Kent, fair and complacent in its thin April green, she tried to think where she had gone wrong with Linnet. And she could not contrive to accuse herself of much. Of course she knew that, broadly speaking, it is always the mother's fault when daughters are 'difficult,' but really, what had she left undone or done amiss with the child? She *could* not see it; and, suspecting herself of moral stupidity, she relapsed into a vague sense of pain and failure.

They were familiar sensations. Walter had criticised and derided her, with a cool friendliness that was almost more wounding than real unkindness, for years. She had got accustomed to that from Walter. Of course he was very brilliant, and she was only just fairly intelligent, except in her own line. It was rather enervating, but she had more or less accepted it, from him. But when it came to trying to accept it from Linnet, her own child, she just couldn't do it. The pain had become overwhelming. Why, if she was a failure, should she stay there to eat her humiliation like bread, day in and day out? Indignant tears sprang to her eyes. No! she was right to go.

Wiping her eyes behind *The Times* again – it would be awful to let a strange parson see her cry – she restored her pretty nose skilfully, and looked resolutely out of the window. It would really be better not to think of all these things in the train; they upset one, and it was part of her careful plan that neither she nor anyone else should appear in the least upset. While Walter made up his mind, everything was to seem quite normal. She began to read *The Times* once more; glancing vaguely down the social column, a paragraph caught her eye:

> Lady Kilmichael has left England to visit her mother, Lady Grierson, at Antibes. No correspondence will be forwarded.

Oh! They had been very quick about putting it in. Well, it did look absolutely normal. And she had told Mother to expect her later, but that she was going to sketch a little first, wandering about as the whim took her. Gina had been told the same thing, and had willingly agreed to cope with Linnet; Mrs Hanbury liked and admired Linnet; she thought her strong-minded and intelligent, not like the usual run of vapid chits. And the servants had all been told the same story, and accepted it. Nobody knew – except Walter, who would know most definitely when he came back from New York next week and got her letter. But by then she would be clear away, in Dalmatia, which no one had ever heard of and where nobody ever went. She looked again at the decorous paragraph in *The Times*, with a certain satisfaction in the completeness of her arrangements. All perfectly normal.

But in her comfortable room at her Aunt Gina's, Linnet was at that moment writing to her dearest friend as follows:

I'm here. Mums has gone abroad. She has given out that she is going to Gags at Antibes, but it's my private belief that she has rootled off alone to paint somewhere, and that she won't come back for a good long time. She and Poppy have got frightfully on each other's nerves. This is to be kept *entirely under your hat*, and I know I can rely on you, but I think Mums has heard a bit too much lately about Our Mrs Barum. I don't myself believe there's anything *in* it, but Poppy is a most frightful fool about some things, and doesn't seem to see that Mums might well think there was, the way he trails the woman round and parades her intelligence. Personally I don't think women should *be* economists; it makes them awful to look at; and those professional women are nearly always the most frightful vamps at heart – haven't you noticed it? I don't know what means they use.

Poor Mums – I am sorry for her. She and Poppy are both darlings really, but *so* incompetent about one another. And really it will be a bit of a relief to be with Aunt G. this season. I don't know *why* I find those two such a strain – Mums especially. She *doesn't* interfere, she *doesn't* cut one out with one's boyfriends, like your hag of an Aunt does poor Angela; and she's pretty good about one's clothes and hair. I give her all that. But she *watches* one. I think what I can't bear is her trying to say the right thing to me, and waiting to see if she has – and then thinking she hasn't. Whereas Aunt G. doesn't give a blow for me, or *what* I think or feel – so restful.

Thus casually, thus directly, the rising generation put its scarlet-tipped finger on the sorest secret spot in the older generation's mind. On the Channel steamer, wrapped in a white coat of clipped lambskin, standing at the rail where the sea-wind made one's eyes stream anyhow, Lady Kilmichael stared at the pearly receding buttresses of the English coast and thought about Mrs Barum and Walter. There is something about crossing the Channel which for people of a certain type (and especially for the non-seasick) promotes melancholy reflections, or deeper reflections anyhow. One leaves one's home so definitely by sea! No crossing of a land frontier gives the same sense of severance. Those white cliffs, fading mistily behind her in the April sunshine, made Grace Kilmichael wonder if she were really leaving England for good.

It all depended on what Walter decided. If – if he really *did* care about Rose Barum, she wouldn't stand in his way. It was so glaringly indecent to hold on to one's husband if he wanted someone else. The trouble was that she didn't know what Walter did want, and this was one of those questions you really *couldn't* ask. Perhaps Walter would merely have said, coldly, that she had worked herself up. She ought to have been able to tell by observation, but she *couldn't* bring herself to observe! She simply looked the other way – had been looking the other way for months now. And anyhow Walter was so undemonstrative, so terribly detached – he was a bad subject for observation. Rose Barum – her mind, in pain, shifted unwillingly to Rose Barum – she seemed a strange person to be attractive. In spite of her dark complexion – naughty Linnet would call her 'the swarthy phenomenon,' because Walter had once said that Mrs Barum's brain was a phenomenon in a woman – she wasn't a Jewess; only married to a Jew. That was the worst of being an economist, Lady Kilmichael thought – Jews sort of cropped up all round you. No – that was a Nazi way of thinking; she ought not to think that. She must be fair. Only Mrs Barum was really *plain*; and she was worse than plain, she was rather fat, and hadn't the wits to realise that fat women ought to wear their clothes very loose, to look at all possible. Her sleeves! (Lady Kilmichael's expression at that moment became one of very decided distaste – the irrational and unconscious contempt of the slender woman for the stout.) And her voice, so metallic and loud, enunciating facts about currency in dominating streams at the dinner table; and her jerky, abrupt manner. No one *could* imagine her the sort of person to attract Walter. But she was incredibly able, she worked like a horse, he said – no doubt she was very useful to him. He *said* that, and one must be fair.

Better not think about Mrs Barum either; it was really such a strain going on being fair. She strolled round the deck, went below and attended to her face, came on deck again. She was relieved when they manoeuvred into port, and she could think about the Customs and find her sleeper, and pay a huge tip to get it changed, because it was over the axle. The mere sound of French in her ears, the blue-bloused porters, lightened her mood, shifted her thoughts; the sight of the white notices on the long coaches, with names which led the mind right across Europe – Milan, Trieste, Beograd, Istanbul – gave her a little thrilled sense of space and travel. At least she was going to get far away from it all, and see lovely places.

Sitting in the dining car, eating a late lunch, she watched the landscape of North France, so simplified, so definite in its greenness and whiteness, with a clearer, a more Latin light over it than England knows, compose and recompose itself into pictures which in turns cried out to be painted. Oh, no wonder the French landscapists had got where they had – further than anyone else in the world! The very countryside would teach one to paint, in France. Well, now she would be able to paint, as much as she liked, and without perpetual teasing comments; as soon as she felt like it, she would get her things from Mother's and begin again. But for the moment she would just rest, and content herself with those little line sketches of places, with a short paragraph of description, for which three American papers had made her such a startling contract. Another instance of the completeness of her arrangements, she thought, with a faint touch of complacency, that contract; for the next six months those two or three little sketches a week would cover her expenses anywhere she chose to go, and if by ill luck she did run into people, the contract would give her a marvellous excuse. It was wonderful to be so independent, at last. Not that she had ever lacked for anything, these last years – Walter gave her plenty of money; but he was so critical of how she spent it. Perhaps being an economist helped to make one economical.

Thinking about Walter, her complacency faded again. His attitude to her painting had made her really unhappy, because, look at it as she would, she could not make it seem generous; and she hated to think of Walter as ungenerous. She had been learning to be a painter when they married; he knew that, he knew it was her chosen profession. Of course she dropped it then; it was only when the boys were nearly grown up and Linnet at school, and they had become rich, and Walter himself was so often away in America or Australia, organising people's currencies and things for them, that she had really begun again; very tentatively at first. How he had laughed when he heard that she was working at the Slade! Well, she didn't mind that – at least, she was accustomed to it; it was his attitude to her success that she minded. For after two or three years at the Slade, and a few stolen periods in Moru's *atelier* in Paris, Lady Kilmichael had had a prodigious, a wholly phenomenal success. Her first important picture, 'Conversation Piece in a Garden', after being hung on the line in the Salon, had been bought by a big Paris dealer and sold to the Metropolitan Museum in New York; her second, 'Business as Usual' (inspired by Walter and some financiers smoking cigars and discussing the Gold Standard in the garden at Netherstoke), had won the 'Femina' Gold Medal, and was now being exhibited on loan in Australia. She had had the luck to create a new fashion in pictures, which had 'caught on'; she could, if she had chosen, have spent all her time now painting statesmen and beauties in their everyday clothes, beside their own herbaceous borders.

But she hadn't chosen. That was why, she thought painfully, as she sat in the train, gazing out through fresh tears at the logically simple countryside of France, it was really unfair of Walter to have been so disagreeable about her success. She had kept her painting strictly subordinated to her main job, to being a wife and mother: entertaining economists for Walter, and chits for the boys; spending the holidays with them and with Linnet. It wasn't as though she had neglected all that. And she had called herself 'Grace Stanway', her middle name, not Grace Kilmichael, and kept her growing fame hidden as well as she could. But Walter hadn't shown the pleasure she expected at this success which had come on her like something out of a fairy tale; he had been tepid, he had been teasing. 'Where is your Mother?' she would hear him say to Linnet, in his rich cultivated voice, coming in – 'in pursuit of Art, I suppose?' 'Well Grace, how are the masterpieces getting on?' he would ask her. And that made her feel guilty; try as she would, she couldn't free herself from her dependence on Walter's judgement and on her family's attitude. Even Linnet, in these last unhappy months, had teased her about her painting, been wittily derisive, following her Father's example. The boys were merely indifferent, except to the benefits which flowed from her work. 'Buck up and finish the old picture, Mums darling – I want a new car' was their very uncomplicated line. They gazed dumbly at her work on the easel, but raced off to the Academy to count the crowds in front of it when it was hung, at last, there too. 'Well done the jolly old public – you couldn't get near Mum's latest spot of horticulture,' they would proclaim triumphantly on their return. 'Do you like it, darling?' she would say sometimes, wistfully, to Teddy, turning from a nearly completed canvas to wipe her fingers on a rag, when the first gong summoned her, distractingly, to get ready for luncheon. 'Looks all right to me – when shall you finish it?' Teddy would answer. 'Buck up and clean yourself, Miss Stanway; you know you're coming to Hurlingham this afternoon,' he would say, pushing her towards the door. Oh, the boys were rather sweet – a smile crept round her faintly, correctly reddened mouth at the thought of the boys; they weren't very interested, but there was no edge on their teasing.

So all across France, lying more picture-like than ever in the deepening afternoon light, she continued her reminiscent argument with herself; now wondering, with Walter as with Linnet, how she was in fault, where she had gone wrong, how failed him, to bring things to this unhappy pass, now thinking with faint resentment that she had done all she could; till the white dome of the Sacré Coeur loomed up on the hill above the city's haze, like a snow-mountain or a gigantic pearl, and she knew that they were nearing Paris. She looked at it with the usual emotions – astonishment at its beauty, its height, and pleasure at the mere thought it always brought of being again in Paris, which she loved. She looked at her watch – there *might* just be time to get round to Rosenthal's Gallery and see those new things of Gillani's. She rang the bell for the sleeping-car attendant and told him that she would rejoin the train at the Gare de Lyon. The attendant, remembering the tip he had received at Boulogne, bowed and promised to lock Madame's carriage.

As Lady Kilmichael walked out through the Nord station to get a taxi, she looked as little like the common conception of an artist as can well be imagined. Her dark clothes were of that distinguished simplicity, so unobtrusive as almost to render the wearer invisible, which well-bred women affect for the street; only her height and slenderness marked her out in any way from any hundred of other well-dressed, quietly good-looking, grey-eyed Englishwomen, with nice complexions and faultless hair.

While the taxi rattled through the sunny streets of Paris, noisy with a different noise, busy with a different liveliness from the streets of London, she sniffed the air, with its burden of unwonted smells, and her spirits rose a little. Delicious Paris! And it would be nice to see Gillani's stuff. But at the Rosenthal Gallery disappointment awaited her. The doors were closed; a vast limousine glittered, rich and sombre, before them. As she turned away, with the curious sense of incredulity which attends an unexpected disappointment, the door half-opened, and a short elderly man, with a grizzled well-trimmed beard and pince-nez, came out. He glanced at her, looked again, brightened into a positive effulgence of delighted recognition and came up to her, hat in hand. '*Mademoiselle Stanway! Quel plaisir inattendu!*' With a start she recognised M. Breuil, the dealer who occupied himself, to use his own phrase, with her pictures.

M. Breuil was one of those dealers who are something more than the mere name implies. He was something of a critic and a genuine connoisseur as well; he had a gallery of his own; he discovered painters, and if he thought well, 'made' them. He had discovered and 'made' Miss Stanway, rescuing her work from the degrading nullity of the Salon and placing it with success in select shows of modern art in his own gallery, and in London; he sold it cleverly. He knew quite well that it was not *absolutely* first-class – if it had been, it would have been far harder to sell; but she had the gift, undoubtedly, Mlle Stanway; she was a very fluent artist; and he had made of her a person to be reckoned with. She did far too little work – but that, too, kept prices up. M. Breuil himself was emphatically also a person to be reckoned with. Now, as he stood talking to Lady Kilmichael on the steps of Rosenthal's, while his immense limousine purred below, other late departers from the gallery pointed him out to one another in respectful undertones – '*C'est le vieux Breuil, celui-là aux cheveux gris*'; and '*Tiens!*' said their hearers, impressed.

M. Breuil was charmed to see 'Miss Stanway.' He had a great deal to say, and said it very fast indeed, in rather charming guttural tones. He had no idea that she was in Paris; she must come tomorrow and see how well 'Afternoon Tea' looked in his new show; it was having a success formidable and unheard-of – moreover, he had a lot of commissions for her. Could she lunch with him tomorrow? It was some time before Lady Kilmichael could get in enough words at a stretch to make him understand that she was not, strictly speaking, in Paris at all, but passing through – leaving, indeed, in under three hours. At this desolating intelligence M. Breuil became Napoleonic. In that case, he said, leading her down the steps, they must at once talk business; shepherding her into the car, he swept her off to his gallery for a glass of sherry; drinking the sherry, still talking to her, he nevertheless contrived to convey to his factotum precise instructions about a restaurant, a table and an early dinner of three courses. And would she, he asked, allow him also to invite Count Schiaparelli? Who was insistent, determined, that he must have a Stanway of his wife, his son and his daughter-in-law, in their miraculous garden outside Tours.

Lady Kilmichael declined the Count, with unusual firmness. She was tired, her toilette was unsuitable, her plans uncertain. M. Breuil must tell her about it, and she would think, and write. Then a picture caught her eye, and she rose and went over to it, glass in hand – surely, she said, this was someone new? And immediately she was engulfed in the delightful business of appreciating, criticising, seeing and enjoying the work of others, with a very acute connoisseur beside her. Back again in this happy familiar world, all her faculties expanded; here she was not stupid or a failure; the ferocity with which M. Breuil controverted some of her opinions was in itself the sincerest flattery. And there was plenty of the more direct thing too. Over the very perfect little dinner to which the limousine presently bore them off, M.

Breuil told her of the advance in her latest work, the greater fluidity and smoothness in her grouping, the more assured treatment of the figures and characterisation. '*Cela avance – de toile en toile, il y a des progrès – même très marqués,*' he averred. And now, in Italy, what was she going to paint? How many pictures would she do? He had a little plan – for a one-man show of her work next winter, in his smaller gallery, combined with a big show – a collection of the later Impressionists. The collection was an important one; to be associated with it would advertise her yet more; success was assured, '*mais cela rehaussera encore plus les prix*'; buyers would be there from all over the world. (M. Breuil was a man of business as well as a connoisseur.)

He was, therefore, the more shocked at his client's vagueness and unpracticalness when she told him that for the next few weeks she did not mean to paint. '*Pas une toile!*' she declared, to his horror. The little sketches for the American papers he derided as sheer waste of time – '*à moins que vous ne travaillez un peu votre architecture. C'est là que vous manquez un peu de force, d'assurance.*' But she must rest, she told him – later on, presently, she would paint again – might even come back to Paris to do the Schiaparelli family. Ah well, to rest, M. Breuil understood the necessity; he too was *surmené*; his bronchitis had afflicted him this winter; he was going on a cruise, very soon – '*le médecin y insiste.*' To sustain her on her journey, he made the *maître d'hôtel* put up a special flask of '75 brandy; when they arrived at the station the factotum was waiting at the door of her coach with an immense bouquet of white orchids and red roses. M. Breuil kissed her hand in farewell, and the sleeping-car attendant ushered her, flowers and all, into her sleeper. Lady Kilmichael, sitting down, suddenly caught sight of *The Times* lying on the seat. She remembered how she had hidden her tears behind it only that morning, in the train from Victoria. Oddly enough, she did not feel in the least like crying now.

TWO

The great figure of the Madonna dominates the apse of the basilica at Torcello, her black draperies sweeping downwards across the golden mosaic curve of the semi-dome, mosaic tears falling down her pale and tragic face. The figure is so vast, its unrelieved black so solitary, there in the golden dome, as to make it one of the most moving things in the world. So Grace Kilmichael thought, sitting in the empty church staring at it, her Ruskin in her hand; she found herself pondering on why Ruskin, who was so moved by Torcello, had so caught the whole touching wonder of the place, should have devoted pages to the pulpit, and barely mentioned the Virgin! She had been reading the great chapter that morning as she rowed across from Venice in a gondola, past Murano, past Burano; now looking ahead to the pale confusion of low shores and dim hills, now looking backwards to the outline of Venice itself, a clear tracery of spires and domes etched above the floor of the sea. People could make fun of Ruskin as much as they liked, but if some of his art criticism was nonsense, it was noble nonsense, and that chapter one of the great splendours of English prose. Book in hand, she had spent the morning wandering round the island and climbing the Campanile, trying to make the neat buildings of today – the small Museum, the house which proffers coffee down on the narrow *fondamento* where the gondolas tie up – fit in with the desolation which Ruskin found and described. She couldn't do it, really – except for the two churches, it was all too different; and presently she gave up the attempt and simply surrendered herself to the lost and lazy charm of the place – the wild rosemary scenting the muddy shores, the wild asparagus feathering over the still waters of the narrow inlets, the peasants cutting hay in the scraps of meadow between the buildings. The scythe-blades sweeping down the small bright familiar flowers, among fragments of stone and marble carved in strange shapes, gave her an idea for a picture, and she made one or two careful studies – it was *really* a pity she had brought no painting things, sent them all to Antibes. If only she had even some watercolours to make notes! While she sketched, the peasants came and looked on, and said '*Molto bene!*' loudly and cheerfully; a very old man, warming his frail body in the sun, leant on a stick beside her and told her that he was over ninety. Lady Kilmichael, sketching away, gave him a lira and a cigarette, and told him that her children's *Nonno* was of the same age; she felt warmly to the old man, he reminded her of Walter's father, whom she loved dearly.

Now and again a motor launch arrived from Venice, and the sunny isolation of this quiet friendly place was broken by an influx of tourists, who were swept breathlessly through both churches, through the museum, and off again. They appeared to be allowed forty minutes in which to 'do' Torcello. Each time, when they had gone, and only the voices of the peasants and the swish of the scythes broke the sunny stillness, Lady Kilmichael settled down into a deepened sense of contentment. She had been here for hours, and felt almost an inhabitant compared to the tourists on the launches. Altogether, that morning, she was content. This journey was being rather a success. Tucked away in an obscure pension overlooking the Giudecca, she had evaded all acquaintances; even her friend Lady Roseneath, who had a Palazzo on the Grand Canal in which she collected all visitors to Venice. She had had a narrow escape, though, from Lady Roseneath one day, in the Merceria; and only saved herself by nipping very swiftly into a small dark shop, and bending her head over a counterful of brightly coloured braces, till all danger was past. She had spent a happy week, sightseeing, pottering and sketching; Venice was marvellous, her freedom more marvellous still. And the paintings! How small, as an artist, they made one feel! Her little trumpery people in their bright garden settings, nothing to them but the contrast of their modernity of clothes and attitude with the perennial, the timeless and effortless perfection of the flowers – what were they in comparison to the maturity of conception exhibited by these grave Madonnas and wise-lipped Doges? Feeling small, Grace Kilmichael felt happy – she was like that; especially since there was nothing personal in the noble superiority of Tintoretto and Bellini, no deliberate putting of her down. And remembering some laughing flick of Walter's, she would wince then – but catching sight of another glorious picture, she would forget Walter and go and stand before it, lost in pleasure.

The freedom was really the most astonishing part. When she had ricked her neck for some time examining a ceiling panel, one day in the Ducal Palace, she noticed an elderly German in spectacles quietly lying on his back on the floor, observing the ceiling in comfort. Lady Kilmichael had not the courage to follow his example there and then, but she went early next morning, when the place was nearly empty, and rather timidly lay down on *her* back. It was perfect! One rested, and one saw. And no one paid the smallest attention. So, unhurried and unscolded, Lady Kilmichael lay down all over Venice to gaze at ceilings – and whenever she did so she tasted her freedom triumphantly. For what *would* Walter or Linnet have said?

But when she had eaten a belated lunch at Torcello, in a sunny corner, and went to look at the church, somehow or other the sight of the great Madonna had dimmed her contentment, and brought back the recollection of her private disquiets. Sitting there now, forgetting Ruskin and his views on pulpits, she thought of Walter. Walter must be back by now – back for two or three days. He would have got her letter. She wondered what he would make of it – what his answer would be. A sudden chill of fear ran over her, startling her by its violence – suppose he did take her at her word, and ended the thing? For a moment her world rocked about her – her safe, her accustomed world, of the boys and Linnet, and Walter and his tiresomeness and his amusingness, the whole fabric of her life. To lose all that was not conceivable. And in her panic she felt that she had been mad to write, mad to come away.

She pulled herself together presently, and summoned pride to her aid. No – if Walter wanted Rose Barum or really couldn't bear her, Grace, she was better away. She would wait, and not write – do nothing, let it all slide. She was *very* happy here, she told herself – happier than she had been for years. She would not worry. And she began to study the Madonna again, conscientiously. But the Madonna is not the best of companions for wives and mothers who have abandoned their families – immense, still, sorrow-stricken and quietly accepting sorrow, there she stands – timeless, the mother who cannot escape her motherhood, and would not if she could. And looking at her, Lady Kilmichael, instead of thinking about Byzantine tendencies in art, as she had meant to do, began to think about Linnet. She hoped the child was happy with Gina, and Gina being *reasonably* careful about what she did – not letting her motor too wildly with that headlong Herbert boy, in his car with the long nose – she didn't really at all like that boy; and discouraging her from going to dinner without her stockings in the wrong houses – at Lady Netherhampton's, for example. Darling Linnet! She was so lovely and so sweet, but she knew so little, really. Oh, how she hoped she was all right.

Lady Kilmichael was at all times subject to these rushes of maternal feeling, even unprompted by the presence of the Madonna; and they generally issued in an impulse to do something for one of the children. But the older children get, the more difficult it is to find anything which they really at all *want* done for them, and the enfeebled impulse is liable to be finally extinguished in a letter – frequently a letter which arouses a faint, if amused, irritation in the recipient. The Edwardian mother who wrote to her soldier son, sitting fever-ridden and solitary among his black troops in the jungles of Nigeria –'I hope, my dearest boy, you aren't going in for too much of that horrid betting and gambling,' has her parallels today, and closer home.

Lady Kilmichael, however, was fortunate in finding almost at once, and even in so improbable a place as Torcello, something which she could do, not for Linnet, but for Nigel. Emerging from the high-lit chill of the basilica into the hot and brilliant sunshine outside, she went round with a vague intention of making a drawing of the apse – pottered through the priest's garden, where among the trim fruit trees and beds of salads she found no quite appropriate position for a sketch, and so passed out into the grassy meadow beyond. There, having found the perfect aspect, she looked about for something to sit on among the fragments of marble heaped casually at the edge of the field. And there, to her immense astonishment, she came on one of Nigel's stones. It was a long narrow piece of greyish *pietra dura*, broken off at one end, and carved throughout its length in a curious intricate scroll pattern of flat thongs plaited and twisted in and out of one another, like immensely elaborate basket-work, forming a general design of squares, circles and triangles. It was, so far as Lady Kilmichael could see, exactly like the patterns on those incised tomb slabs and crosses of the Western Highlands of which Nigel was always making rubbings on linen and 'squeezes' in Barcelona paper. Nigel was a good deal of an archaeologist, and some of his mother's happiest days had been spent under the sycamores and ash trees of small lonely West Highland churchyards, clearing the turf and nettles off half-buried stones, scrubbing them clean with a brush and the bucket out of the Minister's kitchen; or on windy days holding the length of calico down firmly, while Nigel rubbed and rubbed with a piece of cobbler's wax. But she had always been led to suppose that these stones were peculiar to the West Coast of Scotland and the Isle of Man, save for a few Irish crosses showing the same type of design – and here in Italy, at Torcello, she suddenly found one of the most familiar patterns of all. She could not be mistaken – she had seen far too many rubbings, scrubbed far too many stones herself. It was most surprising and unexpected. Nigel would be thrilled. But knowing Nigel's Cambridge caution, she realised that nothing short of ocular demonstration would convince him; and abandoning the apse, she sat down on a broken capital covered with acanthus leaves, and began to make a sketch of the scroll-work stone, happy again to be doing something for one of the children.

But while Lady Kilmichael was sketching in Torcello, Linnet in London was again writing to her best friend:

> I'm sure I was right about Mums, and that there *is* some funny business going on. For one thing, she hasn't written, and you know how terrifically they write as a rule. And when Poppy got back the other day, he came flying round here in no end of a well-restrained flap – Where's your Mother? I told him she'd gone to Gags, though I didn't believe it; and as a matter of fact she hasn't. Because when I popped in yesterday for some clothes, Grimes said, Would I take a foreign telegram for the master over the instrument? – silly old porpoise, he's getting so deaf, he's useless on the telephone. And it was from Gags – 'Expecting Grace any day, but no address.' So you see he must have wired. Meanwhile I gather our Rose is holding his hand – Grimes asked if I should be staying to lunch, and when I asked if Poppy was alone, he made his super-butler

face and said 'Mrs Barum was expected.' So I beat it. How I loathe that woman! I hope Mums will have the guts to stick it out for a good long time, till she gets rubbed off; I can't believe that will last forever. But Mums is so terribly soft – and I daresay that fidgets Poppy just like it does me.

The drawing of the stone took longer than Grace Kilmichael expected. It was extraordinarily difficult to get all those complicated interlacings correct. As she sat concentrated on her work, she was made vaguely aware of the arrival of yet another launch by a distant swirl of tourists round the two churches, and of voices in the distance other than the pleasant nasal tones of the peasants. But the tourists seldom came round the east end of the basilica, and she was startled when someone close by said – 'I beg your pardon, but could you bear to shift for a moment?'

She looked up. A young man without a hat, holding a tripod camera in one hand, was standing a few yards behind her.

'I want to get the apse from just here, and a figure in front will dwarf it,' said the young man explanatorily. 'Do you mind?' He was civil, but not particularly apologetic, she noticed; he spoke in a peculiar impersonal, rather drawling tone.

'No, of course not,' she said, rising and moving away. But it was getting late, and she wanted to go on with her drawing; she began to tug at the piece of carved stone, to shift it to another position, out of the camera's line of fire. 'Here, let me help,' said the young man abruptly, and together they lifted the stone a few feet to one side, and Lady Kilmichael sat down to work again. The young man, as she did so, glanced at her sketchbook, and then at the stone. 'You've got that wrong,' he said, in that same impersonal voice; 'look – here' – he touched the drawing with his finger.

'Oh, so I have,' said Lady Kilmichael. 'Thank you.' She rubbed that piece out, and began it afresh, while the young man paced, and peered, and clicked; she assumed that the interruption was over. But presently he came up to her again.

'I'll put it back for you now,' he said.

'Oh no, thank you – it's all right here,' she answered.

'But I want to get another from this side,' said the young man, in the same explanatory and unapologetic manner, 'and a figure dwarfs it completely.'

'Oh, very well,' said Lady Kilmichael – he was rather an off-hand young man, she thought, though his clothes and speech appeared to belong to the class to which she was accustomed. While he moved the stone back to its old place, she looked at him more carefully. He was very young, probably not more than twenty-two, she decided, with blue eyes and a mop of curly straw-coloured hair; his face was burned a bright raspberry pink by the sun, a most unbecoming combination; in addition, this youthful face, which should have been cheerful, wore a markedly dissatisfied expression. He was not a very taking person, she felt. But while Lady Kilmichael looked at the young man, the young man, when she reseated herself amid mutual and rather cold thanks, looked at her sketchbook. 'You've got it wrong *again*,' he exclaimed. 'Don't you see? That one goes under, not over – and then out here – look, so.'

'So it does. How stupid of me,' said Lady Kilmichael, blushing a little – she still blushed, in spite of her forty-two years, when anything embarrassed her. She set to work once more, while the dissatisfied young man returned to his photography; the stone was a horrible thing to draw – it was more like mathematics than anything else, with all those interlacing lines. When she got one right, it made another come wrong. However, that was better now. She held her sketchbook away, examining it – and suddenly found the young man by her side.

'No, I'm not going to ask you to move any more,' he said, with a faint grin. 'I've done now. I came to say Thank you.' He glanced at the drawing and then at the stone. 'Oh, but look here,' he burst out, '*now* you haven't got it right! This is hopeless!' He pulled out a pencil, and taking the book from her, drew a couple of lines rapidly. 'There – like that – and here – so.'

Lady Kilmichael watched him 'I can't think why I can't get it right,' she said rather regretfully, watching his assured strokes.

'Nor can I,' said the young man, looking as he spoke at the stone – 'perhaps you're not accustomed to drawing. Oh – you've got that bit wrong too. Shall I do it for you?' he said, looking now at her. 'It won't take me long, and these things are no good unless they're done accurately.'

Lady Kilmichael agreed to both these propositions, and the young man sat down and began to draw the stone with quick, careful strokes – dotting, measuring and planning as he went. Grace looked on, a little envious of his precision, a little amused at his suggestion that she was not accustomed to drawing. He was an odd creature – so young, so self-assured. She noticed that the shadows were lengthening; the air was getting cooler, and the marshy smell of the inlets came strongly to them as they sat; it would soon be time to be starting back, she thought regretfully. Several times she heard an impatient hooting from beyond the churches, but she paid no attention, and presently it ceased. The young man, too, found the stone a bit of a teaser, it seemed; even he had to make one or two erasures – it took him longer than she expected. But at last it was done to his satisfaction, and he gave her back the book. While she thanked him, he glanced at his watch.

'Lord! The launch!' he exclaimed in dismay. 'It should have gone half an hour ago.' And before she could utter a word he snatched up his camera and was off, running like a deer across the meadow, till he disappeared round the corner of the basilica.

Lady Kilmichael followed more slowly, feeling guilty. Probably those hoots had represented the cluckings of the launch over its lost passenger. She had never thought of that at the time. Sure enough, when she got down to the *fondamento* no launch was visible, and the young man was standing disconsolate in the centre of a gesticulating group which included her two *gondolieri.* 'It's gone – and it seems it was the last today,' he said as she approached – and now his red face under the yellow hair looked not only dissatisfied but tragic.

'You can come back with me – I have a gondola,' said Lady Kilmichael.

'How long will that take?' the young man asked gloomily.

Two hours, she told him.

'My miserable aunt! I shall be late for dinner again,' he said, more gloomily than ever. 'I was late yesterday too,' he added.

Lady Kilmichael was not sure whether the 'miserable aunt' was a person or an ejaculation, but did not ask. She apologised and commiserated, but there was nothing to be done; it was already nearly seven and nothing could get the young man back to Venice in time for dinner at eight. 'Well, I must lump it,' he said dejectedly. And then all of a sudden something in the whole situation seemed to amuse him. He put his head on one side, looked full at Lady Kilmichael, and laughed. 'What a happy day!' he said.

THREE

Italians have the amiable trait of always being willing to do a fellow tradesman a good turn at someone else's expense, and this was doubtless the motive which prompted Giovanni, the gondolier, to suggest to Lady Kilmichael that before leaving the Signora should take a cup of coffee at the little *trattoria* just across the inlet from the landing stage. 'Good idea,' said the young man when she put this suggestion to him.

Grace was hungry, and glad of his concurrence; they would not get back to Venice much before nine in any case. Giovanni poled them across the few yards of still water, shattering the reflections of the white buildings, the pink roofs and the soft green hedges of tea plant which bordered the little inlet, to the inn, where they sat under a trellis of vines in the garden. It was very still; the water lapped against the stonework below them; further down the inlet a moorhen paddled across from the greenery on one side to the greenery on the other; when the disturbance created by the gondola's passage had subsided, the pinkish shape of Santa Fosca, with its roof of rayed tiles so nearly matching its delicate small bricks, re-formed itself, still moving very gently, on the clear surface. While they waited for their coffee the young man looked consideringly at his companion, and said 'Why did you want a drawing of that particular stone?'

Lady Kilmichael explained about West Highland tomb slabs, and how exciting and extraordinary it was to find one of those patterns carved on a stone in Torcello. 'Of course this bit is only a detail, really – as a rule the tombstones have a sword down the middle for a man, or a cross for an ecclesiastic, with this scrolly stuff at the sides; and sometimes there's a galley at the foot, or a book and shears. And the later ones even have figures, and animals, like stags and hounds.' She further explained how, without calico, it was impossible to make a rubbing, as she would have liked to do. The young man seemed interested in all she had to say, and asked several rather intelligent questions. Of what date were the stones? Oh, fifteenth or sixteenth century, as a rule, she told him; but unless there was an inscription, as on MacMillan's Cross, they were very hard to date with any accuracy. Eventually – 'I suppose you are an archaeologist,' he said, again considering her with his head on one side. Sitting there under the trellis, with the low sun casting blue shadows from the vine leaves on her white dress, Lady Kilmichael looked no more like an archaeologist than like an artist; she had taken off her hat, and her hair, a little ruffled by the light breeze, lay in brown waves, untouched with grey, round her face; her interest in the subject of the stones had made her open her eyes very wide – she looked both pretty and animated. But she disclaimed archaeology – 'I wanted it for my son – he's the archaeologist. I don't really know anything about it.'

'You seem to know rather a lot,' said the young man. Still looking at her – 'Where's your son at school?' he asked.

'He isn't at school – he's at Cambridge.'

The young man's face of astonishment at this announcement made her laugh – a rather nice low laugh. The young man, however, did not even smile – he continued to contemplate her with unmoved gravity and said 'Well, you don't look it,' rather repressively. While they drank their coffee he asked if she had found any other fragments of the same sort of pattern elsewhere in Torcello. No – she had been all round both the basilica and Santa Fosca, and had seen no traces of it. 'What about the Museum?' he asked.

Lady Kilmichael had not been to the Museum. This the young man thought wrong – there were some good things in the

Museum. 'Let's just look round there, before we go – shall we?' he said. So they called to Giovanni, and were poled back, breaking up the reflections again. The Museum was by now closed, and the custodian trimming roses in his garden – but he was easily persuaded to reopen it when the young man, in fluent Italian, represented that the Signora was a noted archaeologist, giving her another fleeting grin as he did so. When he grinned his face lost its dissatisfied look, and became rather attractive, in spite of the deplorable combination of his red skin and yellow hair. They went in, and in the fading light gazed at the various objects, mostly Roman, which were set out in the small rooms – but there were no scroll-work patterns to be seen. Presently Lady Kilmichael came to a halt before something – the young man, who had been wandering about by himself, came up to see what she had found. 'Is that some of it?' he asked.

It was not. It was a small cinerary urn, with an inscription in lovely clear Roman lettering between two graceful wreaths. A piece was broken out of the top, so that the first two lines were incomplete. Standing by her, the young man read it:

'OLIM N . . .
NATI SUM . . .
NUNC QUIETI SUMUS
UT FUIMUS
CURA RELICTA, VALE ET TU'

It dated from the second century.

'I must copy that,' said Lady Kilmichael suddenly. But she had left her sketchbook in the gondola. 'I'll do it – I've got a book,' said the young man; 'perhaps I'd better,' he added, and grinned at her again. He pulled a small sketchbook out of his pocket, and copied the inscription, imitating the lettering, she observed, very beautifully and carefully. She stood looking on, thinking how odd he was, with his discontented face and his extraordinary assurance – she had never met anyone who asked questions so freely; she was afraid that he would ask her why she wanted that inscription copied, that he would laugh at her if she told him, and that she would feel a fool if she did not. But when he had finished he did not ask her anything – he put away his book, she tipped the custodian, and they went down and took their places in the gondola. Giovanni and his second oarsman pushed off, and once more the image of Santa Fosca in the still water was broken by their passage, while Grace Kilmichael looked her last at the beautiful reality on the shore – the lovely slope of the low roofs against the central lantern, the delicate brickwork, the slender arches and pillars – all in that strange shade of brownish pink, like a peach stone, enriched now by the evening light almost to rose colour. The young man gazed too, his face no longer discontented, but almost sad. It was only when they had passed down the inlet into the main channel leading out to the lagoon, and of all the buildings of Torcello only the Campanile showed above the grey shores, that he spoke. 'Do you mind telling me why you wanted that thing copied?'

A certain hesitancy with which the question was put surprised Lady Kilmichael – in her surprise she answered at once, truthfully: 'I had an idea that I should like the last part on my tombstone.'

The young man stared at her in silence for some moments. Then he looked away, out to the low blue horizons opening in front, to left, to right of them, as they emerged into the lagoon; when he spoke, he appeared to be addressing the distant silhouette of Burano far ahead. 'O Care left behind, to thee also farewell,' he said – 'not a bad epitaph at all.' He turned to her again – 'Why do you know Latin?' he asked, as if to change the subject.

'My Father liked us to know it,' said Lady Kilmichael. 'He said it was the only way to understand the difference between the classical and the romantic in literature,' she added, unnecessarily.

Something in the way that question about the inscription had been asked and answered had put her almost at her ease with the strange young man; his grave considering silence on the subject of her taking farewell of Care had a curious – sensitiveness was perhaps the word – about it which made her suddenly feel almost confident in speaking to him.

Now it was something quite new for Grace Kilmichael to feel in the least secure or at her ease with the young, either male or female. Like so many women of her generation, in her heart she was afraid of them. Youth nowadays has many weapons in its armoury with which to defeat middle age. The young – usually with great charm, and (outside one's own family) invariably with the utmost civility – tolerated middle age perhaps, were courteous to it, but left it feeling that they despised both it and its methods; they dismissed its sanctities with gay derision, quite unaware that they were holy – laughed their way through secret shrines of which the stricken owners were too shy even to acknowledge the existence. With all their charm and courtesy, the young contrived to make you feel small – and if you loved them, wounded you. All this had puzzled and troubled Grace Kilmichael for some time, and lately, on account of Linnet, more than ever. She did not fawn upon the young, like many of her contemporaries – partly out of a sort of moral fastidiousness, partly because she was too shy to make advances; she was friendly and kind to them, but she never felt that she really understood them, and had latterly decided that she need never hope to.

It was all so different from her own youth. Then, the middle-aged were extremely high-hat – what an expression! but Teddy always used it – about the young; they thought them foolish; 'young and foolish' was the regular phrase. And the young did not very openly protest. But now the boot was on the other foot; it was the young who thought the elderly nitwits (Teddy again!) and made their opinion very clear. As a matter of fact Grace did not think the young *were* particularly foolish – often they were rather shrewd; painfully so, indeed. Had her mother's generation been wrong about the inseparableness of youth and foolishness, or had the odium of folly in itself made her generation foolish? And were the new young right or mistaken in their assumption about the close connection between ineptitude and middle age? She never could be sure. Anyhow, one thing was certain – taking them by and large, the young had now got the upper hand (rather like servants, Lady Kilmichael thought); parents were afraid of their children's judgements, afraid of being failures with their own offspring; when things went wrong, it was the parent who suffered the pangs of humiliation, as she was doing even now over Linnet – Linnet suffered no pangs at all, that she could see. And this fear of one's children's criticism paralysed intercourse – of that she was certain.

It was therefore with considerable surprise that Lady Kilmichael found herself talking with anything like freedom to a person as young as the yellow-headed boy beside her in the gondola. Abandoning the subject of Latin, they presently began to talk about Torcello, and Lady Kilmichael, rather hesitatingly, mentioned Ruskin – she knew that Ruskin was now completely out of date. The young man had heard of Ruskin, but knew nothing about the Torcello chapter – Lady Kilmichael said he ought to read it, and when he said he would get hold of it produced the book.

'Why don't you read it to me? We've nothing on earth to do,' said the young man – 'if it's as good as you say, it ought to go well aloud.'

So she began, a little nervously at first, then as the splendour of thought and prose took its wonted hold of her, with increasing clearness and emphasis. She wanted to skip the pulpit paragraphs, but the young man would not allow this; indeed he made her read the remarks about the 'meanness and diminutiveness of the speaker' twice, with a satisfied grin. But as the sentences rolled on, magnificent in their sonorous simplicity, to the comparison of this exiles' church with a ship, an ark of refuge in the midst of the prevailing destruction, he ceased to grin, and listened quietly. As she approached the end, Grace Kilmichael nerved herself to do justice to the great closing sentence – she paused for a moment, and lifted her eyes from the book to the low marshy shores, the reaches of water between spanned with the long lines of weed-hung sea-stained poles which mark the channels. Then she read on. 'And if the stranger would yet learn in what spirit it was that the dominion of Venice was begun, and in what strength she went forth conquering and to conquer, let him not seek to estimate the wealth of her arsenals or the number of her armies, nor look upon the pageantry of her palaces, nor enter into the secrets of her councils; but let him ascend the highest tier of the stern ledges that sweep round the altar of Torcello, and then, looking as the pilot did of old along the marble ribs of the goodly temple-ship, let him repeople its veined deck with the shadows of its dead mariners, and strive to feel in himself the strength of heart that was kindled within them, when first, after the pillars of it had settled in the sand, and the roof of it had been closed against the angry sky that was still reddened by the fires of their homesteads – first, within the shelter of its knitted walls, amidst the murmur of the waves and the beating of the wings of the seabirds round the rock that was strange to them – rose that ancient hymn, in the power of their gathered voices:

> 'The Sea is His, and He made it,
> And His hands prepared the dry land.'

The young man said nothing for a little while when she had finished. Lady Kilmichael, closing the book, stole a glance at him – she was half afraid, from his silence, that this chapter which moved her so much had missed fire. But when he did speak, it was quite satisfying – 'I wish I'd read that back there in the church,' he said, waving a hand behind them.

'I did,' said Lady Kilmichael.

'I don't know why no one put me on to it,' he said, a little discontentedly.

'I thought everyone read *The Stones of Venice* here,' said Grace.

The young man did not reply to this. Presently he spoke again. 'All the same, you know, Mr Ruskin was pulling rather a long bow. How long do you suppose it took to build that church? – if it's the original one, which I should say was extremely doubtful. Ten, fifteen years? Well, the Goths or Huns must have found out some pretty slow-combustion methods for burning homesteads if the sky was still reddened with them by the time the roof was put on. What?' he said, cocking his head on one side and looking at her, with amusement on his face.

'I didn't say anything,' said Grace, feeling a little chilled.

'No, but what *do* you say?' said the young man.

Grace thought for a moment. At home she would very likely have let the case for Mr Ruskin go by default; but some unwonted impulse, as well as something disarming about the young man's smile, spurred her on to express her thought.

'I think in point of actual months and weeks, and bricks and mortar – the technical side of history – it may be as great nonsense as you think it,' she said, 'but history has an untechnical side too. Ruskin is talking, as he says himself, about the spirit in which Venice was begun – and I think that sentence probably gives as true a picture of that as could be given.'

'Of course it's amazing to do it in one sentence at all,' said the young man – 'one superb sentence!' He looked enquiringly at her – 'You don't mind my being facetious about it, do you? I'm sure you're right, or he is, about the spiritual side of history, and I don't think that nonsense, really.'

Grace said nothing. The novelty of having one of the young

show himself apologetic about making fun of the things she cared for startled her almost out of the capacity for speech. He *was* an odd young man! The next minute – 'You look cold,' he said suddenly; 'hadn't you better put a coat on?'

Lady Kilmichael thought she had better. The sun had set, and a fresh wind had sprung up from the south-west, ruffling the darkening water before them; Giovanni and his companion were straining at their long oars; little waves slapped with gay ferocity and a small cold noise against the piles which marked the channel. The young man helped her into her white lambskin coat; Giovanni nodded and grinned approvingly – '*Fa freddo,*' he observed – '*Ha ragione, il signorino.*' The young man turned with an expression of exasperation to Lady Kilmichael – 'Always the Signorino!' he said. 'It's my hair!' Lady Kilmichael looked at his hair. Its yellowness and curliness did make him look very young – perhaps she was wrong about his age. But she soon looked away again. Sky, sea and shores were, as it were, assembling and gathering themselves together for the pageant of a Venetian sunset. The whole western half of the heavens was full of a golden glow, throwing a tawny lustre on the steely blue of the wind-ruffled waters; on the mainland shore, to the north, the trees stood up, an incredible bronze-green, with blue hills behind. It was unpaintable, of course – too vast, too glorious, too violent; but her soul rose in her at the sight. In silence, as she looked, the young man waved his hand at it all, like a conductor conducting – after a few moments he spoke. 'What an orchestra!' he said. She nodded, and they rowed on, light and colour moving like music round them as they went.

Off Murano the wind dropped. Giovanni and his companion, encouraged, began to sing; Lady Kilmichael sat watching, against the faint yellow glow in the west which was all that remained of the sunset, the dark shape of Venice ahead of them, its lights drawing nearer and nearer over the water. They had been silent for some time, and she was thinking that she would soon have seen the last of her odd companion, whom she had picked up in such an odd way, when the young man put one of his abrupt questions – 'Do you look at the pictures here at all?'

'Yes, most of the time,' she answered.

'Which do you like best?'

'Tintoretto's "Paradise", in the Ducal Palace,' Grace replied, without hesitation.

'So do I – how odd. I never found anyone else before who did,' said the young man. 'It is incredibly lovely, but I thought no one but me thought so. Can you tell me why you like it so much?'

'I like the thing it describes and the way it describes it,' she answered. 'If Heaven is like anything, it's like that – a white light, and ring upon ring of faces turned up to something they adore. It's like the second movement of the Ninth Symphony – Beethoven is talking about the same place, only the music gets it even clearer.' She stopped, a little embarrassed at having said so much; it was too dark to see the young man's face. But when he answered she was reassured.

'I know the part you mean,' he said. 'I rather prefer to keep music and pictures apart, but those two do belong together.' Then she heard him chuckle. 'If it comes to that, you know, that chapter of Ruskin is like Elgar, religiosity and all.'

Grace laughed. He had to make fun of everything, but somehow he did it very painlessly; and he was quite right – Ruskin's prose *was* rather like Elgar. She admitted it. They went on talking about pictures; they were still talking about them, eagerly and in agreement, when the gondola slipped under one of the bridges on the Fondamenta Nuove and shot through the dim-lit maze of canals. The boy suggested, rather tentatively, that he should see her home; but Lady Kilmichael would not allow this; she was taking no risks, and even a stray boy had better not know where she was staying. She asked if the Piazzetta would do for him, and he said it would. Then they went on discussing pictures. Some key seemed to have been turned between them suddenly, for their conversation, so spasmodic and uncertain before, now ran like a river. The boy knew a lot – and as the gondola nosed its way in among its tethered fellows to the Piazzetta steps, Lady Kilmichael in her turn put a last question. 'Do you paint yourself?' she asked.

'No, I don't,' said the young man abruptly. He shook hands with her. 'Thank you frightfully,' he said, and sprang out. Standing on the landing stage, above the bobbing gondola, his yellow head shining in the light from a lamp behind him, he spoke again, in tones of the most extraordinary bitterness. 'But doing it is the only thing in the world I care about. Good night!' He ran up the steps and was gone.

And only then did Lady Kilmichael remember that he had never given her the copy he had made of the inscription on the cinerary urn! She would have shouted, but what could she shout? She had no idea of his name. She got out hurriedly, ran up the steps, and looked about for a yellow head. But the Piazzetta was crowded, as it usually is on a fine evening; and though she walked as far as the entrance to the Piazza, there was no sign of him. She returned to the gondola and was borne home to her little pension. Such supper as it afforded was long past, and when she had washed she went out to a minute restaurant close by, and sat at a small table on a flagged *calle*, among gondoliers and shopkeepers, and ate macaroni and salad, to the characteristic Venetian accompaniment of a clatter of feet on the flagstones, re-echoed to and fro between the high houses. And while she ate she went over the day in her mind – the solitary and beautiful row out, the loveliness of Torcello, the finding of the stone and the odd encounter with the boy, the lost inscription, and their talk on that highly conversational row home. But two things remained predominant in her thoughts – the boy's discontented expression, and the extraordinary bitterness in his voice when he told her at parting that he cared more for painting than anything else, and yet did not paint. There was some puzzle here – and she would never know the solution now. She was still thinking of this when she went to bed. It was a long time since Lady Kilmichael had expended so much speculation on any human being besides Walter, the boys, and Linnet.

FOUR

The *Adriatica* steamers, which take the traveller in the utmost comfort down the Dalmatian coast, leave Venice at the uncompromising hour of 6.30 A.M. Soon after six on a grey and chilly morning Lady Kilmichael went on board. She had postponed her departure from Venice for a few days in order to await the arrival of her painting things, for which she had telegraphed to her mother at Antibes; she had suddenly decided that she could not go on any longer without painting. She had had the things consigned to the Yugo-Slavia Express Agency's offices at Venice, and put 'No letters, please' at the end of the telegram; but of course Mother always did what she chose and not what one asked her, and when the uniformed official of the Yugo-Slavia Express Agency stepped up to her, cap in hand, and pointed out the two large packages which bore her name, he handed her also a telegram, and a long fat envelope, obviously bursting with correspondence. This put Grace into a flutter. There would certainly be a letter from Walter, and what would it say? And what should *she* say? She opened the telegram with trembling fingers, but it was only from Mother:

> Dearest child where are you and when do you think of coming here you ought really to write feel it a little inconsiderate Walter constantly telegraphing and even using telephone so disturbing and fearfully extravagant please send date of arrival or else some address to pacify W. you know how persistent he always is longing to see you of course dear child be careful of water salads in Venice thought best to send letters best love Mother.

How like Mother that was! And how letters, and still more telegrams from her always carried one back to one's own youth – right into the past, with all the old sensations of dependence, vexation and amusement. She began to stuff the many sheets of this fantastic missive back into their inadequate envelope – really, it was all very well for Mother to talk of Walter's extravagance! – thinking all at once that she must find a tip for the man, and get her luggage sent down to her cabin, and that if there was another passenger in it she would have to try and find a quiet corner somewhere where she could face that other envelope, the terrifying one with the letters in, when a rich deep voice, a familiar voice, hailed her – 'Dearest Grace, who ever would have thought of finding *you* here?' – and she turned to find herself face to face with Lady Roseneath.

This was very awkward indeed – so awkward that Lady Kilmichael entirely forgot about both letter and luggage for the moment. For she had now not only to explain her solitary presence in Venice to her old friend, but also her studied absence, for nearly a fortnight, from that old friend's hospitable palazzo; and furthermore, she must (it was essential; Lady Roseneath was a prodigious correspondent) cover her future tracks, if there were such things, from her amiable curiosity. Embracing her old friend, then, warmly, far more warmly than was usual with her, she took a lightning and unprecedented decision – to lie, and to lie copiously and efficiently. It was the only thing to do, and she did it. She was on her way, she said, to Greece (you could get to Greece from Dalmatia, she knew, even if it meant going by Brindisi, and after all she *might* go there). The contract came out, handy and pat as a cork out of a bottle – such a marvellous contract, far too good to miss; and she had always wanted to see Greece. And to slip down the Dalmatian coast by sea was such a picturesque way of going. By the time the inevitable reproaches came, Lady Kilmichael had so warmed to her unwonted occupation of telling fibs that she produced a statement about 'only a few nights; such a terrible headache after the train; so much to see – she simply *had* to do one or two sketches' (the contract again) as glibly as if it had been the truth. Indeed, she was appalled to find how well she lied. Lady Roseneath accepted it all; she was deeply impressed by the contract – 'My dear, you're so clever!' she said admiringly. She was not nearly so pertinacious in her questions, either, as Grace had feared, and after a few almost perfunctory enquiries for dear Walter and darling Linnet, enquiries which were easily parried, she allowed the reason for this lack of curiosity to appear. Lady Roseneath had a grievance. A nephew was staying with her – 'Louise Humphries's boy; you know – she married the General; a most tiresome, uncompromising man. Retired now, of course – and *that's* the greatest bore for Louise; it wasn't so bad when he was in India, or even at the War Office, but now he's at home all day long, and my dear! the life he leads them all!'

Lady Kilmichael made a sound indicative of comprehension, and tried to slip a tip into the expectant goldcuffed hand of the Yugo-Slavia Express Agency man without relaxing her appearance of polite attention – time was passing, and she was not even sure if all her luggage had come on board. She managed the tip, while Lady Roseneath flowed on about her nephew – such nonsense, going to Dalmatia – as if there weren't plenty of architecture to see in Venice! And now that she had got up – at this hour! – to see him off, of course he had gone and disappeared – Heaven knew where! She hoped he *was* on board. 'He's too impossibly vague and scrambly, my dear – do see him safely off at Spalato. And *so* self-centred and tiresome. All these last few days he's been doing – imagine what? Sitting in the lounges of hotels looking for some girl he met on one of his expeditions! Out for lunch, out for tea – wouldn't come to either of my receptions this week; no, he must find this girl. Too absurd.'

All this time, as she spoke, Lady Roseneath was surveying the crowd on deck – passengers, hotel porters, officers of the ship smartly uniformed in white – vainly trying to catch sight of her strayed nephew. The porters now began to leave, but still she talked on.

'Do be kind to him. Poor boy, I pity him really. The fact is, he's got—'

'Booooop!' went the siren of the vessel, drowning her voice; her mouth continued to move, but what her nephew had got was lost on Lady Kilmichael. 'Oughtn't you to go ashore?' Grace suggested, when the deafening noise was over.

'Oh, there's no hurry – they're very slow on these boats. Well, as you see, that's what's the matter with him, and of course, as a result, he's lost—'

'Boooooooop!' went the siren again – and again Lady Roseneath's lips moved in serene futility against the din, leaving Grace as completely uninformed about what the nephew had lost as she was about what he had got. When the siren ceased, Lady Roseneath interrupted her own discourse with a sudden cry – 'Nicholas! Nicholas!' and made an eager pounce among the crowd. 'Here he is!' she said triumphantly, catching a figure by the arm – 'Nicholas, I want to introduce you to my friend Lady Kilmichael.' And she led up the young man from Torcello.

Startled, Grace held out her hand. Looking as discontented as ever, the young man took it; he said 'How do you do?' without a sign of recognition – then, very deliberately, closed one eye, the eye furthest from Lady Roseneath.

The siren hooted again. An officer came up and interrupted Lady Roseneath's final farewells – still talking, she was somehow bustled off the ship. Lady Kilmichael, shivering a little in her white coat, stood at the rail for a few moments, and waved politely – then she turned away. Now she really must get to her cabin and face that envelope and its contents. But she found the boy at her elbow at once.

'This is distinct luck,' he said, looking much less discontented. 'I thought I'd lost you for good, and should never be able to give you this' – and pulling out a pocketbook, he handed her the copy of the inscription. 'I forgot it that night – we were talking so,' he went on. 'I did a bit of a search for you, but the hotels in Venice were full of tall women in white woolly coats, and none of them were you!' He grinned, reminiscently. 'I maddened Aunt a good deal about you. Where were you? Did you go away?'

'No, I was at my pension,' said Grace, amused in spite of her preoccupation to find herself the object of the search which had caused Lady Roseneath so much annoyance, and also by the boy's casual and minimising account of it.

'It must have been a very obscure pension,' said the boy. Grace could not help smiling – so he had tried the pensions too!

'I am very sorry you should have taken so much trouble,' she said. 'You shouldn't have bothered.'

'I thought you wanted the thing,' said he, looking discontented again.

'I did – very much; I'm so glad to have it at last,' she said hastily – he really mustn't be disappointed. 'Thank you *very* much.' And again she started towards the steps which led down towards the cabins. The boy followed – wasn't she coming to have some breakfast? Lady Kilmichael said no, not yet; she was going to find her cabin. 'Are you going to Trieste?' he called after her, as she descended the steps.

'No, to Spalato,' she answered, and escaped.

Sitting on the bed in her white-panelled cabin, of which she proved to be the sole occupant, Lady Kilmichael opened the fat envelope. Yes – there was a letter from Walter, and one from

Linnet too. With a nervous need to fortify herself against the unknown, she lit a cigarette; then rose, pulled off her hat and straightened her hair. A strange mixture of emotions swept through her in those moments; fear, the same fear that had seized her in the basilica at Torcello, mixed oddly with old resentments; a little touch of stubborn pride, tenderness too – the helpless tenderness that the sight of Walter's firm scholarly writing, curiously beautiful, always brought on an envelope with her name. Such wonderful words envelopes like that had once contained! They flocked into her mind, now, like a cloud of tender doves – lovely, simple, caressing words; she remembered them so well, though it was long since she had seen or heard them. The doves were flown – just when, just why, she could not tell; but gradually they had vanished, and there was no such music now in the place where they had been. An empty dove-cote, a cooling hearth – pictures like those rose in her mind as she sat, the envelope still unopened in her hands, while the piles bordering the channel moved swiftly past the portholes. Then she opened the letter.

If Walter Kilmichael had written then with any hint of tenderness, or of distress – perhaps even of anger, which might have betrayed distress or pain, his wife would almost certainly have melted, got off the boat at Trieste, and taken the first train home on the heels of a telegram. But the letter contained none of these things. It was a chilly affair, breathing a balanced resentment, administering a reasoned rebuke to tiresome and unworthy folly; its tone was superior and undisturbed; the phrase 'working yourself up' occurred in it. It made no answer to her ultimatum, merely brushed it aside with something like contempt. Walter did indeed ask her plans, demanded an address, suggested a return; there were people coming to London who would need entertaining; her place, it was suggested, was at home. 'Surely you can paint here, if you must paint – you have your studio,' he wrote.

After reading it Grace Kilmichael sat in profound dejection, tinged with resentment. The letter answered nothing, settled nothing, altered nothing; it left everything exactly where it was before. Walter did not even take her seriously – there was only the old enervating superiority and contempt. Must she go back to all that? Was it her duty? She opened Linnet's letter, thirstily – she longed for news of the child.

Linnet's communications to her mother were apt to be brief. This one was:

Dear Mums,

I hope you are having a lovely time. This season is being the usual hurtle. Quite fun. Aunt G. says I ought really to have a car of my own – however we contrive somehow. James is a literary creature and I bribe him with books; so long as he can sit under an arc light and read David Garnett, he doesn't care *what* time he drives me home; unlike old Judd! Poppy is back – he seems just as usual. Apparently the Americans won't take his advice – also just as usual. He is rather sour about them. A major disaster has overtaken my evening cloak – we were driving back from Cambridge with Billy and encountered one of those tar sprayers; of course the tar was cold at that hour of the morning, but still it stuck! My green organdie was involved too. That doesn't so much matter, but the cloak is vital – Aunt G. suggested combing one out of M't Marks, off the hook, so I did. This involved opening an account – I hope that's all right? My overdraft was too large to pay.

I hope you are painting a lot and liking it.

Much love,

Linnet.

P.S. – I see no earthly reason why you should hurry home if you are working – Poppy and I and everyone are functioning perfectly.'

Grace read this letter twice, and the second time smiles stirred about her mouth. Linnet was certainly all right. Careless, elliptical little puss! – of course there had been an accident, though she didn't say so; but then they never did say things definitely. And what could she, Grace, do, if she were at home? Linnet would still hoosh about the countryside in young men's cars in the small hours. How like her, too, to find out the weak place in the armour of Gina's second chauffeur, and use it for her own ends! Grace smiled again – what a taking child she was. And this was a *kind* letter, even to her mother. She glanced again at the postscript. It almost looked – yes, really it almost looked as if Linnet knew or guessed that her Father was urging a return, and had put in her little neat casual oar to say it wasn't necessary; it almost looked as if Linnet, for once, was on her Mother's side. But there Lady Kilmichael pulled herself up vigorously. No, that was nonsense, and would be wrong even if it weren't; she always tried so hard to present a united parental front to the children, never to let them think that there were sides to take. True, Walter was a difficult person to be part of a united front *with*; but still, she had tried. However, the main fact was clear; Linnet didn't need her and was all right. No duty there was involved.

She read Walter's letter again – and then put it away in her despatch-case, locking the lid with a certain firmness. No – she would not go back. To go back now would be to stultify the tremendous moral effort she had made in coming away, perhaps the biggest effort she had ever made in her life. It was no good going back until something was settled, until Walter had seen, indeed, that there was anything *to* settle. And there was more to it than that. In this fortnight of freedom she had begun to see, vaguely and dimly, that there was something she must do about herself before she returned, if she was not to be swamped again in the old subservience and discouragement, which after all made no one happy. What needed doing, exactly, was still all cloudy and uncertain – clear thought, as has already been observed, was not Lady Kilmichael's strong suit. But during her happy days in Venice she had still, at intervals, gone on asking herself the questions she had asked on the journey to Paris – where she had gone wrong with Walter and Linnet? – and she had begun to get an idea, not of what the answer was, but, so to speak, in what county the answer might be looked for. She had never thought Linnet, or Walter, wholly or even mainly in fault – she had also looked, always, for her own mistakes to account for their painful behaviour towards her. But she had looked for actual things said or done, and the new idea was nothing less than this, that what provoked their attitude was less anything she said or did, than what she *was*. And what was more, she had become certain that freedom had something to do with it. Out here, because she was free, she was *all right*; she could look at everything more directly, without the confusion engendered by pain and timidity. She felt sure she would manage better if she could remain free. But how that was to be achieved she could not tell; freedom at home was almost inconceivable. In her painting she did indeed escape into liberty, but into another world, whence she was perpetually dragged back to the daily life in which, like Rousseau's Universal Man, she was forever in chains.

Lady Kilmichael, though she did not realise it, was beginning (rather late in the day) to feel the pressure of one of the more peculiar aspects of English life – the moral and intellectual subordination of women to their husbands. This phenomenon is of course not universal, but it is common enough to strike the observant Continental or American with amazement. And the attempt to define logically the causes from which it springs almost always ends in failure, because the English are not a logical people, and most of their profoundest instincts elude definition, as a very intelligent Dutchman has recently discovered. We may tell the observant American that it is due to our Teutonic ancestry, and that he will find the same thing in Germany; we may suggest that it originated with Puritanism and takes its Oriental colour from the traditions of the Old Testament; sociologists may point out that it is mainly a middle-class phenomenon, little exhibited in poorer households, where the daily work of her hands makes the labourer's wife queen in a small kingdom; feminists will seek to prove that it is due entirely to lack of female education and the economic subjection of women. Much or all of this may well be true; men have long been better educated than women, and their work, at least in the professional classes, tended to widen the intellectual gulf between them and their womenkind; while before legislation removed some of the gravest of married women's economic disabilities, they were in a singularly helpless position – the wife whose husband was allowed by law to take her income, her jewels and even her children, and hand them over to a rival, had some reason to feel rather subordinate.

But all this is too heavy, too definite, too pronounced; much of it no longer fits. A married woman's property is now secure to her; females receive a fair education, vote, have careers. The women of England no longer march from the altar to the tomb with the words 'And to obey' sounding continually in their hearts, and the phrase 'your Father knows best' forever on their lips. Queen Victoria is not only dead, but, as an ideal of domestic life, dethroned. And yet, tenuous, elusive, but tenacious, this tradition of inferiority persists – subtly imposed by the husbands; tacitly and often unconsciously acquiesced in by the wives. Their views, somehow, are worth less than men's; the moral initiative has passed from them; in some strange way – whether consciously or not – they are subordinate.

Now this subjection was tiresome and fatiguing enough while it was subjection to one person only, the husband; but for Lady Kilmichael's generation it had suddenly become subjection to their children as well, and when it reached that stage it became insupportable. What was really moving Grace Kilmichael, as she sat in her little white stateroom, was a dawning consciousness of her need to think and act as an independent creature, along her own lines, though she did not as yet clearly envisage it. But it was a vague conviction of where the trouble lay, and of the urgency of her need to deal with it in herself and by herself, which made her lock her despatch-case so firmly on Walter's letter, and decide not to return to England, and not to answer it.

Linnet's letter, however, she would, she must answer. But not, if possible, from Trieste. Perhaps she could do something about that. Putting on her hat again, she went to the saloon to get some coffee. In the passage she encountered one of the white-uniformed officers; with conspicuous gallantry and a brilliant display of teeth he asked if he could help her in any way? (Lady Kilmichael's clothes and figure, and a curious rather appealing youthfulness about her expression, were very apt to produce this effect on strange men.) In her halting but rather pretty Italian she said that perhaps he could – would it be possible to get letters posted, not in Trieste but in Venice? But most easily, he told her, studying her at the same time with evident curiosity as to what this charming creature had to conceal – the letters could be taken back to Venice and posted there. So Lady Kilmichael drank her coffee with a freer mind, and then went back to her stateroom and wrote to her Mother ('Dearest Mother') and then to Linnet ('My darling child'). But she told neither of them where she was going, nor did she give any hint of a return either to London or to Antibes. And to Walter she did not write at all.

FIVE

When Lady Kilmichael went to have lunch after leaving Trieste she encountered Lady Roseneath's nephew at the entrance to the saloon, and they went in and sat together. The other passengers appeared to be mostly Germans and Czechs – there was no one she knew. One face struck her as vaguely familiar – that of an oldish man in spectacles and a suit of unmistakeably Teutonic cut, who had tucked his napkin into his collar to eat his lunch. He had a remarkable head, very large, and of a certain nobility of structure, made superficially ridiculous by a bald top and a surrounding fringe of thick black hair, like a tonsure; his rugged face was full of a fiery intelligence; he ate his melon with ferocity, like a man destroying enemies. Grace was sure she had seen him before, but could not remember the place or occasion.

When a chance acquaintanceship is renewed after an interval, it makes a curious jump forward towards intimacy, merely by virtue, it would seem, of the gap. As Lady Kilmichael sat at lunch now with the yellow-headed young man, she felt almost as if he were an old friend; they shared a past, if it was only one afternoon and evening long – what was more, they shared a secret from their only common acquaintance. It was true that their intercourse had now lost that quality of free irresponsibility, almost as of disembodied spirits, which belongs to conversation with a total stranger – and Grace would definitely have preferred him not to know her name. But she had never actually met his people, and she could only trust that the young man was not – on the whole it seemed unlikely – on terms of intimate correspondence with his Aunt. Any doubts she might have had on this head were soon set at rest. As they ate their melon – 'Why do you know my Aunt?' he began, with his usual method of free enquiry.

'Oh, she's an old friend of mine,' said Grace.

'Not a real friend?' he pursued.

'Yes, we were at school together,' said Grace, amused by his pertinacity, 'and we have always kept it up.' His questions made her ask herself how much of a friend, really, she felt Lucia Roseneath to be – a thing she had never questioned before; but – 'I'm very fond of her,' she added loyally.

'Oh, come – you can hardly be that!' he expostulated. 'She's really a bore, you know.'

Grace was shocked by this. 'I expect our tastes differ,' she said rather coldly.

'I wonder. I'm not sure that they do, much,' said this extraordinary young man. 'You only say that, don't you, because you don't think a nice little boy ought to talk so about his Aunt.' Grace half-smiled. He as it were pounced on the smile, triumphantly. 'If you're so fond of her, why didn't you go to see her in Venice?' he went on. 'You were there over a week, and never went near her. I've got you there!' He looked at her very contentedly.

He had rather 'got' her, since she couldn't explain her real reason for avoiding the friend she was so fond of. Grace did her best, but the memory of the lies she had told to her old friend only that morning cramped her style, and made her efforts sound most unconvincing, even to herself. As for the young man, he laughed.

'The fact is,' he said, 'Aunt really bores me, and she bores you. Why is it unkind to recognise it? She only put me up to please my Mother, and I shall write her an excellent Collins (which will give her much more pleasure than my visit) and that will end it. What's wrong with that?'

Grace found it hard to say, to this pertinacious and analytical youth. She had a feeling that it was always wrong for the young to be critical of the old. So she merely said: 'So long as you don't hurt her feelings, I suppose it doesn't matter,' in a rather indifferent voice.

The young man was curiously roused by this. 'Of course I don't hurt her feelings! I bore her quite as much as she bores me, and she makes no bones about letting me see it. I'm young, so my feelings don't matter! In fact I believe lots of people think it's good for the young to have their feelings lacerated!' He paused for a moment. 'I am really rather careful about people's feelings,' he went on in a different tone, looking at her seriously.

Before Grace could reply, the book which she had brought in with her slipped from her lap. The young man stooped to pick it up for her, and caught sight of the title. 'Oh, you've got Graham Jackson!' he exclaimed. 'Volume One – have you got all three with you?'

Grace said she had.

'Wonderful. Can I borrow them? It's the only book for Dalmatian architecture.'

'It seems to be the only guidebook of any sort for Dalmatia in English,' said Grace, thinking of the vain enquiries she had made in London before starting. Really there were more guide-books for the Sahara, she had felt.

'Oh no, it isn't!' said the young man. 'You just look at this,' and he pulled out of his pocket a small book closely resembling a Baedeker, on the cover of which was printed 'Guide-Handbook for Istria, Dalmatie and the Ionian Islands.' 'There you are – if you want to visit the Ionian Islands at any time, here is the book of the words!'

'I never can remember which the Ionian Islands are,' Lady Kilmichael said, handing back the book.

'Can't you?' said the young man. 'They're Corfu & Co.'

As they lingered over their coffee, the man in spectacles

passed close to their table, going out. 'The Ducal Palace!' Lady Kilmichael exclaimed.

'What?' asked the young man, not unnaturally astonished.

'That man – *that's* where I saw him.' She had suddenly recognised the black-haired man as the bold individual whose example she had followed in the matter of lying on the floor to look at ceilings. She explained this to Nicholas Humphries – he showed no sign of disapproval; on the contrary, he seemed rather impressed, and Grace had a passing wonder whether the young did not disapprove of things as such, but only as done by their parents.

When they went on deck after lunch, Humphries led Lady Kilmichael to two well-placed chairs with a Burberry thrown over them, explaining that he had kept one for her all the morning. Lady Kilmichael sat with her sketchbook on her lap, idly enjoying the sun, the sea and the sense of anticipation and adventure. Dalmatia – Illyria – lovely names for a place she was sure was lovely, a place she had always longed to see. Her companion sat immersed in the volume of Sir T. Graham Jackson's work which he had seen at lunch. Now and then, though, he raised his head from the book, looked at her in a half-considering, half-questioning way for a moment or two, and then, without saying anything, went back to his reading. It was almost as if he were trying to make up his mind about her, or about something to do with her. This struck Lady Kilmichael as very odd. Young people naturally never regarded her with the smallest interest; she was accustomed to seeing the expression of civil attention, the due of the older generation, come across their faces like a mask when they spoke to her. She began to speculate about him again – especially his bitter strange words about painting on the steps of the Piazzetta; she wondered if she would learn any more about what lay behind that. Hardly – they would reach Spalato at six-thirty tomorrow morning, and then, no doubt, she would see no more of him. It was rather tantalising that Lady Roseneath's only two communications which promised to throw any light on the reasons for his discontent should have been lost, owing to her unfortunate habit of talking through the siren. What was it that he had 'got'? And what had he 'lost'? she wondered, looking at his yellow head bent over the book, and his red profile. For the first time, now, she considered his face attentively, in detail. He was not really so plain, apart from his colouring; the nose was good, jutting boldly from the face; the mouth almost beautiful, with lips closing in a firm level line. Apart from his too frequent expression of discontent and unhappiness, it was quite a good face.

Perhaps aware of her scrutiny, the young man presently raised his head again. His glance fell on the sketchbook in her lap. 'May I look?' he said – and stretching out his hand, took it from her knee. Slipping off the elastic band, he began to turn the pages.

He only turned three or four, and as he did so a curious change came over his expression. He turned back to the beginning, and went through the same ones a second time. Then he looked up at her with a sort of incredulous surprise. 'Is this *your* book?' he asked.

'Yes, of course – whose should it be?' she answered, her face suddenly charming with amusement.

'But these are very good,' he said, in slow astonished tones.

Grace laughed out. 'Why shouldn't they be good?' she asked. For some reason his astonishment was not in the least offensive.

'Because – that stone at Torcello; you couldn't draw that at all,' he said.

'I know – I'm no good at that complicated mathematical stuff,' she said. 'But I can draw places and people all right.'

'But these are *really* good – they're like a professional's,' he said.

'Why shouldn't I be a professional!' said Grace, still laughing.

The young man said nothing – he turned back to the sketchbook, and now went all through it, slowly and carefully. Presently – 'Who did you work with?' he asked.

'At the Slade; part of the time with Tonks – and now and then in Paris with Moru.'

'I thought perhaps Tonks,' he said. 'I don't know Moru's work so well; so much of it is in private hands. Do you show in London?'

'No, hardly at all – in Paris mostly,' said Grace. She was beginning to get a little nervous; the boy knew rather too much. It was tiresome enough that he should know her as Lady Kilmichael – if he tumbled to the fact that she was also Grace Stanway he might really begin to talk, or rather write, and her whereabouts be given away. It was stupid of her to have let him see the sketchbook at all. She stretched out her hand for it, in her turn; he gave it up, and she closed it.

'It's odd I shouldn't have seen any of your things, all the same,' he said. 'I generally nose round a bit among the modern stuff, and I've been in Paris once or twice lately. Where do you show there?'

'Oh, here and there – wherever I can get in,' said Lady Kilmichael, hurriedly and untruthfully. Really today was being a terrible day for lies and concealments.

'Kilmichael – Kilmichael,' said the young man, frowning and looking out to sea. 'No, I can't remember a single thing.'

Grace felt guilty – she minded lying about her painting more than about her plans. Partly out of genuine interest, partly to deflect him from the subject, so strewn with difficulties, of her own work, she said hurriedly, 'You seem very much interested in painting – why are you not going to be a painter?'

'Because I've got to be an architect,' he said shortly. Grace realised that she had said the wrong thing, and made some futile and amiable remark about that being very interesting too.

'It isn't to me – I hate the idea,' said the boy, his face more deeply discontented than ever.

'But you are interested in architecture,' said Grace, trying, after the manner of the middle-aged, to look on the bright side, and to make youth look on it too. Youth in this case, however, fairly scowled at her.

'I'm interested in architectural types and development, but not in sanitary fittings,' he said. 'Do you mind if we don't talk about it?' he added, in a cold bitter tone.

'Of course – certainly,' said Grace, a little stiffly. He really was *very* offhand. But pity always triumphed in Lady Kilmichael over her – never very robust – sense of what was due to her, and the sight of the boy's unhappy resentful face touched her almost at once. 'I'm sorry,' she added simply.

This slight episode produced a check to their intercourse, which was only terminated by the boy's asking her to come and have tea with him in the deck lounge – so obvious an act of reparation that Lady Kilmichael accepted at once. The tea was rather oddly interrupted by the sight of the great Roman amphitheatre at Pola, more or less peering in at them through the glazed windows of the lounge. Young Humphries, finding that they had twenty minutes at Pola, dragged Lady Kilmichael off to see it. But they missed the way, had to scale a wall and drop six feet down into the amphitheatre, and then nearly missed the steamer. For while they stood in the empty grassy space, enclosed by the huge outer shell of the building, rising four storeys high, which is all that is left today, some chance remark of Nicholas's drew down on him the attention of the black-haired stranger whom they had seen at lunch; and in a moment the two were deep in an archaeological discussion, which Lady Kilmichael tried in vain to break up. The first siren sounded as they left the amphitheatre, and they had to run like beaglers down the interminable quay, Lady Kilmichael, who in her – or rather

Nicholas's – hurry had left her bag on board, reflecting as she ran how excessively disagreeable it would be to be left in Pola (as seemed extremely probable) without her hat, luggage, money, tickets or passport. The other passengers, pleased spectators of the race, clustered above at the rail as the three of them went up the gangway, just when it was on the point of being raised; Lady Kilmichael was uncomfortably conscious of being hatless, breathless, flushed, and dishevelled as to hair. She was quite unaware of how becoming and indeed rejuvenating an effect this had on her appearance. The lively officer, however, standing at the head of the gangway, was clearly aware of it; he eyed her with amused admiration as she came up. '*La donna e mobile!*' he said, and laughed, showing his handsome teeth. As for young Humphries, like the German mopping his streaming face, he grinned at her with a sort of triumphant proprietary amusement which reminded her sharply of the way Teddy and Nigel always grinned at her when they had managed to ruffle her hair or somehow upset her composure.

'You can run!' he said – and then, as at Torcello, he made his favourite comment: 'What a happy day!'

SIX

It *was* rather a day, whether happy or not, Lady Kilmichael reflected, as she lay in a bath of hot salt water before dinner; it seemed more like a fortnight than twelve hours since the morning, so varied were the things that had happened. Her unexpected meeting with Lucia Roseneath; telling lies; Walter's letter, and her struggle and decision not to return; more lies to the boy about her painting; his vexation on the subject of his career – finally the ludicrous Pola escapade. It was not at all like a day at home! And it was odd, having thought and felt so intensely about Walter and Linnet all the morning, to have had time to think so little – indeed really not at all – about them all the afternoon. Was this – to forget about her family – a part of the freedom she was vaguely seeking? She was not sure – what was certain was that it had been a very long day, and that with another 6.30 A.M. start tomorrow, she should go to bed extremely early.

But Lady Kilmichael's day was not yet over, however retrospectively she might think of it, nor did she go to bed in the least early. It was perhaps natural, after they had shared in that race along the quay at Pola, that the man in spectacles should come up to her when she appeared in the deck lounge before dinner, square his heels, bow, and ask her to do him the honour of taking an *aperitif* with him. Lady Kilmichael accepted this piece of casual board-ship civility, and they sat drinking white 'Cora' vermouth; while they talked she studied his face, and wished again that she could draw it. It was a thoroughly Rembrandt face – furrowed, rugged, intellectual with a touch of mysticism, like so many of Rembrandt's sitters, fine unmistakeable lines of impatience, even of harshness, round the mouth, a surprising hint of benevolence about the eyes – a face full of contrasts which were not yet denials, for they were unified by the curious but most definite impression of goodness which it gave. He was undoubtedly, from his accent, either a German or an Austrian; and belonging, she judged, to one of the more liberal professions.

He began by asking whether her exertions had fatigued her unduly, and next enquired where she was going. (Everyone, Lady Kilmichael noted, seemed to want to know where she was going – it was a universal question.) Spalato, she told him. He immediately became authoritative. There were certain things there which she must see. (She noticed with amusement that he instantly assumed in her a violent interest in the monuments of past ages – a natural assumption, perhaps, in view of her recent efforts to see the amphitheatre, which he had witnessed.) 'For one thing, *gnädige Frau*, you must see the Museum. Everyone sees the Diokletianische Palast, and that is well – it is unique. But the Museum you must see also, and few people even know that it exists.' He went on to explain how it owed its excellence entirely to the energy and devotion of one man, the old Abbé B—, who had spent a lifetime acquiring treasures, raising funds, getting a building erected, collecting an adequate staff. The account caught Grace's imagination – she was thrilled to learn that the old man was still there, working away. 'Yes, go and see him, *gnädige Frau*; it will give him pleasure.'

The black-haired man – she and young Humphries, over their belated and interrupted tea, had decided that he was a professor, and referred to him as such – displayed so much learning that she was about to ask him whether the basilica at Torcello *was* the original building or not when he startled her by saying – 'Your son is very intelligent and well-instructed about architecture.'

'He isn't my son,' she said, amused and a little defensive.

'Oh, pardon! But you travel together?'

'No, not really – only this little bit. He's a nephew of a very old friend of mine,' she added, glad for once that day to be able to furnish an explanation which was perfectly true.

She repeated the Professor's remark to young Humphries at dinner; she felt that he wanted bucking up, encouragement, from whatever source. The maternal instinct, never far below the surface in Grace Kilmichael, had begun to raise its head again; this young man wanted helping somehow – she wished she could help him; when he grinned at her and talked like the boys, she caught herself feeling – most oddly – almost as if he were one of her own children.

When dinner was over, she said she thought she would go to bed.

'Oh, you can't *now* – you'd get the most appalling indigestion!' said the young man. 'Come on deck,' he urged. She fetched her white coat, and they went up. It was nearly dark; a fresh wind whipped the black glossy surface of the water into broken planes – one or two stars already showed, but out to sea a low line of orange still bordered the western horizon. 'There's no Venice against it tonight,' said the boy, with his conductor's gesture at the dying sunset.

'No. I like it better without, I think,' said Grace.

'Do you? Why?'

'It's freer,' she said. She had only meant the sense of unobstructed space, of openness, but he took it up otherwise.

'Do you want freedom?' he asked.

'Yes, I suppose so, from some things,' she answered thoughtfully. It was odd that he should ask her that question just then.

'Care, perhaps?' he said, and she could hear the smile with which he said it.

'No, not care yet,' she said, smiling too, 'it's too soon for that.'

'I should have thought you *were* rather free, by now,' he said, in a different tone. 'At least people can't interfere with you at every turn.'

Oh, can't they? Grace thought – aloud she only said: 'People can *always* interfere with one at every turn – that's not a thing you ever get away from.'

The boy made no answer, and they stood in silence for some time, leaning side by side on the rail, watching the dark water. His mind, Grace felt sure, was on his own troubles, though his speech had skirted round them; his silence held some other impulse too, but she was not sure what. Encouraged by the turn their talk had taken, she gave way to a compassionate impulse of her own – to try and release his sense of grievance somehow. Choosing her words rather carefully this time, she said – 'I am sorry I vexed you this afternoon by what I said about your work – I'm afraid I was very stupid about it.'

He turned his head towards her. 'You know the funny thing was, I had been trying to make up my mind to talk to you about it,' he said. 'Even before I knew that you painted. But when you began, somehow I couldn't. Are you ever like that?'

'I don't know – I daresay,' said Grace. (So that was why he had kept on looking at her in that considering way.) 'Do you want to talk about it now?' she asked.

'Yes, I do,' he said, 'if you'll let me, that is, after this afternoon.'

'Of course – I want to know very much. I've been wondering about it ever since that night in Venice,' she said, anxious to make it clear that her interest was sincere.

He did not begin at once, however. He stood staring at the west, which had now faded to an astonishing silvery green; the light from the windows of the saloon shone from behind on his yellow head – his face was in shadow. At last – 'It's all one of those silly muddles, not having known what one wanted to do soon enough. But how *can* one know when one's frightfully young? If I'd got in first with the painting idea I daresay I might have got away with it. As it was, my sister beat me.' He paused. 'I'd better tell you about us; my mother always says I'm so incredibly muddled in my speech! There's only me and my sister – she's a year older than me, and good-looking, and clever – she's really rather a flyer. I should like you to meet her.'

Grace said that she should like to meet her very much.

'Well, there is always this question of what one is to do,' he pursued. 'You might think that was more or less one's own affair! However! Well, thank God the Army was ruled out, because I have a funny tummy. That's why I'm starting anything so late – at Oxford it rather knocked me out for a year. And that gave Celia her chance, incidentally. But the really unlucky thing was that when I was a very small boy I was rather good at drawing buildings – churches and ruins and all that; and I thought it was the buildings I liked and not the drawing. So the legend grew up – Little Nicky wanted to be an architect. And when I found out that I didn't, do you think I could change the legend? Why *is* it,' he burst out, 'that people will go on holding you down to your old ideas when they're as dead as mutton? Do *all* parents do it? Even my mother, who really is rather good in most ways, can't get that out of her head. 'But dearest boy, you used to *want* to be an architect!' She must have said that two hundred times! I *know* I used – but I don't now!'

Grace wondered wildly for a moment whether Nigel had really stopped caring about archaeology long since, and whether Teddy now violently resented the recognised prospect of his going into business. However, for the moment that wasn't the point. 'How did you find out that you wanted to paint?' she asked, in her soft voice.

'I got keener and keener about it all the time I was at Oxford,' he said – 'I got into the way of doing a good bit of sketching in the vacs, and I put in some time at the Ruskin School, in the terms.'

'That's very sound. Well, then what happened?' Grace asked.

'Well, when my tummy began to play me up, I had an operation, and went abroad to get over it – to various places in the Midi, Vence amongst others. And there I fell in with a painting lot, and rather got down to it. I actually worked for six months with Zarini. It was then I decided that I wanted to go in for it, definitely. But by that time Little Sister had made up her mind that *she* was going to be a painter, and had made a start at the Slade. And the parent struck absolutely at *two* painters in the family.'

It *was* rather gloomy for the General, Lady Kilmichael reflected. But she said nothing.

'That's the sort of irrational idea that people get hold of, and simply *clasp*,' he went on. 'Why not let *ten* children be artists, if they're good artists? But the maddening thing in this case is that Celia really isn't any good at it, and never will be. She's quite incapable of drawing. It's just a stunt. She'd had three seasons and was at a loose end, and wanted something to take up. It was a poor choice,' he said impartially, 'because it's just about the one thing she's not clever at.'

Lady Kilmichael here risked asking an obvious but rather offensive question. 'Are you sure that you would be – are – any good at it; painting, I mean?'

'Zarini thought so,' he said. 'He was quite firm about it. Of course he's youngish still, but he's pretty well recognised. You know him, I expect.'

'No, I don't.'

'But you know his work?'

'Hardly at all – but that doesn't mean anything,' she said. 'I'm not really in with painters much. I just paint. It's rather a side issue with me,' she explained, anxious to account for her ignorance of Zarini. She had just heard M. Breuil, or Moru, or someone, mention him as a Corsican who was coming on, and might make a great noise some day; but what she *did* know, for all her professed ignorance of the world of artists, was how often these future great noises die away unheard.

The young man, however, was deflected from his main theme by her last words. 'I don't see how painting *can* be a side issue, if you care about it at all,' he said firmly.

'It may have to be, if you've got other things to do,' said Grace.

'What sort of things?' he asked, with his usual pertinacity in questioning.

'Oh, a family, and a house and all that,' she said, on a rather weary inflection that was almost a sigh. '*Il faut du temps pour être femme*,' she quoted gaily, to cover up the sigh.

But apparently it did not escape the boy – he was very quick about some things. 'Oh, is that the care you wanted to leave behind?' he asked. 'Is it all that you want freedom from?'

For a second Grace was tempted to use his own words of the afternoon – 'Do you mind if we don't talk about that?' But that wasn't fair – one must be gentle with the young, however awkward their questions were.

'Of course I should like to have more time for painting,' she said evasively. 'But go on about your work – have you actually begun to be an architect?'

'No – I start in the autumn at the Institute,' he said. 'And then go into Lothbury's office. I'm keeping this term free to look round here and Greece – the Institute doesn't think much of it, but Lothbury is rather keen on people taking an intelligent interest in the past.'

'And there's no chance of getting out of it?' Grace asked.

'Do you know my Father?' the boy said. His tone was an answer in itself.

Grace's mind leapt back to Lady Roseneath's remarks that very morning about her brother-in-law – together with the boy's words they summoned up for her an uncomfortably vivid picture of the retired soldier, devoting his superabundant leisure to leading his family a life. She made no attempt to answer such an obviously rhetorical question. 'I'm sorry,' was all she found to say.

'If it was only my Mother, it would be easy enough,' said the young man, with an attempt at casualness that was almost painful to listen to, 'and again, if it weren't for my Mother, I think I should have forced it through, very likely. But as it is, I've had to let it go. However.'

That word 'however,' the one philosophical utterance of the generation to which the creatures she loved best in the world belonged, struck on Lady Kilmichael's ear with a familiarity which made it at once comic and pathetic. The boys always used it in cheerful resignation. Linnet was constantly saying it on those many and bitter occasions when she had proved, by a lengthy argument, how utterly unreasonable and even unpleasant her Mother was. Hearing it now on Nicholas's lips, a wave of pity swept over Lady Kilmichael – pity for the boy beside her, pity for the thwarted Linnet in the past; the pity she always felt so keenly even when holding conscientiously and tenaciously to some righteous point of her own. Always, then, much sharper than her personal hurt at Linnet's bitter words, was the pain of the child's unhappy disappointed face. And here was another unhappy child. Somehow or other she *must* try to comfort him.

'How does your Mother make it more difficult, exactly?' she asked.

'Because it all comes back on her, one way or another, if I have a showdown with my Father,' he said. 'I oughtn't to bore you with all this, but if you know Aunt Lucia you must know most of what there is to know about my parents already, so it isn't giving anything away. And it's rather a help to talk about it to someone who understands; as you paint yourself – even as a side issue!' – she could hear his grin again – 'I'm sure you do understand.' He paused, and drummed thoughtfully with his fingers on the rail. Grace waited – she liked him for his hesitation to discuss his family troubles with a stranger, even in what she realised to be his rather dire need.

'My Father and I are rather a mess,' he brought out presently. 'I daresay it's partly my fault, but not altogether. You see he lives in a world of his own; but the trouble is, he tries to make everyone else live in it too. And I don't fit into it. So we don't get on too brilliantly.' He paused, and Grace tried, irrationally, to remember the very odd word Walter always used for the modern habit of understatement. What was it? – 'my' – something.

'My Mother and I *do* get on,' the boy pursued, 'and left to herself she'd have been perfectly all right about this. But she gives in to him in the most absurd way; she simply can't stand up to him. You see he thinks her a fool, which she isn't; anyhow she wasn't born one. But he's told her she was for so long that she's really come to believe she is, and she acts accordingly; she never will oppose his judgement in anything. It's too silly. Especially as the money is nearly all hers.'

It was the last remark which struck Grace most. She had had a passing wonder, as she listened, whether she herself was really less foolish than Walter thought, and whether her own intelligence might not have been weakened by the constant weight of suggestion. But that little remark about the money fairly hit her, it showed so clearly the difference between her own youth and youth today. Like most of the boy's statements, it was made quite detachedly. But she and her brothers and sisters had never argued things out in that coldly clearsighted way – indeed, till her marriage settlements were drawn up she had never known where such money as there was in her family came from. Did her own children, she wondered, the boys and Linnet, see her and Walter with equal clearness, and argue out their respective incomes, intelligence and merits? A little uncomfortably, she had to suppose that they did.

Aloud, 'Is money much of a difficulty?' she asked, anxious, since they had got so far, to grasp the problem thoroughly.

'Not really, in the least – only with my Father. He has all sorts of ideas about it, even if there's plenty,' said the boy. 'That's why it's a pity I couldn't have got a bit farther on. If I could have made enough to keep myself, or done enough to show that I really *could* bring it off, it's just possible it might have been all right. As it is, it's too late, without a row that would break my Mother up. She's not at all strong.'

'I see,' said Grace thoughtfully. She did indeed see it all, clearly, and she was considerably moved by the way the boy spoke of his mother, impersonal though it was. He was a good unselfish child in some ways, anyhow. 'It's all very difficult,' she said. And then suddenly she laughed. She had let that sentence slip out, without remembering how the children had picked on it as one of her characteristic phrases – they always quoted it at her, now, whenever she displayed any irresolution. The young man turned his head towards her, surprised at her laughter; she hastened to explain. Nicholas Humphries, hearing how 'it's all very difficult' had become a family slogan, laughed too. 'I shouldn't think your family had much trouble with you,' he said.

But Grace Kilmichael had taken a sudden resolution. She would at least see his stuff, and try to judge it for herself.

'I should like to see some of your work,' she said. 'Have you got anything here?'

'That's very good of you,' he said, 'but actually I've nothing with me. I've really only been photographing – I've tried to put the other thing out of my head, as it wasn't any good.'

Nothing at all, Grace asked, no sketches, even? Yes, there were one or two sketches he hadn't been able to resist doing at Chioggia, but that was all. Well, let her see those, Grace said. Eager and nervous, he went below to fetch them.

Grace remained on deck. She was thinking of what she had

heard. Here was another family where there was, as the boy said, 'a mess.' She and Linnet, she supposed, were a mess too; perhaps Linnet called it that. And yet she *did* love the child so! How was it? Did she too try to make everyone round her live in her own world? She couldn't quite think that. And the boy had said she couldn't be much trouble to her family. What a point of view! Grace thought, smiling in the dark. But he was young, too; he ought to know.

But while Lady Kilmichael stood at the rail of a steamer in the Adriatic, thinking about the young, and Nicholas Humphries routed feverishly in a suitcase below for his sketches, to show to the strange woman who painted so well and understood so much, Linnet was again writing to her best friend.

Aunt Gina and I had a prize row today – all about James. She said he'd only had three hours sleep per night, for a fortnight. Poor James! So I gave him my autographed copy of *Brave New World*, and I believe he'd sit up *all* night for a month on the strength of that. 'Eoh Miss!' he kept on saying, 'that's a prize, that is.'

You know the funny thing is I don't mind having rows with Aunt Gina a bit. She blackguards me, and I blackguard her back (as much as I think suitable in a p.g.!) and then we reach a *modus*, and that's that. But it doesn't fray one. Neither of us minds. Whereas rows with Mums are simply frightful, because though she doesn't *say* half what Aunt G. does, she minds the existence of a row so terribly. At least I suppose that's it. Anyhow it's awful. And when I tell Aunt G. *why* I did X or Y, she takes it in, and just says, well I'm not to again – and that is also that. Whereas Mums always begins to think about my moral character and latent tendencies to evil, and is simply blinded by fuss over all that to the plain good reason I had *then* for doing *so*. Which makes it all so complicated. Do you suppose it's the fact of being a parent which makes people so hopeless at understanding things, or was Mums specially born like it? Because she's really rather a lamb in some ways.

Poppy by the way is in a proper fever over Mums. He keeps asking if I've heard from her, which I haven't. Gags wrote that she believed she was in Venice, or going to be – but it all seems pretty vague.

Standing at the rail, waiting for the boy, Lady Kilmichael noticed all at once how sweet the air was. The wind had fallen light, and it was warmer; she guessed that in the dark they had entered some sheltered channel between the innumerable islands of that coast and were near the land, for the delicate breath of land scents, aromatic, flowery, faint, came to her as she stood. But she could see nothing. And then Nicholas Humphries was beside her again.

'Here you are,' he said. 'But come for'ard a moment, on the other side; there are lights ahead – I believe we're going into some harbour.'

Lady Kilmichael followed him round to the port side, where they leant on the forward rail. Sure enough, a twinkle of lights showed ahead, low down by the water, but nothing else. And then, suddenly, a miracle happened. From above their heads the ship's searchlight sprang out, and drew up out of the darkness before them a picture of a town, as if some vast creative hand had raised up a great painted canvas from the floor of the night. There was a quay, thronged with people – behind it a white square, a white church, a tall white campanile with a red spire, and white houses running up the hill behind. An immense plane tree stood at one side of the square, throwing its shadow across the ivory whiteness of the houses and the rich façade of the church. In the strong white light the whole scene was beautiful with a strange theatrical beauty – the green of the great tree, even the brightly coloured clothes of the people on the quay were clearly visible, but with a certain quality of unreality about them; the shadows were dead black, lacking the daylight hint of purple or blue. It was so startling, so lovely, that Lady Kilmichael was speechless. Nor did the boy say anything – he merely waved his hand at it, with that musical gesture which was becoming familiar to her. Slowly they steamed in, while the incredible picture, framed in the surrounding blackness, became more and more detailed and clear. At last the boy spoke.

'If one could paint that – *really* paint it – you'd have done something, wouldn't you?' he said slowly.

'Yes,' said Grace. As they got nearer still – 'Let's go!' he said abruptly. 'It's changing.'

They went into the lounge. It was almost deserted by this time. The boy put down a little heap of sketches on a table, and then sat looking on while Lady Kilmichael examined them. She went through them slowly and carefully. Most were of buildings; these were accurate, delicate, very good of their rather pedestrian sort – what she called 'French exercises.' But at the bottom of the pile she came on two or three which really startled her. One was of a group of women under the apse of the church at Chioggia, their long black shawls brilliant against the pinkish buff of the building, laughing over a funny story told by one of them – the vivid self-satisfied face of the teller, the abandonment to mirth of the rest, were brilliantly, astonishingly done, even in the slight watercolour. There was another of an old man asleep in a moored boat, as immobile as his vessel, and a little boy, intensely awake, looking longingly at the fruit stalls on the *fondamento* behind. Over these two she lingered a long time. Yes – they were most unusual; gesture, colour, grouping, all showed a vitality, combined with a sense of form, which was really astonishing in a beginner. But could he get it across in a bigger picture, in oils? That was the question. She looked up, about to speak, and saw his eyes fixed on her with an intensity which was almost painful. She spoke quickly, to chase away that eager anxiety.

'They're good, Mr Humphries,' she said.

'They're only sketches,' he said with evident relief. 'I wish you could see some of my bigger things.'

'So do I,' said Grace. She sat thinking, weighing a question in her mind; through the window, as the steamer moved, she caught a momentary distorted glimpse of the white campanile, still illuminated. It recalled the boy's words as they stood together outside, and somehow that memory clinched her resolution.

'How long are you going to be in Spalato?' she asked.

'As long as I like. Why?'

'I mean to stay there at least a week,' she said, 'and a lot of the time I shall be making drawings, not painting. I wondered if you would care to use my things and do a small picture or two while I'm there. I could tell better from something in oil, with more purpose in it; something that worked out a definite scheme.'

The boy stared at her. 'Do you mean that? Of course I'd like to – better than anything. You really think they're good enough to make it worthwhile to see more?'

'To see that much more, anyhow,' said Grace. 'I can't really tell from these.'

'That's good of you,' he said – 'really frightfully good. I will – I'll begin tomorrow.'

'Then you'd better go to bed now – it's after eleven,' she said, handing him back the sketches. 'I must, anyhow.' She rose, and held out her hand. 'Good night, Mr Humphries,' she said.

He took her hand. 'My name,' he said, 'is Nicholas. I wish you'd use it.'

'All right,' she said, 'I will. Good night.' And went off to bed. As she lay down in her little white stateroom and switched off the light, a curious thought visited her. She had only wanted to comfort an unhappy child; but what she had actually done, by her offer of help to Nicholas, was to range herself on the side of the young against their parents. How very odd. Still thinking how odd it was, Lady Kilmichael fell asleep.

SEVEN

The city of Spalato has one feature in common with, strangely enough, the village of Avebury in Wiltshire. That hamlet presents the unusual spectacle, not of an ancient monument in a village, but of a village in an ancient monument, lying as it does enclosed in its huge prehistoric circle. In the same way the old town of Spalato is enclosed complete within the four walls of the palace which the Emperor Diocletian, the slave's son who became master of the world, built for the years of his retirement on the seashore of his native province. There it stands, this country residence of sixteen hundred years ago – its great walls still rising to a height of four storeys; its two temples, smothered in carving of a spring-like freshness and grace of design, still roofed and weatherproof; its streets and squares still ennobled with the tall and graceful colonnades which spring so airily from the pavement; its great gateways still looking down on the incomings and outgoings of its occupants. But in and through and round and over this Roman structure, stuck, gummed and crammed like the work of a mason bee against the old stonework, are the shops, the houses and the churches of its more recent inhabitants; along the peristyle, now the Piazza, shop signs peer out between the arches of the colonnades; on the long façade which looks out over the sea the green shutters of private residents are flung back against the pillars, now embedded in masonry, of the old crypto-porticus, the great loggia'ed gallery which was the glory of the place at the time of its building, the exciting innovation of the imperial owner. Whole dwellings, and even a chapel, have been tunnelled out in the mighty thickness of the walls themselves, like rabbit burrows in a turf dyke; they say the place now holds three thousand souls. But in this extraordinary huddle of buildings, the accretion of thirteen hundred years, the original palace remains as it were fossilised, like a winged insect in amber or some strange fish in stone; preserved as no other structure of its age or size has been in Europe, save the buried buildings of Herculaneum and Pompeii. When in the seventh century the scattered inhabitants of Salona crept back from their starved exile in the islands to seek a livelihood on the mainland, and took shelter, not among the ruins of their city, but within the unshakeable walls of that great four-square structure which dominated the shore, they were, all unconsciously, initiating a work of preservation on a scale unknown to the Commission on Ancient Monuments.

Today the city of Spalato has overflowed its ancient boundaries. Outside Diocletian's walls, mainly to the west, a modern town has sprung up, with broad streets and large whitish buildings resembling the newer parts of Munich, where charabancs and motors carry the tourist to and fro, and petrol fumes and the ping of telephone bells are on the air. But still the traveller, arriving by sea, is arrested on the very quay by the sight of that great stretch of palace façade, rising over the masts of the inner harbour in a splendid unity, a single mighty completeness of design dominating the whole town.

The morning of Lady Kilmichael's arrival at Spalato was wet, and the steamer threaded its way in among the islands through grey streams of rain falling on low grey shores and a still grey sea. She herself was packed and dressed by six – but seeing no sign of Nicholas Humphries among the few sleepy-eyed passengers in the lounge and saloon, mindful of Lady Roseneath's injunctions she sent a steward to dig him out, with an amused sense of familiarity – it was so usual to be seeing that the young really managed to do what they intended to do! At six-twenty-nine he appeared, sleepy, manifestly unshaven, hatless as usual, accompanied by several rather distended valises, a number of loose coats and a knapsack from which various objects protruded untidily – the very model of the incompetent traveller. His appearance moved her to a smile as she said 'Good morning, Nicholas.'

'Good morning,' he replied, with that curious gravity of his. The boat was a few minutes late, and as she manœuvred into port they stood in the door of the lounge, staring through the rain at the town. 'There it is,' Grace murmured, half to herself, thus saluting the palace front, which even at that unpromising and chilly hour appeared both noble and splendid to her.

'Where are you staying?' Nicholas asked, as they stood on the quay, watching the luggage come ashore, and feeling the rain filtering down their necks. The Ritz-Splendide, she told him. Mr Humphries, too, it appeared, was staying at the Ritz-Splendide, and thither, with two featureless Czech passengers, a motorbus, bearing these impressive names along its sides, presently bore them.

When Lady Kilmichael descended in search of breakfast she found Nicholas Humphries in the dining room; he beckoned her urgently to his table.

'I've ordered coffee for you,' he said. 'This is not really a *good* hotel,' he went on. 'There's nowhere to sit but there' – he indicated a sort of loggia outside the windows, full of wicker chairs, onto whose concrete floor puddles were seeping from the adjoining pavement – 'and the water won't be bath-hot for another two hours, I'm told.' However, the young man said, one could always paint – and he asked if he might go through her things and get together what he needed. He was evidently feverishly eager to begin at once. Of course he could, Grace told him; but she for her part had no intention of attempting to begin work till it was fine enough to sit out of doors – she was going to look at Spalato. And then she asked him to let her have back that volume of Graham Jackson, to use as a guidebook. He sprang up and went off to his room to fetch it; he returned presently with a profoundly crestfallen expression.

'I haven't got it,' he said. 'I've been through everything. I must have left it on the boat.'

'Oh, Mr Humphries, you haven't!' Grace felt ready to cry at this *contretemps.* Through her fatigue, the discomfort of the hotel and the disappointment of the cheerless weather, she had supported herself with the thought of a quiet morning in the Duomo or the Baptistery, sitting in a corner with the book on her knee, studying with its help all the details of doors, font or pulpit – the sort of morning she had so often, and so contentedly, spent lately in Venice with Mr Ruskin. She looked therefore at the young man with large and lamentable eyes.

'I'm afraid so,' he said. 'I am most terribly sorry. I remember putting it down in that lounge place before dinner, and then afterwards we got talking, and I forgot all about it. I say, don't look at me like that!' he exclaimed, putting out his hand and touching her arm. 'I know it wasn't so good, but I didn't mean to, you know. Are you really angry?'

'No, of course not,' said Grace, recovering herself. 'I can get it back, I expect. Only it's rather a bore not to have it here. But don't worry – I know it was an accident,' she said.

'It was abysmally stupid of me,' he said, 'only I got so keen on the painting idea last night that I forgot everything else.' He crumbled a roll, embarrassed. 'I couldn't go to sleep for thinking of it – that's why I was so late this morning,' he brought out. 'But you won't go back on that, because I've been such an owl?'

'No, no – don't be absurd,' said Grace, rather touched by this. 'I'll go and telegraph for it,' she said, getting up.

He rose too. 'I say—' he said, on a detaining inflection.

'Yes?' said Grace, turning back.

'I know I deserve anything, but *must* you call me Mr Humphries?' he asked, as they stood by the table. Grace had to laugh at his expression, it was so quaint a mixture of the comical and the remorseful.

'No – you shall go on being Nicholas,' she said, gaily and good-naturedly, with a smile. Lady Kilmichael sometimes smiled with her eyes, and when she did, partly because her eyes were very beautiful, and partly because then some part of herself – her simplicity, her generosity, her real goodness – appeared in them, her smile at such moments was of quite astonishing sweetness. Across the table, she so smiled at Nicholas Humphries now. To her surprise he did not smile back – the comical expression left his face, and he stood looking gravely at her. She could not be expected to know the effect that her smile, coming on top of the episode of the lost book, produced on him. It reduced the young man, as he himself would have said, to pulp. He left the chilly dining room of the Hotel Ritz-Splendide definitely in the first stages of a subjugation.

Lady Kilmichael had already learned that on the Eastern shores of the Adriatic the traveller will find the Yugo-Slavia Express Agency his most present help in trouble, and it was accordingly to their office that she applied for help about her lost book. The matter, it appeared, was not so disastrous. The boat would reach Dubrovnik at two-thirty that day, and would be back at Spalato about midnight. Yes, the Agency would catch the commander with a telegram at Dubrovnik, the book would be preserved, and returned to her by breakfast time the day after. Young Humphries, who had come with her, insisted on paying for the telegram, and then, shrouded in mackintoshes, they proceeded to explore the town, their only guide that red handbook which treats also of the Ionian Islands.

It was a day, definitely, as Nicholas said, for indoor sight-seeing, and they splashed through the dripping Piazza straight to the Duomo. This lovely octagonal building, certainly the temple of Jupiter, possibly also the mausoleum of Diocletian, and indubitably pagan, has been turned, by the simple method of applying, in appropriate positions, an altar, a pulpit and a campanile, into a very fair Christian church. But still it remains utterly Roman in spirit and conception. The little fat boys who drive chariots and bestride horses in the frieze are Loves, not cherubs; and from two medallions above the altar stare out, half-seen in the bluish gloom, the grim faces of, it is alleged, Diocletian and his consort.

All these things Nicholas and Lady Kilmichael studied with interest. Rather to her surprise, she found that Nicholas really knew a great deal about classical architecture; and what he knew he put intelligently and well, making the various points of departure from the normal Roman type of building clear, without being either heavy or technical. He led her eagerly from one thing to the next, talking much more rapidly and confidently than she had heard him do hitherto. At last they turned to the wonderful thirteenth-century doors, with Guvina's panels in carved wood, and here Lady Kilmichael made the discovery that the scroll-work of the main cross-framing showed a pattern rather like the foliage on some of her West Highland stones; identical it was not, but like it was – like enough to arouse her curiosity. Then they turned up their collars, crossed the Piazza again, and made their way to the little temple of Aesculapius, now the Baptistery. As they went in through that great doorway, whose architraves are carved so richly with flowers and foliage and curious little animals that it is as if the whole life of a spring meadow were concentrated there in stone, Nicholas halted suddenly, his eye caught by something. In a moment he called to Grace, who had gone in – 'Lady Kilmichael! Come and look at this.'

She went back. 'Look here – here's that pattern again,' he said, pointing to the architrave. 'It's almost exactly like the Duomo doors – do you think old Guvina copied this?'

Grace examined it, frowning a little, as she did when she was puzzled or interested. Was he sure it was exactly like? It certainly resembled it.

'Well, we'll soon see,' he said. 'I'll go and draw the other, and bring it back to compare' – and off he went before she could stop him, his yellow head shining down the dark rainy little street. Grace went into the Baptistery again. There was a lot of carving on the altar, and here also she found scroll-work tantalisingly like her familiar designs. If only she had got Graham Jackson, to find out the date! How very tiresome to be without it. But she could not find it in her heart to feel seriously impatient with Nicholas, who was joining in her pattern-hunt with such zest and intelligence, and had so readily gone off to get wetter than ever in that cause. She sat on the floor and drew one of the likelier pieces, and then the barrel-vaulted stone roof of the little temple – perfectly content, thinking happily of how she and Nigel would later go over her notes and sketches, till Nicholas returned.

'There you are,' he said, handing her his sketchbook with another of his beautifully precise and careful drawings of two sections of the cross-frame. They went out to the doorway and compared it. There could be no doubt about it – the master carver of the thirteenth century had drawn his inspiration from the Roman work of nine hundred years earlier. This, from Lady Kilmichael's point of view, only made the resemblance to the Highland stones more puzzling than ever. Thirteenth-century work might be almost contemporary with some of them – fourth-century work was not.

'Anyhow, it isn't precisely the same pattern,' she said. 'I wish I'd got some photographs with me, and I could show you.'

'Why don't you write to your son – Nigel, is he? – and ask

him to send you some?' young Humphries most reasonably asked.

'Oh' – Lady Kilmichael, embarrassed, blushed, while she sought for some excuse for not writing to Nigel. There came into her mind a sudden certainty, a sort of determination imposed from without, that to this boy with the honest face she could not and would not lie again. He was staring at her now – fascinated, though she didn't know it, by the phenomenon of the blush – with a clear-eyed attention that embarrassed her more than ever.

'No – I'm not going to tell him anything about it till I've got more evidence,' she said firmly. 'He might think it was just a hare I was starting; Nigel is very accurate and careful himself.'

'Are you afraid of him?' Nicholas asked, looking amused.

Goodness, how sharp the creature was! She *was* a little afraid of Nigel – he was far more like Walter than either Teddy or Linnet.

'I don't like not to do things thoroughly for him,' she temporised.

'You might easily have been afraid of him – my Mamma is terrified of Celia,' the young man observed calmly.

Grace had it on the tip of her tongue to ask why Mrs Humphries was afraid of her daughter – it might help her with her own problems to know, she thought. But time was getting on, and she wanted to find the little chapel of St. Martin, hollowed out in the thickness of the Palace wall, of which she had already read before Nicholas had carried off the book. So she let it go for the time being, and they studied the Ionian Islands together, till they made out roughly where the Martins-Kapelle was, somewhere near the Porta Ferrea. But in the warren of small alleys and closes it was almost impossible to find one's way, and they were reduced to asking an old man in a little dark dirty shop full of sausages and spaghetti. Nicholas tackled him in Italian, but he merely looked blank and vague. Lady Kilmichael then tried him in German, and this succeeded. Yes, he knew the Martins-Kapelle, and would take her to it; but, he said, looking rather sourly at Nicholas, it was no good the Herr Sohn coming, because the chapel now belonged to a sisterhood, and the nuns wouldn't let him in. Lady Kilmichael conveyed this information to Nicholas, who knew no German, and they arranged to meet for lunch later at the restaurant in the Piazza; then the young man went off, and Lady Kilmichael followed her guide.

Certainly she would never have found the Martins-Kapelle alone. They wandered in and out of passages and alleys, climbed up flights of steps which brought them out on the open top of the Palace wall, walked along it, and descended again – what an extraordinary place it was! Eventually Lady Kilmichael found herself standing before a door in a whitewashed corridor, which might well have been part of the interior of a house, but apparently wasn't; here, after ringing a bell, the old man left her. Lady Kilmichael waited – no one came – she rang again. At length the door was opened by a white-coiffed nun; Lady Kilmichael this time addressed her in German, but the nun merely looked blank and vague. Along the coast of Dalmatia there is always this extreme uncertainty as to whether the person one addresses will answer to German or Italian, if indeed to either. As a rule, men who were of an age to do military service before the War speak some German, which they picked up during their enforced term in the Austrian army, when Dalmatia was still a province of the Dual Monarchy. But the age-long tradition of Italian influence and Italian culture all along the coast is still persistent, and numbers of both men and women speak Italian as readily as their native Serbo-Croat. In spite of successive waves of invasion and colonisation by Slavonic tribes – Serbs, Slovenes, Croats – the old Roman cities of the coast have always clung tenaciously to their Latin heritage of blood, speech, laws and culture; the coin of the country today is the *dinar*, lineal descendant of the Latin *denarius*; the boats which bring wine in from the islands bear a strong resemblance to Roman galleys, with their low waists, their high poops and prows; the faces of the old women who sit selling lettuces and spring onions in the morning vegetable market in the Piazza delle Erbe at Ragusa are like Roman cameos of the best period, with their hawk-like profiles, close-lipped chiselled mouths, arched eyebrows and boldly set eyeballs. Strong as Jugo-Slav nationalist feeling may be today, the traveller cannot but feel himself, here, upon a classic shore.

Lady Kilmichael, unaware of all this, nevertheless tried the nun with Italian, with success. She was admitted, and led through more whitewashed corridors till, opening a small door, the nun ushered her into the chapel itself.

Lady Kilmichael's first thought was that if dolls' houses were ever fitted with private chapels, they would be rather like this one. Hollowed out of the thickness of the wall, the whole place was no bigger than a section of a fair-sized passage. Against each wall, in which one or two little windows were pierced, was a row of prayer desks, at the further end a small altar; the space before the altar was railed off from the desks by a rood screen or iconostasis of carved grey stone. The whole thing was minute, complete, ancient, and somehow touching, in the same way that a child's dress of two or three centuries ago is touching. But this tiny sanctuary had enshrined human prayers and human worship, not for a couple of centuries, but for a thousand years, and enshrined it still – the little lamp yet burned before the altar, incense hung faintly on the air, and when Grace presently asked permission to remain for some time and sketch, the calm-faced nun, having acceded to her request, knelt down quietly at one of the desks and prayed, with folded hands and bent head.

Lady Kilmichael's desire to sketch the Martins-Kapelle did not arise from its age, its holiness or its minute size, sensitive though she was to all these. In fact she did not really want to sketch the chapel itself at all. What she wanted was to make a drawing of the iconostasis. For carved in the hard closely grained grey stone she had found, precise, exact and indubitable, one of the best-known patterns of West Highland tomb slabs – the serpentine stem, with the three-lobed leaf fitting so elegantly into each curve of the loops. This is one of the most characteristic designs of all; used sometimes singly, more often doubled to form a series of circles with an object like a fig leaf in each, it occurs in lonely churchyards from Stornoway to Kintyre, from Barra in the Hebrides to Loch Awe. And here, beyond the possibility of mistake, it was, in a chapel of the ninth or tenth century in Spalato. Thrilled by this discovery, she sat down and drew it, with care and precision, thinking as she worked that she *must* somehow find out the actual date of the iconostasis, and must also try to get some light thrown on the puzzle of how that pattern came to be there. Who could she ask? Of course! – the curator of the Museum, the venerable Abbé B—, of whom the German on the boat had spoken. To the Museum she would go, that very afternoon, and try to get hold of him.

She finished her sketch, and then sat on for a few minutes in that quiet place, reluctant to leave it. Lady Kilmichael was one of those people who in a strange church are always prompted to pray. This wish came over her now; and as it did so she remembered the last time she had sat in a church, at Torcello. Then fear and unhappiness had been too strong in her for her to think, she supposed, of praying – anyhow she had not prayed, but had fled from the great Madonna. Now it was different; she had a feeling, unformulated but nevertheless strong, that she was learning something, getting somewhere; learning about freedom, learning about herself – not merely selfishly throwing her hand in, in resentment and despair. She felt – irrationally perhaps – *hopeful*. She slipped to her knees. Her darling Linnet, her darling boys, Walter – they were after all her own, her dearest and her best. Her thought just brushed that other child, with the yellow head and the unhappy eyes, to whose troubles she had so curiously been made a party. But she put it aside – he was not, so to speak, hers. No foreknowledge touched her then of a day when she would pray for Nicholas. One on each side of the tiny chapel aisle, in the thickness of a Roman palace wall, the nun and the Englishwoman prayed together.

EIGHT

For those whose imaginations can be touched at all by the sense of the past, there are few greater pleasures than to make an historical discovery for themselves, and on the spot. To know too much about a place beforehand may actually be a mistake, since it robs the traveller of this particular thrill of exploration and discovery – a thrill much keener than the satisfaction which the well-primed sightseer derives merely from recognising anticipated objects one by one. For Lady Kilmichael the loss of her book was really a blessing in disguise; owing to its absence, Spalato afforded her precisely this pleasure, this thrill.

Rather late, she appeared in the little restaurant in the Piazza where she was to meet Nicholas for lunch; he was sitting looking resigned at a table in the low hot room, steamy with food and the damp clothes of the patrons. She apologised, described the chapel – 'And look at this!' and she drew out her sketchbook with the drawing of the iconostasis.

'Not *another* pattern?' said the young man, rather gloomily, taking it to examine.

'Yes – such a beauty. And absolutely unmistakeable,' she said eagerly. 'I *must* go to the Museum this afternoon and find out about the date.' Then his tone, rather belatedly, penetrated her enthusiastic preoccupation. 'Does this all bore you very much?' she asked, rather wistfully.

'No no,' he said quickly, 'not a bit. I love it really. I was only teasing.' He smiled at her, a very nice smile. 'It only amuses me a little to see you get so eager about it. You don't mind my thinking that funny, do you?' he asked, cocking his head at her, in a very engaging way.

'No,' said Grace serenely. 'The children always think I'm funny. Now tell me where you went.'

Nicholas too had had a fruitful morning. He had gone to the Porta Aurea, the great northern gate, where his curiosity had been aroused by seeing on the wall of the inner court of the gateway, near a small door, a blue and white tin notice – 'No. 1, Porta Aurea.'

'It looked like a house number in a street,' he said, 'but there was no house to be seen, only the door in the wall. I thought I must go into this, so I rang the bell.'

'You didn't really?' Lady Kilmichael interjected.

'Of course I did! I wanted to find out where the house was. A young man came down, and, thank God, he spoke Italian, so I asked him if he would show me his house. He was frightfully pleased, and took me all over it. You go up a lot of stairs in pitch dark to a sort of first floor, and there are three or four little rooms all on different levels – a kitchen, and a place where an old party was ironing clothes, and one or two bedrooms – I can't remember, and anyhow, there were onions and washing hanging up in *all* the rooms. But they are all very narrow, because they're burrowed right out of the heart of the gateway walls, just like your chapel. It was a most extraordinary place. So now I've been to call at Number One Porta Aurea, Spalato, and I know what it's like inside.'

He was very satisfied with himself, and Lady Kilmichael rather envied him this insight into the domestic life of the Spalatans – or Splits, as Nicholas called them. He suggested that one day they should 'do the Splits' thoroughly, together, and see how many houses they could get into. Then he described the rest of his morning. He had gone out onto the sea front, to examine the south façade of the Palace. 'It reminded me of parts of Edinburgh or Bath,' he said – 'all those houses somehow combined into one whole. Has it ever struck you,' he went on, 'what a peculiar feature that is of Palladian domestic architecture in England – the way a whole row of houses was built as a single unit, with a great pediment in the middle and often higher houses at the ends, to carry out the idea? Adelphi Terrace, for instance. On the Continent they tended much more to treat each individual house as an architectural unit in their Renaissance building.'

Lady Kilmichael had never thought of this for herself, but on recalling certain foreign towns, and also Adam Street and John Street, Adelphi, she realised the justness of Nicholas's observation, and agreed.

'Adelphi Terrace and all that is Adam, isn't it?' she said.

'Of course. The Adam brothers practically *were* Palladian building in England,' said Nicholas, making one of the sweeping assertions of youth. 'Anyhow, they coloured the whole thing. But it's odd to find something so like it here, that has happened by accident and is partly, at least, sixteen hundred years old.'

Lady Kilmichael again agreed; but how little odd it was, she was very soon to find out. After lunch, she insisted on a return to the hotel to change into dry shoes, and then, in a taxi, they set out for the Museum, Nicholas making fun of her for fussing about wet feet.

'They were cold,' said Grace defensively. 'I hate cold feet.'

'I had an old Uncle who hated them too,' said Nicholas, beginning to grin. 'We were staying there once, and there was a huge dinner party, and someone started talking about cold feet, their cause and cure. And in one of those pauses – you know, when one hears every word – Uncle Nicholas, who was frightfully absent-minded, suddenly boomed out in the most innocent way – "My wife has the coldest feet of any woman I ever slept with!" My Mother was appalled.'

He glanced rather shyly at Lady Kilmichael after telling this story, to see how she would take it. One of the rather crucial moments in any relationship between two highly civilised people is the making of the first even slightly *risqué* joke. Nothing kills an incipient liking more effectually, rouses a more violent sense of affront and distaste, than to have an impropriety, however funny, forced on one by a person from whom one is not yet ready to accept it. On the other hand, the first sharing of a slightly improper joke marks a definite step forward in any acquaintance. In this instance Nicholas Humphries had judged exactly right – the story itself, and the rather shy comicality of his expression as he told it, amused Grace Kilmichael enormously. And she rightly regarded his telling it as a mark of confidence. One of the things which always made her feel that perhaps she and Linnet were not quite a hopeless 'mess' was the fact that Linnet, even during those last cruel months, always came flying to tell her Mother the latest in the way of good stories, however hair-raising. Remembering this – 'Didn't your Mother see that it was funny?' she asked Nicholas.

'Not at the time – she was too shattered. Celia and I persuaded her to see it afterwards,' he answered. 'You see my Father can't bear that sort of joke, and for years my Mother felt it unconscientious to be amused by what he would disapprove of. It's really Celia who's cured her of that; if anything, she's more afraid of Celia now than of Father, so Celia is training her up bit by bit.'

'Why is your Mother afraid of Celia?' Lady Kilmichael asked, putting now the question she had deferred that morning. She awaited the answer with an eager expectancy that would have surprised the boy if he had realised it.

'Oh, she puts it across her, one way and another,' he answered airily. 'It's partly because she's rather clever, and she uses her cleverness to do Mother down, now and again. But really I think it's more that she keeps her at a distance. My Mother likes to pet and spoil people, and run round doing things for them, and to know everything they're up to and help them do it. *I* don't mind that – I think it's rather sweet,' the young man said simply, with an indescribable mixture of detachment and affection in his tone, 'but Celia won't stand for any of it. She keeps Mother in her place. I'm really the only person she's allowed to spoil,' he said, looking amused.

'But why does Celia mind being spoilt?' Grace asked, with almost painful interest. Linnet had lately – oh, so completely! – kept her own Mother at a distance, and Grace had so often and so bitterly wondered why. Perhaps from this member of Linnet's generation she might learn the answer.

'It fusses her,' said Nicholas readily. 'She's quite able to do everything for herself now, in just the way she wants, and she doesn't want someone else to do it for her even in some better way. She isn't a child any more – that's what my Mother always forgets, though it's not for lack of being told! You see, really in a way,' he went on, more slowly, 'I suppose Celia is right when she says that it's largely self-indulgence on Mother's part. She's trying to do things for Celia that Celia doesn't in the least *want* done, because she herself enjoys doing them. Only *I* think Celia is rather too brutal about it. *I* don't really want to have my bed choked with hot-water bottles whenever I sneeze, and be given whiskies and lemon last thing; or to have my suits forever reft away to be cleaned, and all that. If I want a whisky I can ask the butler for it; and I *am* really capable of looking out my own trains for that complicated journey, sixty miles up to London! But I don't mind letting my Mother do all these things, because she adores doing them. She doesn't get too much fun,' he said, 'and it doesn't fidget me like it does Celia. Hullo, here we are.'

The taxi had drawn up at a gateway. Passing through, they found a garden surrounded by cloisters, in which were set out sarcophagi, friezes, inscriptions, statues and fragments of statues – a most un-museum like place. A large modern building on the further side they rightly guessed to be the Museum proper. On their way thither Nicholas spotted two more pieces of stone carved with patterns like the fragment at Torcello. At the Museum Lady Kilmichael enquired for the Abbé B—, and was presently confronted by a courteous little old gentleman with white hair and a rather unclerical black suit; to him she explained her mission, and showed him, by way of illustration, the two carved stones in the cloister which Nicholas had found. The Abbé examined these objects through his pince-nez, and then turned to Lady Kilmichael. The man she must see, he said, was his young colleague, Dr Rajitch, who knew all about these patterns, and was indeed writing a book on them. If she would step back to the Museum, he would send for him. He himself, he courteously explained, was chiefly interested in the *Roman* antiquities. Lady Kilmichael, equally courteous, spoke with admiration of the arrangement of these in the cloister, and with enthusiasm of the Palace. The old man was delighted; he led her into the library, a large fine room, well lit and beautifully arranged, and began to spread out on the tables some of his most cherished treasures in the way of books. At these Nicholas and Grace gazed with interest, and indeed with some embarrassment, as the eager old *savant* piled up more and more tomes in front of them – books on the Palace in Latin, in Italian, in German. At last he plumped down a great folio volume before Lady Kilmichael, saying pleasantly – 'The finest illustrations of all are in this – and it was written by an Englishman! See, here – and here' – opening the book in the middle and showing some superb engravings of the Baptistery and the Porta Aurea. 'Now I fetch Doctor Rajitch' – and he stepped briskly out of the room.

'Isn't he sweet?' said Nicholas, looking up at Lady Kilmichael across the table. She didn't answer – she was absorbed in the big book of engravings. 'Nicholas!' she said a moment later in a startled tone – 'Come and look at this!'

He rose and went round to her, to see what she had found that surprised her so much. She had turned back to the title page – leaning over her shoulder he read, in heavy type, the author's name –

Robert Adam
1764

'Do you *see*?' she said, turning and looking up at him with astonished eyes – 'Robert Adam himself! He was here – he drew all this. No wonder the Palace front – you said at lunch it reminded you of English buildings that the Adams had done. Of course it does, if he made such a study of this place! It would be bound to colour his work. Isn't it wonderful to find that out, here? Did *you* know he'd ever been here?'

Nicholas did not, and in his heart of hearts he was a good deal impressed, both by the fact of the connection between Robert Adam and Spalato, and by Lady Kilmichael's promptness in spotting it. But he was almost more impressed by his new friend's delightful enthusiasm for such matters – a thing he was not in the least prepared for in women. She really *was* rather a remarkable person. And his heart warming to her for all this, being the child of his century he merely said, in a very neutral voice – 'M'm – yes; Diocletian's palace the direct ancestor of the Adelphi! It is quite a thought, isn't it?'

Grace was a little chilled. She knew that he thought her enthusiasm over her stones merely funny, and her own family's attitude to her interests had prepared her for that. But this was architecture, his own subject, and she had expected him to be rather pleased. At this check to her eagerness she realised suddenly that she was cold and tired, that the hotel would be chilly when she got back to it, that she was in a strange town, where she knew no one except this perverse boy, and that it was pouring with rain. She looked down at the book again, and began to turn the pages. 'Well, *I* think it's rather wonderful,' she said – and though she tried to speak cheerfully, her voice, in spite of herself, held a note of reproach.

To her great astonishment, Nicholas suddenly patted her shoulder, several little quick pats, in the 'There – there – there' manner that one uses to console a child. 'Of course it is! I think so too, really,' he said, poking his head round to see her face, and grinning at her. 'Only you're so—'

He had no time to finish his sentence. At that moment – '*Voici Monsieur le Docteur Rajitch!*' said the Abbé, bustling back into the library. Lady Kilmichael stood up to greet the newcomer, a stout young man with very fair hair and immense spectacles. Dr Rajitch only spoke German besides his native Serbo-Croat; on learning that she spoke it also, he begged her to do him the favour to step into his room, where he had all his photographs and materials. 'Your son will perhaps amuse himself among the collections,' said the Abbé in French. Nicholas saluted this relationship with raised eyebrows, but Grace felt unequal to coping with it at the moment, and was borne off by Dr Rajitch to his sanctum.

There followed for Lady Kilmichael a most strenuous afternoon, sustaining a highly technical conversation in an unfamiliar tongue. And on the whole it was singularly inconclusive. Dr Rajitch was writing, he told her, a book on these very patterns in which she was so much interested, to be entitled – 'The Universal European Entwined Ornament-Motives.' He traced for her on a marked map their distribution on the Continent – all through the Balkans, up the Adriatic coast to Northern Italy, and right across the Lombard plain into Southern France; down the Italian peninsula as far as Ravenna, which was full of them, and a little further – in Southern Italy not at all. Nor, to his knowledge, were any such 'motives' to be found in Central or Northern Europe, nor in the Iberian peninsula.

How watertight the compartments of knowledge were, Grace thought. Here on the one hand was Nigel, studying these patterns as a Scottish-Irish development of art; and on the other Dr Rajitch, quite prepared to write a book on their 'universal' European character, but wholly ignoring the tremendous flowering of such ornament on the western coasts of the British Isles. When her turn came, she described the abundance of such work in Britain: the great crosses of Ireland; the similar crosses on the West Coast of Scotland; above all, the wealth of incised tomb slabs bearing the same designs, not only in the important ecclesiastical centres such as Iona, Saddell and Kiells, but in small and obscure country churchyards all up and down the coast, from the Clyde to the Butt of Lewis. She produced her drawing of the iconostasis in the Martins-Kapelle, and extracted from him the information that the Martins-Kapelle was either ninth or tenth century, no one knew which for certain, and that the iconostasis might be contemporary or might not – probably was.

But Dr Rajitch was not to be turned aside by the Martins-Kapelle. He was at once thrilled and appalled, it seemed to Grace, to learn that his ornament-motives extended to what he called 'the Atlantic coastal lands of Europe,' especially to Ireland; this discovery would not only necessitate a fresh chapter in his book, but might call for a modification of his theory as to their distribution. Ever since Torcello Grace had been wondering how the designs found their way from Argyllshire to the Adriatic – Dr Rajitch now began, audibly, to speculate how they might have found their way from the Adriatic to Argyll. It was Lady Kilmichael's first personal introduction to the continental outlook. She had never thought of Great Britain as an 'Atlantic coastal land,' an obscure and outlying fringe of Europe. Like many English people she tended unconsciously, in her heart of hearts, to think of Europe, taking it by and large, as a Dark Continent, full of foreigners – very civilised, but still foreigners. Being an artist, and having spent a good deal of time in France, she felt this less than many people, and hardly extended it to the French; but her reaction to Dr Rajitch's point of view, here in Jugo-Slavia, in a way revealed her own feeling to herself, and she was amused by it.

Dr Rajitch surprised her by another manifestation of the continental outlook too – the extraordinary respect accorded to Ireland as a centre of culture, of art and religion during the Dark Ages. It was Ireland which bothered Dr Rajitch most. Ireland, he said rather gloomily, might conceivably have been the fountainhead, the original source of entwined ornament-motives; Ireland and not Asia; and the designs might have been carried over Europe in illuminated manuscripts, as Irish scholarship had been carried. But no – on second thought the dates did not fit; if the period she gave him for the Irish crosses was correct, Ravenna and the Balkan work was far earlier. For the moment the problem of Ireland remained insoluble – as did the strange gap in Central Europe, extending from Northern Italy almost to the Roman Wall, in which no entwined ornament-motives were to be found. And that was all there was to be said. Dr Rajitch begged for photographs of the Irish and Scottish Stones, which Lady Kilmichael promised, in due course, to send him; and they exchanged cards – a little doubtfully on Grace's part. But the curator of the Museum in Spalato could hardly be a menace! And then – considerably enlightened, but rather more tired than before – she took her leave, and went to see what had become of Nicholas. Good heavens! it was half-past five – she had been stewing with that Professor for over two hours. What had that poor boy been doing with himself?

Nicholas had been doing something rather unwonted, for him – quite spontaneously taking a good deal of trouble for somebody else. He wandered through the museum for some time, but after an hour his interest was exhausted, and he began, rather gloomily, to look at his watch and feel that he was wasting his time. He had hoped to get down to painting at once, at Spalato – at least to get what materials he wanted together today, to prepare a canvas and choose a subject, so that he might begin without delay on the morrow. And here was the whole day being wasted, frittered away over those dim patterns which enthralled Lady Kilmichael so. How funny of her to care so much about them – but evidently she knew a lot. She wasn't in the least like ordinary people (ordinary parents, he meant), what with her painting, and this passion for a rather specialised archaeology. Ordinary people fussed over their houses and children, and gave tea parties and dinner parties, and read novels; but they never seemed to be ferociously interested in anything which took them out of an armchair – only in D. H. Lawrence, whom they discussed by the hour together. Extraordinary! He himself could see nothing whatever in Lawrence – he didn't like novels to be so clinical; and most of his friends felt the same. It was very much one up to Lady K. that she had never mentioned D. H. Lawrence so far – as a rule older people simply rubbed your nose in him from the word go; one of the more hateful of older people's many futile and boring assumptions about one as a member of the genus 'young' was that one was interested in D. H. Lawrence! But she was much too intelligent for that – she was very intelligent. Only so funnily eager! How thrilled she had been over Robert Adam. He hadn't meant to dash her about that – he was rather an idiot, sometimes! Of course the connection between Spalato and the Adam buildings in England was really exciting, and it was most spry of her to spot it. He hoped she wasn't really soured – especially when she'd been such an angel about his losing her book.

So meditating, Nicholas had wandered out into the cloister, where his eye was presently caught by the two stones. It occurred to him that she would be sure to want drawings of these for Nigel, and a combined impulse of remorse, admiration and affection caused him to pull out his sketchbook and spend the rest of that damp and chilly afternoon sitting on the cloister parapet, muttering to himself about the extreme probability of his getting piles, and making two very beautiful drawings. They *were* brutes to draw! But she would be sure to want them, and to be pleased with him for having done them; she would say 'Oh *thank* you, Nicholas,' with her soft emphasis. She made the name Nicholas, which he loathed, sound rather nice. Turning up the collar of his mackintosh, the owner of that name worked with unremitting diligence.

NINE

'Yes, but I still don't quite like it, Nicholas. All that foreground is too flat; it's too much the same quality as the wall and the tower. You want to make more difference between flowers and stone. Why don't you use another brush for that part? And I think you'd do better with a little green in the paint for that – there's always a green tone about the white of flowers. I don't like that shadow from the column, either.'

'What's wrong with it?'

'You've got it too like the tower shadow – don't you see? It's nearer – well then, bring it forward.' She waved her hand at it. 'And I should get some red into the picture, here, and here – that will help to pull the whole thing together, and warm it up. If you can get all that better I think it will really be rather good.'

'You're a hard taskmistress, Lady K.! I was rather pleased with it.'

'No, I don't feel you've quite got it, my dear child. It wants pulling together. I know it's difficult, all that white on white – but you *did* choose it!'

'And you *did* think I couldn't do it, didn't you?' said Nicholas, screwing himself round on the camp stool to grin up at Lady Kilmichael, as she stood behind him, studying the canvas on the easel. 'And you're quite surprised that Little Nicky has done it even as well as he has!'

'Yes – but it's not the least use for Little Nicky' – the warmth of an imperceptible smile came into her voice on the two words – 'to half-paint things. You must *see* a subject properly, the essentials of it; and then get them into a picture. It's no good painting shapeless unselected masses of objects.'

They were on the broad *fondamento* at Traü, outside the Porta Marina, over which the Lion of S. Mark, in his little penthouse, presides with such a singularly coy and lamb-like expression. Immediately to the right a projecting piece of the city wall cuts off the view abruptly – to the left the sea, the hills and shores beyond showed blue and pearl-like as a milky opal, faintly traced with the masts of ships moored below the quayside; the long vista was closed at the further end by the creamy polygonal mass of the Camerlengo tower, part of the old Venetian fortifications, its heavy crenellated battlements crumbling here and there – in the foreground that white column whose shadow was bothering Nicholas rose, abrupt and solitary, from the pavement. That view up the *fondamento* is at all times one of the loveliest aspects of the lovely little island town, but in the month of May a strange enchantment is added. The inhabitants of Traü then cut, in their mainland fields, the harvest of the starry white flowers of *Chrysanthemum cinerariaefolium*, from which insect powder is made, and spread them out on mats to dry in the sun all along the *fondamento*, so that the whole of that immense space is floored, not with cobbles or flagstones, but with flowers. There was something incredibly lovely about that pale pavement of blossom, spreading up to the foot of the white column, and stretching away towards the creamy mass of the tower beyond, under the tender blue of the North Adriatic sky – a strange blue, washed with silver, as if it had taken its tone from the silvery white of the limestone hills, the pale rocks of that arid coast. And it was this aspect of Traü which Nicholas had elected to paint.

It was his second picture, and he had already spent a couple of days on it. He had begun with a brilliant little painting of three women in the pottery market outside the former Porta Aenea at Spalato, which he had finished in a day – a painting so good that Grace was astonished. It seemed that he really could make a picture as well as a sketch; make a whole out of his subject, with the solidity of the actual somehow welded and fused into the significance of a design. This, for her, was the essential thing, and it looked as if Nicholas had got it. Technical accomplishment of course he still lacked, except for his draughtsmanship, which was already astonishing; his sense of colour seemed to her weak too. But that he was worth helping she felt sure. After that first picture she insisted on going to Traü, to get fresh material for her own sketches for the American contract. She found plenty. The little mediaeval town, filling its island to the brim like one of those toy cities in ivory with painted roofs, set in a border of looking glass, was so full of delicious things to draw that she hardly knew where to begin. And there Nicholas had fixed on the view along the *fondamento*, with the flowers, the column and the tower, as the thing he would and must paint next. Grace had thought it overambitious, and said so; lovely in itself, all those different planes and tones of creamy white, in the soft clear light, might be difficult to make anything of, she considered. But Nicholas had persisted, and had tackled it with a measure of success that surprised her. It gave, indeed, just the measure of his success that she was now become so critical – was forcing him towards such a high degree of excellence, of completeness. If he had failed, as she expected, she would have encouraged him and left him alone.

They had fallen into a sort of routine of work, quickly and almost without noticing it. The buses from Spalato to Traü were slow, and at awkward times; the hire of a car and chauffeur was exorbitant. Nicholas, suddenly displaying a quite unexpected resourcefulness, had thereupon routed out, through the agency of one of his sitters in the pottery market, a rather dilapidated Peugeot car which he managed to hire without a driver for quite a reasonable sum. Every day, in this, they drove over to Traü, where he parked it on the small piazza by the bridge; they worked all the morning, took a long luncheon interval at the little restaurant on the quay, sitting under the shade of the awning, and then, if they had the energy, filled up their sketch-books for an hour or so in the afternoon. At four or thereabouts they knocked off, and armed with Grace's tea basket drove somewhere for a picnic and a little sightseeing, only returning at dark to Spalato, to dine at the restaurant in the Piazza, and then to sit outside it, drinking coffee or beer, watching the shadows flung by the street lamps repeating the grace of the colonnades in black along the white pavement, and the octagonal lantern of Diocletian's mausoleum grey against the stars.

Grace loved these expeditions. The landscape of Dalmatia, as they gradually revealed it to her, was a perpetually renewed enchantment. She could not get over the fact that the prevailing colour of that coast should be white. Shades, gradations of tone of course there were, but the impression was of a white landscape; and the summits of the mountains, above the last traces of vegetation, were really white, like paper or cream. And in what subtle ways these white hills took their colour from the light and atmosphere about them! On lowering days they showed a sullen grey, featureless and dull; at noon, in sunshine, they had the warmth of ivory; there was a moment at evening when, most strange of all, as the light left the sky all the solidity of rock and stone deserted them, and they melted into the sky, became invisible, lost in one incredible tender tone, like a shadowy pearl. She was charmed too with the near-at-hand details of the landscape – the grace of olive trees, the patches of bright flowers, goats browsing among ruins, the dark flame-like shapes of cypresses round some monastery – and for a background, always, that delicate opalescent blue of the sea and the shores of bays and islands.

Whether working or sightseeing, of course she and Nicholas talked. It is surprising the amount of talk that two people will get through during a week of solid *tête-à-tête*. Now in modern life it is an extreme rarity, outside marriage, to get a week of uninterrupted companionship with any human being. Nicholas was too inexperienced to realise this, and Lady Kilmichael too interested in other things to think about it one way or the other. She was absorbed in her sketches, in seeking out the various bits of entwined ornament-motives to which Dr Rajitch had directed her, and above all in Nicholas's painting. These interests, half separate and half in common, made their companionship a delightfully rational and natural thing. But there was little that Grace did not now know about the General, his wife and Celia; and Nicholas for his part had gained a very lively impression of Nigel, Teddy and Linnet, from the little remarks, half deprecating, half complacent, which Lady Kilmichael let fall about her children from time to time.

But such external details, though illuminating, were not the most important fruits of these days spent together by this very oddly assorted couple. They were getting to know not only the details of each other's lives, but getting to know one another – a different thing. The process of getting to know anyone is not merely a matter of listening, watching and understanding. M. Maurois has pointed out how, in any new relationship, we feel an unconscious need to create, as it were, a new picture, a new edition of ourselves to present to the fresh person who claims our interest; for them, we in a strange sense wish to, and do, start life anew. Grace Kilmichael was not analytical enough to recognise either this wish or this process in herself, but she was unconsciously doing it. All she realised was that she was finding this new friendship strangely interesting. It is a fact, not always recognised, that married women of her generation are apt to have singularly few independent relationships. They are probably on terms of intimacy with a few women, friends of their youth with whom they have 'kept up,' as Grace had kept up with Lady Roseneath; but outside their own families with few other people, and with men hardly at all. This lack of experience in human relationships is one of the factors which most handicaps them in their dealings with the young, now that the old-fashioned stereotyped relation between parents and children has broken down. Today each family creates a new relationship for itself, on a fresh and individual pattern and on its own merits. And many women, unused to this delightful task, and utterly at sea without the formal landmarks of family behaviour which guided their own youth in relation to their mothers, flounder, helpless and distressed. Married women so often become more an institution than a person – to their own families a wife or a mother, to other people the wife or the mother of somebody else. Apart from her painting, Grace Kilmichael had been an institution for years. She didn't mind it; she hadn't really noticed it; but when Nicholas Humphries started treating her as a person, being interested in her as herself, 'Lady K.', and not as Nigel's or Teddy's or Linnet's mother, or as the brilliant Sir Walter Kilmichael's nice wife, she *did* notice it. She found it something quite new and rather delightful. And entirely without conscious intention, without being aware of it, the presentation of herself which she was making to Nicholas was, in some subtle way, more personal and less 'institutional' than it would have been if she had met him in her London house, as a friend of Linnet's or Nigel's.

But what she was very clearly aware of was the extraordinary interest of all she was learning from Nicholas about those mysterious and baffling creatures, the young. His accounts of his family, his day-to-day attitude to people, books, and things, all threw a flood of light for her on the new generation. And whenever she got what Teddy would have called a 'slant' on such matters, she thought of Linnet, and of herself and Linnet. This very morning, while she sketched the fish market at Traü, she had been thinking again of what Nicholas had said on the way to the Museum about Mrs Humphries' spoiling of her children being really a form of self-indulgence. She had always meant to talk to him again about it, but somehow she never had – there had been so many other things to talk about. Was there so much self-indulgence in doing things for one's children? When they were small, anyhow, what one did for them was often arduous and exhausting, and at the time, and to the doer, felt much more like self-sacrifice! But that was all over – now was the point. And as her pencil sped and her eye travelled from her paper to her subject and back, her mind ran over various recent episodes with Linnet, which had roused that young person's reprobation, seeing them in the light of Celia and her mother. With considerably more detachment than ever before, Lady Kilmichael examined her motives as well as her actions – detachment was a habit she was catching from Nicholas. Yes, she did often remind Linnet to write her Collinses; she knew she would do them in the end, but she wanted her to do them promptly; it was more polite, it was obviously better to write them at once. But when she enquired within herself *why* she wanted Linnet to be polite, she was forced to admit the existence of a self-regarding motive – she wanted Linnet, her daughter, in a sense her own creation, to be thought polite; to do her credit, and not discredit. So there was *that* to it! Of course when she or the boys *did* come and ask to have this or that done for them – 'you're rather a hand at that, Miss Stanway' – it was the dearest pleasure, the tenderest flattery. Well, she told herself, with stubborn instinctive common sense, that was natural and quite all right. But trains and things – Nicholas had spoken of them; Linnet was always missing trains or engagements through sheer fecklessness, and sometimes the things she missed were important. Was one then never to say – if you don't start now you'll be late? Must one stand by and see them do things really badly, for lack of a word?

It was at this point in her discussion with herself that Nicholas's voice had summoned her – 'Lady K. Could you spare a second to come and look?' Now, standing behind him, making her comments, the thought came into her mind – in painting anyhow one couldn't let people do things badly – one had to try to make them see what was wrong, indicate the right way. She was doing that now, vigorously, far more vigorously than she usually remonstrated with Linnet, and Nicholas didn't mind a bit! Of course painting was different, somehow. But why was it different?

Before she could answer that question, Nicholas replied to her last criticism.

'No, I know – but I think I have got the main points of this taped now, if I only get this pernicious floral effect right, don't you? – and the shadow?'

'Yes, I do.' She glanced at her watch. 'Nicholas, how long do you think you'll be? You know we're going to Clissa, and it's a good long way. Are you likely to get it finished before lunch, do you think?'

'I daresay, if lunch can be two-ish – but it doesn't matter if I haven't – I can go on with it tomorrow.'

'I thought we might want to spend the day at Clissa tomorrow, if we like it,' said Grace.

'We can spend the day after there just as well, can't we?' returned Nicholas, working the recommended green into a white mass on his – or rather Lady Kilmichael's – palette.

Grace didn't answer at once. Actually apart from Clissa, the hill fortress commanding the pass into the interior, up beyond Salona, she felt that she had seen most of Spalato and its environs, and rather wanted to move on to Ragusa. Oh well, there was really no hurry – one day was as good as another; time hardly counted on this magic shore. They could talk about that later.

'We'll see,' she said easily. And leaving Nicholas to his painting she went off to the Duomo to draw the little business-like cherubs, with faces like immature but immensely determined stockbrokers, who thrust their flambeaux so menacingly through the false doors in the panelling in the Capella Orsini. She thought about the picture she had just been criticising. It was good. She herself would have tackled it differently: concentrated on all those related masses of white, put the emphasis there, made everything else subsidiary. Nicholas hadn't – he had stressed the architectural quality, shoved the architectural detail at you in a way that she felt was out of proportion; and like most draughtsmen he tended to paint in lines. The picture had precision, too much precision – and too little atmosphere; he had rather missed the quality of warmth and light which to her eye was so much there. It was a *young* person's picture; it gave him away – that over-precision was a reflection of the artificial rigidity of someone not sure of himself, a person afraid to surrender to warmth and light – a young person, in fact! But then he was insensitive to colour; that was his weak spot; there he most needed to develop both his perception and his technique. But one must let that come, gradually; one couldn't interfere too much. She could help him – a little – to paint what he saw; she couldn't dictate to him about what he was to see. Moru had been so skilful about that – she wished the child could have worked with Moru. '*Mais demandez cela à vos propres yeux!*' he used to say, in answer to requests for advice; though he taught so much, he always respected a person's individual vision.

Her own phrase hit her, as one's own phrases sometimes do. To respect a person's individual vision! And abandoning the winged infant stockbrokers, she sat back and thought – Was it just what she didn't do with Linnet? Must one do that, even with one's own children, for whom one was so much responsible? And even if Linnet's individual vision was of a person who habitually sent belated Collinses and missed important trains, and left expensive pochettes and gloves scattered all over London, like a top dressing over a flower bed? Up to a point she had abstained from criticism – but largely because the results of criticism were so painful; from fear, not from any settled principle. She decided to talk to Nicholas about it – he was very clear-headed. And she went back to the formidable cherubs.

But even while she drew their resolute faces, Linnet, that formidable child, was communing on paper with her best friend.

It's really rather extraordinary about Mums. I had a letter from her the other day, from Venice – just 'Venice,' like that; no address. She sent me a cheque for my cloak, the late lamented, and urged a velvet (which wasn't much good, as I'd already got a *lamé*) and generally wrote a rather sweet letter. But she never said where she was going, or where she was, bar Venice. I told Poppy, because he is really getting into rather a state about her, and he put Aunt Gina up to write tactfully to that God-awful Roseneath woman, who lives in Venice, to find out about her movements. But we haven't heard yet. I gather Poppy has more or less been driven into a state of confidante-ing with Aunt Gina, and I hope to goodness she takes the opportunity to give him a home truth or two about Our Rose. I'm not at all sure that she hasn't, because they had a sort of conference the other day, before the Roseneath letter went off, and Poppy came out looking most soured. And next day when I was lunching with him, Grimes came in and announced 'Mrs Barum on the telephone,' in his most unctuous voice – and I heard Poppy being firmly unable to do at least six things she wanted him to.

Aunt Gina takes Mum's absence rather calmly, it seems to me. I wonder if she's really been in on it all along. She adores Mums. But she is getting worried about Poppy. He rather overdid it in the States, and he isn't sleeping, I gather. She's nagging him to see Sir John Lord, but you know what parents are. If *we* cut our fingers, off with us to Lord Dawson of Penn! But they themselves go on quietly dying of cancer or something, without a word to anyone, till the hearse is practically at the door.

When Lady Kilmichael had finished the cherubs in the Duomo she went out through the Porta Marina onto the *fondamento* again. Nicholas was painting away furiously, and not wishing to disturb him, she went quietly across to the steps at the quayside and sat down to wait. A sort of lane had been left between the mats of flowers, leading from the steps to the fishmarket, but on both sides of her they lay thick. She plunged her hand idly into the soft white mass, picking up the dull creamy heads, sniffing their sharp, rather medicinal smell, and letting them fall again – now and then she glanced at Nicholas, and thought what a good picture she could do of him sitting there, working, his yellow head such a sharp note of colour in its white surroundings, above the dark patch of his own shadow. But she was too tired and lazy even to make a sketch of him – she had been working hard all the morning; and instead she began to think again about his painting. The very fact that it was so good was beginning to present her with rather a problem. She had very little doubt that he could become a good painter; but if his family was determined that he should not, that he must be an architect, was she justified in encouraging him to paint – helping him, teaching him? These two pictures had been a test, an experiment, and quite legitimate; but if he wanted to come on to Ragusa, as she felt pretty sure he would, and go on painting, ought she to let him? It was more than 'letting': he would be using her things, he would demand her help; she would be, most directly, aiding and abetting him in a course of which his parents disapproved. But if he had it in him to do really good work, wasn't it almost a crime to prevent his talent from developing? And at the moment the thing was very much in her hands, she knew that; she had not yet delivered her official verdict on his two pictures, but she realised that that verdict would be in the nature of a casting vote. She had observed during the past week a growing dependence on her judgement on the young man's part, not only in what concerned painting – he was always asking her opinion on this matter and on that, listening with respect, reverting to her former pronouncements; in spite of his growing freedom about teasing her, delightfully and childishly, he depended on her. If her verdict was unfavourable or discouraging, it would more or less settle the painting question, for the time being at any rate. When they met, his parents' decision had been accepted, however unhappily – it was her rash offer to let him show what he could do which had reopened the question. But how could she deliver an unfavourable verdict, when she believed that here was a solid, even an unusual talent?

The artist and the parent thus met and battled in Lady Kilmichael, as she sat on the quay at Traü. And neither would give way. But if anything the artist was the more truculent. And presently the parent turned traitor to some extent. Glancing again at the figure by the easel, content, absorbed, eager, she remembered the listless unhappy young man she had met at Torcello, and contrasted him with the gay companion of the last few days, full of nonsense and high spirits from morning till night. And from some inarticulate depths of consciousness a conviction, unformulated but strong, rose to the working level of her mind – that painting did something more important for Nicholas than the mere gratifying of a wish; that this form of work and liberty of expression straightened out in him something that was tangled, set free in him something that, shut up, turned bad and poisoned him from below. She could not explain this certainty, even to herself – but it existed. Then how could she, could anyone in their senses, with a heart in their body, return a child deliberately to that prison of dejection and gloom?

There was only one thing to be done, she decided at last – they must have it out, and she must make him let his Mother, at any rate, know that he was painting again. But that – oh dear, that meant letters, and possibly her whereabouts given away! Still, there was no reason to suppose that Mrs Humphries would be in any way in touch with Walter or Gina, though they had plenty of common acquaintances. She couldn't really ask Nicholas not to mention her name. Or could she? No, not without giving a reason, and she couldn't give her reason. She must just take the risk. At least then it would all be open and above board. She would not be the slave of her fears!

Her resolution taken, she felt relieved. She took off her hat, lit a cigarette, and sat looking out over the blue water and the pale shore opposite. Lovely, lovely place, Dalmatia! Every now and then she glanced round at Nicholas, still at work – and each time she did so, she felt that her decision was the right one.

TEN

To get to Clissa from Traü one follows at first the shore road towards Spalato, along that strip of fertile coast sheltered from the *bora*, the bitter north wind, by the mountains behind, and ennobled with the seven fortresses, each with a village at its foot, which still recall the dominion of Venice in the days of her power. At Salona the road forks; the right-hand branch crosses the Giadro towards Spalato, the left-hand one passes through the modern village of Salona, and then climbs in great loops towards Clissa and the pass.

They halted for tea as soon as they were clear of the plain, just where the road begins to climb, on a little patch of smooth turf under two gnarled and ancient olive trees, whose roots grasped an angle of ruined wall. Here Nicholas lit the Primus stove and set out the tea things, two tasks which he now insisted on performing as a matter of routine; then he went off to look for wildflowers – he knew a good deal about wildflowers and they were, he said, a useful counterblast to the stones. Grace remained to watch the kettle. She took off her hat, and leaning her head against the wall, looked through half-closed eyes at the scene before her – the fine pattern cut by the thin olive leaves against the sky, their little shadows moving over the tea things set out on the turf, itself patterned with small dead leaves, silvery-brown – below, the plain spread out in the evening sunshine, with the sea beyond. And for the second time that day a phrase of her own arrested her attention. Suddenly the thought, 'this is like an idyll,' drifted into her head – and having drifted, stayed; the words stood up like a small signpost in her mind. Yes, it was idyllic, this life she and Nicholas were leading, of hard work and pleasant idleness, of meals in the open air, and – of late – of most serene and unclouded companionship. And for the first time the rarity, the unusual quality of the whole thing struck her. It was very odd that she should find herself wandering through Illyria with this delightful boy. (Nicholas had by now definitely assumed the status of a delightful boy.) But it was more than odd; it had the unexpectedness and simplicity, the tranquil naturalness of some Greek story, set in a clear pastoral landscape. Complete even to the goats, she thought, shooing away an intrusive Nannie and a couple of snow-white kids, which came and sniffed at the tea things. The kettle was nearly boiling – in a moment she must call Nicholas. Pulling out her case, she powdered her nose, rather absent-mindedly – she was getting quite brown with all this marvellous sun! She looked up from the little mirror to see Nicholas standing in front of her.

'You don't do much of that, do you?' he said, glancing at the pretty shagreen object with a certain hostility.

'No, I don't. I can't be bothered to do it very thoroughly,' said Grace, putting the flap-jack away. 'It takes so long.'

'Thank goodness you don't,' he said, regarding her thoughtfully. 'I do hate it so. I can't think why women make up as they do.' He sat down beside her. 'Does Linnet do it much?' he asked.

'Yes – about the usual amount for her age.'

'Red nails?'

'Yes, red nails.'

'Pity,' he said judgementally. 'I like the sound of your Linnet, bar that. Why do you let her?'

'It isn't easy to stop them doing things, unless they're actually wrong,' said Grace. 'And besides, I'm not sure that it's fair.'

'How do you mean, fair? I should have thought it was unfair to let a girl of nineteen – that's what she is, isn't it? – make a sight of herself. Or has she got a very bad complexion?' he asked, with practical interest.

'No, a very pretty one,' said Grace.

'How you do adore her, don't you?' he said, looking at her with amusement. 'Do you know that you always smile a little when you talk about her?'

'No, I didn't.' Grace's tone, not unkindly, rather brushed this aside. 'But Nicholas, the thing is this – I was wondering about it this morning, after I'd been looking at your picture. In painting, teaching a person, one has to let them go their own way to a great extent. I can't dictate to you how you're to see a thing – I can only help you to do what you're already trying to do, and have seen for yourself. And mayn't it be the same, in a way, with one's children? That one must let them go their own way, and be the person they want to be – at least in small things?'

'I don't know. No, I shouldn't have thought so,' said Nicholas. 'I should have said it was just in the small things you ought to dragoon them for their own good. It's no injury to anyone to be sent to school. There's all the difference in the world between teaching people how to behave and dress and all that, and trying to shape their lives for them. That's what seems to me intolerable, and really wrong – interfering in the big things. Hullo, that kettle's boiling.'

This was a new point of view to Grace, and while Nicholas made the tea she considered it. It was the very importance of the big things that had always seemed to her the justification for parental control there, hard as it sometimes was to exercise. But it was rather startling to find Nicholas a champion of discipline in minor matters. And her thoughts went back to his remarks about Celia and her Mother, and her own meditations on them.

'Then you think one ought to force them to be tidy, and catch trains, and things of that sort,' she asked, 'however cross it makes them?'

'Certainly. But surely Linnet isn't often cross with you?' he said, studying her face.

'Oh yes, she is – and I've been wondering how far it was my fault. Do you remember what you said going to the Museum, about your Mother doing things for Celia being a sort of self-indulgence? I've been wondering since then if my wanting Linnet to be – well, rather perfect – wasn't a form of self-indulgence too.'

He looked at her thoughtfully, saying nothing. At last – 'I should think you were entitled to expect a rather perfect daughter,' he said. 'But I think you're getting this muddled up, Lady K. Discipline is one thing, and fussing round is another. What Celia hates is being fussed round. And then there's the whole business, there, of she and my Mother being across one another. Mother's frightened of her, and so she isn't quite straight with her; that's what really maddens Celia. She's often afraid to ask Celia outright about a thing, so she steers round the subject, and sort of lies out for her. Of course Celia sees what she's up to, and she loathes it.'

'But they loathe being asked things outright, too,' said Grace, remembering how disastrous were the results with Linnet when she did occasionally break her rule of not asking anything unless she was told of it first – the cold offhand tone, the few careless uninformative words, the icy reproof in the whole manner; worst of all, the clam-like silence on *every* subject for days afterwards. And she remembered, with a curious sense of guilt, occasions when she had 'lain out' for Linnet too. They had provoked no explosion at the time; but had Linnet also seen through them, and been maddened as Celia was maddened? Remembering all this, the old pain returned sharply, and with it the old questions she asked herself so perpetually and so vainly at home; and on a sudden impulse, she slipped one of them out – 'I wonder *why* they don't want to tell us things?'

'I think very often they do want to,' Nicholas returned readily. 'And they would if people left them alone. But no one likes being catechised. It's this assumption that parents have a right to know that rots everything up. There must be a proper way of asking just the right questions, if only one's parents could tumble to it. I shouldn't mind what you asked me – in fact I tell you all sorts of things without being asked, because I like to.'

'I'm not your Mother, though,' said Grace.

'Sez you!' was Nicholas's reply to this exercise in the obvious; Grace laughed. 'Lady K., you know you do make most frightful bromides sometimes. Why do you?'

'I don't know – I don't think before I speak,' said Grace, quite unoffended. 'But Nicholas, why don't you mind telling me things? Could you tell me?'

'Well – apart from the great truth you've just enunciated – I think it's because you don't treat me like a child,' he said, looking thoughtfully in front of him. 'I don't generally tell people of your age about anything, mothers or not. But you see you treat me like a person. If only parents could learn to treat their children like people, when they grow up! But the trouble is they don't *really* believe that their own children ever do grow up; I'm sure at the back of her mind my Mother always thinks of me and Celia as tots,'

Grace laughed a little – Nicholas's very considerable length, stretched on the grass beside her, was extremely un-tot-like. He turned his head at her laugh, and looked up into her face.

'You don't make me feel how young I am all the time,' he pursued. 'If you only knew how loathsome it is to be made to feel young! Most people never let you forget it for a minute. You aren't like that.'

Grace recognised that this was true. Her normal method with young people was to talk 'rather ordinarily,' as she herself put it, to them, partly because her natural modesty gave her no sense of a pedestal from which to patronise, partly out of an instinctive fastidiousness. But though she had all along thought of Nicholas as a child – at first as an unhappy child – her very sense of his need of encouragement had made her talk to him even more 'ordinarily' than usual; she had deliberately put him entirely on an equality in all her dealings with him. She had wondered a little if this would spoil him, make him tiresome, recalling his assurance and offhandness when they first met; but in her strong sense of his need she had risked it. And the risk had been justified – his response had been an extreme openness and even freedom in his speech and behaviour to her, but he had never been uppish; his criticisms, his teasing, were always made in an ingenuous confiding manner which she found rather charming. Indeed there was a subtle flattery about his openness with her which in its turn made her more at ease than she had ever expected to be with anyone of his age; she sometimes spoke her own thoughts to him in a way that surprised herself. It was very restful, not to have to watch your step all the time, to be so careful of giving offence, as she was forced to be with her own offspring.

'No, I know I'm not,' she said, reverting to his last remark. She smiled a very little. 'I think I spoil you rather, Nicholas.'

'I think you do,' he said, looking at her now with immense gravity. Then he gave his sudden grin. 'I adore being spoilt! That's what's so nice. But I hope I don't' – he paused, and looked away, out over the plain to the sea – 'I hope I don't ever seem to you to take advantage of that, in any way. You would bite me if I did, wouldn't you?' he said, turning to her again. 'I rely on you for that. This growing-up business is really very difficult, you know.'

Grace was touched by this admission, coming on top of his emphatic statements about being grown-up. For the first time she received a direct hint of how superficial may be the apparent assurance of youth, caught a glimpse of youth's vague resentment with age for having so many cards in its hands, so much greater certainty and ease in dealing with life. This was quite a new idea. But her immediate response was the quick and certain one which generosity dictated; Lady Kilmichael's thoughts might halt and hesitate, but her instinct was winged.

'No,' she said decidedly. 'You do everything just right, so far, my dear child. And if you don't, ever, I *will* bite you! But look, if we're going to see anything at Clissa I think we ought to go on, don't you?'

'Yes. Back to the treadmill!' said Nicholas, sitting up and beginning to put the tea things together. But his tone told her that he was perfectly satisfied.

The fortress of Clissa sprawls along the narrow summit of a ridge between the road and the valley. The drop to the road is steep but short, commanding the pass absolutely; on the valley side a garrison could almost drop stones through a couple of hundred feet of clear air into the chimneys of the village which lies immediately below, smothered in a delicate foam of olive trees. A roughly cobbled track leads up through the gateway and along the ridge, from building to building, from level to level – the rock space on which the buildings are perched is so narrow and so irregular that from inside the place resembles a village street on a steep tilt, rather than a fortress. It is completely empty and desolate now – bats infest the roof of the chapel, the coloured and stencilled plaster of the finer apartments breaks off, or hangs by a thread in loose pieces; wildflowers stray in over the deserted doorsills, unchecked, and plant themselves wherever a fault or angle in the white stone gives them foothold. Only the roofs are for the most part still sound, and for the best of reasons; the weakness of the fortress was always its water supply, and the roof of each building was made flat, within a low parapet, to catch and keep what Heaven let fall in the way of rain. Seen from above, those flat cemented roofs, with a little hole in one corner for the water to drain off by to a cistern below, are a pitiful reminder of the privations of former sieges – privations to which King Bela of Hungary's two daughters succumbed in the year 1242, when they were immured for safety at Clissa during the Tartar invasion.

The Peugeot, not without trouble and anxiety, was coaxed and hustled up the long steep loops of road below the pass. 'Wonderful marvellous us!' observed Nicholas in a flat self-satisfied tone, as he finally brought it to rest, boiling and steaming, at the roadside. This was his stock phrase wherewith to register any minor triumph over circumstances, and the complete and vacuous folly of it always amused Lady Kilmichael. He peered at her now to see if she were smiling, and finding that she was, permitted himself a grin in response, as they set off to explore the fortress.

Lady Kilmichael's chief impression of Clissa, afterwards, was of the flowers. As for Nicholas, he was absorbed in them at once. The cliff beside the gateway was draped with pendent cushiony masses of a snow-white cerastium, with silver foliage almost as pale as the blooms; he was off after this instantly, clambering up the rocks like a large clumsy cat. Meanwhile, beside the track, she found again a pink flower whose bright rose-colour had intrigued them all the way up the road, when they dared not check the Peugeot to gather it – a goat's beard, it proved to be, also with silvery stalks and foliage, and opening its inflorescences on a most ingenious plan, first the outer florets of the ray alone, afterwards the rest; so that there seemed to be flowers of two patterns on a single root. Inside they found it everywhere, standing stiffly in the cracks, its pink heads erect against the white walls, disputing for sustenance with great sprawls of henbane. And all about the little courts and steps of the fortress they found another and a lovelier thing still – the pale pink convolvulus, with trumpets the colour of apple blossom, whose trailing silver foliage is cut like the leaves of an eschscholtzia; indeed they thought at first that it was a climbing eschscholtzia, wreathing walls and rocks with its delicate pink and silvery grace. *C. elegantissimus*, botanists call it – and for once their description is apt. Here at Clissa, for the first time, Nicholas and Lady Kilmichael were confronted, in its full beauty and strangeness, with that most exquisite feature of a limestone flora – the prevailing silver colour of leaves and stalks, all that on other soils is green. Nicholas in particular was enchanted, and gave only the most perfunctory attention to the buildings or their history, or even to the marvellous view; when Lady Kilmichael sat and imagined the feelings of the two Hungarian princesses, watching from narrow windows the Tartar hordes on their small savage ponies pouring past like a dark evil river, and spreading out over the plain below, Nicholas cheerfully interrupted her to exhibit the palest yellow alyssum ever seen, primrose-pale and of course silver-leaved, which he had found on one of the towers.

They lingered so long that when Lady Kilmichael at last looked at her watch, and called out 'Nicholas! Do you realise what time it is?' they found that there was very little hope of getting the Peugeot back to Spalato in anything like reasonable time for dinner – even, as Nicholas said, with gravitation to assist. They had passed one restaurant as they came up, only a couple of hundred yards down the road, and almost opposite the fortress another modest 'Restauraćija' sign offered an immediate solution to the food problem. They chose the latter, and went across to try it out in hopes of supper.

The *restauraćija* proved to be fully as modest as its sign, a little bare barn-like place with the humblest of tables and chairs. But it possessed a 'terrace' – in other words an unparapeted square of concrete reached by a flight of steps, which commanded the very wonderful view; and to the terrace they betook themselves to have supper. This, when it came, matched both inn and sign: macaroni soup full of garlic and swimming with strong-flavoured herbs, raw smoked ham, bread thickly peppered with caraway seeds and *maigre* cheese. Lady Kilmichael, healthy, hungry, and accustomed to odd food in odd places, enjoyed every mouthful; Nicholas subjected each item to a careful scrutiny, made searching enquiries about it from his companion, and then ate about half, groaning and predicting disaster. His digestion, as Grace had already discovered, was something of a familiar to him – no doubt because of his previous illness; 'my tummy' often seemed to her to sit at table, an almost visible third, whose probable reactions to a meal were canvassed in advance and deplored subsequently. This made her a little impatient, even while it amused her; Nicholas was like any old gentleman over his inside. His fussiness about food was quite the maturest thing about him – that and his curious flashes of perception; they fitted very oddly with his singular general *youngness.* Remembering Lady Roseneath, she sometimes wondered if a weak inside was what he had 'got,' or a sound digestion what he had 'lost' – but it couldn't be both! Thinking of this now, she smiled to herself.

'What's amusing?' Nicholas enquired.

'You – fussing about your food! Do eat it up and forget about it. Look at Mount Mossor!'

Nicholas looked. Above the valley, filling silently with blue shadows, above the dim lavender of the open plain below rose the great limestone mass, glowing in the evening light. But that white rock glowed true and clear, without any hint of purple or bronze; the great curved stratifications showed as a pure incandescence, the colour of burning peat, purest of all the many tones of flame. As they looked at it she knew that he had at last forgotten about his food, forgotten everything but the beauty he looked on; she received then, as so often, an extraordinary impression of the strength of his feeling about the thing they both beheld, though how communicated, how known, she could not tell. For all he said was 'Mossor's good,' when he at last returned his attention to his plate. But her sense of this strength of feeling in him reminded her of the problem of his painting, and as they ate their cheese she embarked on it.

'I think I shall go on to Ragusa on Thursday, Nicholas,' she began.

'That will suit me all right,' he returned. 'Where shall we stay? I hope there's some rather more savoury hostelry than our friend the Ritz. There ought to be some pretty good things to paint there too.'

'I want to talk to you about your painting,' said Grace, nerving herself for an effort – she felt that this might be going to be a difficult business, and fell involuntarily into the rather portentous tone and manner which parents employ to tackle a difficult business. Nicholas was startled by it.

'I say, do you think it quite hopelessly bad?' he asked, beginning to fiddle his bread, and looking anxiously at her.

'No, I think it's very definitely good,' she answered.

'You think that if I went on with it I might get somewhere?'

'Yes, I do. I think if you were really to work at it you might go a long way. But Nicholas—'

'You really think that!' he interrupted. 'That's rather bracing, you know, for me.'

'Yes, but I want you to think sensibly about this. If you've promised, if it's settled that you are going to be an architect and not an artist, is it a very good plan for you to go on painting now? Won't it rather unsettle you? Is it really worth your while to take it up seriously again?'

He stared at her. 'Worth my while? Of course it's infinitely worth my while, every bit that I can do and learn, if I'm really not fooling myself in thinking that I can ever be any good. What can you mean?' He paused, and a dejected uncertain look came into his face. 'Are you saying all this because you don't want to go on being bothered with teaching me? Of course there's no reason why you should. You only said to let you see what I could do; I remember. Only somehow I thought perhaps you were going to let me go on working, if you thought me any good.' He fiddled his bread again, more violently than ever; she saw that his fingers were actually trembling, emotional creature that he was. 'I'm sorry,' he said in a moment in a colder tone – 'I'm afraid I've been an awful bore, mopping up your time and using your canvases. But I was going to get you some more, you know.'

'My dear child, don't be absurd,' said Grace, warmly and decidedly. 'There's nothing I should enjoy more than to go on helping you – as far as I can; I know nothing about teaching, you know. But even if you think it worthwhile to go on now, you must see that it's rather difficult for me to aid and abet you in doing something that your parents disapprove of, and that it's settled you should give up. Isn't it?'

Nicholas's face lightened considerably at this speech. He put his head on one side, and the beginnings of a grin appeared, slowly.

'Oh, that's it, is it?' he said. 'Solidarity of the parents! But Lady K., surely the fact that I'm going to be an architect doesn't make it wrong for me to do a spot of painting now and then, in my holidays? This is a sort of holiday, you know.' He looked at her in a very coaxing way; she made a negative gesture with her head.

'It's all very difficult, isn't it?' he said, before she could speak. Grace laughed in spite of herself. 'Listen, Lady K.,' he went on. 'I've said I'll be an architect, and as I must, I will. But nothing is irrevocable, is it? And if there's really something *in* my painting, I ought to go on with it, as and when I can. Nothing will stop me, now I know it's possibly some good. And in time I might get good enough to make a living at it – if I did that half my Father's objection would be gone. So it's more than worth my while to take this chance of working with you, if you can bear it.

It's very odd,' he pursued, 'but for some reason I seem to be getting on more with you even than I did with Zarini; I'm enjoying working with you, and you seem to have a way of hitting the nail on the head about certain things – colour, and emphasis – that he hadn't, although he's so much better known. So you see it's really a tremendous chance for me, your being here,' he concluded.

'Yes, I see,' said Grace. 'Very well, Nicholas, you shall go on working, but on one condition – you must let your Mother know that you are painting, seriously, while you are out here. I won't do it otherwise.'

'The clean breast, in fact?'

'Yes, the clean breast.' She laughed.

'That's easy,' he said. 'I'll write tonight. She won't really mind! I'll order some more canvases too, from the S.A.A. in Venice; they're quite good. You're *sure* it won't be a bore helping me?' he asked earnestly.

'Of course not.'

'You are frightfully good to me, you know,' he said, gazing at her across the table with a steady intensity which she found almost embarrassing.

'My dearest child, I like doing it,' she said, thoughtlessly using her customary form of address to her own children. He continued to look at her in silence.

'Why do you worry about my Mother?' he asked at last. 'Apart from parental solidarity? You don't know her.'

'Because—' Grace looked away from his intent eyes, out over the plain, fading now almost into invisibility. Why did she worry about Mrs Humphries? She did – but even more, in this, she was worrying about Nicholas himself. She didn't want him to behave in a way which, if it happened with Teddy or Nigel, she would mind – mind, not for her sake, but for theirs. There were intangible loyalties, sincerities beyond any technical definition;

to infringe them injured the soul. She had only said what she wouldn't do; but she was really thinking of what he *couldn't* do – what she mustn't let him do.

'Because if you let her know about this,' she said at length, 'nothing will be spoiled between you and her; and nothing in you will be—' she hesitated – 'well, damaged. You see there are all sorts of things which are much more important than what one actually does – interior things: I can't explain. But they are what really matters – they're *all* that matters.'

She spoke with conviction, imprecise as her words were – with a conviction which surprised herself. She felt suddenly that this was a thing she *knew*; something in her spoke with authority. She sat looking out over the darkening plain, strangely untroubled by the usual doubts and hesitations which she felt with Linnet or the boys, as to how her words would be received, even if she had, improbably, made her meaning clear. And because she had spoken with conviction, if incompetently, her meaning was received and accepted, as the utterance of conviction usually is.

'I see,' said Nicholas, and that was all. But it sufficed. She knew that he not only saw, but believed; that on that intangible battlefield where she was accustomed to meet only with reverses, she had gained an easy victory. Why had it been easy? She must think that out.

Suddenly, from somewhere below, the sound of a violin came up out of the gathering darkness – long slow notes, carrying a melody curiously restrained, withdrawn, remote, as though reluctant to disclose some secret. Grace recognised it – the opening bars of Strauss's 'Morgen.' It must be a gramophone at the lower restaurant – who would be playing 'Morgen' here? In a moment the voice would come in – she hoped it was the Schumann record.

'I'm sure I know this – what is it?' Nicholas murmured, leaning across to her.

'Morgen – listen!' She held up her hand, as the words began. It *was* Elizabeth Schumann. Clear and pure, the voice wound through the complex harmonies, poured out the beautiful words with that matchless integrity of interpretation, gradually unfolding the melody's secret – the gravity at the heart of bliss. It was a song which always moved Grace, by its quality of indescribable security and reassurance, of absolute confidence in human love. She sat listening, watching the shadowy outline of the fortress opposite standing up against the great bulk of Mount Mossor, which had faded now to the colour of a pale pearl against the pale sky, feeling rather than thinking – confidence! – in love, in affection – and how lacking she was in it! Towards Walter, towards them all; she was afraid, she had so little faith.

And to the shore, the wide-flung, blue horizon
Speechless and slow, we shall go down together.

Yes, that was it – that confident simplicity, she thought, as the violin filled the pause with completed harmony:

Deep in each other's eyes will look, in wonder
While on us sinks our rapture's helpless silence.

Oh, heavenly completion! Where had it gone, for her? Where and why? As the violin reverted again to the opening melody, sealed up the secret once more, something made her look back at Nicholas. Dark as it was, she could see that his eyes were still on her face.

'I wish I knew German,' he said, as it ended. 'What does it say?'

'Oh, I'll sing it to you sometime – it is translated,' she said.

'I was wondering what it was making you think about,' he said.

But Lady Kilmichael did not tell him. Nor did it occur to her to ask what Strauss's secretive melody had made Nicholas think about.

ELEVEN

Lady Kilmichael was sitting in the open street beside Onofrio di la Cava's fountain at Ragusa, painting the long vista down the Stradone. It was one o'clock, and she would get no lunch till two; it was hot, and her head ached a little with the glare off the white roadway, the houses, the white towers above the houses. There was, however, a reason for this peculiar arrangement about luncheon. During the midday hours at Ragusa business ceases entirely – from twelve till three-thirty the shops are shut; the inhabitants retire, first to eat and then to take a siesta, and the streets become as empty as those of a northern city at three o'clock in the morning. She wanted to get the whole of the Stradone, with the alternating blocks of sunlight and shadow, and the buildings at the further end – and in order to get an unimpeded view of its entire length, she had to work in the hours after twelve, when the usual throng of passers-by had ebbed away. Nicholas was doing the same thing in the Piazza at the other end of the town, and they were to meet for lunch. He had procured himself an easel, some canvases and brushes, and a rather limited supply of paints from Venice – which supply he augmented, shamelessly, by raids on Lady Kilmichael's tubes; but he had forgotten a palette – it was inevitable that Nicholas should have forgotten something! This calamity had been retrieved, rather oddly and unexpectedly, during a visit to the principal chemist. Nicholas had run out of a medicament called Maclean's Powder, with which he was wont to soothe his fractious inside, and wanted more. The chemist only spoke German, and Grace was roped in to explain the nature and properties of Maclean's Powder. In Ragusa, unfortunately, that valuable product did not exist; but the chemist, who was alert and intelligent, volunteered to 'make something up' if Nicholas's symptoms were fully explained to him. By the end of the highly technical conversation which ensued, all the parties were on the most confidential terms possible; it was only natural that the chemist should enquire the reason for his clients' presence in Ragusa and the length of their stay; though he would probably have done this anyhow, after the friendly fashion of the place. On hearing that they were artists, he evinced a certain surprise, at least as regarded Lady Kilmichael – 'the lady also?' – and the utmost interest; he painted himself, it appeared. Grace at once bethought her to ask him whether one could obtain a palette in Ragusa, explaining Nicholas's dilemma. '*Unmöglich!*' (Impossible) he declared; but then he volunteered to lend the young gentleman his own. No, he would not need it – he never painted during the business months, only on his holiday in September and October, when he took his small yacht for cruises among the islands. So, equipped with the yachting chemist's palette, Nicholas was painting at one end of the town while Lady Kilmichael painted at the other.

The street was certainly empty enough to satisfy Lady Kilmichael or anyone else. A beggar and a boy slept in a narrow strip of shade along the steps of Onofrio's fountain, that curiously beautiful and unexpected structure, with its domed centre like a beehive hut; to her left a dog was snoozing on the steps of San Salvatore, the lovely little barrel-vaulted church vowed by the Senate after the first earthquake of 1520 – and vowed in vain, since most of the town was shaken down in the appalling disaster of nearly 150 years later; a cat was licking herself in the entrance to the Franciscan monastery next door; behind the fountain, by the guardhouse, a sentry stood, now and then shifting his feet uneasily, and sweating in his thick field-grey uniform – a country lad, accustomed to goatskin slippers, baggy homespun trousers, and sleeveless jacket, the tight hot clothing and heavy boots irked him miserably. Except for these, there was not a living thing in sight. Right down the broad street the stately square houses, all rebuilt alike after the second great earthquake of 1667, slept, half in sun and half in shadow, in their beautiful uniformity of design – four arched entrances below, four tall windows above, smaller windows above those again, and two little dormers projecting from the warm pinkish-brown tiling of the roofs. In all the arched entrances the shutters were drawn down – Madame Lina Amandi had withdrawn her embroidered jackets, her brilliantly coloured woven bags and stuffs, her old peasant costumes, into the dark recesses of her shop, leaving only a few strings of red and green slippers dangling like onions before her door; M. Kraljic had bundled his handbags of antique gold embroidery, his silver-inlaid cups and ewers with their Arabic patterns, his trays of earrings and crucifixes in gilt filigree, his heavy belts and bracelets of silver chain-work, into his little stuffy room crowded with chests and ottomans, and was now drinking muddy fragrant Turkish coffee among them in the gloom; behind his closed shutters the yachting chemist was drinking coffee of the German brand, equally fragrant but unmuddy, and reading an oldish copy of the *Berliner Tageblatt*; across the street Signor Lassi, the photographer, in a black skullcap and black alpaca jacket, had put on his spectacles to read the latest number of an Italian archaeological review over a postprandial glass of vermouth – he, like Mme Amandi, left his less valued commodities to languish before his door, and under his wide sunblinds pendant frames of picture postcards swung, very slightly, when a faint air moved along the street. From the state of the Stradone, in fact, an inhabitant of Ragusa would instantly have deduced one thing – that today was not a day when a ship bearing a Mediterranean cruise was anchored either off Pasquale di Michele's fifteenth-century mole, which still protects the inner harbour outside the Porta Ploce, or in the roadstead at Gruz, the modern harbour a couple of miles away over the hill. On such days, and on such days only, the inhabitants of Ragusa, true to their great commercial past, sacrifice the siesta to trade, and keep their shops open even through the noon-tide hours to catch the stream of tourists off the vessel.

The Stradone is, so to speak, the ground floor of Ragusa. On either side of it, the city climbs a hill – to landward the Monte Sergio, to seaward the Monte Peline. And where the city climbs, there also climb the walls, following its irregular outline up hill and down dale, with superb dignity and solidity – swinging out along the cliffs to seaward, themselves as white and high as cliffs; dropping to mirror themselves in the still waters of the harbour; climbing again abruptly by the Dominican monastery to contour Monte Sergio, among palms, cypresses, and the fantastic growths of agaves and cactuses, to drop once more to the northern gate by the Borgo – with square bastions and round bastions, square towers and round towers, and bulging half-isolated masses like the Torre Menze, which rises like a huge two-storey wedding-cake, heavily trimmed with crenellations, from the half-tropical vegetation at its foot. Along the level between the hills the Stradone runs straight from the Porta Pile on the north to the Porta Ploce on the south; it is in fact really the old coast road, which formerly, so cramped was the space between sea and mountains, passed right through the city on its way from north to south.

It was very still in the Stradone. The water trickling into the fountain from the curious masks empanelled between its little pillars, the scrape of the sentry's boots, an occasional burst of laughter from behind the guardhouse wall, were the only sounds which broke the silence. Lady Kilmichael's head ached more and more, and presently she gave it up. She bundled her tubes into her box, wiped and put away her knife and brushes, and then carried her canvas, easel and all, into the cloister of the Franciscan monastery close by, where she set it down in a corner. A monk, snoozing among the roses and orange trees of the cloister garden, looked up, nodded at her amiably, and closed his eyes again. He didn't mind – nobody minded anything here, Grace thought comfortably. Already she felt pleasantly at home and familiar with the main landmarks of the little city, though how well she would come to know it she did not then guess. She picked up her box and stool from by the fountain, and went off to the appointed restaurant to wait for Nicholas and lunch.

The restaurant lay some little way up on the seaward side of the town. From a small narrow street one entered a small courtyard, overhung by a huge walnut tree, with one or two tables set about its trunk – in one corner, a flight of steps led up to a minute stone terrace, on which a single table stood by itself; in another an open door led into a dark hovel-like building – the kitchen, in which unpromising edifice food of the most unexpected perfection and deliciousness was prepared. Grace and Nicholas owed their knowledge of this place to the yachting chemist, who told them that they would find there the best food in Ragusa – which was true.

The restaurant was empty when Grace arrived – it was half-past one, an hour when all good Ragusei have eaten. She went up and sat down at the table on the terrace, and ordered a vermouth – the dark syrupy vermouth of Dalmatia, of which a quart can be bought for about eight pence. The proprietor, who cooked, entertained his patrons, and waited on them in need, came up and discussed her lunch with her; Lady Kilmichael ordered *spini di mare*, a peculiarly heavenly form of crab, with a special sauce, for herself, and veal in white wine for Nicholas – all to be ready at five minutes past two. Then, sipping her vermouth, she leant back and rested. It was cool there, and pleasant, so close up under the greenness of the great tree, in the quiet courtyard; small encouraging noises of wood and metal issued from the kitchen, otherwise it was very still.

But Lady Kilmichael's thoughts were not so pleasant as her surroundings. Last night had been horrible! No wonder her head ached, she thought, the colour coming into her cheeks at the recollection. That really odious man! She had thought she would never get away from him. And then how humiliating – and how prickly – hiding there in the bushes by the roadside while he blundered about, cursing and searching, till at last he took himself off. And by that time the last tram from Gruz had gone, and she had had to walk the whole length of the road over the hill, ruining her evening shoes on the sharp white fragments of limestone. Worst of all, when she got into the Hotel Imperial, disreputably late, with her wrecked shoes and those incriminating prickles still clinging to her shawl, to be met by Nicholas, waiting up for her with a white and comminatory face. Ridiculous child! Why couldn't he have come too, if he was so anxious about her? Then it couldn't have happened. But to have stayed away in a sulk, and then so absurdly to sit up for her, and after asking rather nervously if she was all right, to say, as he did, 'I gather I was right' before he went off to his room – that was really intolerable! Who could have foreseen that a man like that, an officer, well-mannered and even witty, would have behaved so? And to a woman of her age? That Nicholas had apparently foreseen it was almost the most vexatious part of all.

The fact was that Lady Kilmichael had got herself into a rather unpleasant adventure. The day after their arrival at Ragusa she and Nicholas had made the round of the city walls. They had found this walk, one of the loveliest in the world, to be hedged about with such restrictions and difficulties as befit so paradisal a promenade; they must produce their passports, they must get their permits in advance, they must go at certain hours and not at others, a soldier must accompany them all the way. Escorted by a perspiring Croatian recruit – who spoke no known language, but politely insisted on carrying Grace's jacket, which he held at arm's length, by the neck, like a duck – they had made that wonderful circuit: looked down into the green and shady cloister of the Franciscans, and the green and sunny cloister of the Dominicans; been dazzled by the white mainland slopes, with gay villa roofs appearing between the green of palms and myrtles and the silver of olives and agaves; had seen the piled roofs of the town, all of the same dim pink, like peach stones, dipping down to the Stradone and rising, sharp-edged with black shadow, up the further slope; above all, from one end of the city to the other, had looked across at the great ramparts along which they had come, standing out like the battlements of Heaven against a sea and a sky bluer than stone or flower or anything else on earth.

Of course Grace wanted to paint a picture from the walls. She found, on applying at the Commandant's Office, that this was against all the rules. The Commandant was away, but his deputy, a bulky well-nourished officer in the late thirties, explained the matter to her with great civility, on a vine-trellised veranda overlooking a courtyard. The Deputy Commandant spoke good German, and Grace, who had set her heart on doing a particular picture, used all her arts to persuade him to make an exception in her favour – she was accustomed to having exceptions made in favour of Sir Walter's wife – while Nicholas sat by, scowling. In the end she was successful; she got a special permit, and when the stout officer then begged the honour of their presence at dinner at his villa over by Gruz, Grace thought it only decent to accept. Nicholas, however, curtly and uncompromisingly refused – giving as his reason, when Grace remonstrated with him afterwards, that anyone could see from a mile off that the fellow was a bounder, and not to be trusted an inch. His estimate unfortunately proved to be correct. Lady Kilmichael went alone; she was entertained, properly enough, by the officer and his wife at dinner – but the officer's potations were rather liberal and when, in her thoughtless British innocence, she accepted his escort back to the tram, there was a tiresome episode on the dark path among the thick thorny bushes. Grace did not like being kissed by strange foreigners at all – she was frightened and indignant. Luckily her dress was dark, and the man so tipsy that she fairly easily eluded him. But it had all been most disagreeable.

The puzzling part about the whole thing was Nicholas's behaviour. He had still been in the deepest sulks this morning. Grace was not only puzzled; she was rather disappointed. Nicholas had never shown ill humour like this before – indeed his consistent sweet temper, this last fortnight, had attracted her very much. The thought had sometimes crossed her mind – though she banished it hurriedly as scheming and vulgar – of how well he would do for Linnet. He was well-informed, reasonably sensible; he had ideas, he was amusing, he was clearly affectionate and hitherto sweet-tempered. And he came of nice people, in the peculiar sense in which the English use the word nice – meaning thereby, not that a family is necessarily either amiable or amusing, but merely that it possesses a certain degree of good breeding. It was true that there was something rather childish, undeveloped about him – Grace couldn't exactly say what; but she felt that he would develop, was developing. But this black temper, this stubbornness – oh dear, they were not nice at all. *Why* wouldn't he come with her last night? After her easy moral victory at Clissa Lady Kilmichael had rather got into the habit of expecting easy victories with Nicholas – she had begun to speak her mind on various subjects, and, though sometimes disagreeing at first, in the end he usually accepted her views. Which made this last performance all the more unaccountable. And forgetting for the moment the immediate occasion of their disagreement, she fell back into another train of speculation – why she did have easy victories with Nicholas. When she spoke with conviction to him, he accepted it; perhaps if she spoke with equal conviction to Linnet, Linnet would accept it. But she couldn't – hadn't, anyhow; with Linnet she was afraid, she had not the self-confidence that she had now with Nicholas.

Self-confidence – that was the thing she needed! It was a thing which, up to a point, everyone needed – must *have*, to carry them through things. And she fell to thinking how odd it was that Linnet should have done so much, more really than anyone else, to destroy her, Grace's, self-confidence, when she remembered all the time and thought which she herself had given to fostering, with the most delicate tenderness and care, the child's self-esteem. For Linnet, who was now, at nineteen, finished, delicious, poised, had not always been any of these things – at fifteen she had been almost plain, with features too big for her face, an overgrown figure that she didn't know how to carry, and unruly nondescript hair; intelligent and honest enough, moreover, to be well aware of these shortcomings. But by praising her for the things she did well, dressing her becomingly, repeating nice things said about her, and pointing out where she had gained morally or conspicuously done right, her mother had built up, as it were, in the child that moderate degree of self-approval without which no human being can face the world adequately. It seemed a strange cruelty that no sooner was the edifice complete than Linnet should turn round and start to shatter the same fabric in her mother. Why was it? For Linnet was not cruel – Lady Kilmichael flung back the thought – though she might behave cruelly from lack of knowledge or understanding. As usual now, Lady Kilmichael turned to Nicholas for a clue to help her to solve Linnet, and found a possible one in the thing she had first divined in him on the way up to Clissa – youth's vague resentment at being at such a disadvantage compared to age. Did Linnet too feel that growing up was a difficult business, and try unconsciously to support and reassure herself, in her inexperience and uncertainty, by 'taking down' the person whose superior equipment would press most immediately and heavily on her? Seek to establish her independence as a personality – all unwittingly – by breaking up her Mother's self-confidence? Was that it? In the light of this new idea Lady Kilmichael as it were stared at the figure of her daughter, for once without either emotion or resentment. That would explain a lot. It would explain nearly everything. Yes – it might be so – though Linnet was far less tentative and unsure than Nicholas, although so much younger. And if one understood that, and allowed for it, one might stop being either hurt or afraid, knowing the rather touching cause; one might even be rather tenderly amused; more, one might try not to press so heavily, not to know so much more – or at least to avoid obtruding one's knowledge. But the main thing would be that, understanding, one would stop being hurt and afraid. And then, of course, one would be self-confident, with Linnet anyhow.

At that her thoughts swung round to Walter. Was it conceivable that she should ever regain her self-confidence there? That she should say what she thought and felt to him fearlessly? Once she had – long ago; to think of doing it now was an idea which checked and almost dizzied her. To talk to Walter without thinking – without even worrying about whether he thought her a fool or not; that would be freedom indeed! And suddenly she remembered a remark of Nicholas's about his Mother, that poor lady whose lot seemed to have so many features in common with her own. He had spoken of her shyness socially, and had added – 'But when my Mamma has had her ego burnished by one or two successes, she will take on anyone.' That absurd phrase was curiously apt – one's ego *was* burnished by success.

But how many, and what shattering successes would her ego need to burnish it up to the point of taking on Walter?

It is probable that Lady Kilmichael, for all her humility and simplicity, would not have been so puzzled by Nicholas's behaviour – would indeed long ago have seen what was happening to him, if she had not been so obsessed by her own problems in connection with Walter and Linnet. But her habit of regarding the young man rather as a quarry of enlightenment for herself than as a person whose relations with her might require attention and care had made her even more blind, in this case, than the usual run of virtuous married Englishwomen, whose emotional blindness is a continental portent. However, his ill temper with her over the Deputy Commandant's dinner had at last focussed her attention on his attitude to herself, and when illumination came, she was able to take it in.

Nicholas turned up soon after two, slung off into a corner a miscellaneous load of canvases and equipment, and sat down at the table. 'It's hot,' he said, mopping his face.

'How did you get on?' Grace asked.

'Oh, not too badly. Would you like to see?' There was a certain effort in his manner – it was clear that he wanted to resume normal relations, and found the initial steps embarrassing.

'Yes, rather. Signor Antonio!' Grace called, as Nicholas began to undo his canvas. The patron appeared at the hovel door, saw Nicholas, and crying '*Subito!*' withdrew again. Nicholas propped his picture on a chair in front of Grace – she studied it carefully.

'You've been using the knife a lot,' she said at length.

'Yes – I thought I'd try that out. What do you think?'

'Rather good, really. You've got a good deal more light into it. That figure is frightfully good.'

'Yes, I liked him myself. He came and sat down outside the café, and he was such fun I put him in. Mercifully he stayed for ages. Hullo, here's the food.'

This interchange lightened the atmosphere considerably. Presently Nicholas asked how Grace had got on.

'I left off – it was so hot.'

'You're tired,' he said, looking at her.

'Not really – only a bit of a headache. It's the sun, I think.'

'I don't,' said he, abruptly. He began to crumble his bread, in that nervous fashion she had come to know. 'Lady K.,' he said then, without looking up, 'I'm sorry. I was a brute and a fool to let you go alone last night. But you're' – he paused, and looked up at her with something like misery in his eyes – 'you're all *right*, aren't you?'

Lady Kilmichael's winged instinct told her a number of things in that one instant, but as usual she dealt first with the immediate need.

'Goodness yes,' she said lightly. 'He only got tipsy and tried to kiss me. Luckily he was *so* tipsy that it was fairly easy to hide. But by the time he'd gone, the tram had gone too.' She paused. 'You were quite right,' she went on, with a slight effort, 'but I wish you'd been there, all the same.'

'Don't!' he said. Then, without looking up – 'If you *could* forgive me for what I – said, when you came in – I should feel better. But I don't know that I could, if I were you.'

'Please don't worry about that, Nicholas,' said Grace, easily. (Easy does it – to be easy was the thing.) 'You were worried and upset; I know you didn't mean it. Very well' – as he opened his mouth to speak – 'Yes, I forgive you. There – is that plain enough?'

'Thank you,' he said, and for some time they ate in silence, though Grace trembled for the effect on Nicholas's inside of mouthfuls swallowed in such circumstances. At last he spoke again, in a manner that was less strained.

'I don't suppose you realise how hard I find it to behave properly to you,' he said, with a curious meditative candour.

'You see I know really that I ought to treat you with tremendous respect, because you're so much older and so on – but actually when you're with me I forget about all that, and only think of you as someone about five years older than me. So I rather forget myself. That's no excuse, of course,' he finished.

Nothing he could have said at that moment could have surprised Grace more. The truth was dawning on her – and with it a quite violent sense of the improbability, the fantastic absurdity of such a thing happening to anyone of her age.

'That's very curious,' was all she found to say.

'Yes, isn't it?' said Nicholas simply. 'When I first saw you at Torcello,' he pursued, 'I remember how astounded I was when you told me that Nigel was at Cambridge, in that *trattoria* place.' He looked across at her. 'You look rather the same now,' he said, 'with those shadows on your dress. That's the same frock, isn't it?'

Grace looked, almost with surprise, at her dress. It was the same. 'Yes,' she said.

'But I began to forget, even then, rowing back to Venice,' he went on. 'When you were so shy about Ruskin. I didn't know then how shy you are!' And his grin, irrepressibly, peeped out again.

'Was I shy about Ruskin?' Grace asked, interested in spite of herself.

'Oh *yes*. You read it beautifully, but you were as shy over it as a person at school. That intrigued me rather. So did your being so knowing about your stones – people of your age, women, I mean, don't generally go in for archaeology. And then your wanting that rather peculiar inscription for your epitaph – that was very intriguing too. In fact altogether you were a puzzle.'

'I should have thought I was a very simple person,' said Grace, who was not accustomed to being regarded as an enigma.

'So you are, in one way. That's the greatest puzzle of the lot,' said Nicholas firmly. 'I *was* bored,' he went on – 'when I thought I should never see you again and learn any of the answers.'

Grace was surprised by the acuteness of her curiosity to know what answers, if any, he had learned; but some feeling which was not shyness restrained her from asking. 'You must have a very speculative mind,' she said lightly.

'Don't you ever speculate about people you meet?'

'I did a little about you,' she answered, feeling her present incurious attitude to be faintly dishonest.

'Oh, what did you think of me?' he asked, with an eager confiding interest which was somehow an extreme gesture of intimacy.

'I thought you very offhand,' said Grace, 'and rather unhappy.' She smiled, remembering Torcello. 'You *were* gloomy that day,' she said.

'Was I completely awful?' Nicholas asked.

'Not completely,' said Lady Kilmichael.

TWELVE

That conversation with Nicholas in the little restaurant in the Via del Levante gave Grace Kilmichael a good deal to think about. It left her convinced of the rather embarrassing fact of Nicholas being mildly in love with her. Even more than his temper, his distress and his apology, what carried conviction to her was the way he had talked about their first meeting at Torcello. Lady Kilmichael had once been young; she had been – as indeed she still was – pretty; Walter Kilmichael had been the successful last-comer in a very considerable train of adorers. She had not forgotten all the symptoms of the disease – she knew quite well what it meant when people began to recall first impressions. There is a particular tone and way of doing that – a tender curiosity, an artless self-revelation, an amused anxiety about the past combined with present security – for *now* it is all right, *now* we are safe, *now* we can give ourselves away, fearlessly – which belongs, unmistakably, to the early, serene and unconscious stage of love; and in just that tone and that way Nicholas had talked. There could be no mistake about it; ludicrous as it seemed, there it was.

There is a distinct tendency among Englishwomen of a very normal type rather to shy away from the emotion of love when directed towards themselves, unless they happen to have fallen in love on their own account first. Once married, to shy becomes a duty as well as, so to speak, a pleasure; it is what society expects of them. Only, curiously enough, an exception is ordinarily made in favour of the devotions of young men to older married women: these are regarded as an arrangement socially sound, formative to the young man and innocuous to the married woman, who has other fish – a husband and a family – to fry. The frying of the family is supposed to keep her out of harm's way. On the whole this view is a sane one; and Grace, aware of it, though she might be surprised, did not feel called upon to be shocked by Nicholas's state, accustomed as she was to regulate her life and even her thoughts by conventional standards. But the married woman, if she is a person of any sensibility, may be somewhat embarrassed by such a situation. She may feel rather a fool. Grace felt a fool. In so far as she thought about herself at all, she was very profoundly embarrassed. She remembered all the things that Linnet and the boys were wont to say about older women who went in for baby-snatching, and they made her blush. She was so old; she was old enough to be his mother! It really was ridiculous – only she felt that it was she who was ridiculous, not Nicholas. Dear child, there was nothing in the least ridiculous about him. But she would have to do something about it, somehow.

She argued it all out with herself that evening, on her balcony at the Imperial. It was a warm night, with no moon; prodigious southern stars burned over the sea; she could hear a little noise of waves from the rocks round the foot of the fortress of San Lorenzo, whose bulk stood up into the stars, except when the trams from Gruz clanged past, their brakes screaming down the hill. The air was sweet with flowers from the garden below, where the fronds of the great palms curved, black or golden, as the light from the street lamps struck them; away to the left, by the Porta Pile, the city walls glimmered shadowily from the same illumination. Sitting by the balustrade, her chin on her hand, she thought of Nicholas. It was very slight, she thought, and would soon pass off; probably he didn't realise it himself – in fact she was pretty sure he didn't; he would hardly have talked just like that about Torcello if he had. It was not in the least a serious matter; the only important thing was to deal with it lightly enough, cleverly enough, for it not to become serious. It would not be a bad plan, though, for them to separate fairly soon, if that could be managed without what Grace called 'making a business of it.' To make a business of it would be fatal. Only she didn't quite see how to get away from Nicholas without some form of business-making. He was perfectly free, for weeks to come, to go wherever he chose; and she felt pretty sure that he would choose to go wherever she went, unless formally notified that his presence was undesired. It was, in fact, all very difficult! And at that quotation from herself she laughed – softly, but aloud.

The laugh brought Nicholas out onto his balcony next door; he looked very childish in his pyjamas, with his hair all standing up on end after his bath.

'What's funny?' he asked.

'Something was very difficult,' said Grace gaily.

'You on the horns of a dilemma?' he said. 'What is it? Can I help? I'm full of ideas.'

'No, I don't think you can, my dear child. It's nothing vital.'

'I often have admirable ideas on un-vital subjects,' he said, sitting on the balustrade and swinging his legs over, so that his feet dangled above the lamp-lit roses and oleanders below. 'You'd better come clean, Lady K. – I'm sure I can help.'

'Nicholas, you'll catch cold if you sit out there after your bath. You ought to go to bed,' said Grace.

'You're talking exactly like my Mamma,' he said, turning round and grinning at her. 'Maternal strategy! Send the child off if he starts asking awkward questions!'

'Well, if we're going to Ombla tomorrow I shall go to bed, anyhow,' said Grace, and went. Oh no, it wasn't a bit serious, she said to herself; and the only thing was to go on – just as easily as that! – till something turned up and gave her a chance to withdraw.

The Ombla is one of those Dalmatian rivers which, like so many other features of that strange coast, startles the traveller into a sense of enchanted unbelief. It appears just beyond the entrance to the harbour at Gruz as a broad estuary between white tree-flecked hills, and curves up a valley, southwards, till it reaches a point almost behind Ragusa itself. From this point the valley continues, stretching away to the south-east, but the astonished visitor presently realises that the river does not – except for a few small streams, the valley is dry. Out from under a white limestone cliff on the north side, through a jungle of wild figs and pomegranates, the river issues in a torrent, ice-cold, green and clear as glass, and within a hundred yards of its source broadening out to the width of the Thames at Oxford. It swings out into the middle of the valley floor and then flows gently between the broad *fondamento* of the village of Komolac – usually, but mistakenly, referred to by foreigners as Ombla; divides to embrace the low island opposite the deserted bathing establishment, and then, once more a single stream, takes its short and beautiful course to the sea. But the sudden appearance of this great mass of clear water out of the solid hillside fills the stranger with an Arabian-Nights sense of illusion, made all the stronger by the peaceable village activity which so soon encloses it – the wine boats from the islands moored to the quay opposite Pavlé Burié's famous cellars, the restaurant with its tables and cheerful loiterers, the little skiffs, which replace a bridge in the communal life of the place, passing across from side to side, casually oared by schoolchildren, monks, market women or anyone else whose business takes him from one half of Komolac to the other.

There are various ways of getting to Ombla. Participators in cruises are herded thither in a launch; the inhabitants go in a small bus from Gruz, which bumps and rattles along the road on the south bank; the discerning and fortunate charter a rowboat, also at Gruz, for a derisory sum, and go by water, in solitude, able to land wherever the whim takes them, and to float down on the swift current in the evening. Lady Kilmichael and Nicholas took this last way. Nicholas, again displaying his uncanny resource about means of transport, unearthed in the harbour at Gruz an old Italian-speaking boatman whose skiff was stepped for a mast, and who vowed that he was expert in the manipulation of a sail. This proved to be an overstatement: both mast and sail were unspeakably one-horse affairs, and Nicholas had to do the lion's share in getting them rigged; once the sail was up and had caught the breeze, and the little craft began to move out across the sunny harbour, the ancient mariner quietly handed the tiller to Lady Kilmichael and the sheet to Nicholas, asked for a cigarette, and retired to the bows, where he sat, smoking, spitting and humming to himself, leaving his passengers to manage their navigation as they chose.

It was delicious on the water. The sun was hot, but not too hot; and after they had rounded the blunt angle of the land and were fairly in the estuary, the boat skimmed along with a beam wind. To Grace Kilmichael, whose sailing had been done mostly in Hebridean waters, past rather featureless shores coloured in the dim duns, greens and buffs of that moisture-shadowed climate, it was strange to see under the arch of a sail white sun-bleached hills, vivid at the base with olives and cypresses and rich evergreen shrubs; and instead of the uniform stone-and-slate buildings of the Highlands, gleaming white or yellow houses with glowing pink roofs. In the strong sunlight, everything gleamed and glowed with a hot brilliance, as if enamelled. At the bend of the river the breeze, cut off by the hills, failed them, and they had to row. The current was strong, and though Nicholas took an oar their progress was slow and arduous. Some distance below the island, where the stream, in its narrowed bed, flows with particular violence, the boatman startled them by suddenly remarking 'River 'ere run bloody fast,' in clear English. And he suggested – now in Italian – a landing on the north bank. Then they could walk round to the source of the river, and follow the road back to Komolac, whither he would take the unladen boat to meet them for the return journey. So they put in near a small steep hill covered with trees and surmounted by a campanile, and, still leaving the boatman's sudden burst into Anglo-Saxon unexplained, they landed; the boat pushed off again, and they were left with their afternoon to themselves.

They found their way up to the road, and walked along it; it soon left the river, and led them through a green country, with olive trees everywhere, and here and there a thicket of pomegranates, whose fierce scarlet flowers flamed among their pale leaves. It was hot, and presently they halted to make tea, early though it was, on a bank shaded by a group of arbutus, the small waxy white flowers dangling like bell-shaped pearls among the dark foliage and the green and scarlet berries, with their fine granulated surface. Not less remarkable than the arbutus, however, were the flowers on that bank. There were, as Nicholas pointed out to Grace, three kinds of sage alone – one of a blue as deep as indigo, one pale and clear like a forget-me-not, a third with very large flowers the colour of apple blossom – and all with thick silver-white foliage. Where the soil was thinner, the pink-and-silver convolvulus sprawled everywhere; the little meadow at their feet was thick with the delicate puce flowers of the wild gladiolus; and the air was sweet with a strong fragrance which they traced at last to the rocks above the bank, which were smothered in tufts of a bushy white thyme with flowers twice as large as the English variety.

Nicholas became so absorbed in the flowers that Grace had some difficulty in dragging him on to find the source of the Ombla; he made her empty the tea out of the kettle, curtailing her last cup or two, in order that he might use it as a vasculum in which to carry his finds. Drag him on, however, at last she did, up the dusty white road, with the hills growing higher and nearer above them, till at last they were close in under the cliff-like heights. Grace had expected to be warned at a distance of the presence of the river by a roaring of waters, but they came on the source almost unawares; for it is in a singular silence that the Ombla issues from its subterranean bed. They stood on the bridge which here crosses it, watching the water swelling and twisting past below them, smooth and solid as glass, and with a glass-like quality about the recurrent shapes of its curves and eddies, perpetually dissolving, perpetually renewed in the same design. The overhanging masses of wild fig trees masked the actual exit – but there, a few yards away, was the living rock, and here the river; a conjunction dramatic enough to satisfy Lady Kilmichael's most eager expectations. It was not exactly beautiful, but it was almost incredible; and as she watched it she tasted that very deep-seated human satisfaction of beholding a portent.

But Nature in Dalmatia is singularly open-handed, and distributes beauties as well as wonders with lavish impartiality. Within a few hundred paces of the source of the Ombla they came on a thing which Grace was to remember all her life, as much for its beauty as its incredibility. The road here swung round to the right, pushed out towards the valley by a spur of the mountainside; some distance above the road the slopes of this spur rose steeply, broken by ledges and shallow gullies, the rocks of the usual tone of silvery pearl colour. And all over the ledges of these pearly rocks, as thick as they could stand, grew big pale-blue irises, a foot or more high, sumptuous as those in an English border, their leaves almost as silver as the rocks, their unopened buds standing up like violet spears among the delicate pallor of the fully opened flowers – *Iris pallida dalmatica*, familiar to every gardener, growing in unimaginable profusion in its native habitat. Now to see an English garden flower smothering a rocky mountainside is a sufficient wonder, especially if the rocks are of silver colour and the flowers a silvery blue; and Nature, feeling that she had done enough, might well have been content to leave it at that. But she had a last wonder, a final beauty to add. In the cracks and fissures another flower grew, blue also, spreading out over the steep slabs between the ledges in flat cushions as much as a yard across – a low-growing woody plant, smothered in small close flower-heads of a deep chalky blue, the shade beloved of the painter Nattier. Anything more lovely than these low compact masses of just the same tone of colour, but a deeper shade, flattened on the white rocks as a foil and companion to the flaunting splendour of the irises, cannot be conceived.

Nicholas and Lady Kilmichael, strolling up the lower slopes in search of flowers, first came on the cushions of the blue plant. Then they caught sight of the irises, and by little paths, white-floored stone shoots and shallow gullies they scrambled up to one of the broad ledges, where above, below and all round them the flowers stood thick. 'Good heavens!' said Grace, and dropping down upon a stone, she stared incredulously about her. The white rocks, the flowers, their blade-like silvered leaves all glowed in the strong sunshine with an effect that was quite literally dazzling. Nicholas sat down beside her. He said nothing – he did not even sketch his gesture; but, as before, she was aware of the strong current of feeling set flowing within him. And this time, with a curious precision and certainty, she was aware of something more – how her own presence increased and heightened his delight, his response. Unspoken and unexpressed, this awareness grew and deepened, and with it her own pleasure in the sight. And for a short space of time, forgetting everything else, she gave herself up to this wordless sympathy, this peculiar accord between them, which made of the shared moment something more delicate and wonderful than it could have been for either alone.

Presently, with a curious movement of his shoulders, as of a dog who shakes himself, Nicholas got up, and clambered off to examine the low blue plant, while Grace sat still, glad of the rest, now looking up at the iris-clad mountainside behind her, now at the view in front. How lovely, and what an impossible thing to paint, she thought, noting how the flower heads cut a sort of stencil of pale lilac across the foreshortened landscape of the valley. In a picture, that would be affected, impossible, without beauty – and she fell to thinking, as she often did, about the limitations which painting imposed, and the mysterious process by which, within those limitations, the great artists produced a quality of beauty and significance which often transcended the actual. But they could only do that by accepting the limitations.

'I think it must be one of the *Boraginaceae*,' said Nicholas, coming back and sitting down beside her with a loose flop. He continued to examine a sprig of the plant through a small lens. 'It looks like an evergreen. Look at it.'

Grace took the sprig, painfully certain that she would have no views as to whether it was one of the *Boraginaceae* or not. It had a tough woody stem like heather, with small dull-green leaves set close along it – the flower heads curled over tightly at the top, and the unopened buds were of a blue much deeper than the rest. It was unlike anything which she had ever seen; there was a delicate precision about its smallness, firmness and accuracy of design which charmed her.

'It's very lovely,' she said thoughtfully. 'I wish one could grow it at home.'

'I must come up here again with a pick and get a root,' said Nicholas decidedly. 'They go so deep, a knife's no use.'

Grace looked at her watch. 'I think we ought to go on. But we will come back. Goodness, how lovely it is.'

'It is a place, isn't it?' said Nicholas, looking approvingly round him. They scrambled down to the road again, and followed it round the curve of the river to the village, looking with pleasure at the gardens round the houses, the oleanders before the inn, the innumerable little boats moored along the *fondamento*, which was also the main street. Two or three villas stood a little way back from the road, in larger gardens, more or less screened by rich shrubs – one of these attracted their attention because it had a monkey puzzle. 'What a thing to plant in Ombla!' said Grace. 'We shall have to find Rudolf now,' observed Nicholas, scrutinising the boats in turn. 'Oh, there he is.'

'I'm hot – I should like a cup of coffee before we go back,' said Grace. 'Ask him where we can get it, Nicholas. Oh, this *is* a nice place.'

The old boatman, who was snoozing in his craft some distance beyond the inn, indicated the last house in the village – the Signora Orlando there, he said, served coffees. He would bring the boat down. They strolled on in search of the Signora Orlando, Grace increasingly delighted with her surroundings. It was all so clean, so fresh, so simple, this village, among the sunny fields, with the river making soft sounds to itself as it hurried by, deep and clear; there was something homely about the spectacle of the bus, waiting empty in the shade at the side of the road; it was all very quiet. The idea came to her that if only there were a pub of any sort, it would be a divine place to stay. But the inn among the oleanders hardly looked habitable – those minute country places were really only wine shops, as a rule.

The last house stood right on the *fondamento*, within a few feet of the water. A dark-haired woman, whom they took to be the Signora Orlando, responded to their knock, and, readily promising coffee, led them round to a garden at the side of the house, where little tables stood on the raked gravel, under trellises of roses and vines supported by small stone pillars. Oleanders and pomegranates stood in groups about the garden, the flower beds were fragrant with stocks and brilliant with snapdragons; further away from the house, grass paths ran between pergolas of ramblers – a high hedge enclosed the whole. Somewhere close by nightingales were singing; loud, sweet and fervent as the sunshine, their song filled the air like a clear light made audible. And drinking her coffee, again Grace thought – what a divine place to stay! If the Signora had a room or two, and would agree, what could be more perfect? Besides – yes, if the Signora could only spare *one* room, it would give her just the opportunity she wanted to leave Nicholas, for a time, anyhow. It would not be making a business; nothing could be more natural than that she should seize a chance to come and stay in this heavenly spot, and she could go over to Ragusa now and then to keep an eye on his work. The more she thought about this scheme, the better it seemed to her; and presently, making some excuse, she sought out the Signora in the house. Did she ever, Grace asked, take guests for a short time? The Signora looked a little startled, but after a moment's hesitation smiled and said '*Perchè no?*' (Why not?) Grace, encouraged by this amiability, explained that she would like to come, by herself, and stay there to paint. '*Perchè no?* said the Signora again. Could she then look at a room, Grace pursued. With another smiling '*Perchè no?*' the Signora led her up a broad wooden staircase and along a wide landing, all scrubbed, Grace noted, to a white spotlessness, and threw open the door of a room. Grace went in, and examined it with delight. It was a corner room, with one window looking out on the river, the island, and its black groups of cypresses; the other window looked inland, across the fields to the ridge of hills which separates the Ombla valley from Ragusa and the sea, their lower slopes blurred with the soft grey of olive trees. The floor was bare, except for a couple of bright native rugs, and as spotless as the stairs and landing; there were two beds with, astonishingly, box-spring mattresses; there was also a wardrobe, a marble-topped washstand and a wicker armchair. It was all anyone could need; its very simplicity was delightful, and the view from those two windows riches in abundance. Were there other rooms? Only one, opposite, but the Signora's niece was living in that – she could, however, be ejected. Grace explained that she would need a second room to paint in, and took the niece's room as well, for the purpose; having thus made her solitude secure, as she hoped, she broached the question of meals, and was taken downstairs and shown a small cement-floored room, looking on the garden, where she could eat alone instead of in the main restaurant in front. And price? For the first time the Signora hesitated – she had never had a permanent guest before; but after some consultation with a white-haired crone in the kitchen across the passage, she returned and rather deprecatingly suggested for complete board, lodging and attendance, a sum in *dinars* which amounted to about 5*s.* 3*d.* a day. Grace nearly laughed – to live in such a paradise for such a price! She agreed, however, gravely, and then asked if she could come as soon as tomorrow? For the last time – '*Perché no?*' said the Signora. So with the simplicity of some event in the *Pilgrim's Progress* the whole thing was settled, and Grace returned to the garden.

'What ages you've been,' said Nicholas.

'I know – I was seeing the house. Nicholas, I'm coming out here to stay.'

'Oh, do they take people?'

'They never have, but she's going to take me. I want to paint here.'

'How many rooms has she got? Can I come too?'

'No, I'm afraid not,' said Grace, feeling slightly guilty. 'She's only got one bedroom free, and I've taken that – and got another room to paint in.'

'What a bore!' he said. 'I should like to come too. It's a good place.'

'You can always come over by the bus, and I shall be coming into Ragusa a lot,' said Grace cheerfully. 'It's only a few miles.'

'What do you suppose the food's like?' Nicholas enquired, rather gloomily.

'Oh, completely native, I should think. But *I* like that.'

'I expect you'll be poisoned,' he said, more gloomily still. 'When do you come?'

'Tomorrow.'

'But you haven't finished your picture of the Stradone,' he protested.

'No – I shall leave that with you and come in and finish it one day. But I want to do a thing of those irises before they're over,' said Grace, seizing on an inspired excuse for her precipitate move. Nicholas appeared to accept it, and presently they left, with a warm exchange of *À riveder-la's* between Grace and the Signora. The boatman was waiting at the steps outside, and they set off down the river, Lady Kilmichael glancing back at the square house and its trellised garden with infinite satisfaction in the thought of her return the very next day. Nicholas still looked rather dejected, and to distract him she said, as they swept rapidly down on the swift current past the island – 'Nicholas, we must find out why he talks English. Do ask him.'

'Oh yes – so we must; I'd forgotten that.'

The boatman's Italian, though fluent, was very bad. However Nicholas presently elicited the information that he was *vecchio piroscafo*, as he called it. This, literally, means 'old steamship'; the fact, it appeared, was that he had been a deckhand on tramp steamers, and had actually spent several years in the coastwise trade from Cardiff, where he had acquired a few words of English, including the national adjective. 'Really, you know,' Nicholas said to Grace, 'bloody has taken the place that God-damn used to hold. I wonder when Continentals will start calling us "les bloodies" as they used to call us "les Goddams".' The *vecchio piroscafo*, catching the last word, nodded and grinned – 'Goddam, goddam!' he said, delighted to show his knowledge. The ice thus pleasantly broken, he became extremely chatty, and volunteered various items of local information; as that the Signor Orlando worked for Pavlé Burié, the wine merchant, and that the monastery on the north shore belonged to the Franciscani. He praised Grace's steering, and flourished a few compliments on her appearance. 'Rudolf's getting quite matey,' observed Nicholas. Grace laughed. 'I think he probably had one or two at the inn, don't you?' she said.

Whether that were the cause, or whether it was merely the instinct, common to all watermen, to sing on the smallest provocation, 'Rudolf' presently volunteered a song, and poured out '*O sole mio*' in a voice which, though nasal, was powerful and not unpleasing. Grace asked him then for a song of his own country, and he sang two or three – strange airs, monotonous and even uncouth to northern ears, but with a haunting quality in their curious intervals. The sun had set, and it was very still; the current carried them along smoothly between the pale hills, while those strange songs rang out over the darkly shining river with the peculiar resonance of a voice over water. Presently the old man asked Grace to sing an English song. Grace had rather a pretty voice, trained by much part-singing to a simple accuracy and purity; she sang 'The Water of Tyne', first carefully explaining the plot to the old man. He was delighted, and asked for another. And then Nicholas remembered something. 'You've never sung me "Morgen",' he said; 'you promised at Clissa to sing it to me in English. Sing it now – I want to know what it's about. It's such an intriguing tune.'

'It will be horrible without the accompaniment,' objected Grace.

'Never mind – please!'

So Grace sang it.

'And oh, the sun will shine again tomorrow!
And still my feet along that path will lead me
Where we, the happy ones, shall be united
There in the fragrant pinewood's sun-breathing centre.
And to the shore, the wide-flung, blue horizon
Speechless and slow, we shall go down together –
Deep in each other's eyes will look, in wonder
While on us sinks our rapture's helpless silence.'

The old boatman applauded when she had finished, but Nicholas said 'Thank you,' and nothing else. They had passed the bend now, and ahead of them the darkening river broadened to the open sea, where a faint glow lay along the horizon. He sat looking at it, his head turned away; and this time it was Lady Kilmichael who wondered what he was thinking about. But she did not ask.

THIRTEEN

Lady Kilmichael was sitting high up on the slopes above the source of the Ombla, painting the irises. She was working very fast – always, with her, a sign of interior well-being. Deliberately, but swiftly, she transferred to her canvas those militant cohorts – the leaves like swords, the buds like spears, the flowers like an army with banners – which covered the white rocks, in the fierce light, with something of the glitter of an invading host. That light, that whiteness, that intensity of heat and coolness of colour – what a thing to paint! But what a picture, if it came off! And it was coming off.

She had been at Komolac three days, and she was deeply content to be there. It was with something of the sense of slipping into clear water that she woke, in the mornings, in her bare room, seeing from one window the long shadows of the cypresses cutting across the shafts of early light, from the other the olive trees detaching themselves with unwonted precision against a hillside which the morning sun made faintly golden. She lay in bed watching them, her lovely empty day spread out ahead of her wide and still as a lake, which she could explore in any direction; it seemed to her then that she had never been happier, never so free. Watching a parti-coloured flock of pigeons swing out over the river, circle and wheel back over the roofs of the village, she felt that here at last she was as unencumbered as they. All day and all night the river spoke gently under her windows; all day and all night the nightingales sang with a loud intense rapture of which their song in cool English spinneys is but a thin echo. And as she was astonished at the fervour of their singing, so she was astonished at the intensity of her own contentment. She had forgotten that it was possible to be so actively, so eagerly happy.

There were no material drawbacks to check her pleasure, either. The house was perfectly clean – every inch of every floor was scrubbed daily. The food, as she had surmised, was completely indigenous and strange – each meal was like a voyage into uncharted seas – but it was also delicious. Now she sat down to roast kid smothered in chopped rosemary; now to thick rolled pancakes stuffed with raw ham, fennel and hard-boiled eggs; everything was full of strange herbs, strange flavours. And the Signor Orlando, finding that she took an interest in wines, brought her back daily from Pavlé Burié's establishment some new thing to try – the red wine of Lacroma, heavy, of a Burgundy type, or one or other of the varieties of Grk, a white wine which at its best has something of the quality of sherry, with some other and more elusive subtlety added. Pavlé Burié's office was the big building outside which the bus stopped, in the intervals of hurtling to and fro along the river road to Gruz; his cellars were further up the village, beyond the inn – one day she was to see over them. In Pavlé Burié's office was the nearest approach to a public telephone in Komolac; she had been up once into the big barn-like room to speak to Nicholas. He sounded cheerful and even a little elated; he enquired very particularly as to her movements, what she was painting and in what light, but he made no complaints of solitude, and she was satisfied about him. For the present he had clearly accepted their separation, and was perfectly all right.

She thought about him a good deal, nevertheless. From here, at a distance, she was able to see the whole thing more clearly and with greater detachment. Her sense of embarrassment lessened; in fact she began to regard that as rather an unworthy thing, remembering the simplicity of his affection – it was as artless as a child's. Of course she reviewed her own conduct, asking herself – familiar question! – whether she had been in any way at fault. Had she been too easy, too free, given and accepted teasing too readily? With unusual robustness she decided that she had not. No! She had, quite deliberately, taken the line of treating him as an equal and contemporary, for the specific purpose of restoring his self-confidence, giving him encouragement. But on the whole she could not feel that that treatment had been a mistake; it had, as Teddy would say, 'done its stuff'; Nicholas was undoubtedly happier, more equable, more poised than he had been when they first met. She began now to think of him apart from his relation to herself – it was much easier to do this, to stand his character up against the wall and look at it, when he was not always about, teasing, cajoling, interrupting her with demands for an opinion, for advice about his work. She was puzzled by that combination in him of considerable intellectual maturity and childishness of character. His mind was interesting, a more interesting mind than Teddy's; perhaps as interesting as Nigel's, because it was more experimental. But how odd to realise that he was actually older than they! One thought of him instinctively as years younger. And in a curious flash of insight it struck her that his childishness seemed almost *deliberate*; as though because of some failure of courage, of realisation, he clung to it. He was – yes, *dependent* was the word.

Another thing which Lady Kilmichael now looked at clearly for the first time was exactly how much importance she attached to Nicholas. She had long recognised, with the utmost readiness and freedom, that she was extremely fond of him – his very need and dependence had attached her. But looking back over the past three weeks she was rather startled to find how much she had enjoyed and valued him as a companion, quite apart from all the valuable information he afforded her about the young. At the time she had hardly realised this – consciously she had chiefly thought of him as an unhappy child in need of consolation, and as a searchlight thrown on the ways of youth; she now saw that this was not the whole of it. In spite of the years which separated them, she had found him a most satisfying friend – and quite without vanity, with the most extreme simplicity. She was a little surprised at this.

She need not have been. The old are too apt to forget that age alone is not the decisive or even the most important factor in any relationship. As a rule the decisive factor is community of feeling or interest, and what contribution one person has to bring to life as a whole, as it exists for the other. What makes this contribution valuable is partly experience, and still more the use made of experience, a question with which age has little or nothing to do. The stockbroker of sixty-six does not necessarily bring a richer contribution to life, by virtue of his extra forty years, than, say, one of our young modern adventurers in the early twenties. On the other hand what makes the young modern adventurers' contribution to contemporary life so rich and gay is not alone the fact that they have canoed and waded through the Matto Grosso, or flown and joggled on motor-buses across China or Africa – it is the use they have made of those experiences: the lively enquiring mind, watching its own reactions, and those of others, forever checking theory against reality – amused, inquisitive, intelligent, sceptical and ardent. Nicholas Humphries was no great adventurer, but he did stand possessed of this special quality of their common generation, the sceptical intelligence combined with ardour, the irreverent debunking spirit, which will surrender to the genuine, but only to that. He did make use of such experience as he had, examining it, checking it, testing it; Lady Kilmichael on the other hand, in common with many women of her generation, had made remarkably little use of her experience. It had been impressed upon her in youth that experience was necessary and valuable, but no one had ever told her what to do with it; it was something which you apparently acquired in large or small packets, like Lux, and then put away in a cupboard. Experience so treated does indeed leave a sort of sediment of knowledge – the mere possession of those stored packets may give a certain confidence; but it does not make a very vivid contribution to life, and intellectually Grace Kilmichael and Nicholas Humphries were not so far apart as one might have supposed.

Lady Kilmichael was thinking about Nicholas while she sat eating her lunch – dry bread, olives, goats'-milk cheese and white wine – on a hot rock on the sunny slope. But the conclusion of the matter was satisfaction: here she was, happy, and so free! – he was all right, and the problem of what to do about it all shelved for the time. So she thought of him with affection and content, untroubled – and while she did so Linnet was writing to her best friend again:

> Aunt Gina has triumphed at last – Poppy *did* see Sir John Lord on Tuesday. Apparently he really is in a pretty dicky state – 'nervous exhaustion' and all that. He's got to go on a cruise. The crushing part is that he and Aunt Gina want me to go too – though what help I'm likely to be to a case of nervous exhaustion I can't think! According to Mums I'm quite enough to produce it! However. I see I shall have to go, though – Poppy can be a bit roughshod at times. Of course if I thought I *should* be the faintest use I wouldn't mind, though it will mean no Ascot and all sorts of things. Too withering.
>
> Oh, Aunt Gina heard from that terrific Lady Roseneath. She *did* see Mums in Venice, but only for a minute; she was going off on some boat to Greece, to paint and all that. The cruise goes to Greece. Wouldn't it be supreme if we were to bump into her! I rather wish she would write – I'm sure it's largely fuss about her that is rotting up Poppy's nerves. Not

but what in a way I feel he's bought it, with all that business about Rose. Our Rose by the way seems to me to be fading rather fast. I have an idea that she volunteered to go on the cruise too and was turned down, and that I'm being roped in to eliminate all necessity for her presence. I'm not sure – but I shouldn't wonder. In a way, you know, I've sometimes thought that Mums would be in a stronger position if *she* had a boyfriend – but anything of that sort is simply unbelievable in connection with Mums, and anyhow if she had one she wouldn't know what on earth to do with him.

Lady Kilmichael had not quite finished painting when her 'porter' appeared, an immature relation of the Signora's, who for a few *dinars* daily carried her things to and from the village. He was a healthy sturdy freckled urchin, with a head of bleached dusty hair, and bare feet thrust into the usual local slippers – a heel and sole of goatskin with the hair still on, and 'uppers' of fine cord laced through the sole and rather intricately plaited all up the instep. He sat whistling on a rock till she was ready to start, and then, laden, preceded her down the steep path. He took a short cut to the village through the fields, and Grace presently found herself passing down a lane under the high thick hedge of the villa which had the monkey puzzle in its garden. A wooden door in this hedge stood open, and as she passed she glanced in. She caught a glimpse of an immense ilex with a stone seat under it, groups of sea buckthorn with pale pink rambler roses wandering through their silver foliage, standing round a fountain playing into a parapeted pool. Even from that hurried glance she got an impression of a garden created with unusual taste; she walked on vaguely surprised, for a monkey puzzle is not usually associated in English minds with taste in garden planning. Out on the *fondamento* she walked slowly, loitering with deliberate pleasure; the schoolchildren were returning to their homes on the other side of the river, and it amused her to watch the casual and competent way in which quite small mites unmoored a boat, rowed themselves across, and tied it up on the further bank. Grace had already discovered that as regards boats, the sense of *meum* and *tuum* was very slight in Komolac; anyone who wished to cross the river took the first boat he came to, rowed over, and left it on the further side – someone else was sure to be returning shortly, and would bring it (or some other boat) back again. As she approached the Orlando house she thought with happy anticipation of her evening to come – warm hours in the garden with a book, another delicious meal, a little gossip perhaps with the Signora; but in the main, solitude and freedom. No Nicholas, no problems – just an idle evening of peace. With a sense of homecoming she turned into the garden – there under the vines, roughing-in a charcoal outline on a canvas and looking very completely at home, sat Nicholas.

He got up when he saw her, came over with his rather slow walk and stood in front of her, looking at her with immovable gravity. 'Good afternoon,' he said at length.

'Oh, my dear child, have you come out for tea? I'm so sorry I wasn't in,' said Grace, very considerably taken aback by this apparition.

'No – I'm staying here too,' said Nicholas serenely.

'Not here, in the house?' said Grace, almost aghast.

The young man burst out laughing at her expression. 'Oh, Lady K., would it be so appalling if I were? You look completely shattered.'

'Not a bit – what nonsense!' said Grace, recovering herself. 'Only there isn't room. What do you mean, Nicholas? Where are you staying? At the inn?'

'No, not at the inn.' He cocked his head at her, enjoying her still evident discomfiture.

'Well, where then?' she asked, a little impatiently. She sat down on the trellis parapet, threw off her hat, and pushed back her hair with a faintly weary gesture.

'Oh, Lady K., it is a shame to tease you! But you are so funny when you're nearly cross – I always long to make you quite cross, and see what happens! No, listen,' he said, as she made a movement to rise, putting his hand on her arm, 'I've planted myself on the villa.'

'What villa?'

'The monkey puzzle villa – Villa Araucaria, I presume.'

'But that's a private house.'

'I know – but the venerable owner is away, and his equally venerable housekeeper is allowed sometimes to take Doctor Halther's friends as PGs to reduce expenses. So she's taken *me* as a PG.'

'But you aren't a friend of Doctor Halther – whoever he may be – are you?' objected Grace.

'No – but she thinks I am,' he said, grinning.

'Nicholas, you are crazy!' said Grace, half impatient and half amused. 'What on earth will happen if he turns up?'

'He won't turn up – he's just been here. He only left a week ago, and he never comes twice in the same spring the old party says. He's gone off to Greece.'

Grace remembered, inconsequently, that Lady Roseneath no doubt believed that she herself was in Greece at that very moment, and it made her feel somehow that Greece offered a rather slender security. But all she said was – 'How did you find all this out?'

'From the bus conductor and the inn keeper. Everyone in Komolac knows all about everyone else's affairs! I've done a lot of sleuthing here in the mornings, the last two days, while you've been painting up the hill,' said he, looking very complacent.

'Is *that* why you were so interested in my picture – and the light?' said Grace.

'Yes, of course – little Machiavelli! And once I'd found all that out, nothing was easier than to march up to the door with a card and get off with Maria; she talks Italian, thank God. I'm Mr Humphries, a young English friend of Doctor Halther's, who met him in Vienna last year. He belongs in Vienna – he's a philosopher. I got away with it completely. Wonderful marvellous us!' He chuckled with the most disarming self-satisfaction, but Grace could not altogether respond; this was just the sort of irresponsible prank the young *would* play; and such pranks nearly always led to tiresome consequences in the end. And what now became of her precious freedom and solitude? The problem of dealing wisely with Nicholas was shoved neatly and firmly onto her shoulders again, like a well-placed knapsack.

'Well, I hope it will be all right,' she said, rather despondently.

'Don't look so worried, Lady K.,' he said, coming and sitting down by her, and leaning forward so that he could look into her face. 'Of course it will be all right! And you wanted me to come if I could, didn't you?'

For some reason the artless confidence of that question made Grace Kilmichael feel ready to burst into tears. She so much *didn't* want him there just then, and he was so certain that she did! It was like the absolute confidence of the child in the affection, the interest and sympathy of the parent – the most complete security that human love knows; and it gave her the measure at once of the innocence and the depth of his affection.

'Of course I did, dear child – only I think this is rather a risky way of getting here,' she said, after the slightest possible hesitation.

But Nicholas had noticed the hesitation. He sat for some time, gazing at her with that sort of searching gravity peculiar to him. At last – 'Lady K., tell me honestly – did you want me not to come?' he said. 'I never thought of that, or I'd have stayed in Ragusa. Please tell me. You see' – he paused, looked away, and with a certain determination looked back at her again – 'I enjoy working with you and being with you so much that I don't always think of you, and that I may be a bore to you, because I'm so young and all that. And you're so frightfully nice, so angelic to me, that I forget to think about it more than ever. Will you tell me honestly?' he said.

Looking into those determined eyes, anxious, but intent on the truth, Grace Kilmichael could not lie. But neither could she shatter that affectionate security. There was just one true word which in that moment she could say, and she said it. 'I have never been bored by you once, Nicholas,' she said, as gravely as he.

He gleamed then with a sort of startled happiness that almost frightened her. '*That's* all right,' he said. And suddenly he grinned – 'I wish my Father could hear you! Now I'm going to make you some tea. Where's the basket?' And he was off into the house, where she could hear him wheedling the Signora for milk and cakes, and trampling upstairs to her room to find the tea basket. Peals of female mirth travelled about in his wake. Grace could not help smiling as she listened. But even as she smiled she sighed a little. With that one true sentence she had fastened the knapsack of her problem onto her back more firmly than ever.

FOURTEEN

There were certain peculiarities about the domestic régime at the Restauraĉija Tete Mare – the official style and title of the Orlandos' restaurant – which Grace Kilmichael could never quite fathom. There was the question of the white-haired crone, for instance. She occupied a position of apparent authority, or at least of oracular wisdom, for she was consulted by the Signora on all knotty points, such as Grace's *en pension* terms; on the other hand she performed all the most menial tasks, peeling vegetables, chopping herbs, getting in the kindling and washing up the dishes and cooking pots. Everyone called her Teta (Aunt), and Grace sometimes wondered if she was the Aunt Mary who gave its name to the place; but everyone, even the Signora's niece, ordered her about. (The niece was the assistant schoolmistress.) Teta only spoke Serbo-Croat, so Grace could not question her directly. Then Teta's ordering of her own life aroused Grace's curiosity. Why, for instance, did she rise at five o'clock every morning to wash up last night's pots and pans? This was a matter of personal concern to Grace, since these purifications took place in a small half-basement yard immediately under her window, and the splash of water and clatter of metal re-echoed as off a sounding board from the walls of the small enclosed space, mounted daily to her ears and woke her up. If the crone had gone on working steadily till seven-thirty, when the rest of the household arose, Grace could have understood her zeal and extolled it, but she did not; after half an hour of scouring and clattering she crept off, nodding her white head, and for the next two hours silence reigned, except for the river, the nightingales and vague cheerful village noises in the distance.

Sometimes Grace fell asleep again after this disturbance, sometimes she did not; she didn't mind in either case – she slept marvellously at Komolac. But every morning she wondered afresh what the old woman did between half-past five and half-past seven. If, as Grace believed, from certain light creakings on the stairs, she crept back to bed again, why on earth did she get up at that extraordinary hour?

A couple of mornings after Nicholas's unexpected reappearance in Komolac, Grace lay in bed, as usual asking herself this question. And a sudden idle impulse prompted her to get up and find out. It was a perfect morning, and she was far too wide awake to go to sleep again; she might just as well go out, and have a long siesta in the afternoon. Quietly she washed in cold water, dressed, and put on a pair of tennis shoes – she had already discovered that any form of nailed or leather sole was agony on the steep rough limestone paths; then, taking up her hat and stuffing a few small-denomination notes into her pocket in case of emergencies, she crept softly downstairs.

Teta had finished her morning task at the pump by this time, but Grace made a cautious examination of the premises to see if she was anywhere else downstairs – she was not. In the front restaurant the bottles were locked up in the cupboard behind the counter, the chairs piled neatly on the tables; the family sitting room was empty, so was Grace's own little dining room. She went into the kitchen. Not a soul was there; the door into the yard stood open, and the pigeons had come in to forage – stepping delicately on their little pink feet, they were pecking at some fragments of bread, the crusts and ends off the long stick-shaped loaves, which lay heaped in a large dish on the white scrubbed table. Grace stepped out into the yard. The air was divine, cool and fresh as water; the sun was barely up, and a faint glow in the sky made the light tender to everything. It was a perfect morning for a walk. And the thought suddenly struck her – why not walk in to Ragusa along the aqueduct, that 'Acquedotto Promenade' so strongly recommended by the book on the Ionian Islands? She had not done that yet, and there was a lot she still wished to see in Ragusa – the Memling in the Duomo, the Titian and the Nicolo Ragusanos in the Dominican church. She *would* – and come back on the bus. It was just after half-past five now – she would get in to Ragusa by seven-thirty. Passing back through the kitchen to go out – the yard had no exit – she bethought her to take one or two of the stale bits of bread to eat on the way; the pigeons, indignant at this intrusion on their claims, sidestepped with little angry flutters, and then walked back to give small soft vicious pecks at her hand. Laughing, Grace flourished her crusts at them before she put them in her pockets and went out.

The aqueduct, really only a pipeline in a solid concrete bed, lies fairly high up on the slopes of the ridge between Komolac and Ragusa, and follows round the contours of the hill till it reaches a point above the town, a distance of some seven or eight miles. Grace found a path through the level fields in the valley, crossed the road, and took a stony track up the slope beyond, through the olive trees. The low sun, striking level through the branches, lit up the silver undersides of the small fine leaves, so that the olive groves were filled with a sort of delicate illumination. Down in the fields a low growth of bay and myrtles bordered every path, as brambles border field paths in England; up here there were still myrtles, and great clumps of *Phlomis fruticosa*, a plant with bright yellow flowers and felt-like silver foliage, which brushed her skirts as she passed. What a countryside, she thought, which has bay and myrtle for brambles and phlomis for nettles, and pomegranates and arbutus for hazels and hawthorns! The richness and strangeness of flower and tree, in a land so arid, bleached as white as weathered bones, struck powerfully on her imagination. Presently she reached the aqueduct, and turned right along it; here she was above the olives, out on the open hill, and here a new wonder filled her with startled delight. The rocky hillside was covered with cistuses, purple and white, and the flowers were opening in the early sunlight, damp and crinkled still as a butterfly newly emerged from its dark chrysalis. For three or four hours that stretch of hillside would be bright with clouds of bloom, frail and ephemeral as butterflies – they would fall by noon. In Dalmatia these dry open slopes of the *phrygana* level are above all the place of flowers – in spring they are one vast rock garden filled with cistuses, irises, brooms and alliums; a rock garden on such a scale of size, richness and variety as no words can make credible. And on this May morning Lady Kilmichael's path led her along the lower edge of one of these slopes, just where it blends gradually into the evergreen richness of the *macchie.* Every few yards some new flower entailed a pause and an exclamation of wonder and delight. Now it was a clover, furry and silver of leaf, with enormous flower heads of maroon and cream; now a patch of alliums, with great reddish-purple balls of bloom two inches across; now a dozen or more grape-hyacinths, standing in a miniature valley between grey rocks – but puce-coloured, not blue. As for the brooms, they were everywhere – some upstanding, stiff and yellow, with sparse blooms most delicately shaped and set, some cream-coloured and drooping. She gathered a little of everything for Nicholas – she collected flowers for Nicholas now just as she collected stones for Nigel, or embroideries for Linnet.

This thought occurred to her when, after an hour's walking, she stopped to rest. It was not yet seven, but she was already glad to sit in the shade of a small tufted pine tree beside the path. Munching with relish one of her crusts, dry and full of caraway seeds as it was, she glanced at the bunch of flowers beside her, and smiled. Yes, Nicholas might really be one of the children, the way she now collected things for him! Dear Nicholas – he had been very nice since he came back to Komolac; but what she ought to do next she did not know. She had tried to withdraw herself, and he had defeated that intention. Perhaps it was really better – separation sometimes poked people up, made them more aware of their own feelings; and the last thing she wanted to do was to poke him up. And looking down through the pines and myrtles at the emerald line of the Ombla, flowing below her, she thought for the twentieth time how strange it was that he should be so fond of her – a woman old enough to be his mother; not realising how much her own attitude, so nearly that of a mother to a child, had had to do with creating this affection.

'I will love them and believe in them, whatever they are and whatever they do, because they are mine' – that, unconscious but unescapable, is the attitude of parents. And whether mistakenly expressed, or not expressed at all, this attitude gives a most lovely sense of assurance, of certainty – in this one relationship spontaneous, in all others hard to come by, the fruit of cultivation and intention; a sense of assurance on which youth rests, supported; the safe base, paradoxically enough, from which it launches its merry and irresponsible onslaughts on authority and the tiresomeness of age. Something of this sense of reassurance Nicholas Humphries had from the outset had with Lady Kilmichael, just because there was so much of the maternal in her attitude; with her he was fearless and secure, feeling no need to fence and defend himself. He realised her age in theory – he knew perfectly well that she had sons almost as old as he; but as he had told her that day at the restaurant in Ragusa, when she was actually with him the years fell away, and she became the delightful friend; much wiser than he, infinitely wonderful in character, such a rock of safety and affection as his mother might be, a wellspring of more skilful happiness than his contemporaries could bring – lovely in person and most dear. But though Grace Kilmichael had caught a glimpse of this certainty and confidence in her affection, which more than anything else bound him to her, when he had so naïvely assumed that she wished him to rejoin her at Komolac, she was too little accustomed to thinking things out to see that just there lay the main clue to the whole business.

She rose presently and followed the aqueduct round the hill along the estuary, through the villa gardens above the harbour at Gruz, till she came at last to one of the flights of steps which lead down through agaves, palms and roses to the Borgo. In spite of her crusts on the hillside she was hungry already, and she went in through the Porta Pile and along the Stradone to the restaurant in the Piazza, where she ordered rolls and coffee. It was only half-past seven, but all the shops were already open. Lina Amandi's jackets and embroideries swung above the pavement, a brilliant mass of colour; M. Kraljic was flicking his trays of earrings with a bunch of hen's feathers; Signor Lassi, the photographer, was examining some negatives outside his front door, holding them up to the cool glitter of the early sky. How sensible it was, she thought, drinking her coffee outside the restaurant, for a whole city thus to rise early, work during these cool delicious morning hours, and then rest through the midday heat. The bells of the Duomo and San Biagio chimed eight – perhaps it was rather too early to disturb the Dominicans; and when she had paid for her coffee she went off to the Duomo. But instead of taking the direct way thither, she went round through the Piazza delle Erbe.

The morning vegetable market is another peculiar feature of the life of Ragusa. There is not a greengrocer's shop in the whole place – fruit, salads and vegetables of all sorts are sold in the market between 7 and 10.30 A.M., and thereafter simply are not sold at all. The market women pack up their baskets and return to the country, taking their unsold produce with them, and the shopper who has failed to make her purchases while the market was open must either borrow from a neighbour, or wait till next day.

Grace lingered there for some time, watching the women with their Roman faces under their white-kerchiefed heads bargaining, gossiping, joking, exchanging what was evidently the liveliest repartee in high screaming rather nasal tones. There was plenty of what Nicholas called 'fancy dress' in the Piazza delle Erbe. Neat serving-women in full dark skirts, white aprons, bodices with short puffed sleeves and dark sleeveless jackets embroidered round the armholes, paused by the stalls, basket on arm – fingering the aubergines, opening the flageolets to see if they were tender, examining the salads critically – while the vendors, similarly, but rather more brightly and dirtily dressed, screeched reassurance at them with flashing eyes and southern gestures. Regretting bitterly that she had not brought her sketch-book, Grace at last went into the Duomo.

Mass was going on in several of the chapels when she went in, and she sat down to take her bearings. The paintings above the different altars were all uncovered at this early hour – the curtains which later protect them from the strong light, and are so reluctantly withdrawn by the sacristan for the midday visitor, were pulled to one side. Having discovered the Memling, she went and knelt in front of it, and looked her fill. It was a lovely thing, and almost certainly genuine – the long filbert nails were highly characteristic, she thought. Then she moved on to another chapel and examined the altarpiece there, and then to still others. No one paid any attention; the church was full of coming and going – above the pattering drone of the priests' hurried syllables there was a perpetual soft scuffle of feet on stone as people passed in and out: market women who had left their stalls in the care of a friend to come and say the rosary, boys and girls on their way to the college further up the hill who slipped in, crossed themselves with holy water, heard five minutes of a mass and slipped out again. It was all very homely, casual and free – she had no sense of being an intruder. She was tired with her walk, and glad to rest, and when she had seen all the pictures and Mass was over, she still sat on, watching the sacristan draw the curtains and fuss about, in the almost empty church. It was quiet now; undisturbed, her thoughts strayed into familiar channels – to Walter, to the children, and at last to Nicholas. But imperceptibly the tone of her thoughts had altered since she knelt in the Martins-Kapelle at Spalato. Walter and the children – this time they were not 'after all' hers; they were just *hers*, her treasure and her joy – she found the current of her affection setting towards them full and clear, without checks and barriers of resentments or doubts. How strange! How had this come about? Was this the beginning of freedom, she wondered, or just a momentary impulse? She caught herself actually contemplating writing to Walter – it *would* be nice to hear how they all were! But there she pulled herself up. No – she must wait, be sure; she knew her own impulses, and how little they were to be trusted to wear well and durably. But in the meantime, how blessed was this sense of fearless love and affection, so confident and free!

And with the idea of confidence, her thoughts turned to Nicholas. With curious vividness his image rose in her mind – his yellow head, his red face, his teasing grin, his eyes, whether searching or trustful, so steady in their gaze. Dear child! This time she did not put the thought of him aside – now he was very much hers; and when presently, unable as usual to resist the impulse to pray, she knelt in the Duomo, she prayed chiefly for Nicholas.

It was past nine o'clock when she emerged again, and after the cool dim church the heat and light hit her like a blow. She went down across the Piazza to the monastery of the Dominicans.

There she gained admittance to the church, and ignoring the urgency of the sacristan that she should admire the Titian, went and sat before the paintings of Nicolo Ragusano, that lovely creative spirit thrown up out of due time by the little free republic. Two unique things Ragusa has given to the world – the painter Nicolo, and the word 'argosy,' which is merely a corruption of Ragosy, the name by which her trading vessels were known in all the ports of Europe and the Levant in the sixteenth century, when under her Spanish Alliance a contingent of her ships sailed up the Channel with the Armada. Caught away into delight, Grace sat before Nicolo's gracious saints, the pure flow of their draperies somehow emphasising the still perfection of their hands and faces, statue-like in their raised golden backgrounds, touched with that remoteness which is the Byzantine heritage. She forgot the time, and went on forgetting what she had forgotten all the morning, that she had promised to sit to Nicholas in the Tete Mare garden at half-past ten. It was only when the bells in the Campanile overhead raised a sudden clamour for the hour of ten that with a flash of dismay she remembered this, and fled.

There was a bus from Gruz to Komolac at ten-thirty, and luck favouring her in the matter of a tram, she managed to catch it. The Komolac bus, as was stated plainly above its door, was constructed to carry fourteen persons, but twenty-six passengers were already inside it when Grace arrived – mostly market-women sitting on each other's laps, their baskets, tied up in pale flowered aprons, piled all over the roof. Loudly and cheerfully they beckoned her in, pushed her along between them, and planted her firmly on someone's knee. Lady Kilmichael, looking round to see who it was who was thus affording her a seat, found herself sitting on the lap of a Franciscan monk; he smiled and nodded very complacently to her. The driver started his engine, came in and gave Lady Kilmichael a ticket, and mounted to his seat. At the same moment all the women in the bus crossed themselves fervently, and then crossed themselves twice more, nodding once to their neighbour on the right, once to their neighbour on the left as they did so. It reminded Grace of drinking healths at a German wedding. Fascinated by this unwonted ritual, she took no part in it – this, however, could not be allowed; the woman who had pushed her down on to the monk's lap seized her hand and made the sign of the cross for her, the correct number of times, while the others applauded.

Before the drive to Komolac was over Lady Kilmichael felt that the precaution of crossing oneself was one which was certainly worth taking. The road was narrow, rutted and stony, and full of sharp bends; round these the driver shot at top speed, while the passengers lurched to and fro and bumped against one another. But nobody minded. The monk very amiably clasped Grace firmly round the middle from behind, to steady her, making intelligent conversation in French at the same time – a manifestation of impersonality and politeness which struck her as the very flower of good manners. The market women screamed gibes at one another at the pitch of their voices; the noise was really deafening, and by way of a hint the three men passengers, who each had a woman on his lap, ostentatiously tore up their bus tickets, rolled them into pellets and stuffed them into their ears. This witticism produced fresh paroxysms of mirth. The bus stopped opposite the steep tree-clad hill of Rožat, where Grace and Nicholas had landed on their sail up the Ombla, and the monk and one of the men got out – a little boat was waiting for them at the riverbank below the road. Grace saw it pull out across the current as they moved on again. At length they drew up outside Pavlé Burié's office; the women descended, and still screaming and laughing collected their baskets as the driver handed them down off the roof one by one. What nice happy people they were, Grace thought, as she too got out; but goodness, what voices! No wonder her head ached. Her bunch of flowers was squashed and wilted, after being carried in her hand for so long – they wouldn't be much good to Nicholas. Tired, remorseful at her lateness, she felt vaguely dispirited as she hurried along the *fondamento* – a very common reaction to rising at five in the morning.

Nicholas was sitting in the garden, rather idly mixing paint on his palette. 'Nicholas, I *am* so sorry! I forgot all about it,' she said rather breathlessly as she came in.

'What happened to you?' he asked, getting up.

'I walked to Ragusa to look at the pictures, and I forgot. I'm terribly sorry,' she said, sitting down on the parapet.

'You *walked* to Ragusa! What on earth for?'

'Because it was so early, and such a lovely morning.'

'What time did you start?'

'Half-past five. Of course I could have been back in time if I'd thought. But never mind – we can begin now – there's more than an hour before lunch.'

He stood looking down at her. 'You don't look in the least fit to sit,' he said. 'Have you got a headache?'

'No.'

He stared hard at her. 'You're telling a story,' he said accusingly, 'you *have* got one. You'd better go up and lie down on your bed till lunch.'

'No, really, Nicholas, there's no need for that. I'll have some coffee or something while I sit, and I shall be quite all right.'

'Well, I shan't paint you now, in any case, so you may as well rest,' he said rather dourly, beginning to put his things together. 'We can do it just as well this afternoon.'

Vanquished by his firmness, Grace gave way. She settled that he should stay to lunch, so that they could begin immediately afterwards, and then went up to her room, put on a dressing gown and lay down. Oh, it was heavenly to lie still and shut her eyes. What a pity she hadn't pulled down the venetian blinds – but she couldn't be bothered to move.

There was a knock at the door. '*Avanti!*' she called – it was probably the Signora, come as usual to mother her. The door opened and Nicholas came in, carrying a glass of white wine on a tin tray.

'You'd better have this,' he said, 'otherwise you won't be able to digest your lunch.' As she thanked him and began to sip it, he looked round the room. 'Don't you want those blinds down a bit?' he asked. 'There's a terrific glare.'

'Oh, thank you – yes, I wish you would,' she said. His mixture of thoughtfulness and disapproval suddenly reminded her of Walter, and this amused her. Pulling down the blind of the landward window, he paused. 'Hullo! There's a most posh car coming up the road,' he observed.

'Tourists,' said Grace indifferently. The wine and the fatigue together were making her sleepy. Dear boy – it was so sensible of him to have made her do this. As she handed him back the glass – 'Thank you frightfully,' she said, 'it is darling of you to look after me like this, Nicholas, when I've been so tiresome.'

He stood holding the glass, looking at her. 'As far as that goes—' he said slowly, and stopped. 'You go to sleep!' he said, and went out, shutting the door softly behind him.

That evening about seven o'clock Nicholas and Lady Kilmichael were sitting among the oleanders outside the inn, taking a glass of wine together. This was a recognised practice in Komolac, and it amused them to conform to it; they had already found that one heard more amusing things about village concerns at that time and place than during all the rest of the day. They had had a satisfactory sitting in the afternoon; Grace was pleasantly tired, and both were in the most serene of humours. The evening light lay golden over Rožat, with its pines and its campanile, across the river; and seeing it, Grace was reminded to tell Nicholas about the monk in the bus. 'He ended up by asking me to tea,' she was saying, when she broke off suddenly, with an exclamation of surprise, and stared up the *fondamento* behind Nicholas's head.

'What is it?' he asked.

'There's the Professor!' she said, astonished. 'What can he be doing here?'

Nicholas looked round. Sure enough, down the road towards them came their fellow traveller from the steamer. He was dressed in a cool-looking suit of a peculiar buff shade of alpaca, and wore a panama hat – he looked more German than ever. As he approached it was clear that he had already seen them – he came straight up to their table, but even before he reached it, a premonition of the truth flashed into Grace's mind. He raised his hat, squared his heels and bowed to her. 'Since we meet again, *gnädige Frau*,' he said, 'allow me to introduce myself – Dr Julius Halther.' And then, rather more formally, he turned to Nicholas. 'My young friend Mr Humphries, of Vienna, I presume?'

FIFTEEN

Nicholas had risen when the Professor approached their table, with a look of pleasure; his expression changed to one of almost laughable dismay on hearing the name Halther. Lady Kilmichael sat wondering how on earth he would extricate himself from this situation. When directly addressed, she saw his face somehow harden into resolution; then with a gravity and formality equal to the older man's, and at the same time with a sort of respectful firmness he bowed and said:

'Yes, sir. A rather futuristic conception, but I hope a true one. Will you take a glass of wine?'

The Professor gave him one of his keen looks. Grace had an impression that he was searching for impertinence and failed to find it, for after a moment he broke into a laugh, and patted the young man on the shoulder.

'*Ausgezeichnet! Na ja*, I am prepared to hope so too! Thanks,' he said, sitting down in the chair which Nicholas drew out for him – then he sat looking from one to the other, with a sardonic amusement in his rugged face.

'So you like Komolac enough to stay here, *gnädige Frau*?' he said, as Nicholas went to call for another glass.

'Yes, I love it – it's so quiet,' she said. Lady Kilmichael was if anything more embarrassed than Nicholas by this encounter. This was exactly what she had foreseen! No one ever went to Greece who said they were going there, she thought, almost resentfully. And now what was she to say to this strange Austrian, into whose house Nicholas has inserted himself on false pretences? With the grave courtesy which was the one invulnerable part of her rather inadequate technique for living she said – 'I am so very sorry about this; I am afraid it is most inconvenient for you that Mr Humphries should have come to the villa. But he can go back at once to Ragusa – there is a bus at eight-thirty.'

Dr Halther continued to look sardonic, but he made no direct reply to her statement. 'Let him explain, *gnädige Frau* – he is old enough,' he said.

And Nicholas, at this moment returning with the landlord and more wine, proceeded to justify this assumption. Raising his glass politely to the Doctor – '*Prost!*' he said. Now this is a rather characteristic Viennese formula for health-drinking, and Dr Halther's expression relaxed. 'Ah, so you know *Vienna* at least?' he said.

'Yes, sir – a little.' Then he plunged into it. 'I must ask your pardon for my intrusion. The fact is that Lady Kilmichael is helping me with my painting, and when she came out here there wasn't room for me at the Orlandos', and I wanted to be nearby, so I looked round for somewhere to stay, and your house seemed to be the only place.' He paused – the Doctor said nothing, and he went on – 'I do apologise, sir, for taking your name in vain. It was a gross untruth, really. But I thought that if your house was empty anyhow, I should do you no harm by fibbing about you.'

'What is this, fibbing?' the Doctor interjected.

'Saying what isn't true,' Nicholas explained, with the utmost candour. 'You see I wanted to come very much,' he pursued. 'I'm doing a portrait of Lady Kilmichael. But of course I'll clear out at once, now. And I do hope, sir, that you will accept my apologies.'

He made this explanation very simply and nicely; Dr Halther listened to it with the expression of one who reserves judgement till he has heard all the evidence. When Nicholas had finished:

'This portrait – where is it?' he said.

'At the Tete Mare – I'm doing it in the garden there.'

'May one see?' Dr Halther asked, turning to Lady Kilmichael.

'Certainly, if Mr Humphries doesn't mind,' said Grace. So presently they all trooped down to the Tete Mare, and Nicholas brought out his canvas. The Doctor studied it for a long time in silence, looking now and then at Lady Kilmichael, and turning back to the half-finished portrait again. Nicholas had painted her sitting sideways at one of the little tables, with a cup of coffee in front of her; the shadows of the vine leaves in the trellis fell over her dress – behind, one of the flower beds glowed in full sunlight. Lady Kilmichael, who like many slender women with long backs never stood if she could possibly sit, had dropped into a chair for the inspection, and sat now, unconsciously, in an attitude very much like her pose in the picture – one elbow on the table, her head tilted slightly back, showing the beautiful relation of jaw to throat, one of the subtlest forms of human beauty – watching the two men with an expression of rather meditative enquiry. It was a common look of hers – she spent so much of her life watching people and wondering about them; and already Nicholas had caught some hint of it in his portrait.

'This shall be good,' Dr Halther at last pronounced, emphatically. 'It is remarkable already. With whom do you study?'

'I had six months with Zarini, sir.' Nicholas brought out Zarini's name with his usual complacency at having studied with so great a man; Dr Halther's reaction to it, however, was unexpected.

'Zarini? Bah!' he said, tapping the edge of the canvas. 'He has never painted such a picture, and never shall – *nicht im Leben!* He is all tricks – the knife, the point of the brush! Tricks – they make no picture. Here too are some tricks' – he tapped the canvas again – 'but here also is a picture.'

Grace was surprised by his authoritative manner. He spoke as if he took painting seriously. The next moment he turned with an air of finality to the young man, who stood looking faintly bewildered, between this rough handling of one of his idols, and the praise of his own work.

'This must be finished,' he said, sharply, as if it was an order. 'Till it is complete at least, you stay with me. *Einverstanden?*'

'Thank you very much, sir. I ask nothing better,' said Nicholas. And when the two men presently walked back to the villa together, Grace was left marvelling at the capacity of people of Nicholas's age for pulling off the most impossible situations. Once again, in his own phrase, Nicholas had 'got away with it completely'; whilst she had wasted a considerable amount of worry over a contingency which, when it finally arose, he had handled without the smallest trouble.

Rather to her surprise, Nicholas informed her during their sitting next morning of his host's intention of calling on her in the afternoon. Nicholas was in considerable spirits; he painted fast, and not in his usual silence – a little trickle of cheerful remarks punctuated his work. Dr Halther, Grace learned, was rather a card; he was a terrific talker, they had talked half the night; he knew a lot about painting, and had some first-rate pictures – he was altogether good value. Clearly they had got on well together; Grace was pleased. She awaited her visitor that afternoon with a little stir of interest and anticipation.

Dr Halther arrived at about four o'clock, in his yellow suit and his panama hat; he refused coffee, saying that he never took it before five-thirty; and after a few minutes, with his usual abrupt definiteness, he suggested that they should take a walk. Grace agreed, and they set out up the valley, towards a small hill which rose steep and isolated among the level fields, its gentler slopes covered with cypresses, growing in open groups of all ages and sizes, from hoary ancestral trees with huge silvery trunks to delicate slips of seedlings only a few feet high – they reminded her of patriarchal families, where several generations kept house together. Among the trees the rocky soil was covered with a pale wiry turf, set here and there with great clumps of the silver phlomis and a big spurge, with greenish-silver leaves and coral-red stalks, carrying enormous flower heads of primrose yellow – there was something almost unnaturally pictorial about this pale background of buff and silver, set with the spectacular darkness and formality of the cypresses. Asking if she minded a climb, Dr Halther led Lady Kilmichael up among them. He walked, as he apparently did everything, with immense energy, moving so fast that Grace found it all she could do to keep up with him. The summit of the little hill was crowned with a small battered-looking chapel, and here, to her relief, Dr Halther suggested a pause to look at the view. Sitting on the stone steps of the platform before the door, the whole of Komolac was spread out below them, river, street and houses, neat and small in the afternoon sunshine; Dr Halther pointed out the villa, dominated by the uncouth and unmistakeable shape of the monkey tree. 'But for the hedge, one might almost see Mr Humphries at work,' he said, with a short chuckle. And added 'That is a very nice young man.'

'Yes, isn't he?' replied Grace.

'He paints remarkably well,' the Doctor went on – 'he tells me that you teach him now?'

'Yes – I have been helping him as much as I could these last three weeks – in fact all the time since we last saw you,' said Grace.

'Ah, yes – you told me then that you did not travel together, but now you do?' he said, looking at her keenly, with a hint of amusement.

'Yes – it all happened rather oddly,' said Grace. For some reason she was not ruffled by his amusement, nor embarrassed by his obvious curiosity as to why she and Nicholas were still together; she found herself quite willing to tell him how it had come about, and did so; the boy's accidental discovery that she painted, his difficulties with his family, and her sudden resolve to let him show what he could do. 'He was so unhappy, I felt I must do something about it,' she said, turning her clear gaze to Dr Halther.

'Do you always feel you must do something about it, if people are unhappy?' he asked, with that mixture of benevolence and irony in his expression.

'Generally – don't you?' she asked.

'I am apt to ask myself first if I shall not in the end do as much harm as good,' he said drily. 'You, I expect, do not ask yourself this.'

'I did quite soon, that time,' said Grace, and described her dilemma, in view of his promise to his parents to give up painting, when she discovered that Nicholas's talent was a thing which must be taken seriously.

'No doubt – one sees at once that he has a great gift. Well, and then you did what? Decided to let him sacrifice his parents to his art?'

'Not exactly. But you see there was something besides his art,' said Grace earnestly. 'When I met him first he was more than unhappy – he was all at odds with everything.'

'What is this – at odds?' the Doctor interjected.

'Well – how can I explain? He was like a piece of knotted string then, all taut and tangled; and in the first week that he was painting he became different – as if half the knots had been undone. I felt – I find it hard to explain – that being able to paint was doing something to him, inside, that really needed doing, and that probably his parents didn't realise it. We don't realise a great many things. His art *is* important, but this was more important than his art.'

'I see you are something of a psychologist,' the Doctor observed.

'I? Good heavens, no! I hardly know anything about psychology, and most of it seems to me really rather silly,' said Grace frankly.

He laughed. 'We shall discuss psychology another day. In

every case, I think you make an accurate deduction about this young man. Well, what did you do about his parents?'

'I said he must write and tell his Mother that he was working with me.'

'And his Frau Mamma says what?'

'I don't know,' said Grace, startled. It suddenly occurred to her that she had never asked Nicholas what Mrs Humphries' reactions had been to his letter from Spalato. The episode of the Deputy Commandant and her subsequent discovery about Nicholas's state of mind had put the other matter entirely out of her head. 'I forgot to ask him,' she said. 'I will.'

The Doctor smiled – if such a sarcastic grimace could be called a smile. '*Na, jedenfalls* for three weeks now he paints, and you teach him. And he is better, happier, with fewer knots? You find him unhappy, and you do something about it, and now it is all much better? You have done him good? Yes?'

Dr Halther put this machine-gun fire of questions, all the time peering at her from under his eyebrows with a certain insistence which, coupled with that hint of amusement, began to disconcert Lady Kilmichael a little. She answered with a slight hesitation.

'Yes – I think so. Oh yes, he is *much* happier and more easy in himself than he was.'

'H'm,' said the Doctor. 'As to that, I think you are right. You have resolved a conflict for him, and given him a liberation. But it is on your responsibility, not on his. So it is perhaps not so valid.' He took out a cheroot, and saying 'You permit?' lit it. To Grace, watching the puffs of blue smoke curling up between her and the panorama of the sunlit fields, came the thought that the effect of this rather odd conversation was, curiously enough, to make the whole question of Nicholas and his difficulties much clearer to herself than it had been yet, though the Professor – why couldn't she stop thinking of him as the Professor? – asked questions rather than expounded. He *did* ask questions! The next moment, having got his cheroot going, he turned to her again, and went on, as if there had been no pause – 'But it can happen sometimes that one shall only exchange one conflict for another. Is he now in love with you, this young man?'

Lady Kilmichael hesitated again. She did not want to give Nicholas away to a person who was almost a stranger, but under the scrutiny of those remorseless eyes she felt the futility of lying.

'I have occasionally thought so – but I may be mistaken,' she said evasively. 'Young men do sometimes get these sort of attachments, but they don't amount to anything.'

Dr Halther's ironic grin appeared again.

'Of course he is! I have seen this already. I wanted only to find out if *you* know – and if you are honest!'

'Yes – well, he is,' she said.

'Much?'

'I really don't know how much. It seems so strange that he should be at all,' she said simply, now returning the Doctor's look steadily.

'Strange? *Um Gottes Willen*, why is it strange?' Dr Halther burst out. 'He is young, he is sensitive, he is unhappy – and he spends now several weeks with a woman like you! What shall he do but fall in love? You did not foresee this? But, *meine gnädigste*, what then *did* you expect?'

'Not that,' said Grace, startled by this outburst. 'I did not expect it in the least.' She hesitated an instant and then said, with a directness which had a certain dignity – 'Compared to him, I am so old.'

'So old!' The Doctor looked at her, and gave a sort of yelp of impatient laughter. '*Gnädige Frau*, if you think you shall not still be fallen in love with, your great age has not brought you much wisdom!'

'No, I am afraid that is true,' said Grace, still with that disarming directness. 'I am in a muddle about a great many things, besides Mr Humphries. I don't think I am at all clever about people. But I am still rather surprised that anyone so young as he should fall in love with me. After all, I am old enough to be his mother.'

Dr Halther looked thoughtfully at her, at this; when he spoke again, it was rather more gently.

'Pardon!' he said, still abruptly. 'I think you will be insincere with me – I am wrong. All women are insincere, but some will be, and some will not! I think you will not. But to be sincere one must first think clearly – *nicht wahr?*'

'Of course. But I'm not very good at it,' said Grace, unresentfully. She was vaguely surprised at her own lack of resentment at the Doctor's methods; but something about him – some purity of intention, some detachment from ordinary social values – seemed to preclude resentment. She was even aware of a certain relief at having the question of Nicholas treated with such drastic precision, after her own confused meditations; and by someone whom she felt instinctively to be trustworthy.

'Look then,' said the Doctor, spreading out before him a large square hand with blunt-tipped fingers, as if it were a diagram of young men in love, and tapping it with his cheroot – 'why must you be surprised that a young man shall fall in love with a woman much older than he? You know very well that in love there are always two elements, the romantic, the ideal, as well as the physical – and for young people it is usually the former that is the most important. From type to type this varies, which element shall predominate, but *im allgemein* this is true; the heart and mind will worship first, and afterwards only the body, when one is young. This is clear?'

'Yes.'

'Very well. And in an older woman there is more for the heart, the mind, to enjoy and love, than in a young girl; and because of her age, her position, the senses are longer left at peace – they do not intrude and interrupt so soon. So the love of the *Karakter* can expand fully. However such a relationship shall develop later, it is thus in the beginning. But this is very satisfying to a young man, with his mind wide like a nest bird's mouth for knowledge, for experience! Why then is it strange?'

'One hears of it happening, of course,' she said thoughtfully. 'But it seemed strange that it should happen to oneself.'

'That is because you do not think clearly, especially about yourself. People do not willingly think clearly about themselves. It is not strange at all. It happens often – it would happen more often if the opportunity did not lack. How many young men travel for a month, alone with a woman to whom they are no relation? Yet I have known many cases of young men who fall in love even with women who are really old and extremely ugly – which you are not. In this case, it could not well be otherwise.'

Grace was silent. Put like that, it all sounded as inevitable as a mathematical proposition. Apparently she had made as much of a muddle of Nicholas, with whom she had seemed to get on so easily and so well, as she had of her own family. A little discouraged –

'I see. I suppose I should have foreseen it,' she said. 'The last thing I intended was to do him any harm. I am afraid I have been very stupid about him.'

'It is not stupidity – it is lack of thought. You have not the habit of first asking, 'If I act thus, what shall the result of my action be?' But why shall this do young Humphries any harm, to love you? Most probably it will do him a great deal of good. It gives him perhaps a new conflict – I cannot say; he can have already another emotion in his life. But such a relation can be the most important in a whole existence. You remember Benjamin Constant and Madame de Charrière.'

'Yes – but I'm not very like Zélide,' said Grace.

He smiled. 'No, I too think not, though I do not know you yet. But please do not mistake. I have not said that I think the result of your action unfortunate. What is really strange is that, to you, it should have been unforeseen.'

'But one doesn't go about asking oneself if people are going to fall in love with one,' said Grace, in a tone of faint protest, after a moment's pause.

He gave her an odd look. 'In your case, I think it would be advisable to ask oneself this,' he observed, drily. 'Do you tell me that no one now makes love to you? Apart from young Humphries?'

The unlucky memory of the Deputy Commandant checked the stout denial which Lady Kilmichael would have given a month before. Her blush appeared. 'Not often,' she said.

Dr Halther studied her blush. 'I gather you live in England,' was all he said. He rose. 'Shall we return, now?' he asked.

Grace rose too. 'Just one thing,' she said. 'Doctor Halther, I make so many mistakes; what do you think I ought to do now about Mr Humphries?'

He looked at the view, blew out a cloud of smoke, and then looked back at her.

'Let him finish his portrait,' he said. 'This at least shall be good.'

They talked about flowers on the way back. Passing down through the cypresses Grace picked a piece of the great silver-leaved spurge, in case Nicholas had missed it. He had begun a *hortus siccus* of Dalmatian flowers – the loose sheets of blotting-paper (procured from Signor Lassi, the photographer) reposed between boards under a pile of weighty objects in her painting room at the Tete Mare; she was always bumping into it, and whenever she did so she was reminded of the twins' habit of parking the bulkier apparatus of their hobbies either in her morning room or in the studio, instead of in their own sitting room. When she gathered the spray now – '*Euphorbia dendroides*,' Dr Halther remarked.

'Oh, is it? Do you know the names of all the flowers here?' she asked.

'Most of them' – and it seemed that he did, for all the way back he told her the name of each flower that they passed. At the villa gate he asked her to come in and take coffee – Grace declined, saying that she must do some work herself; she promised, however, to have tea there on the following day. As she walked back along the *fondamento* she thought, of course, about the conversation which she had just had with the Professor. He was very abrupt! But it seemed to her also that he was reliable and wise – that was her main impression of him. One could learn a lot from a man like that, who would insist on thinking clearly, who tore away all the veils of reserve and shyness and conventional humility, and left nothing but facts, bleak and gaunt as the figures in an El Greco picture. Why did she think of an El Greco? she wondered. Was there a hint of distortion, too, in his view of life? Anyhow she would like to hear him talk on all sorts of subjects, besides Nicholas. But why wouldn't he tell her what to do about Nicholas? She was aware of a definite refusal there. Did he not know what she ought to do, or wouldn't he tell her? It was rather tiresome; she did very much want to know.

There was a sound of rapid feet behind her; a hand was pushed unceremoniously through her arm, and there was Nicholas himself.

'Why didn't you come in?' he said. 'Why did you bolt off like that?'

'I didn't bolt – I want to do some work.'

'I wanted you to see my picture,' he said. 'I've started a most priceless one of Maria giving the Professor what-for! She tongues him like anything if he doesn't eat his food or change his underclothes – she was doing it this morning.'

'I can see it tomorrow – I'm coming to tea,' said Grace.

'Yes, I know. Am I coming to supper tonight?'

'I think perhaps *not*; I must work.' Then a thought struck her. 'Nicholas, what did your Mother say about the painting when you wrote to her about it? You remember you promised to, at Clissa.'

'Yes – and I did; I wrote that same night. But the odd thing is that she's never said a word about it. The Jug Agency forwarded a letter from her from Split yesterday, too, but she never mentioned it. That's rather funny.'

'You're sure you *did* write?'

'Of course I'm sure. Why are you so suspicious, Lady K.?'

'You really wrote the sort of letter I meant you to write – a letter that needed an answer?'

'Yes – really and truly. It *is* very odd.' He paused, and looked down at his suit, with an expression suddenly doubtful. 'I suppose I posted it,' he said, and began to feel in his inner pockets. Out came a miscellaneous collection of papers – the bill for his paints and canvases, not paid; a receipt from the Hotel Imperial at Ragusa; a menu from the inn at Spalato, on which Grace had drawn an idle sketch of him one night – and among them, unstamped, rather dirty, the corners bent, a letter with the name of the Ritz-Splendide printed on the flap of the envelope. This he held out to her in silence, with guilty eyes.

'Nicholas, you are hopeless! No, that really *is* wrong of you,' she said, as he put on his coaxing expression, cocking his head on one side. 'You've made me work with you really on false pretences! You know that I should not have done it unless I believed you had written.' She was surprised herself at the keenness of her vexation at this discovery.

He looked at her in silence, flushing. 'You know I didn't mean to hold it up,' he said at length. 'I remember now – I hadn't a stamp, and you'd gone to bed, and I left it till the morning and forgot.' His expression changed. 'It is my fault, Lady Kilmichael, and I am very sorry – but I don't think you ought to use that expression about me. You can hardly believe that I did it intentionally.' His voice was very cold – the letter shook in his fingers; Grace realised that he was bitterly angry. It was nearly a month since he had called her 'Lady Kilmichael.'

'No – I oughtn't,' she said at once. 'I am sorry I said that – I take it back. But you do see that you are exceptionally tiresome, don't you? That I feel that I've been put in a completely false position, even if you didn't do it intentionally?' Having apologised, she felt, as people are apt to do, that she was thereby entitled to show her vexation freely.

He looked at her again, and said nothing for some moments. At last – 'When you really *are* cross, it isn't funny,' he said slowly. 'But I deserve it. That wasn't so good. I am very sorry. Good night.' He turned to go.

'Good night,' said Lady Kilmichael, and walked on towards the Orlandos'. Suddenly she noticed that she was still carrying the piece of spurge which she had picked for Nicholas. Ridiculously, the sight of it brought the tears into her eyes. Really, she was absurd this afternoon, she thought impatiently – the least thing upset her. But she remembered how she had picked it to give him pleasure, and all she had done in the end was to be unfair and unkind to him, to part almost in anger. She glanced back. Nicholas was still standing in the white roadway, looking after her; there was something rather desolate about his solitary figure, with the yellow head. She had a strong impulse to go back, to give him the spurge and heal this small breach. But she resisted it, and went slowly on. She thought that she was making this decision in the light of the Professor's remarks about weighing the probable result of one's action, and not because she did not want, for some reason, to confront Nicholas again just then. Perhaps she was right.

SIXTEEN

'Goodness, what a view!'

'That big mountain over there is whiter even than Mossor. Lady K., this is rather a place.'

Nicholas and Lady Kilmichael were standing on the crest of the mountainous ridge which overhangs the Ombla valley on the north. Behind, they could look clear over the valley and the low intervening hill to the sea and the islands; but it was the view in front of them which drew forth these exclamations. It was one of the strangest they had ever seen – an upland plateau of greyish-white rock, sloping away very gradually in front of them, and rising again beyond to great bleached mountains, white with the dull whiteness of paper or ashes. Slope beyond slope, range upon arid range, this vast pale landscape stretched away into the furthest distance, as empty and almost as desiccated as a slag heap; near at hand the broken rocks were skinned over in places with a low scrub of rusty dwarf oak and juniper, only three or four feet high; but this scanty shrubby vegetation merely added to the prevailing sense of drought and desolation. There was not a house, an animal or a human being in sight – it was like looking on the skeleton of a world which had perished in a fire. They were in fact seeing for the first time a typical stretch of *karst* country, the high limestone tract which with a few interruptions stretches all down the hinterland of the Adriatic coast, from Trieste to the Bocche di Cattaro. It was a startling contrast to the cultivated valley behind them, the iris-and-cistus-clad slopes up which they had just climbed; they had passed almost at a stride from a hillside brilliant as a garden to this bleak wilderness. Nevertheless, it had beauty, though of so strange a sort. 'It's like being in the moon,' Nicholas presently remarked – and Lady Kilmichael could only agree.

The climb up had taken them two hours, and they were both hot and thirsty. Nicholas suggested a preliminary lunch where they were, before setting out to explore the plateau, and they sat down to eat it under the crumbling wall of a small ruined building, affording some shelter from the wind, which at this height was keen in spite of the hot sun. Nicholas hazarded the suggestion that the building might at one time have been a frontier post – 'Halther says that the old frontier between Dalmatia and Herzegovina ran along this ridge, and it was a great place for smugglers.'

'Then when we go down there we shall be in Herzegovina,' said Grace, waving her hand vaguely at the sloping plateau in front of her. 'What fun! But Nicholas, it is a *queer* place, isn't it?'

It was queer. It was unnatural to see any tract of country so empty. There was something oppressive about the very solitude. Small paths winding between the rocks and the patches of scrub showed that humanity – or goats – sometimes passed that way, but there was no sign of them now. The whole place gave Lady Kilmichael a feeling of being a survivor on a deserted planet.

This expedition into the interior had been Nicholas's idea, engendered by some chance remarks of Dr Halther's about the scenery and vegetation of the plateau; and Grace, faintly remorseful still about her vexation over the business of the letter, had at once agreed to go too, when he suggested it at tea in the villa garden the previous day. That tea had been enlightening in one or two respects. For the first time Lady Kilmichael had seen Nicholas, under no special stress of circumstances, in company other than her own; and she had been struck by how much more mature, more independent and upstanding he showed himself in the society of the older man. More dispassionately than was usual with her, she registered this. After tea, Dr Halther had escorted her back to the Tete Mare, and on the way he said, with his usual abruptness:

'You have asked me yesterday what you shall now do about young Humphries. I have not told you, because I did not know; also it is better that one should decide for oneself how one shall act. But today I know more. Last night we have spoken about you.'

'Yes?' said Grace, rather breathlessly. She was slightly appalled to think of Dr Halther cross-examining Nicholas as he had cross-examined her.

'Yes. We speak only generally,' he said. 'But it is clear to me that he does not at all realise that he loves you. It is what I said yesterday. He thinks that it is your painting, your goodness of heart, your wisdom that he admires.'

'Not my wisdom, surely?' said Grace, startled into hitting on the irrelevant with even more accuracy than usual.

Dr Halther gave her a fine smile. 'He said wisdom. But that is not the point, *gnädige Frau.* While he does not know, there is little that you can do but display goodness of heart, and wisdom.' He smiled again. 'But you cannot hope that he will not presently find out. Sooner or later, something shall show him. And then you will have to decide what you shall do.'

As she sat now, drinking Dr Halther's lager beer at the edge of the plateau, Grace was thinking about his words. Nothing could have been more easy and unembarrassed than Nicholas's manner on the walk up, and she wondered if this revelation were really so imminent as he supposed. Actually it was almost upon them. Nicholas had agreed that the place was queer, had rejected a *salami* sausage of Maria's providing, and had embarked on some bread and cheese, when suddenly he turned his head rather quickly and said 'What's that?'

Grace looked round too. They were on a sort of saddle, and to their left the ridge rose considerably higher; there the oak scrub was thicker too. Up on this slope, almost hidden by the bushes, she caught a glimpse of several figures moving towards them. Owing to the scrub and the distance, it was impossible to see what they were; now they disappeared for a moment, now bobbed up again somewhere else, but their general direction appeared to be downhill and towards the saddle. For some time Grace and Nicholas watched this oddly anonymous approach with a certain intentness; Grace found herself trying to count the newcomers, but their spasmodic movements made this impossible, and presently they vanished entirely. Nicholas stood up to get a better view; she did the same; but nothing was now to be seen but the brownish scrub growing among the uneven white rocks, and the mountains in the distance – the plateau was again as empty as it had been before. There was something vaguely disquieting about this sudden appearance and disappearance of human beings, in that solitude. 'I wonder where they've gone,' said Grace.

'They may have got into dead ground – it's all very broken. I wonder what they are.'

'Peasants, I suppose.'

Both spoke with a sort of deliberate casualness – neither was willing to admit to anything so obviously ridiculous as fear, or even nervousness, of they knew not what. But both, when they reseated themselves, without a word sat down, not under the wall as they had done before, but on the top of it, where they could see all round them. They went on eating, they talked about the view and the beer, but all the time each noticed, without mentioning it, that the other's eyes were ranging the scrub, to right, to left, and above all behind them. And a little thread of tension, fine and impalpable but strong, was drawn taut between them.

Presently, out into an open space in front of them emerged a curious procession – first a flock of goats, and following them nine or ten girls, each carrying a distaff in her hand, from which she spun yarn as she walked. The girls had kerchiefed heads and long white coats reaching almost to their heels, with a foot of vivid scarlet embroidery at the hem – preceded by their flock, they moved across the landscape with the slow, rather formal grace of figures in an Eastern frieze – beautiful, pastoral, utterly peaceful. And they came from the foot of the slope! At the sight, the little thread of tension broke. Nicholas burst out laughing.

'*That's* all they are,' he said. 'Girls and goats!'

'Oh Nicholas, how lovely their clothes are. Do let's go and try to talk to them.'

'They'll only speak Serbo-Croat'; but he went with her. The girls were as shy as animals – they would stand to stare till the strangers were within a few yards of them, but on any closer approach they moved on, quietly but determinedly, like cows in a field. Lady Kilmichael managed nevertheless to take in the details of their garments – the dress of some dark stuff, the white woollen stockings and string-topped goatskin slippers, the long white homespun coats with that magnificent stretch of embroidery round the bottom, and narrower scarlet bands at the neck and armholes. Pursuing and pursued, goats and humans, the whole company shifted slowly along the ridge, till the girls reached an immense boulder; up this they climbed, and there, perched like cormorants on its summit, they began to sing – a curious monotonous little air in four simple phrases, repeated over and over again, which rose and fell in the clear air, vaguely melancholy as the desolate plateau and the ashen mountains beyond. Nicholas and Lady Kilmichael returned to their interrupted lunch, and this time they again sat under the low wall. Leaning his head against it – 'Why did you sit on top, after we'd first seen them?' Nicholas asked.

'So that I could see behind me. Why did you?'

'Same reason. Were you frightened?' he said, looking rather closely at her.

'Not really – I felt rather uncomfortable,' she said. 'No – I *was* rather frightened, just because I didn't know what they were. It was frightfully silly.'

'Yes – we looked pretty good fools when they showed up,' said Nicholas. And they laughed at themselves, in a sort of warm relaxation from that earlier tension, comparing notes as to how the fear of the unknown had taken them. Both had felt silly all the time; but both had remembered that they were miles from anywhere, in a place of which Dr Halther had said that once up on the plateau, one left Europe and the twentieth century behind, and went back three hundred years into what was really an Asiatic world. To share fear is to share a new form of intimacy; but while Lady Kilmichael, though she treated them with civilised lightness, spoke honestly of her own sensations, Nicholas did not. In those moments when he sat on the top of the wall, eating food he could not taste and discussing beer, he had met fear in a new form. He had visualised danger, not only to himself, but to the woman beside him; his imagination, running ahead to meet the unknown and give it shape, had shown her to him in possible peril from which he could not shield her. And the sharpness of that thought had opened his eyes. A full realisation had not come yet; but as they sat together under the wall, relaxed and easy, he looked at her, up and down, from head to foot, with a sort of bewildered wonder. It was as if he had never seen her before; as if he had never really noticed this face, which was in fact so familiar, which he had even painted – the delicate indeterminate profile, the gentle mouth, the fine soft shadowing round the eyes and modelling round the lips, which give so much quality to a face which has left the unemphasised freshness of youth behind. And as he looked a new feeling, a sort of error which was yet delight, stirred in him – and once when she turned with some laughing remark, he who had so often embarrassed her by his staring lowered his eyes and looked away.

Presently they went on to explore, leaving the knapsack with the remains of the lunch cached in the ruin against their return. A faintly marked stony track led away into the plateau, and they followed this. The absence of soil was what struck them most; the scrub grew in fissures in the living rock, which was broken up into curious shapes, but of earth, properly speaking, there was hardly any to be seen, till they passed a small round hollow in the rocks, some fifty yards across, whose level floor was of soil, and bore a crop of vegetables – one of the *dolines* which are such an odd feature of this country. Later on they came to more *dolines*, but still they saw no house, no village. The track bore round to the east, and high above them on the shoulder of a hill a train came puffing, trailing a sulphurous yellow cloud of smoke – it puffed off into the distance, filling that great space surprisingly with its noise, and disappeared. That must be the line to Trebinje, Nicholas said.

When they had been walking for nearly two hours, Grace suggested a return. Clouds were piling up threateningly among the mountains to the south-east, and they had left their jackets with the lunch. 'Oh, let's go on!' Nicholas begged. 'We ought to see a village, now we've come all this way. Look, there's a road.'

Sure enough, just ahead of them a road lay, winding round among the broken slopes; they went down to it and followed it. Now in one of the *dolines* they saw a donkey tethered, browsing on real grass, which Nicholas took as a sign that there must be a village close by. 'If there is, I hope there's a *kafana* [café] in it,' said Grace. 'I *am* thirsty.'

Nicholas was right. A quarter of a mile further on the road topped a small rise – in the hollow just beyond were several houses, with stone walls and roofs roughly thatched with turf and branches, held in place by stones. They were more like low huts than houses, not built in any order, but each lying tucked into a fold of the ground, from which the roofs alone projected, like the backs of sleeping animals. There was no sign of a *kafana*. On the road just in front of them an old man appeared, dressed in the baggy indigo-blue breeches, sleeveless jacket and little round black cap, perched precariously on one side of his skull, of the Illyrian peasant. 'Everyone up here seems to be in fancy dress,' Nicholas muttered.

'Let's ask him where we can get coffee,' said Grace, and approaching the old man, '*Kafana?*' she said enquiringly.

He shook his head, and waved up towards the railway line above them, saying words they could not understand – it was clear, however, that the *kafana*, if anywhere, was by the railway.

Grace tried again. '*Kafana, kafa*,' she said urgently, and made the motions of drinking.

The peasant by way of answer sat down on a rock by the roadside, and proceeded to address what was evidently a series of questions to them. Nicholas was wearing shorts; the old man poked his bare knees with a gnarled finger that was like the stump of a juniper bush, and extended his own leg, stoutly clothed in a home-made stocking of dark brown sheep's-wool, by way of admonition or comparison, they could not tell which. Grace grew rather impatient – a cold wind was blowing those threatening clouds right over them now, and a spatter of chill raindrops was borne on the wind. 'We really ought to get under cover,' she said, and '*Kafa?*' she repeated to the peasant, urgently. She felt that curious mixture of vexation and powerlessness which comes from the inability to communicate with other human beings.

In reply, the man rose rather reluctantly, and led them down a by-path to what proved to be his own dwelling – two low huts of unmortared stone on either side of a sort of yard which had a goat stall at one end and a shelter full of dried brushwood at the other. In response to his shouts two women appeared, one clearly his wife, the other a rather beautiful girl – both wearing dark stuff dresses, pale aprons, white kerchiefs and heavy silver-gilt earrings. After a long pattering speech in which they caught the words '*izba*' [hut] and '*kafa*,' the woman, with much more amiability than the man, led them into one of the huts, indicated that they were to remain there, and disappeared.

Left to themselves, Nicholas and Lady Kilmichael gazed round them with interest. The hut had no window, and such light as there was entered by the door. The floor was of beaten earth, most of it occupied by a sort of shallow box of planks roughly fastened together and piled with strong-smelling blankets of goats' hair, chocolate-brown in colour and nearly half an inch thick – the bed. There was no other furniture of any sort; a kind of ledge along the edge of the bed afforded the only seat, and strings fastened across from wall to wall, hung with a variety of garments, evidently served the purpose of a wardrobe. Piled in a corner against the stone wall, whose larger interstices were roughly stopped with turf, stood the only objects of any interest or beauty – three or four wooden distaffs whose tops were very richly and carefully carved in rather arabesque patterns. It was a singularly primitive dwelling, comfortless and chilly – the rain, now falling heavily outside, splashed in over the stone door-sill, showing how easily this bedroom floor might be reduced to mud.

Nicholas soon became restless, and in spite of the rain, went out. Lady Kilmichael had embarked on a more careful examination of the carved patterns on the distaffs, in the hope of coming on something related to her West Highland designs, when a call from Nicholas interrupted her – 'Lady K.! Do come over here and watch them – it's rather fun.'

Thus summoned, Grace poked her head out. Nicholas was standing in the door of the hut opposite, and she stepped quickly through the drenching rain and joined him. This second building was evidently the kitchen and living room; like the other it was windowless, floored with earth, and wholly innocent of furniture. At one end was the hearth, a stone slab three feet across – on either side of it the floor was raised about fifteen inches into two low platforms, whose use was indicated by the fact that the old peasant was sitting on one of them; in the darkness of the further end more garments could just be made out, hung from more strings. The woman was stirring the embers; then she flung on a pile of dry brushwood, and kindled it to a blaze with a very ornate pair of bellows. 'I believe we are to have some coffee,' Nicholas murmured to Grace, who had sat down on the platform opposite the old peasant – 'the girl has gone to milk the goats.'

It soon became evident that he was right. From a hole in the wall, rather like an aumbry, the woman presently produced two cooking utensils – one of those tall slender copper saucepans, narrowed at the top, in which pseudo-Turkish coffee is brewed in French restaurants, and a Gold Flake tin with a piece of wire twisted round it to form a handle; from another hole she drew forth a small metal box and a very old-fashioned ornamental Mazawattee tea canister covered with flowered pictures. Coffee and soft sugar were carefully measured out of these into the copper saucepan, which she then filled with water and stood in the hot ashes. The pretty girl now returned with a crock of goats' milk, from which the Gold Flake tin was filled and similarly placed on the hearth. While the girl watched the saucepans the woman reached down a large brightly coloured handkerchief off one of the strings, and spread it on the floor before Lady Kilmichael and Nicholas – from other holes in the wall she fetched two little Turkish coffee cups in tall copper stands, a round flat loaf of bread nearly as dark in colour as the blankets, and about half of a flat and pallid cheese. All these she set out on her improvised tablecloth with the utmost neatness, and when the coffee and milk were ready she poured them into the cups with careful exactitude; then with a singularly gracious gesture she bade her guests fall to, and stood by to watch them eat. The ceremony and care with which the whole thing was done made Grace and Nicholas realise at last what a rarity coffee was to these people, and the extent of their poverty; they felt guilty at having so recklessly provoked this lavish hospitality. However, there was nothing to be done now but to accept it with gratitude, and fall to.

This was not so easily done, for as there were no plates, so there were also no knives, and neither of them carried one. Seeing this difficulty, the woman applied to a tall young man who had come in and stood watching the strangers; he produced from somewhere about his person a sort of dirk with an ornamental but very dirty blade, with which he cut off large lumps from both loaf and cheese. The bread was sour and saltless, the cheese thin and very sour too. Nicholas displayed his usual alarm at any unwonted food – Lady Kilmichael brusquely adjured him not to be a goose, but to eat it up and look polite.

'It's all very well, but there are most filthy marks from his thumb and his knife on this cheese,' protested Nicholas dismally.

'Rubbish! Everyone has to eat a peck of dirt in their life.'

'What I *should* like is a good drink of that milk,' he said, setting down his empty coffee cup.

'Well, try to make them understand.'

This, after a good deal of dumb-show, he succeeded in doing; the girl rather shyly brought the milk crock, and held it to his lips. This time even Grace was appalled – the crock was encrusted with dirt, and successive dried rims inside it showed, like strata, the levels of previous milkings. However, Nicholas drank deeply from the filthy vessel, and said that he now felt better.

All this time their hostess was trying to carry on a conversation with her guests. Grace's chief contribution to this was to touch various objects, hear their names in Serbo-Croat, and repeat them; her repetitions were greeted with laughter and applause. She thus learned that both the brown stockings of the two men, and the fine white ones of the girl, knitted with a broad open-work clock an inch wide up the outside of the leg, were of *ovcavuna* [sheep's wool]; on the other hand the blankets, and a thick dark cloak with a hood, worn by a woman who presently came in and joined the party, were of *dlakakozja* [goats' hair]. All the peasants except the old man displayed an artless friendliness, and even pleasure in this visitation; and by dumb-show – though in her case accompanied by a torrent of words – the woman managed to convey a surprising amount of information about herself and her family. The old man was her husband, the young one wished to marry her daughter; this she did not want; the girl was only thirteen (she counted the years on her fingers). Her gestures towards the two men indicated with dramatic vigour her views of the other sex – 'Oh, *men*!' But when she spoke of her daughter her whole face was illuminated with pride and delight, her harsh nasal tones softened to a warm tenderness, and when, with the utmost simplicity, she illustrated her feelings by drawing the girl's head to her and holding it against her breast, Grace could not but realise that this bare, dirty and archaic hut sheltered a family affection as delicate and ardent as that to be found in any civilisation.

But while Lady Kilmichael was smiling at a mother and daughter in a peasant's hut in Herzegovina, her own daughter, off Gibraltar, was writing a letter in the lurching lounge of the S.S. *Mindora Star*.

Well, here we are. I think it's going to be even more frightful than I thought. I was madly sick in the Bay and so was Poppy, though he swears it's only that he *prefers* to keep flat! A most crushing boatful – what I've seen of them, that is; a quite fearfully Anglo-British General with a red-haired daughter is really the nearest thing to a suitor on board. He's utterly Mbonga – fires on the mob in Poona, way back in '04, at every meal. I long to tell him that I was on safari at Frinton-on-Sea last summer – one day I shall, if this goes on. Still no news of Mums – Poppy has rather closed down on the subject. What I can't understand is *why* Mums has hooshed off like this. I thought people only did it for a grand passion, or out of complete suicidalness. But tho' Rose – she saw us off, by the way – was rather tiresomely *en evidence*, I shouldn't have thought even Mums could have been so misguided as to feel suicidal about her and Poppy. And Mums just *doesn't* go in for passions, grand or otherwise. She's really a family woman.

The rain presently lessened, and Lady Kilmichael and Nicholas began to think of starting home. 'I say, oughtn't we to pay them something? They must be frightfully poor,' said Nicholas.

'No, I'm sure one can't give them money,' Grace replied.

'Why not?'

'I'm certain they'd be terribly affronted – like Highlanders. The only thing would be to give them some *thing*, as a present, if we could. Have you got any object on you?'

Nicholas sought and considered. From the hip pocket of his shorts he finally produced a large clean linen handkerchief, with an 'N' embroidered in one corner.

'That will do,' said Grace. 'I've got this—' She had pulled out a tiny pocket comb in a little Venetian leather case. These things she presented with some formality, the handkerchief to the woman, the comb to the girl. Their delight was touching to see. The woman unfolded the handkerchief, felt its fineness knowingly, and rubbed it against her husband's face that he might feel its softness, while the comb and its case were passed from hand to hand amid loud exclamations of admiration. The 'N' was examined with curiosity – '*Nicolaj*', said Grace, pointing first to the monogram and then to Nicholas.

The woman beamed. '*Nika!*' she said, tapping her own breast; and suddenly stepped forward, threw her arms round Nicholas, and gave him a hearty kiss. Nicholas, rather to Grace's surprise, and very much to her satisfaction, responded with unembarrassed vigour.

'I'd really rather it had been the girl!' he said to her with a grin, as they left the hut and walked up to the road. 'Lady K., though, what very nice people, weren't they? I mean nice on any showing, not just as natives.'

'Yes, they were,' said Grace warmly. She had felt just the same, and rather expanded on the subject. But Nicholas was not very responsive; he soon fell silent – and silent he remained for the rest of the long, damp and chilly walk home. Now and then he turned his head and looked at her; but if she turned to him he looked away, and made only the briefest and most grudging replies to her remarks. Grace was puzzled; he was evidently out of temper, apparently with her, and she could think of no reason for it. Oh well, perhaps he was tired; and she gave up the attempt to talk and walked in silence. Only once more that afternoon did Nicholas volunteer a remark. It was when, at the ruin on the saddle, they picked up the knapsack with the remains of the lunch.

'Pity we didn't take this after all,' he said sourly; 'then we needn't have fed in that place. If that meal doesn't poison us, I don't know what will.'

'Nicholas, you really are absurd about your food,' said Lady Kilmichael. And she really thought he was.

SEVENTEEN

Few people enter for the first time the house of someone whom they have met elsewhere without the expectation of getting some new light on the owner from the mere sight of his intimate surroundings; and Lady Kilmichael walked in through the front door of the villa, on the evening of her day on the plateau, with this sense of expectation well developed. It was strong enough to counterbalance a very considerable fatigue, and a slight and puzzled sense of discouragement about Nicholas. He had occasionally been sulky and unresponsive before, but usually for some ascertainable reason; for his gloomy irritability on the walk home she could not account, and though she told herself that it was absurd to pay any attention to it, she had found her attention, most tiresomely, paying itself to the subject while she dressed. However, it would be amusing to see what Dr Halther's house was like; she vaguely expected it, like himself, to be rather bleak and grim.

She was wrong. The villa was as charming as the garden, which she had already seen, with the excellent armchairs on which men somehow always insist, a few good bits of marquetry, and several first-rate modern pictures. Maria's food was Italianate but delicious, the temperature of the Rhine wine perfect; and after so many weeks in hotels it was delightfully strange to sit at table surrounded by the individual grace of family silver and good glass. Dr Halther, this evening, was as ungrim as his house; he made a very urbane host. They had coffee in the garden, under the ilex by the fountain; the Doctor settled Lady Kilmichael into one of those double swing seats made of canvas, with cushions at her back; he and Nicholas sat on the marble bench. After they had finished their coffee he asked if she liked the piano. 'I usually play for an hour in the evenings – if you care for it?' Lady Kilmichael said that she cared for it very much indeed, and made a movement to rise; the Doctor checked her – the windows were all open, she would hear perfectly, and it was pleasanter out of doors. So she and Nicholas stayed by the fountain, dropping musically in the shadows, and Dr Halther went indoors and played Debussy.

It was delicious in the garden. The storm had passed over long since, and it was still and warm; the sweetness of the stocks and roses filled the air with the peculiar intensity of fragrance of flowers after rain – in the evening light they had the unnatural shadowy vividness of a coloured photograph. The rain had stirred up the nightingales too – near and far, their bubbling ecstasy welled out from the dark shelter of ilexes and cypresses, and through the open windows of the villa there came presently the cool elusive sequences of Debussy's music – ghosts of melody rather than melodies, evocations rather than statements; gleams on water and pale lights in spring skies, a single star, slow waves beating in mist on a deserted shore. Grace leant back in the corner of her seat, listening, watching the leaves of the buckthorns, like little curved pencils, against the sky above her head; in the relaxation of fatigue her attention was fixed on nothing, but some part of her was profoundly aware of all these things – the scent of the flowers, the song of the nightingales, the cool western music, with its memories of her own Atlantic shores. In the shadows under the ilex Nicholas was visible as a rather indeterminate shape, his shirt front, his head and the polish on his shoes concentrating all the light which reached him, and indicating the rest. He had been silent, but not exactly gloomy at dinner; out of a vague desire to re-establish contact Grace said, when a pause came in the music –
'I like Debussy.'

'Do you?'

'Yes. When he thinks of an island, he thinks of the same sort of island as I do – small and low, with pale bents on it, and very little birch trees, and wind blowing; his islands have the same emptiness as mine, and the same sort of strangeness – almost fear.'

Nicholas stood up. 'This marble is most frightfully hard,' he said. 'Is there room for me on your seat?'

Grace thought so, and moved further into the corner to make space for him; he sat down beside her, and stretched his arm along the back.

'Go on about your island,' he said.

'That's all. *L'Isle* made me think of it.'

'What's this he's playing now?'

'*La Fille aux Cheveux de Lin.*'

He sat turned rather towards her. Presently he said, 'Are you tired?'

'Only healthily.'

'You've got shadows under your eyes.'

'Have I? How disagreeable.'

'No, it isn't. I think I shall paint you with smudges under your eyes – it's very becoming to them.' He peered at her in the dusk. 'Altogether your face is more exciting when you're tired, or half-cross,' he said.

'Yours isn't at all nice when you're cross!' said Grace with deliberate lightness. A faint uneasiness, which she imagined to be embarrassment, was beginning to creep over her, tired and inattentive as she was; Nicholas's arm, lying along the seat-back, just brushed her shoulders if she really relaxed into the cushions – and there was a sense of emotional disturbance about him, like the uneasy atmospheric quality of a day which will end in thunder.

'My face is never nice,' he said sombrely. 'People like you have no idea what it's like to go about with a face and hair that put everyone off.'

'Oh, nonsense! Your face isn't in the least off-putting, except when you're cross.'

'Was I very cross this afternoon?'

'Not really – a little glum. Why were you?'

'No real reason.' He stared ahead of him across the darkening garden, and Grace knew that there was a reason, and that if he could find the courage she would hear it. Somehow this was a little frightening – she waited in a suspense that surprised her till he spoke again.

'I think I'm really rather a bestial little boy,' he said slowly.

'Why do you think that?'

'*You* make me think it, primarily,' he said, turning towards her face, so close beside him, shadowy in the dusk. 'I'm a coward, I'm selfish, and I'm not honest.' He paused, and she waited, curiously shaken, for more. The words were unsensational enough, but words are not everything – a strained, almost stern note in his voice which she had never heard before, something even in the way he held his head gave a sense of crisis which was unmistakeable. But what chiefly troubled her was a confused awareness of some movement in herself which was more than the mere recognition of a crisis; something in her was responding to the emotional disturbance in him in the most unexpected way. She knew all sorts of things suddenly; knew that it was not quite an accident that his arm had slipped down off the back of the seat, so that it just rested on her shoulders; knew that at that moment he wanted very badly to kiss her, and that some incredibly small thing would decide whether he did or not; most disconcerting of all, the thought of being kissed by Nicholas actually made her heart beat. In a moment, if he didn't speak again, she would have to say something sensible and soothing, which wouldn't be so easy with this silly pulsation in her throat.

But he did speak again – in a curious speculative tone – 'Why are you so nice to me, Lady K.?' he asked.

Something about the humility and simplicity of the question brought Lady Kilmichael back out of that disquieting emotional spell onto solid ground again – the solid ground of affection and goodwill.

'I think probably because you're so very nice to me, my dear child,' she said, a little uncertainly, but more readily than she would have thought possible. 'You may really be very nasty, but you haven't shown it much so far!' She rose. 'I think it's time I went home. I am tired, actually.'

Dr Halther accepted her early departure without protest. Rather surprisingly without protest, she thought afterwards; did he guess that something might have happened in the garden? Had he even expected something to happen? Crafty old man! Had he had the temerity to arrange it? A touch of indignant colour came into her face at the thought. But she did not spend much time on thinking about the Professor and his motives, long though she remained awake that night. She lay in bed, listening to the nightingales and the river under her window, and asking herself in a sort of exasperated astonishment whether she could really be falling in love with Nicholas.

That young gentleman sauntered round next morning and finished her portrait, in a sitting which was monosyllabic on his side and rather flowingly conversational on hers; any possibility of embarrassment Lady Kilmichael always met with a rather more social manner than usual. At the end he asked her if she liked it. Grace studied the picture carefully. It was unexpectedly good. That idea of concentrating most of the light in the background in those blazing flowers, leaving the figure in shadow, was unusual and curious, but he had brought it off; in that dim filtered light the relaxation of the pose, the tones of dress and skin took on a remarkable quality. There was no over-precision this time, either; though the painting was forcible and direct there was an ease, an expansion about it – the warmth and light were there all right, but used with a stroke of ingenuity that was almost genius to emphasise the quiet meditative aspect of the portrait itself. It was an extraordinary advance on the Traü picture; and remembering how she had thought at the time that that gave away his youth, his uncertainty, she felt suddenly that this portrait revealed, more than he ever could or would reveal in words, some interior development.

'I like it very much,' she said.

'Would you be satisfied with it as a portrait, if you'd come to me as a sitter?'

'I think so.' She narrowed her eyes at it. 'Yes, definitely – and what's more I think Walter would, too.'

He grunted at that, did up the canvas, and took himself off to the villa. It occurred to her when he was gone that he wasn't looking very well – he was paler than usual, and his eyes looked headachy. Probably he was tired after the walk; and he had obviously been in rather a fuss about her last night, which was tiring too. Well really, *she* mustn't let herself get into a fuss as well – that would be too much! She had probably exaggerated her own disturbance – she had been tired and sleepy, and his coming and sitting like that had taken her by surprise, that was all. He was a dear delightful child, and she was very fond of him indeed; but to put it higher than that was to be too irrational. She would start that picture this afternoon, and forget about it all.

She duly started her picture, but she was not to be allowed to forget about herself and Nicholas. After lunch she carried her camp stool and easel a couple of hundred yards out onto the small promontory opposite the island, and set them up in the shade of a single tree. A great bed of pale reeds fringed the shore at this point, and over them the cypresses on the island showed nearly as grey as olives in the high afternoon light; to the right was a glass-green expanse of river, and beyond it the clear pinks and whites of the houses on the further shore. It was rather an exciting subject – she saw it all in tones of buff and cream and green, and as sun-flooded as she could make it; she worked away at her underpainting in pale umber, now and then pausing to listen to a loud babble of notes, more liquid and far more powerful than the nightingales', which broke out from the reeds close by. It was very near, she ought to be able to see the bird, and presently she did, clinging sideways to a reed and pouring out those enormous bubbles of sound from a distended throat of the most vivid coral. It was a bird as big as a thrush, and the same soft brown above, but its whole breast was of that extraordinary colour, as startling as its voice. A lovely creature – by its note and its attitude, a warbler. Suddenly it flew off. Vexed, she turned round to see what had startled it; there behind her, in his Panama hat and pale suit, stood the Professor. 'I disturb?' he asked, raising the hat.

'No no – good afternoon,' Lady Kilmichael replied.

He came and looked at the canvas. 'Ah, you underpaint thoroughly. That is what I like to see. These naked canvases, the grain of the *toile* staring through sea, mountains, human faces – it is *not* painting, this! Young Humphries says you paint professionally; it is your *métier*?'

'As much as a married woman with a family can be said to have a *métier*, yes,' she answered, smiling.

Dr Halther smiled back – he seemed in a benevolent mood that afternoon. 'See, now I learn something!' he said. 'Up till now we meet like spirits in Limbo – I know nothing of you but what I see. How large a family?'

'Three – the boys are twins, and at Cambridge – the girl is younger; she's nineteen.'

Dr Halther appeared to digest this information carefully, while he looked round for something to sit on – he had evidently come prepared for conversation. There was nothing but the ground – eventually he spread out a large bandana handkerchief and seated himself upon it.

'Three children, a husband, and some painting,' he observed. 'This is already quite a full life. And now there is young Humphries too.' He looked a little amused. Grace could think of nothing to say, and was silent. The Doctor lit a cheroot.

'Something has happened,' he said presently, in a different tone. 'He knows.'

The colour, not unobserved, came into Lady Kilmichael's face at this announcement. 'How do you know?' she asked.

'I see it. Did you know?'

'No – not for certain.'

He looked shrewdly at her. 'I am quite certain,' he said. 'Something has happened yesterday which has told him. So now you must answer your question, what shall I do?'

Again Lady Kilmichael was silent. Dr Halther, she knew, would think that she ought to find her own answer; but she was singularly without theories as to how one dealt with young men who were in love with one and knew it, and this disquieting new element of uncertainty about her own feelings for Nicholas made her more hesitant even than usual.

'Is it so difficult?' Dr Halther asked at length.

'Yes – very difficult,' she said, with a sudden smile which for once he could not interpret.

'Why? To me it is simple, if you wish, as I suppose, to do what is best for him, to give him what he most needs?'

'Of course.'

'But *gnädige Frau*, think then! He needs most love, and the experience of love; and this you – older, married – can give him with grace, with beauty, as a younger woman could not. Obviously you give him this.'

'Do you mean have a love affair with him?'

'*Natürlich*. You may have to help him considerably; he is

nervous, reserved, he does not express himself easily. But this is his need, and you can fulfil it. You will be his mistress.'

Lady Kilmichael's principal feeling at this speech was one of astonishment that a man as clever as Dr Halther should be so utterly mistaken. She hardly hesitated at all this time.

'No, I shan't do that,' she said, so decidedly that the Doctor in his turn was surprised.

'And why not?'

'Because that isn't what he wants; not from me. He would be shocked to death at the bare idea.'

'What do you think then that he does want from you?'

'I'm not sure,' said Grace thoughtfully. 'I should think really just kindness, and to be let off his own feelings as lightly as possible, as it were. But I'm sure he doesn't want the other thing.'

Her tone of unhesitating conviction appeared to impress the Doctor. 'How do you know this so surely?' he asked.

'I just know it. They don't want that at that age, not the nice sensitive ones. If they fall in love they only think of getting married. All that other business comes much later, if they *can't* marry. Anyhow about him I'm certain I'm right.'

He looked at her consideringly, and puffed at his cheroot. 'It is possible,' he said at length. 'You English are a most extraordinary people – unlike any other race.' He puffed again; it was clear that he was thinking hard. 'I think I shall speak with him about it,' he said finally.

'For pity's sake don't talk to him like you talk to me!' said Lady Kilmichael, startled out of her usual civil circumspection of speech at the idea.

He looked at her in surprise. 'Do you dislike the way I talk to you?'

'No, as a matter of fact I don't. I think it helps me to have everything put rather brutally, because I'm so woolly-headed.'

'It is brutal, the way I speak to you?' He made the enquiry with judicial detachment.

'Perhaps brutal is the wrong word – unsparing. Anyhow I don't mind. But I think it would upset him terribly. He's a mass of sensitiveness anyhow, and just now, about me, I think you might really hurt him.' She spoke with urgent concern. 'Please be careful with him, Doctor Halther.'

'Very good, *gnädige Frau*, I shall.' He sat looking at her in silence for rather a long time – Grace was sure that some fresh idea was brewing in his mind. At last he asked, 'Is it your husband – his feelings – which stops you from giving yourself to this young man?'

Grace considered. She really hadn't thought about Walter at all yet in connection with Nicholas; until the Doctor made his extraordinary proposition there had been no occasion to.

'Perhaps it would be that partly – but it's more *me*, myself,' she said.

'Are you still in love with your husband?' Dr Halther next asked.

Grace sat looking out over the river. With her eyes she was seeing the clear hot colours of the buildings on the other bank, but the picture that came into her mind, involuntarily, was the sable figure of the great Madonna in the basilica at Torcello, and with it, the memory of her own sudden panic there when she thought that Walter might take her at her word, and disjoin their lives for good. In love – it was a foolish phrase, really, set against that reality, the very thought of whose loss had caused her such terror. But Dr Halther was not a foolish person; though he was so mistaken about Nicholas, she still felt a strong confidence in his real goodness and wisdom. These astonishing questions of his were asked in no spirit of levity or impertinence – it was just that he overrode everything in his drive at the truth; and she had a conviction that not to answer them as truly as she could would be to lose such a chance of enlightenment as might not come to her again. She did her best.

'I don't think people are usually *in love* much, when they've been married over twenty years,' she said. 'It's something rather different. Even if there are difficulties, the other person is somehow more important to you than anyone else in the world – he and the children.'

'And there are difficulties, in your case?'

'Some. I think it's mostly my fault. Walter is very clever, and—'

'Pardon!' Dr Halther interrupted her. 'Your husband is Walter Kilmichael? The economist?'

'Yes.'

He looked at her with increased interest. 'That is a most remarkable man,' he said with emphasis. 'Though economics are not my subject, I read all he writes. He has a beautiful intellect – one of the most beautiful in existence.'

'I know. Well, you have seen me – I'm not like that,' said Grace, with great simplicity. 'I never was a clever woman, and I seem to get stupider every year – except for my painting. Two of the children are clever too, like him – and I – well, somehow I'm not quite equal to them all anymore. When they were younger it didn't seem to – to *show* so much.' She broke off, a little uncertain of her voice; the memory of those years when her stupidity hadn't 'shown' so badly, when to the children she was perfect, and to Walter at least necessary and dear, was rather too much for her just then.

'Why do you mind this, that they think you stupid?' Dr Halther asked, not ungently.

Why did she mind, Grace wondered. The flat reasonableness of Dr Halther's question put her unhappiness in a new and curious light. She thought rather hard before she answered.

'A lot of it is silly, I expect,' she said. 'But being thought stupid is rather disabling. I think it makes me stupider yet, for one thing. And now that they are so critical, I don't think they're so fond of me anymore.'

'You think that they loved you for your intelligence?'

Grace had to smile. 'No one ever did that, I'm sure! No, but Doctor Halther, it does make it difficult – if they don't respect one, it makes it very hard to control them, and that's a thing one *must* do to some extent. And then there's friction, and that makes them dislike one. It's the friction – yes, I see – that does it; but the friction comes because they think that almost everything I say is foolish. That's a *real* difficulty.'

She poured this out, not fast, thinking it out as she went along. Dr Halther listened quietly; when she stopped – 'Do your *sons* dislike you?' he asked.

Goodness, how shrewd he was! 'No – I can't say that. It's worst with Linnet. I – she's such a darling, and *good*, but somehow we *can't* make it work, lately.' Again she was uncertain of her voice.

'Is this why you come abroad, because you are unhappy with your daughter?'

'Partly. The whole thing, really – it was getting worse instead of better, and I felt it was no good going on. I thought it might help me to get right away.' She had elided the question of Rose, deliberately – now that Dr Halther knew who she was, and all about Walter, Rose and Walter must be kept out of it.

'And has it helped, to come away?'

'I think it has, rather. I feel able to think about it all more clearly. Nicholas Humphries has helped me a lot, too.'

'How so?'

'Because he's young, and knows how young people think and feel, and he talks to me as if I were young too. He's taught me a great deal about the things that annoy children in their parents.'

Something in the simplicity of this statement made the Doctor laugh. 'This shall be most useful, no doubt,' he said, 'but you must also be clear on the fundamentals. Thinking for yourself, what have you found out?'

Grace considered again. To garner the fruits of a month's scattered reflections into a handful of sentences has taxed clearer heads than hers. But, as seemed to happen when she was talking to the Professor, his questions released in her conclusions of which she had hardly been aware.

'I've found that I can't do without them, to begin with,' she said. 'I almost thought I might be able to when I came away. But not now – I must go back when I'm ready.'

'What else?'

'That it's more my fault than I thought. There is something in me, in the way I set about everything, that is wrong – but I'm not absolutely certain yet what it is. And besides that, I've begun to find out what it is to feel free, out here – and now I've got to find out how to be free at home. If I could do that, I'm sure I could manage. I thought that was a thing *you* might be able to help me about,' she said, turning to him almost wistfully.

'You have already helped yourself a good deal,' he said. 'You need only to think a little deeper to make it clear. Look – this thing in you which makes your life at home go wrong, is there not the element of *amour propre* in it? Not much, but a little? Is not that why you mind being thought stupid, teased? You are confused in this still; no one was ever loved for their intelligence, and respect is usually reserved, in England anyhow' – he smiled – 'for moral qualities. These you have. I suspect that your children both love and respect you really, but you are made clumsy and *exigeante* by your *amour propre*; you will have them think you also intelligent. Is this true?'

'I must think. Perhaps it is. Does *amour propre* make one afraid of people?'

'More than almost any other quality – it shrinks at a touch.'

Grace nodded, slowly, thinking. Was this what had alienated Walter, bit by bit? Was this what made her lack with Linnet the self-confidence she had had, so surprisingly, with Nicholas? If she could accept both her own stupidity and her family's attitude to it *really* unresentfully, was he perhaps right, and would she nevertheless be able to deal with them all?

'I think you are right,' she said, turning to him. 'I haven't been *content* to be stupid, as it were.'

'You have the word! You must be content with what you are. See – you speak of freedom, but freedom, *gnädige Frau*, is within. It does not live in Dalmatia any more than in London.' He spread out his hand again like a diagram, and tapped it with his cheroot while he spoke. 'What is freedom? It consists in two things: To know each his own limitations and to accept them – that is the same thing as to know *oneself*, and to accept oneself as one is, without fear, or envy, or distaste; and to recognise and accept the conditions under which one lives, also without fear or envy or distaste. When you do this, you shall be free.'

Lady Kilmichael sat silent for some time after that. 'Thank you,' she said at last.

Dr Halther rose, shook his bandana carefully, and replaced it in his pocket. 'Do not be too concerned about your stupidity, *gnädige Frau*,' he said, looking down at her. 'The habit of thought you lack, but this can be learned; and *l'intelligence du cœur* is a very useful quality, which I think you have.' His sardonic grin appeared. 'See, you know what to do about young Humphries for yourself, without any help from me!'

'I only found that out by your suggesting the wrong thing,' said Grace. And when he had gone and she returned to her painting, she thought how curious that was.

She and Nicholas were still in the habit of meeting at the inn between six and seven, for a glass of light wine and 'a tot of village gossip' as he called it; but when she went down that evening he was not there, and she sat with Signor Orlando and the innkeeper, hearing about the export trade in red Lacroma to Glasgow and Oslo, and how unlucky it was that Grk would not travel. She worried a little about Nicholas, remembering his ill looks that morning, and after supper she had almost screwed herself up to the point of walking down to the villa to see how he was when a note was brought to her in the garden. It was from Nicholas; she knew his writing, though she had never had a letter from him. The written word has a quality all its own, and she opened the note with a little tremor of curiosity as to how he would write to her.

Dear Lady K.,

I am off to Ragusa tomorrow early. Now the portrait is done I think I may as well pursue my architectural tour, so I shall get on to Greece as soon as there's a boat – probably via the Bocche. I expect it will enlarge my mind, as they say.

The portrait is for you. I am leaving it here; you can fetch it any time when it is dry. It is rather unworthy, but I want you to have it, as a mild thank-offering for all your help. I have learned quite a lot from you, one way and another – thank you.

Your dear child,

Nicholas Humphries.

Lady Kilmichael put down the note. So that was Nicholas's own solution of the problem over which she and the Professor had differed so acutely that afternoon – to go away. Well, it was probably the most sensible one of all. It wasn't very prettily done – to sever a month's companionship and affection with that rather poverty-stricken little note was slightly ungracious; she was a little chilled. She took up the note and read it again and this time she was less chilled. Her attention was held by the touching absurdity of the signature, with its hint of revolt – who but Nicholas would have thought of calling himself 'Your dear child'? That said most, for and against, of what the rest so determinedly *didn't* say. As she folded it up she noticed a single line written on the back of the sheet. It was scrawled so illegibly that it took her some moments to make it out – so illegibly that when she had at last deciphered it, she wondered if it had not been written so badly on purpose, in a panic lest it should be understood. 'And still my feet' – that was all. But Lady Kilmichael recognised it – the second line of the translation of 'Morgen'; and she remembered the words which followed. Poor child! The note wasn't so poverty-stricken after all. Smiling a little, she put it away and went up to bed. (Of course she couldn't go to the villa now.)

It was only when she was in bed that one thing struck her – Nicholas's destination! She had said she was going to Greece, and she hadn't gone; the Professor had said he was going to Greece, and he hadn't gone; and now Nicholas proposed to go there too.

'Well, if he gets there, he will be the best out of three,' she thought, and fell asleep.

EIGHTEEN

Notes were something of a rarity at the Restauracija Tete Mare, and the arrival of two within twelve hours caused quite an agreeable stir of excitement in the establishment. The second came about eight the next morning, and was carried up to Lady Kilmichael's room by the Signora, followed by Teta and the niece, who remained listening in delightful speculation on the landing outside. Grace had ordered her breakfast in her room overnight, to secure herself against any sudden impulse of going for an early walk and happening to be at the bus-start at half-past seven; from her bed she had heard the bus go roaring off with sensations which surprised her. 'He's only going away – it *can't* hurt like this really' her mind protested. 'You've only known him a month.' But it did hurt, just like that; and she stared out of her window at the cypresses on the island, remembering how free she had felt, watching them, barely a fortnight before; and thinking how futile and humiliating it was to fall in love at her age – till the sight of the venetian blinds across the top of the window reminded her of the day when Nicholas came in to bring her the glass of wine, and let them down for her against the glare. The tears sprang to her eyes, at that; they had been so happy, he had been so sweet. Well, it was over now – and though it was a very silly business on her part, she at least wouldn't pretend about it.

The Signora's knock startled her. '*Avanti!*' she called. The sight of the note startled her still more, brought the colour into her face – as the Signora duly informed Teta and the niece two minutes later; but it was in a strange writing this time, and the signature, which she read first, showed it to be from the Professor.

Dear Lady Kilmichael,

As soon as you can, it would be kind if you would come round to see Mr Humphries. He is very unwell; he vomits constantly and I think he has fever. Maria does her best, but outside her kitchen she is as one of the lower animals, and I am without resources in illness, being a healthy bachelor! I do not think it grave, but it is better that you should see him.

Lady Kilmichael issued a demand for immediate breakfast, sprang out of bed, and began to dress. No wonder he had looked seedy yesterday morning! Probably he had got a chill up on the plateau, or he had eaten something which upset him – his digestion was so groggy. She bundled the very few 'resources' which she had – some bicarbonate of soda, aspirin, a flask of eau-de-cologne, and a thermometer – into a satchel, and after hurriedly swallowing some bread and coffee, while the Signora stood by urging her to take more and deploring the illness of the Signorino, she set off for the villa. It was a brilliant morning, fresher than usual after the storm of the day before; the *fondamento* wore its normal matutinal aspect of rather casual activity, the river glittered in the early sunlight. As she passed Pavlé Burié's office, where the bus was wont to stand, she surprised in her mind a little thread of gladness, twisted in among the vague anxiety – he hadn't after all gone! Greece had failed as a destination again.

Dr Halther met her in the garden. 'You have come quickly,' he said. 'That is good of you.'

'How bad is he?' Grace asked.

Dr Halther shrugged. 'I cannot judge. He is all the time sick. I do not think it is grave, but he is very unwell.'

'When did it begin?'

'In the night, it seems. He ate little last evening, but he had told me that he leaves today, and I attributed this to his state of mind. When Maria went to wake him this morning she found him very sick; he tried to get up, but he could not stand, and must lie down again. She made him some *tisane*, but he vomited it immediately again. I have no thermometer, but I think he has fever also.'

'I've brought a thermometer. Shall I go up to him?'

Dr Halther led the way upstairs. 'You will tell me presently how you think he is,' he said as they went. 'Maria will do anything you tell her and bring you anything you want. I hope it is not much, this sickness.' He opened a door. 'See, I bring you a nurse!' he announced cheerfully, ushering Lady Kilmichael in, and then went out, shutting the door softly behind him.

Nicholas was lying with his knees drawn up and his back to the light; a basin stood on a chair by the bed, and there was a sour smell of sickness in the room. His suitcases and knapsack, three-parts packed, stood about between little heaps of clothes and shoes on the floor; half the drawers in the bureau were open – a more comfortless sick-room Grace had never seen. He turned his head a very little at her entrance and said 'Hullo!' and nothing else. Grace went over to him. 'You poor Nicholas, how horrid this is for you,' she said. 'How do you feel?'

'Beastly,' he said weakly.

'Any pain?'

'All over my front. Oh lord, I'm going to be sick again!' He was – with retchings of great violence. Grace held his head till it was over and he lay back, damp and exhausted, on the pillow. She was shocked by his appearance. His usually red face had a yellowish pallor, his cheeks a look of having fallen in, and there were enormous purplish circles under his eyes. The sweat on his forehead from the exertion of retching was cold under her palm, but his hands were hot. She took out the thermometer, and shook it down. 'Take this,' she said. 'Where's the bathroom?'

'Third door on the right. I say, I hate your bothering with all that.'

'Nonsense – I'm going to make you tidy. Put that in and leave it till I come back.'

'Mmm.'

While he took his temperature Grace found the bathroom, emptied the basin, sought out Maria and demanded some cloths for her own use, a small table, tumblers, eggs and a kettle of boiling water. Then she went back to Nicholas. His temperature was only a hundred and one degrees, but his pulse and his general appearance alarmed her a good deal; he gave her the impression of being really ill.

'When did this begin?'

'I felt sick and queer all yesterday afternoon, but I was only taken short after dinner, when I was getting packed – and then I began to be sick too, and I've gone on more or less ever since.'

'Sick how often?'

'About every quarter of an hour, I should say.'

She reckoned in her head. This had been going on for nine or ten hours. It must be stopped somehow. When Maria brought the kettle she mixed some bicarbonate of soda and gave it to Nicholas. While he sipped it she broke the whites of two eggs carefully into a tumbler, beat them up with a tooth-brush handle, went and fetched some salt and another glass, poured on the water, and strained the mixture through a clean pocket handkerchief.

'What's that brew?'

'Albumen water – it soothes your inside.'

'It looks filthy.'

'It isn't really.'

While she did these things her mind was working fast, taking stock of the situation; thinking what was probably the best treatment, what most urgently needed doing, what must be got from Ragusa. As soon as he had finished the bicarbonate of soda Nicholas was sick again. As she came back from the bathroom she met him coming along the landing, in a sort of staggering run. *That* couldn't be allowed either; something must be arranged. While he was gone she hurriedly made his bed; as soon as he came back and was tucked up again she gave him the albumen water to sip.

'It'll only make me sick again,' he said fretfully.

'Sip it very slowly – it may not. Some of it will stay down anyhow. Besides if you're going to be sick you must have something to be sick with! I'll be back in a moment.'

'Where are you going?'

'Just to ask Doctor Halther for one or two things I want. You've got the basin.'

Downstairs she found Dr Halther writing in a room off the verandah. '*Na, wie geht's?*' he asked.

'I think he's really pretty bad – more than just an upset or a chill. His temperature is only a hundred and one, but he has pain all the time, and this severe sickness. Can one get a doctor?'

'Doctor Karaman is away, and his assistant is a man of little skill. You think it is grave?'

'He certainly ought not to go on being sick like that, and I don't know how to stop it. I should like to give him castor oil, but I hardly dare to without advice.'

'I shall see if there is a doctor,' he said, reaching for his hat. 'I telephone to the Imperial – there can be one among the guests.'

'Wait,' said Grace. 'There are things I need – could you telephone to Herr Hasler for those too?'

'I send the car, if you make a list.'

She made a list for the yachting chemist, with Dr Halther's help; there were one or two items for which she did not know the German word, nor he the English, and she had to explain – 'Obviously, with a temperature, he can't go running along the landing all the time.' When the list was done he took it. 'I am glad you are here,' he said. 'I should not know any of these things.' He smiled at her. 'For a woman who is not clever, you are very competent!'

'I should telephone the list to Hasler before the car goes; he keeps half his stuff in a sort of cellar up the hill, and it always takes him ages to get it out,' said Grace. 'Oh, and please send to the Tete Mare for my tea basket; then I can heat water and all that upstairs whenever I want. And Roberto might bring some more Meta too.'

'I do this.' He went off to summon the 'tremendously posh car' which Nicholas had seen from Lady Kilmichael's window on the day of her walk to Ragusa; and Grace went up to Nicholas again.

'You have been ages,' he said.

'I had to make a list of things from Hasler's. How do you feel?'

'The pain's rather beastly – can one do anything about it?'

She gave him two aspirins, and a hot bottle to put on his stomach – it was all she could think of for the minute. Then she set about what she had longed to do from the first moment she entered the room – unpacked and removed his suitcases, tidied everything up, arranged the small table by his bed. She borrowed a clean basin out of Dr Halther's room for him to wash his face and hands. Nicholas protested at all this – he could get up and do it himself, she needn't bother really. Grace dealt with this attitude at once, firmly; it would have to be dealt with sooner or later, and it was better to do it now and get it over.

'Listen, Nicholas – while you're ill you've got to do exactly what I say, as if I was a trained nurse; I shall do what needs doing for you, just as a nurse would, and you mustn't fuss about it. Do you see? I nursed scores of soldiers during the war; it's nothing new to me. So be a good child and don't worry about it.'

'Am I ill?' he asked.

'I don't think very, but you've got a bit of a temperature, too much to go wandering about with.'

'You'll get tired out, and it's all so beastly for you,' he said, looking at her with a sort of weary concern.

'No I shan't – I'm going to bring up a good chair from the veranda to sit in.'

She did so, but Nicholas was sick again before she got back. Then the tea basket came, brought by her 'porter' from the Tete Mare; she made him a cup of weak tea, but that too he brought up in a few minutes. Grace got more and more alarmed – after each bout of sickness and retching he was more exhausted, and she began to look most impatiently for Dr Halther's return. She got brandy from Maria and gave him some, weak, in boiled water – this seemed to soothe him a little, and while he lay quiet she slipped down to the kitchen and showed Maria how to make barley water.

'Where were you?' he asked when she came back. It was like a sick child's complaint. She told him.

'I'm sure it was that filthy cheese,' he said presently. 'I told you we should be poisoned in that place.'

Grace thought this only too likely, though she did not say so. As the hours passed, and the sickness continued unchecked, she became convinced that it must be a case of poisoning – she remembered, not so much the cheese as the filthy crock from which Nicholas had drunk milk in the *izba* on the plateau. Food poisoning – people died of it sometimes. But what did one *do* for it? If only she knew – if only Dr Halther would come back and bring a doctor! Her sense of helplessness and ignorance grew on her – perhaps everything she was doing was wrong, and there was some quite simple thing which, if only she knew what it was, would stop this appalling sickness. But Dr Halther didn't come back – the chauffeur returned on the bus, bringing the things ordered from the chemist and a scribbled line from his master. There was a French doctor at the Imperial, but he had gone out for the day, it was believed to the Mestrović Mausoleum at Cavtat, and he, Halther, was going after him in the car. With that rather vague hope she had to be content.

All through the afternoon Nicholas got worse. His temperature rose no higher, indeed presently it began to fall, but the sickness went on and on. Grace Kilmichael, clinging blindly, in what was rapidly becoming something like terror, to her theory of giving him something to be sick *with*, plied him with barley water, albumen water, weak brandy and water, weak Benger; but he kept nothing down for more than a few minutes, except occasionally the brandy. The pain became more severe, and with Maria's help she put on hot fomentations; these relieved it, if only temporarily. His pulse was now rapid and weak; his face was greyish-white; the dark circles seemed to cover half of it, and out of them his eyes stared, enormous, following her wherever she went with that curious anxiety which is, though she did not know it, a feature of such illnesses. Although she was constantly occupied, heating things, mixing things, emptying things, washing things up, the hours dragged interminably; Nicholas's eyes, clinging to her like a drowning man's hands for help and relief in this strange world of pain and weakness, seemed like a weight which she dragged after her whenever she moved.

Once, when she had put on a fomentation and came back and sat by the bed, he said – 'I do feel ill, Lady K.'

'You poor child, I am so sorry. I wish I could do something to make you feel better.' She smoothed the sheet, mechanically, as if that would do some good. He put out his hand and took hold of hers. His hold was weak, but there was a sort of desperation in it nevertheless – as with his eyes, Grace had the sense of being clung to by a drowning man. This increased her panic, but she fought it down, and put her other hand over his in a firm clasp. That seemed to soothe him. And for the rest of the day, whenever he wasn't being sick and she was not fetching or making something, he held her hand; each time when she came back to the bed after one of those endless trips to the bathroom, his hand was lying on the quilt, waiting, like a mute pensioner, for hers.

Dr Halther got back about six, bringing with him a Doctor Roget. This gentleman had gone on an expedition, not to Cavtat, but to Cannosa, and had actually passed through Komolac twice that day, had they but known it. But Dr Halther had not known it, and had spent six or seven fruitless and exhausting hours, combing out every resort and restaurant down the coast for one isolated visitor among the spring crowds, returning about five to the Imperial, only to find his quarry quietly sitting there, having returned from his expedition sometime before.

Dr Roget was a small round bearded man with a snappish manner. He stepped rapidly up to the bed and took one glance at Nicholas, who now lay with his eyes closed, his face so fallen away that it was all features, his hair clinging dankly to his forehead. Dr Roget found his pulse, slipped a hand under the bedclothes and felt his abdomen. He shot out questions – when had this begun? How often was he sick? Had he eaten any doubtful food? Grace told him of their meal in the *izba* on the plateau, and the dirty crock from which Nicholas had drunk.

'*Mais que voulez-vous, Madame?*' the Doctor snapped, and led her outside. It was an acute gastroenteritis, he said, from food poisoning. What had she given him since? Anxiously she mentioned all the things she had tried; Dr Roget summed each one up: the albumen water was perfectly right, the brandy and water not wrong, the barley water wrong, but not seriously, the Bengers Food a crime. '*Mais c'est de la folie, cela!*' he snapped, tapping his pince-nez against his forefinger, and looking at her accusingly.

'I am sorry – I did not know *what* to do,' said Lady Kilmichael. She leant against the wall; the thought of her mistake and the sharp scolding suddenly made her realise that she was very tired. 'But if you will tell me what to do now, I will do it,' she said.

One must endeavour to combat the prostration, Dr Roget said – that was now the danger. Had they any glucose? Of course they had not. Did the patient still vomit the brandy? If so, try champagne. '*Et chauffez-le bien*'; blankets and hot bottles. Grace went to fetch these, while Dr Halther opened some champagne – she muffled Nicholas up and gave him the wine in little sips, while the two men talked in low tones outside the room. Presently Dr Roget called her out and asked her a question about the administration of the glucose, for which the chauffeur had gone to telephone. 'If he still vomits, it is the only means to maintain life.' Grace had to admit that she knew nothing about it – 'But give me exact directions and I will do it,' she said again.

He looked her up and down. 'When have you last eaten, Madame?' he asked suddenly.

'I had some soup at twelve,' said Grace. She had been too busy and too anxious to think of a proper meal, and had only had a cup of soup, brought up to the bedroom by Maria.

'You must eat and drink,' he said, less sharply, 'or you will be fit for nothing. Anxiety fatigues.' And he announced his intention of sitting with the patient while she had some food.

Dr Halther took her downstairs. He made her drink some champagne while Maria was bringing soup and an omelette. Grace sat at first in a sort of stupor of weariness, but as the food took effect she began to pay more attention to her surroundings; she was struck then by Dr Halther's look of anxiety and distress.

'Does Dr Roget think it dangerous?' she asked.

'He says it is grave. There is great prostration. It is now so long. If only this *verfluchte Portier* at the Imperial had not misinformed me about Roget!' He sighed heavily. 'Poor boy! I like him so much,' he said, more simply than she had ever heard him speak; there was real affection in his tone, but the context made her heart sink.

'There's Roberto!' she said, springing up, as the chauffeur passed the window. 'Doctor Halther, he ought to fetch the glucose at once now. Shall I tell Dr Roget? I suppose he's going back with the car?'

But Dr Roget did not go back then. When the tall Englishwoman with the tired face came in again with paper and pencil to write down before he left precise directions about this task of which she had no experience, something – perhaps her evident fatigue, perhaps the controlled distress of her manner – moved him to remain. 'I shall stay, and show you at least what to do,' he said, and sent her down again to finish her meal.

Gastroenteritis is not a picturesque illness; few illnesses are really picturesque. Dr Roget, with skilled competence, brought into play those ingenious but ignominious devices of modern science by which the organism can be nourished even when the reluctant stomach rejects whatever it is offered. At last he was driven off to Ragusa, promising to come back early the next morning, and leaving Lady Kilmichael considerably fortified by the precise knowledge of what to do and when to do it, and the certainty of his return. It was all very different from her ignorant and despairing experiments of the afternoon. The vomiting was now rather less frequent; sometimes Nicholas kept the champagne down for as much as half an hour, and his pulse was certainly no feebler; on the other hand his exhaustion seemed greater than ever, he hardly opened his eyes, and his hand lay damp and utterly relaxed on the sheet. All the same, when Dr Halther peeped in about eleven-thirty and suggested that she should go and lie down for an hour while he sat with Nicholas, she felt justified in doing so, and dropped at once into the leaden sleep of exhaustion.

She woke with that unpleasant sense of having the soul dragged up by the roots out of the body which a sudden awakening from deep and insufficient sleep gives. Dr Halther was bending over her.

'He wants you,' he said.

'Is he worse?'

'I do not think so – but he asks for you, and it is in any case almost the hour.'

'All right – I'll come at once.'

Nicholas was lying with his eyes open. 'You've been away so long,' he said, in the sort of whispering half-tone that was all his voice now. 'I'm cold.'

She filled fresh bottles, put on another blanket, gave him brandy. Then she put out the hand-lamp on the table, pulled a spare rug over her knees and sat quietly by the bed. It was just after one; 'the turn of the night,' her old nurse used to call it – and said that Nature turned in her sleep then, and souls escaped that were 'on a loose chain.' Grace shivered a little – certainly it was the time when human strength and vitality were at their lowest ebb. Outside the voice of one distant nightingale, in undimmed ecstasy, was like a light pulse in the heart of the night; she could see the irrational shape of the monkey tree, close outside the window, black and straggling against the grey starlight. Something made her look towards the bed – a gleam of white showed her that Nicholas's eyes were open. She switched on the light again. 'Do you want anything?' she asked.

She had to lean near to hear his answer. 'No, it's all right when you're here.'

'I shall stay here now,' she said.

'Are you very tired?'

'No, hardly at all.'

He shut his eyes, but his fingers just moved; she knew he was looking for her hand, and closed hers over his.

'Try to go to sleep,' she said.

'When you're out of the room, I do miss you so,' he said in that fluttering half-whisper. 'You are so —' Was it 'heavenly' that he said? She couldn't be sure. It didn't matter – she really knew. In his extremity he had become the sick child, uttering what was in his heart. Under a mixed impulse of love and terror she bent down and kissed his forehead. 'I am here – go to sleep, my darling boy,' she whispered.

But just then Nicholas was sick again.

NINETEEN

Dr Roget was rather more reassuring about Nicholas when the car brought him out next morning. There had only been two bouts of sickness in the last three hours, the pulse was stronger, the colour less ashen. He said that when four consecutive hours had passed without sickness they might try giving him glucose to drink, as well as brandy and champagne. But it was only when he came again in the evening that he said the words for which Grace had been waiting all day – 'There is no longer any danger.' He flipped his pince-nez – 'It is short, this *gastro-entérite,* whichever way it goes,' he said practically. 'Tomorrow night, Madame, I hope you may get some repose. But for tonight let him sip the glucose constantly unless he sleeps. And only if he vomits, do as you have done before.'

Grace went upstairs again slowly. So it was all right – he wasn't going to die. She leaned against the wall for a moment before going into the bedroom. Soldiers after a battle must feel as she was feeling, she thought – almost light-headed with fatigue, but vaguely content with victory. Presently she would be able to realise how glad she was, but not now – she was too deadened. If only she could sleep for twenty-four hours! She had slept that afternoon, while Nicholas had a long nap – but she wanted to sleep for weeks and weeks.

'What did he say?' Nicholas asked when she went in. There was a little more tone in his voice.

'That you were much better.'

'I feel better. Can I leave off those beastly things now?'

'Yes.'

'Thank goodness. I do hate them so.'

'I know. Do you want your pillows flopped? They look rather flat.'

'Yes, please.'

She raised him on one arm, shook and turned his pillows and lowered him expertly again.

While she was fetching the brandy he asked suddenly:

'Are you dead?'

'No, not a bit. I had a sleep this afternoon.'

'I do hate your having to do all these appalling chores for me.'

'It's only for a little while. You'll be better very soon.'

He did look much better, she thought, as she gave him his brandy and settled him for the night. When it was all done and she sat down he took her hand again, and held it till he fell asleep.

He slept quite a lot that night, and next day Dr Roget, rubbing his hands, decreed Benger made with water, and said that Lady Kilmichael was to lie down from ten till three, and might try to get some sleep during the night. The Signora and Roberto between them had transferred her more necessary effects from the Tete Mare, and Maria had made her up a bed in the room across the landing from Nicholas. Dr Roget also observed that as soon as the patient was fit to be moved, he had better be taken back to the Imperial at Ragusa. The Frenchman had gone sniffing round the villa kitchen, and flatly pronounced Maria's methods to be more than dubious. 'You must be full of antibodies!' he said to Halther. But Dr Halther only laughed, and said that he had eaten Maria's food for fourteen years without ill effects.

That sleep of five hours made Lady Kilmichael feel a different woman. This was just as well, for she found Nicholas rather miserable and fretful when she went back – his bed was tumbled, his face and hands sticky with perspiration, his nerves on edge. She tidied him up, in spite of his protests – crossness was a sign of convalescence, she hoped.

'I say, that's my eye.'

'Would you rather dry your face yourself?'

But he was too weak to do that. When she was wiping his hands he felt one of hers. 'It's all rough,' he said, examining it.

'I know – it's only the disinfectant in the water.'

He dropped her hand and turned away, hunching his shoulders under the bedclothes. She busied herself making Benger, but when she went to give it to him she saw that he had been crying. She made no remark, but held the feeding cup for him.

'I can't even help being cross to you,' he said weakly, pushing it aside.

'Never mind – take this, there's a good boy, now while it's warm.'

He was a difficult patient. His sensitiveness tormented him at intervals about her fatigue, her roughened hands, and all the drudgery of a sickroom undertaken on his behalf; but his concern emerged chiefly in irritability or distress, which merely added to her burdens. He was at first too weak to read, or even to listen for any length of time – he just lay passively watching her as she moved about, but whenever she sat down he wanted her hand to hold. This whim of his, natural and simple as it was, imposed a curious and painful discipline on Grace Kilmichael. During the acute stage of his illness pity and terror had exercised their usual powers, purging her of all thoughts and feelings but the one passionate desire to conquer the illness, to win; her whole being was concentrated to a spear-point of effort in that struggle. But when the worst was over, in the leisure of a victorious peace other emotions found their way back into the realm of her recognition. She realised now how much she cared for Nicholas – the quality of her terror had shown her that. It was a curious emotion, so gentle, so much compounded with feelings exactly like those she had for Teddy or Nigel, that a few weeks ago she might have managed to deceive herself as to its nature. But she was losing her inclination for self-deception. And this particular circumstance forced her to a clearer understanding. Sitting beside Nicholas, unable to read, or work, or do anything to distract her thoughts, while he played idly with her hand, folding the fingers up and straightening them out again, or tracing the lines on her palm, with the passionless simplicity of a sick child, his touch brought back the recollection of her strange disturbance that evening in the garden, when he sat beside her on the seat; it compelled her, unwillingly, to be aware of feelings which she would rather have kept at bay, made her, so to speak, their prisoner. She was ashamed of having them at all at a time like this, and when he clearly did not; for him now, as for a child, past and future alike were blotted out, and he rested, weak and acquiescent, in the passing moment. It was a relief when any small task took her from the bedside, but she would not invent excuses or tasks – he should not go short of this simple comfort because of what she innocently regarded as her baseness. And gradually something rather important emerged for her out of this – the practical truth of Dr Halther's words on the promontory, when he said that to accept one's character and circumstances, without fear or distaste, was to find freedom. By submitting quietly to this thraldom to sensations of which she was ashamed, she learned that it was possible, even when most imprisoned, to reach a measure of freedom from the most insistent feelings of all, those which the body imposes on us whether we will or no.

This knowledge, however, did not avail her much with the larger issues raised by finding herself in love with Nicholas. There it was, a most uncomfortable fact. With her conventional standards she had not thought it wrong, though it might be awkward, for Nicholas to be in love with her; but she was certain that it was both wrong and undignified for her to be in love with him. And yet she was. It was very – actually the word she used in her own mind about it was 'inconvenient'. Lady Kilmichael had no dramatic sense about herself; it never occurred to her to take herself romantically. She had been driven by distress and pain to one violent action in her life, when she had left home; but this new circumstance she met with her usual flat simplicity. It was 'inconvenient,' but one just dealt with inconvenient things as well as one could. She couldn't go away, as Nicholas in the same strait had tried to do, because she had got to stay and nurse him till he was well. So the only thing was to put it down as far as she could, think about it as little as possible, and get on with the job. She hadn't a great deal of time to think anyhow, just now – she could think it all out later on. It wasn't really much good reminding herself how wrong it was, even, for the moment, because she had got to behave quite normally; and to be what those psychological books which she so much contemned called 'guilt-conscious,' made one tired and embarrassed. So, vaguely humbled within, but practical and serene without, she set her face against analysis, and went quietly on her way.

Dr Halther was a help to her in this. Nicholas's illness had quietly altered the character of their relationship, from the master-and-pupil aspect which it had had at first to a partnership in a common enterprise, in which Lady Kilmichael was admittedly the senior partner. During the bad days the Doctor hung about, waiting for a chance to ask how the boy was; obeyed orders, fetched and carried, trusted and deferred to her. Now, as the convalescence gave Lady Kilmichael more leisure, enabled her to come down to regular meals, and even to sit in the garden for a little sometimes, they found that a certain ease and intimacy had of itself come into being between them; there was casual talk on minor topics, instead of only those Socratic and soul-shattering conversations of the first few days.

But Socratic conversations were not altogether at an end. One day after lunch as they were sitting by the fountain they found themselves discussing Dr Roget. He was apparently a man of some eminence in Paris, and Halther emphasised their good fortune in having found him in their need.

'Yes, I suppose he is clever, but I didn't much like him,' said Grace. 'I didn't feel that he was very' – she hesitated for a word – 'valuable,' she finally brought out. She meant something by that; she had a curious sense, often, that certain people were indefinably valuable, like a rich mine, quite independently of any obvious merits. She had always felt that about Walter – felt it still; she felt it about Nicholas, although apart from his painting she recognised that to all appearance he was just a rather sensitive arrogant boy, subject to alternate fits of moodiness and slightly teasing gaiety. Noticing now that Dr Halther raised his bushy eyebrows at the word, she said something of this to him, but only about Walter. 'It isn't only his cleverness, it's *him*; and it isn't only I who think so – other people notice it too,' she ended.

Dr Halther nodded – a large embracing nod which he used to cover a full comprehension, and by which he economised on many small current phrases. 'Yes – and even philosophy does not tell us with any exactness how we recognise that value in others. Your husband has obvious intellectual qualities, but we are aware of it in people whose qualities we do not yet know. I see it *zum beispiel* in young Humphries, of whom I know very little. It is some fineness in the texture of the soul, which we recognise by what used to be called direct apprehension, now an unfashionable expression.'

Grace knew nothing about direct apprehension, but she was pleased that the Professor should think that Nicholas's soul was of a fine texture.

'Well, I don't think Dr Roget has got it,' she said decidedly.

'He is probably a very different man from your husband,' said Halther, amused.

'Goodness, yes!' But she said no more.

'Do you feel that you get a full share of this value in your husband?' the Doctor asked.

She looked at him, too much at ease now to feel any personal embarrassment at his question.

'I get *a* share,' she said. 'I think people get what they are able to take, of that sort of thing, don't you?'

'This is precisely what I think! But many people, many wives, do not recognise this fact. Especially the wives of very brilliant men are apt to feel that they do not get the share due to them. You do not feel this?'

Grace hesitated a little before she spoke. It would be a help, she felt sure, to talk about herself and Walter to Dr Halther, but a traditional distaste for discussing one's husband with anyone stood in her way.

'Not exactly. The value just *is there*, for those who can take it; and his brilliance – well, that never was my share, you see.'

'You are wise,' Halther said. 'You see clearly the limitations of your share. So many women will not see this, will not be content with the one facet of their husband's character which belongs to them; the side of him which first turned to them and is theirs. They will not recognise this – no, he shall be *all* to them! And when they marry they throw aside their work, their interests, very often their friends – and expect this one man then to fill their whole life, to be friends, interests, occupations to them. It is *Unsinn*! How many men could do this, even with the leisure and the inclination?'

The word inclination made Grace laugh.

'No, but it is true, *gnädige Frau*.'

'Yes, I know it's true – we do tend to do that.' She was wondering which facet of Walter's character it was which really belonged to her, which had first turned to her. None of him seemed to belong to her now!

'Not you, I think,' he said. 'You are much too wise. You leave him free for his work, his friends, and just take your proper share, contentedly.'

Grace did not answer at once. This praise made her ashamed, it was so far from the truth. She wanted Walter's affection, which she felt she had lost; and though she did not resent his work, his preoccupation with economists who seemed to her dull, and gloried secretly in his fame, she *did* grudge his interest in Rose, who could share those things which she could not. She had been really jealous of Rose. It was true that she had her work to occupy her, that she was not as much without resources as some women she knew – but given that advantage, how far from wise she had been! She could not really sit down under the Doctor's encomiums.

'No,' she said at last. 'I'm not like that at all. I'm grudging and discontented and' – she checked the word jealous – 'a failure, really. You are quite mistaken about me.'

'Then I am twice mistaken,' he said cheerfully. Something in the tone of his voice made her look up at him – she had been staring at the jet of the fountain, rising and falling against the silver foliage of the buckthorn, while she spoke. There was a curious illuminated sparkle of amusement in his whole face, as bright and visible as the crystal glitter of the sunlit water drops.

'You're making fun of me!' she said, startled.

'*Verzeihung, gnädige Frau!* It is true – I do this.'

'But why?' She was almost hurt.

'Because I wished that you should speak the truth about yourself and your husband, and I have twice seen that you do not care to do so, to admit that you are unsatisfied. You think that you shall be disloyal. But it is also my impression that it is not only on account of the little daughter that you leave your home. So I use a little art – I have laid a trap for your honesty!'

There was something so benevolent, so nice, about his self-satisfaction as he said this that Grace could not resent it.

'Well, I've fallen into your trap,' she said, smiling – but almost at once her face grew grave again.

'*Gnädige Frau*, may I say something?' She nodded. 'See, I am *Philosoph*, and my work – the work of the philosopher – is to understand the nature of things – the universe, if you will. But of the universe human life is a part, and this too must be understood, and set in its true relation to the rest. To do this is for the individual in itself a liberation; to place oneself in a category can be helpful as well as accurate! One's sorrows then do not darken so much of the sky. But many are unwilling thus to reduce their own importance! And married people are often reluctant, as you are, to speak openly of the facts of their life. This instinct of loyalty is in itself good; but if it shall hinder a recognition of things which are a source of failure and pain – pain, *gnädige Frau*, to *both* – it may be well to put it aside. You have said that you are a failure – do you think that it pleases your husband to have you so?'

It was the fact that Grace Kilmichael, in all her months of self-doubt and self-accusation, had never asked herself that question. She had wondered why Walter had stopped caring for her, why he treated her with such chilly derision, and had asked herself where she was in fault – but it had simply never occurred to her to wonder whether Walter *minded* the terms they were now on. She had felt them to be imposed by him, and had supposed vaguely that he had stopped caring because he wanted to! Under the impact of this new idea, with all the possibilities which it opened up, she sat silent for some time.

'You are quite right,' she said at last, 'about everything. It isn't only Linnet, it is my husband too. And I have wanted to talk to you about it, but I felt – just what you say. But now I should like to – I think I'd better really.'

She paused, trying to get clear in her mind what she wished to say. Dr Halther gave his large comprehending nod again.

'There are two separate things, I think,' she began. 'My husband isn't so fond of me as he was – but perhaps that's only to be expected.' (She still could not bring herself to mention Rose.) 'But because of that, or for some reason, the other thing has begun. I never was clever, but he used not to mind that – if he teased me, he did it nicely; I liked it. But now he does it differently – unsympathetically, somehow. So I've got nervous about it; I seem to have lost my initiative. They can all put me down now, about everything. I feel' – she paused for a word – '*dominated* by them all. I think all the time – 'Will Walter think that silly?' before I say anything; I'm almost afraid to speak about some things. But lately I have thought that that in itself might irritate him.'

Halther looked sardonic. 'It most certainly will! But go on.'

She looked at him, and then looked away again, in front of her, as was her habit when she was thinking as she spoke.

'There isn't much more. I think what you said the other day about *amour propre*, and freedom, will help me about all this. But I haven't had much time yet to think out how, because Nicholas has been ill ever since, and I've been so busy.'

He nodded. '*Gnädige Frau*, here is a point. In this illness you have shown no lack of initiative; here all have depended on you and your judgement. *Nicht wahr*?'

'I suppose so.'

'I think it probable,' he said, 'that in your life at home there are also spheres in which all depend on you, or would wish to – the *ménage*, health – and matters of *conduct, gnädige Frau.* If you have abdicated your authority in these, you have failed your family – and this shall irritate them all, but in chief your husband. It is your *amour propre* – inverted, as we say – which has made you abandon an authority, an initiative, which they really wish you to exercise, whether they realise it or not.'

Some of Nicholas's statements about Mrs Humphries and

Celia darted into Grace's head at this point – they confirmed the Doctor's words.

'I shouldn't wonder if that is true,' she said thoughtfully.

'I would risk much money that it is true!' Halther said emphatically. 'And I believe, *meine Gnädigste*, that I could even suggest the history of this abdication, from the general history of the subject.'

'Do then, please. I should like to hear.'

Out came the Doctor's diagrammatic hand again. 'Look,' he said. 'Physical love in time cools; this is a natural law. But women will not expect this, since they will not be in a category, or study general laws; therefore this most natural thing they take as a personal failure, an individual loss. And they either resent it, or are discouraged by it, or both.' He stopped tapping off his points on his outspread fingers, and looked at her. 'You I think have not resented it, but discouraged by it you have been.'

She nodded, in silence.

'Then you turn to your children, and cling to them. But in time this support also fails you; the children will now be independent, lead their own lives. And again ignoring a universal law, the law of growth, you grasp, hold on to your children; you seek to prolong by force a state which is outgrown and therefore unnatural – and when you fail, as you inevitably must, you are confronted with what seems to you a second personal defeat. And you lose courage then. All the rest flows from that.'

Still Lady Kilmichael was silent. They were hard words, but her heart listened to them.

'Is this true?' he asked her at last, with a sort of gentle doggedness.

'Yes,' she said, turning to him with tears in her eyes. 'It is true.'

Dr Halther smoked in silence for a little while. At last – 'Do you read the Bible?' he asked.

'Sometimes. I know it pretty well.'

'I am not a Christian,' he said, 'but I recognise in Christ a great philosopher, and a greater psychologist. There is a word for you in his teaching. See if you can find it.'

Grace made no answer, beyond a slight nod. Presently she looked at her watch, and got up. 'I must go in,' she said. 'Thank you very much, Doctor Halther. You are very good to me.'

'No – but you shall yourself be "good," as you call it,' he said, as she started to cross the lawn. Grace hardly heard him. She was wondering which word Dr Halther meant. She was almost sure that she knew. And all that afternoon, while she read to Nicholas, she wondered just how the truth would make her free.

It occurred to her that evening, with something of a shock, that they ought to have written to tell the Humphries family of Nicholas's illness. While he had been critically ill there had been no time to think of anything, but during these last few days, since he was out of danger, it ought to have been done. It was very negligent of her not to have thought of it. She mentioned it to Dr Halther at supper. They had gone up together after tea, by Nicholas's urgent wish, to get a root of the blue plant which grew among the irises, and only returned just as Maria was preparing to bring in the soup. Grace ran up to Nicholas, taking the plant with her; while she heated his supper and gave him his tray she answered his questions about it.

'Yes, it is one of the Boragy – whatever-they-ares. It's called *Moltkia petraea*. He says it's a plant of the Tertiary Epoch.'

'What on earth do you mean?'

'I've no idea – I'm only repeating what he said,' said Grace gaily. The walk had done her good; she felt better than she had done for days. 'He said it was a plant of the Tertiary Epoch, and an endogene of the Balkan area, whatever that may be. Anyhow it only grows in this part of the world. He'll tell you about it – he's coming up to see you after dinner.'

'We must get a tin and send it to my Mamma,' said Nicholas. 'She'd love it. I hope it will grow.'

'Well, let me put it in the jug now, and have your supper.' But the mention of 'my Mamma' put the idea of writing into her head, and when she went down she spoke of it to the Professor.

'Yes, this is necessary,' he agreed.

'Will you do it? I'll get you the address.'

'I think you do it much better than I. Moreover I do not know these people.'

'But neither do I.' She was tempted to make him do it; with a little pushing she was sure she could. But some new impulse decided her not to shirk, and when Dr Halther went up to see Nicholas she settled down and wrote to his mother.

And while she wrote to Mrs Humphries, whom she did not know, Linnet was writing, as so often, to her best friend, from the *Mindora Star*:

> We saw Syracuse today. It is quite marvellous. Poppy and I went round with an old Frenchman, one of his favourite Bridge four, who reeled off no end of classical stuff. But Poppy knew rather a lot too – Thucydides and all sorts; I was quite surprised. The General, my dear, had some *military* map of the place – it seems there was a battle there or something – and worked it all out again at dinner with the forks! The girl did a picture – a complete poster, it seemed to me – no drawing whatever, and no depth; but I suppose Mums makes one rather intolerant of amateurs. How soured she would be – the girl I mean – to be called an amateur! She goes to the Slade and feels enormously professional. Quite nice, really; in fact rather a resource – we think the same things funny. She's a niece of that appalling Lady Roseneath, strange as it may seem.
>
> Poppy is much better, but not the old self yet. I believe it's nothing but fuss about Mums that's keeping him back. We

got letters here, but no word of her, of course. People can't *die* now without getting into the papers, as I keep on telling him – but I do think it rather odd of her not to realise that he *would* fuss. They are so funny, those two. He does nothing but trample rather elegantly on Mums when she's there, but when he mislays her completely for a few weeks he nearly dies of worry – and she's utterly taken in by the trampling, and I don't think realises in the least that she *matters* more to him than twenty Roses. Mums isn't at all good at realising things – she's really so madly humble, although she does try to stand on her rights at intervals.

It was perhaps partly this mad humility which made Lady Kilmichael show Nicholas her letter to his mother before she sealed it up. 'Yes – I think that'll do very well,' he said, handing it back to her. 'It won't fuss her – you make it clear it's all over now. But why do you write like that?'

'Like what?'

'As though you'd had nothing to do with it. You might be just a person staying in the village, from that letter; instead of having slaved night and day for me, and ruined your hands!'

'I don't think your Mother would be particularly interested in my hands!' said Grace cheerfully, licking the flap of the envelope.

'*I* shall tell her what a saint you've been, all the same,' he said.

'All right – it will come better from you.' She gave a little laugh. 'I wish Linnet could hear you!'

'Doesn't Linnet see that you're rather an angel?' he asked, with a sort of simple curiosity.

'No, of course not. Nobody does but you, you silly child! Now take this Benger.'

He took it, but after a moment or two of imbibing he removed his lips from the cup, to grin at her with almost his old impudence.

'I bet you the Professor does!' he said.

TWENTY

Lady Kilmichael's own views on her humility did not quite square with Linnet's. During the last days at the villa, before they returned to the Imperial, she was comfortably aware of a sort of fatherly approval in Dr Halther's attitude to her; and she was struck by the fact that this approval, and still more Nicholas's idealising attitude, made her feel much more humble than she had ever felt at home. There, with Walter and Linnet constantly criticising her, she was always on the defensive, justifying herself to herself, seeking excuses, thinking how much she did for them, and how little she was in fault; whereas here, where Nicholas (in the intervals between being distinctly cross and offhand) made it clear that he thought her far more clever and good than she in fact knew herself to be, she was becoming much more honest and clear-sighted about her own faults and weaknesses. Now she was willing and even eager to recognise them. It was very odd! And thus introduced to the uses of appreciation, Lady Kilmichael, in her painstaking fashion, thought it all out. Obviously this linked on to what the Professor had said about *amour propre*; now that her *amour propre* was not wounded, she was all right. But that would not do; one couldn't depend on that sort of nourishment. One must learn what one was like, and then be what one ought, independently of the opinion of other people, whether good or ill. Then one would be free. And thinking this, in little sentences which she said over to herself – it was her way of trying to get things clear – suddenly she laughed. How amused Walter would be at her making this discovery for herself, at her age! Because after all this was a thing that, in other words, one was taught in the schoolroom. Only words, unluckily, taught one so little; it was only when the things happened to oneself, and when the words got into your heart, that they came to have any meaning, and really did you any good. Truth, she thought, all the truths that anyone could need to lead an admirable, a nearly perfect life, lay spread out all round one all the time – but one had got to annex them, as it were, conquer them by force and make them one's own, before one could use them.

She was sitting up on the little hill with the battered chapel on its summit, one hot afternoon, when this particular idea crystallised in her mind – it was perhaps the sunny fields spread out on all sides below her which prompted the form of her reflections about truth. For the last day or two Nicholas had been able to come down and spend some hours in the garden in a deckchair, and she rather gladly left him to Dr Halther's company, and took herself off to walk or sketch. She had been surprised how soon he began to look normal again; his face filled out as if by magic as soon as he stopped being sick – this, Dr Roget had explained, was due to the normal supply of fluid being restored to the body. But she found that his return of strength did not keep pace by any means with the improvement in his appearance – it came back very slowly. Naturally, Roget told her; such a bout knocked a person out pretty thoroughly, and he would need care about food and fatigue for some time to come. But he could well be left now, and she was glad sometimes to be alone. She had taken her sketchbook today, but she was not sketching; she just sat quietly in the shade of the cypresses on the dry pale turf, idly noticing through her thoughts all sorts of little things – the smooth nut-like silvery knobs, almost as bright as silver foil, on the trunks of the larger cypresses; a great vetch with flowers of mixed maroon and lemon-yellow, up and down whose stalks ants were running, for some purpose which she could not guess; the extreme delicacy and grace of a slender blue veronica, with pointed heads of bloom over two inches long – it had a sort of lovely poise, erect, but slightly drooping at the tips; like a firm character which can yet show a gracious flexibility, she thought. The air was full of the faint resinous fragrance of the cypresses, brought out by the sun, and the whirring of the grasshoppers – that scent and that sound, restful and sleepy, seemed so much a part of the air that the fancy came to her that she breathed them in with it. That was the sort of idea for which Dr Halther would remonstrate with her, smiling and shaking his great head – there was no 'clear thought' there! And thinking of him, she remembered their first conversation that other afternoon, up on the chapel steps, only a few yards above where she now sat, when he had so scourged her folly in not foreseeing that Nicholas would fall in love with her. It seemed a long time ago, though really it was not yet a fortnight.

She sighed a little. The illness had caused a lull, a sort of truce to this problem, but as soon as he got well it would have to be faced again. In a way it was beginning again even now. Nicholas might idealise her, but he took it out of her too! As he got better he was increasingly short with her, increasingly restive under her care – and the better he got, the worse this would become. She guessed dimly at the cause, some revolt in him against his own feelings – she could even sympathise with it. She had already less actual nursing to do, and as soon as she got him back to the Imperial, and he was properly on his feet again, she would leave him. She could, she felt, really go home very soon now; she was almost equal to that, and she ought to go.

Lady Kilmichael and Nicholas went back to the Imperial at Ragusa a couple of days later. Grace was startled, when it came to the point, at the liveliness of the regret which she felt at leaving the villa. On the last morning she went down early to fetch something which Nicholas had left under the ilex – she stood there for a moment, looking round her almost with surprise. Dew lay grey on the lawn, and clung mistily to the flowers; the spray fell into the pool with a clear gentle noise. All this – the fountain, the ilex with its marble seat, the buckthorns and the roses were now familiar to her with an intense and individual familiarity. They were really the same this morning as on the day, three weeks ago, when she first glanced in through the villa gate on her way down from painting the irises, and thought that the garden was planned with great taste – but for her they were different. Places and objects which have as it were escorted us through certain experiences take on this individual quality – they become the companions who share our memories. Grace felt this then. She would miss that garden – some part of her would always *belong* there, more than anywhere else in the world. She would miss the Professor too, she thought, as she went back to the house. His wisdom, his clarity of thought, his strength and kindness had not only instructed her, they had in some way supported her too; leaving him, she felt rather small and chilled. She would try to put his precepts into practice, go forward; soon she would be going home, to test her new knowledge among the old surroundings; but a child going to school, she thought, though full to the brim of good advice and good resolutions, must feel much as she felt now.

Roberto drove them in the car. He had taken Grace in once in the morning, with an advance load of luggage, canvases and painting equipment, and she had done some preliminary unpacking in their rooms at the Imperial so that Nicholas should be able to rest undisturbed when he arrived, after the exertion of the drive. She came back to lunch, and immediately afterwards they set out. Dr Halther, in his yellow suit, came with them to the gate. '*Viel Glück* with the painting,' he said to Nicholas. 'Perhaps one day my friend Mr Humphries of Vienna shall be famous!'

'Goodbye,' said Grace, holding out her hand. 'You have been so good to us.'

He bowed over her hand and kissed it. '*Auf Wiedersehen, meine Gnädigste*,' he said. Emerging into the lane outside the villa they found quite a small crowd clustered round the car, waiting to see them off – both the Orlandos, the niece (who would certainly be late for afternoon school), the innkeeper, Grace's little porter, Teta, nodding her white head, Maria, and the bus driver. There were handshakings, cries, farewells; then the car moved slowly out onto the *fondamento*, and gathered speed along it.

'How sweet of them!' said Grace, sitting back after a last wave from the window.

'Mmm,' grunted Nicholas. 'Well, that's that.' As the car turned into the main road she leant out to take a last look at the river, the square bulk of the Restauracija Tete Mare, the whole clean serene prettiness of Komolac, spread out in the afternoon sunshine. She remembered with what pleasure she had seen it on that first afternoon, and with what a sense of satisfaction she had gone there next day, to escape from Nicholas. She had thought she was doing that for his sake; but had some part of her, wiser than the rest, unconsciously prompted that move as an escape from her own feelings, while yet she was unaware of them? She could not tell. Anyhow it hadn't been any good, she thought, leaning back in the car; *that* effort at freedom had come to what Teddy would call a sticky end. She had only been free for three days, after that she had been more involved with Nicholas than ever – and now here she was, committed to looking after him for at least another week, bless him; and entangled in her own emotions into the bargain. Rather helplessly, she wondered what the outcome would be. It *could* have no outcome, really; it would just have to come to an end. And till it came to an end, the only thing was to keep kindness in it. What was he thinking about, staring so fixedly ahead of him? Did he know what she was thinking? He so often did know. And just then Nicholas spoke.

'That's where you sang 'Morgen,' coming down the river,' he said, pointing to the green stream below them. 'I remember that ruined house on the bank; we were passing it as you began.'

'Oh, were we?' said Lady Kilmichael.

The change to Ragusa did Nicholas good. After a few days he was able to begin painting again, a little in the morning and a little in the afternoon. He got two pictures going for the two different lights – one of San Salvatore before lunch, and in the afternoons one of the view down across the deserted Piazza delle Erbe. Grace finished her picture of the Stradone – really it meant practically beginning it all over again, for the quality of the light had altered in the last three weeks; the noonday shadows were shorter, the sunlight hotter and more intense. Then she began one of the Franciscan cloister, at which she worked in the mornings; and in the afternoons she was doing a funny little vista down a small dark street and across the corner of a shadowed square, a vista closed by the façade of the Duomo, brilliantly lit up by the western sun. It was only a hundred yards or so from where Nicholas sat in the Piazza, and she had chosen it partly so that without apparently watching over him she could hunt him away when the shadows got too chilly.

She was sitting there one afternoon, working away, and thinking that she could safely go on for another half-hour at least, when to her surprise as she glanced down towards the Duomo she saw Nicholas go up the steps and into the church. How odd of him! She supposed that he must be going to have a look at the Memling, as she had often urged him to do.

But the sight of him made her put her brush down and begin to think about him again. Since they got back to Ragusa he had been very much withdrawn into himself; the old easy confidence between them was impaired – she felt that she never knew what his mind was up to, now. She guessed that their silence on the subject which must be as much in his thoughts as in hers might be oppressive to him, but so far she could not bring herself to do anything to break it. Halther had said emphatically that she ought to give him a chance to speak – 'some expression such feelings must have, *gnädige Frau*.' But the more she thought about it, the more some instinct told her that it would in the long run be easier for both of them if nothing was said. *Of course* such feelings craved expression – but not only by talking, as a rule! And if once he started to speak of it, she would find it hard, in the face of his sincerity, not to show an equal truth about herself – and that could not help. Married, and twice his age, what could come of it? That was always the point to which she came back. It had never occurred to Lady Kilmichael to take any but the practical view of love. Love ought to lead to marriage – if it didn't do that, it could only lead to disaster or waste. And no exhortations could change her view.

Her thoughts went round it again and again. She felt sure that in this Walter would agree with the Professor; she could hear him saying airily – 'Lord, yes, let the boy go to it and kiss you as much as he likes. Do him all the good in the world.' Walter would think her hesitations foolish, prudish and cowardly. Perhaps they were. If she could be *sure* that free expression would be the best thing for Nicholas, of course she would want him to have it. But her instinct reiterated that between him and her such a thing would be – 'inappropriate' was the modest word her mind found for it. There was a real thing which she and Nicholas had got, improbable though it might seem – a very genuine and happy affection, trust and pleasure in each other. That was all right – that could be glad and permanent. But Lady Kilmichael felt that this other element was somehow fortuitous, an intrusion, with no possible solution or permanence in it; and that to acknowledge it and give it free expression might imperil the rather delicate and valuable thing which they had got.

Presently she saw Nicholas come out of the Duomo again. He

stood on the steps for a moment or two, before he walked slowly down them and disappeared in the direction of the Piazza delle Erbe. Seen at that distance, his solitary and unconscious figure had a curious significance, like that of a person in a film; Grace had a swift impression, as he paused on the great steps, of someone who was lost, adrift – who really did not know which way to turn. The tears sprang to her eyes at the sight – little phrases came crowding to her lips. 'Darling child! Dear love! If only *I* knew, too! But I don't, any more than you.' Then she scolded herself for silliness, wiped her eyes, re-did her face, and bundled her things together – it was getting chilly, and he had been at work quite long enough; they would go and have coffee down at the restaurant opposite San Biagio, in the Piazza.

Nicholas seemed quite ready to knock off when she rejoined him, and they put their canvases and easels into a barber's shop at the corner of the square, as usual. One of the nice things about Ragusa, as Nicholas always said, was the unquestioning readiness of the inhabitants to assist in any enterprise save their own legitimate ones; anybody would knock off whatever he was doing to show the way, give unasked advice about a picture, find a place to bestow it, or produce rags or a stool. Signor Lassi, the photographer, had abandoned his shop to two very immature assistants for a whole hour one morning in order to escort Lady Kilmichael in person to find the little carved fragment set above a door in a wall which is all that is left of the Church of Holy Stephen, the earliest building remaining in the city today.

They had their coffee, and then Nicholas suggested a walk. 'Yes, I'd love to – only not too far – I don't feel very active,' said Grace.

'Are you tired?'

'A tiny bit – I'd like to stretch my legs, but not to go miles,' replied Grace, who wasn't tired in the least, but thought that Nicholas ought not to walk too much. They strolled out through the passage under the belfry tower and skirted the harbour, past the great arched recesses in the walls into which ships were formerly drawn – these are now for the most part walled up, but small doors here and there led into cavernous depths, gloomy and smelling faintly nautical, in which small odd trades were carried on – a tinsmith, a repairer of wine barrels, a sail-maker all functioned there. They lingered a little by the harbour – some wine boats from the islands were drawn up by the quay, and Nicholas commented on their quite extraordinary resemblance to Roman galleys. Then they went up to the Porta Ploce and the coast road, and followed it round below the Monte Sergio – when they were nearly back at the Borgo the sight of one of the many flights of steps leading down from the steep hillside prompted a suggestion from Nicholas that they should go up and see the sunset over the town.

They climbed up, flight after flight, sometimes between walls overhung with palms and roses, sometimes looking down into gardens where houses, washed pink or yellow or pale green, stood luscious as blocks of ice cream among the spears of agaves and the green spiny oddity of cactuses. At last they reached a height where the city lay spread out below them; along the walls the mediaeval strangeness of tower and bastion was defined by transparent blue shadows, blue as the sea beyond; within them the city roofs, blurred with the smoke of evening cooking, glowed like a misty opal. Up here they were still in sunshine, and it was warm – they sat down on a seat, and began talking idly, amusing themselves by trying to pick out various buildings from the huddle of roofs crammed within the walls; they argued about them and laughed, more at ease than they had been for some time.

'There's the Duomo, anyhow,' said Nicholas eventually.

'That's a sitter, with that great dome – I don't count that!' said Lady Kilmichael. Then she remembered something. 'Oh, what did you think of the Memling? I saw you go in there this afternoon. Do you think it's genuine?'

'I didn't see the Memling,' he replied, rather gruffly.

'Oh, didn't you? I thought that was what you went for.'

'No, I just went in.' He paused for a moment, and then said, 'As a matter of fact I was praying for you – or rather I suppose really I was praying for myself in connection with you.'

Grace Kilmichael was startled and moved – the colour stirred in her face; but her habitual impulse to 'keep things light' overtook her, and without giving herself time to think she answered, gently but quite easily – 'I prayed for you in the Duomo too, one day – how funny!'

'When was that?' he asked, turning and looking at her.

'That morning when I walked in from Komolac.'

He continued to look at her, doubtfully – she saw that some question was in his mind. But all he said, after a moment, was – 'How nice of us to be praying for one another!'

He spoke with the most savage sarcasm, but she recognised the reason for that, and what it covered. She made some easy remark about liking to pray for people, and presently suggested a return – 'We shall be late for dinner if we sit here any longer.' But as they dropped down the long flights of steps and walked back to the hotel, neither made any further attempt at conversation. Grace was thinking that Dr Halther would have blamed her for her part in what had just passed. Nicholas had – with evident effort – made an opening, and she, as much from habit as anything else, had quite gently closed it again. Halther would say that this was wrong, that she ought to have made some response which would have enabled Nicholas to let it all out. She wondered – she watched the silent face beside her, and wished that she knew what he was thinking. Was he hurt, disappointed, rebuffed?

The course of Nicholas's thoughts was more complicated. He had actually gone into the Duomo to look at the Memling, because she had so often told him to – but the curtains were drawn over the various altarpieces, and he had no idea which it was; he was tired – he got tired so easily still – and the small frustration checked his impulse; he had sunk into a seat, in the cool empty building, among the dimly burning lamps and tapers and the faint smell of incense. And there the thought of Lady Kilmichael had overtaken him, like one of those single large waves which on a still day sweep without warning far up the startled shore. Small pictures of her sprang out with extraordinary vividness – the way she lifted her head when she laughed, her wide eyes when anything surprised her, the soft tone of remonstrance in which she said 'But Nicholas —' when she disapproved. But for all the clearness of these pictures, she was somehow remote; her image stood on the edge of his life, her hands full of gifts – beauty and tenderness and gentle understanding, and a wisdom which he could not define, but which he felt to be necessary to him. She knew all about that difficult business, life; she had no angles or awkwardnesses; she was beautifully adept at human relationships, in which he was so frequently and so disastrously clumsy. All this, very confusedly and vaguely, he felt; but when his mind turned to himself, what had he to bring, what could he be but a recipient or an encumbrance? And in a quick movement of devotion, mixed with a vague confusion and distress about his personal relation to her, he had slipped to his knees.

But the prayers of youth do not always resolve its difficulties at once, any more than do the prayers of age and wisdom. When Nicholas left the Duomo both his affection and his perplexities were nearer the surface, more insistent, than when he went in – aspirations and renunciations and the sense of unworthiness and eager ardours swept round like bats in his head. When he paused on the cathedral steps, where he was seen by Lady Kilmichael, he said 'Oh hell!' twice, with a long pause between, before he went back to his painting. And when he later sat with her on the seat above the town, that sentence had broken stubbornly through his shyness and his reserve, driven by the urgent confusion within him.

Her answer, so readily and innocently given, had however provoked a fresh train of speculation. As he walked silently beside her, on their way back to the hotel, he was thinking: 'I wonder why she prayed for me. Is it because she is a little fond of me too, or because there is something wrong with me? I wish I had asked – I wish it wasn't so hard to talk to her now. I used to be able to say anything to her, but now all the things I really want to say are too difficult. There *is* plenty wrong with me, goodness knows – I'm selfish and I'm cowardly and I'm weak and I'm not honest. I can't just be nice to people as she is – I'm always afraid: of giving myself away, I suppose. I was hateful to her when I was ill; I am still, sometimes. And it's rather awful of me to want as badly as I do now to kiss her. I wish I didn't – but I do. I suppose if I were honest and less of a coward I should tell her that I am fond of her. But I should feel a fool and presumptuous. And yet I want to – I feel such a liar going on saying nothing. I wonder if she guesses? If she doesn't it might only worry her to tell her. What ought I to do about it? And even if I do tell her, what is there to do about it? I can't marry her – and as she's married I oughtn't to love her, let alone kiss her. What is to come of it?'

So gloomily reasoning, his face (now red again beneath his yellow thatch) firmly set, Nicholas Humphries walked in silence beside Lady Kilmichael. Independently, they had both reached the same point – there was no outcome possible to love between them; for them, as them, there was no solution.

TWENTY-ONE

On the following morning Nicholas was sitting in the open space by Onofrio's fountain, working on his picture of San Salvatore. It was just after twelve, but they were going to lunch late, as usual, in the Via del Levante; Lady Kilmichael was at work in the Franciscan cloister close by. He noticed with rather sour amusement that none of the shops had shut at noon – one of those cruises must be coming in; Lina Amandi's jackets fluttered as freely and as brilliantly as ever before her door. And presently he became aware that the cruise had indeed arrived – little groups of people, obviously English, suddenly appeared in the Stradone, buying postcards, peering at M. Kraljic's trays of earrings, and drawing one another's attention to Mme Amandi's jackets. The official guide passed by on the other side of the fountain to that where Nicholas sat, followed by a rather dejected string of sightseers, who listened bewildered to his mouthed monologue, uttered in a form of English which was quite incomprehensible; Nicholas, absorbed in his work, nevertheless vaguely noted the faces of his listeners, and grinned. He had seen the official guide at his official task before, and knew his utter incompetence – he was always rather sorry for the cruisers, as he called them – only why were they such fools as to cruise, instead of staying in places like Christians?

A tall and very distinguished-looking man, accompanied by a girl, presently detached themselves from the distant group; they stood together for a moment, evidently debating some point – then the man came firmly over towards Nicholas. Nicholas was not surprised – that frequently happened; when despair succeeded to bewilderment the more spirited tourists often abandoned the guide and sought information from him or Lady Kilmichael or any other obvious Briton who was obviously at home in Ragusa. He had personally conducted several tours before now. Sometimes it bored him, but he noticed while they stood arguing that this Englishman had a rather striking face, and that the girl, though too much made up, was exceedingly pretty.

The Englishman, approaching, raised his hat and said civilly – 'I beg your pardon, but could you perhaps tell me what the date of this fountain is, and who built it?' He indicated Onofrio's domed structure.

The precision and intelligence of the question impressed Nicholas. The cruisers usually said 'What *is* that?' about any building which caught their eye.

'It was built by Onofrio di la Cava, about 1437,' he said. 'He brought the water to the town from the Gionchetta.'

'Was he a Dalmatian?'

'No, he came from Naples,' said Nicholas.

The Englishman looked critically at the fountain, pointed out the carving of the little empanelled masks on it to the girl – Nicholas had already decided, from the resemblance, that she was his daughter – and then turned to the young man again.

'Is there any more of this la Cava's work here in Ragusa, do you know?' he asked.

There was the other fountain, Nicholas told him, down on the Piazza – 'but that's rather pulled about now. And two of the capitals in the loggia of the Rectors' Palace are his, too; two beauties.'

'Where is that – the Rectors' Palace?'

'Right down the Stradone' – he pointed – 'and then turn to the right.' But as he spoke he began to put his things together; these people were intelligent, much more so than most – he might as well go down with them. 'If you'll wait one moment, I'll come and show you,' he said.

The Englishman politely urged him not to trouble – if he would tell them the way they could find the palace.

'Yes, but then you won't know which Onofrio's capitals are,' said Nicholas, getting up. 'One second' – and he picked up his canvas and carried it across to Mme Amandi's shop. He often left it there, and with a cheerful word deposited it now, propped on a carved chest, along with his easel and his paintbox. Then he rejoined the tall Englishman and the girl.

'There doesn't appear to be any guidebook to this place; it makes it difficult to find out what to see,' the man observed, after thanking him, as they walked down the Stradone.

'No, there is no local one,' Nicholas replied.

'And as for that alleged guide—!' said the girl.

Nicholas laughed. 'I know that guide! He can't really speak English at all, and he hardly knows anything either. I always pity the tourists who fall into his hands.'

'They ought really to arrange to have a competent guide, since seeing this place is specified as part of the cruise,' the Englishman pursued, rather severely. 'We are very fortunate, but that is not the fault of the Company.'

'There's the Orlando Statue,' Nicholas observed, as they reached the Piazza.

'Who was Orlando,' the girl asked.

'Roland – the name's got turned round. They say Charlemagne had them set up in all the cities of the Empire, as a sort of trademark. There's one in Bremen still, too.'

A number of other tourists, seeing an explanation of the Orlando Statue in progress, drifted up and joined the group. Then Nicholas led his two acquaintances on to the other Onofrio fountain, gathering further followers by the way; by the time he reached the Rectors' Palace a small tail of respectful listeners was hanging on his words wherever he went.

Lady Kilmichael meanwhile had also been involved in the

tourist influx. The guide, with an increasingly dispirited following, came into the Franciscan cloister, where she sat painting the garden, seen through two of the graceful small arches of Mycha di Antivari's exquisite double colonnades. On her canvas the roses and oleanders flowered; beyond the shadowed columns, flatly painted with the brush, the thick leaves of an orange tree, glittering in the high sunlight, were indicated sharply with decided strokes of the palette knife. She, too, glanced pityingly at the bewildered and unhappy tourists, but she was absorbed in her work and paid little attention till she heard a voice behind her say, in a low tone, but with evident astonishment – 'Oh Daddy, *look*! How frightfully good! Do you think we might ask to see it?'

She glanced round. A rather soldierly man in his sixties was standing a few paces away, a girl beside him, both looking towards her picture. Lady Kilmichael's face was at all times singularly unintimidating, and when she turned the girl came forward, with civil hesitation, but a good deal of self-possession, and said – 'Might I look? It's such interesting treatment.'

Lady Kilmichael winced a little inwardly at the *cliché*, but politely gave her permission, and the pair came and examined her picture. 'My daughter paints herself,' said the soldierly man, in complacent explanation. The girl expressed a rather intelligent admiration and asked some quite sensible questions; she clearly had all the jargon at her fingers'-ends. And presently – 'Are there any pictures to see here in Ragusa?' she asked. 'It's so hopeless – there's *no* guidebook, and that guide man really can't speak English at all! We've only got today here, and it's quite distracting not to know what there is to see, let alone *where* it is. Is there anything one really ought not to miss, do you know?'

Thinking, like Nicholas, how insane it was to 'do' Ragusa on a cruise at all, Lady Kilmichael nevertheless became helpful; given the folly of cruising, it was very sensible of the girl to want to be put onto the essentials at once. The Nicolo Ragusanos were the main thing to go for, she said, because you could see him hardly anywhere else; they were in the little chapel of the Dance, out towards Gruz, and in the Dominicans' church. And finding that her new acquaintances had no idea where the Dominicans' church was, she, like Nicholas, took pity on their helplessness; and having given her canvas into the charge of a somnolent friar, led them off down the Stradone to see the Nicolo Ragusanos. On the way she paused to show them the Sponza, or Customs House, with its completely Venetian façade and pious Latin inscription; more stranded tourists, seeing intelligible information going free, fell in behind the soldierly man and his daughter and followed, listening eagerly, when Lady Kilmichael at length led them up past the Porta Ploce and into the Church of the Dominicans.

By the time Nicholas had finished showing his party the Rectors' Palace it was after one o'clock, and he bethought him that he had better go back to the Franciscan cloister and pick up Lady Kilmichael for lunch. He was sufficiently pleased with his two principal companions to suggest that they might possibly lunch together; he was even more attracted by the incisive intelligence of the man than by the prettiness of the girl. Accordingly, having shaken off the tail, except for one very persistent Bishop and his wife, he took the others along to the Franciscani. But no Lady Kilmichael was to be seen – except for a drowsy friar or two, the cloister was empty; her canvas stood in the corner – she must already have gone to the Via del Levante, he supposed. The Bishop and the Englishman, delighted with the delicate colonnades, began to question Nicholas, and they wandered slowly round together. The girl strolled off by herself across the garden – presently she called out, in rather a startled voice – 'Poppy! Come and look at this!'

They went over to her. She was examining Lady Kilmichael's picture intently.

'Poppy, I would swear this was one of G. S.'s! Do look!'

'Nonsense,' said the tall man, without looking – 'you know she's in Greece.'

'We don't *know* she's in Greece,' the girl protested. 'We've only Lady Stick-in-the-Mud's word for it, and anyhow that was ages ago. Look at those flowers, Poppy! There's that red outline round the lit-up petals – no one but her does them like that.'

The Englishman adjusted a pair of pince-nez, and looked, remarking 'No one but *she*,' as he did so.

'And she's used the knife for those leaves and the brush for the buildings, just like she always does,' the girl persisted, pointing, and disregarding his correction of her grammar. 'Poppy!' she gave a little skip of excitement – 'I bet you a hundred *dinars*, or whatever they are, that she *is* here!'

'It isn't unlike, certainly – but it's impossible really to recognise pictures in that way,' the Englishman said. Nicholas had meanwhile been buttonholed by the Bishop, and could only give half an ear to this conversation – he noticed, however, that the Englishman looked slightly disturbed. The argument went on – the next words he heard, as he detached himself from the Bishop and moved back towards them, were – 'Well, if that *isn't* a Stanway, I'll eat my lipstick!'

'I can tell you with certainty that it isn't a Stanway,' Nicholas said with authority, coming up.

'How?'

'Because the artist happens to be a friend of mine.'

A sound of voices, and footsteps on the echoing flagstones proclaimed the entrance of another party into the cloister, but neither Nicholas nor the girl, intent on their argument, looked round.

'Well, who *is* your friend?' she asked, with a sort of undefeated uppishness.

'Her name—' he was beginning repressively, when a sort of

strangled ejaculation interrupted him. The Englishman was staring over their heads as if he had seen a spectre. Nicholas looked behind him. Round the corner of the cloister, followed by a string of tourists, came Lady Kilmichael.

The Englishman's pince-nez dropped and smashed on the flags with a high tinkling noise. He paid no attention. 'Good God, it *is* Grace!' he said. The girl had turned too, and stood staring – after a moment '*What* did I say, Poppy?' she demanded triumphantly, and darted down the cloister crying 'Mums!'

Nicholas was so much taken aback by all this that for a moment he never observed who Lady Kilmichael's immediate companions were. He stood, startled into complete absorption by the beauty of her gesture as she put her arms round the girl, while the Englishman, still ignoring his broken glasses, walked slowly towards them. Nicholas stooped to pick up the pince-nez; as he did so a voice cried 'Daddy! There's Nicky!' He looked up and saw Celia and his Father.

On such occasions coherence is not an outstanding feature.

'Nicholas, what on earth are you doing here? We understood you were in Greece.'

'Well, Grace, this is quite unexpected!'

'Is *this* where you've been all the time, Mums?'

'Darling, how well you look! No, not all the time.' The persistent Bishop and Lady Kilmichael's train, seeing that some exciting encounter was in progress, regretfully but politely melted away. Each family rather drew together, till on Sir Walter's recovering himself sufficiently to look at his watch and mention food, Lady Kilmichael said – 'Nicholas, won't you bring your Father along to the Via del Levante? It won't be so crowded there.'

'Do you know one another, then?' the General enquired, fixing his eyeglass to stare in bewilderment from Lady Kilmichael to Nicholas.

'Oh dear, yes – we've seen no end of one another. Come on, Father, let's go and eat – you must be starving.'

'But your Mother wrote over a fortnight ago that you were going to Greece, Nicholas. You weren't at Ragusa then, but some place with a peculiar name.'

'Komolac, I expect.'

'I daresay,' said the General helplessly, as he found himself being shepherded by his son, with an air of complete confidence, along some very small smelly streets, in company with that artist woman who appeared to be Sir Walter Kilmichael's wife. Though what she was doing here, where her family had certainly had no expectation of finding her, and why she knew Nicholas, was more than he could understand. In his bewilderment he clung firmly to the one point on which he felt on firm ground.

'Then have you been to Greece and come back? I should like to get this clear.'

'No, Father – I never went near Greece – I was taken ill on the day I meant to start.'

'Ill, Nicky? You poor lamb! What was it?' Celia asked, putting in her oar.

'Tummy, as usual,' grunted Nicholas. He didn't like being poor-lamb'ed by Celia any better than being cross-examined by his father.

In the other family Greece also held the field for the time being – it seemed a safe subject in these rather disconcerting moments of unexpected reunion.

'Then have you not been to Greece after all, Grace? Lady Roseneath wrote that you were off there, when she saw you in Venice.'

'No, Walter. This coast is so lovely, and there's so much to paint, that I've just lingered and delayed.' (It all looked so different, seen through Walter's eyes. It had been so inevitable while she was doing it.) 'But what are you cruising for? I'd no idea you meant to do that – no, up this passage; we'll be there in a moment. The food's incredible at this little place.'

'Poppy's been seedy – Sir John Lord sent him cruising.'

'*Really*, Walter? What was it? I *am* sorry.'

'Nothing much – just a bout of insomnia. I only saw Lord to please Gina.'

Then the two conversations coalesced.

'Your Mother said nothing about your being ill. When did this happen, Nicholas? I should have expected to be told.'

'General Humphries, that was my fault,' Lady Kilmichael put in from behind. 'I ought to have written to your wife at once. But while Nicholas was so bad I really hadn't a moment to do anything – and I never thought to make Dr Halther do it. I did write as soon as I remembered, but that was rather late.'

The General stared. 'You were there when he was ill? And is Dr Halther the local doctor? I really don't quite follow.'

'Considering that Lady Kilmichael nursed me for three days and nights on end, practically without lying down—' Nicholas began.

'No, Dr Halther isn't a doctor at all. We were staying with him – at least Nicholas was. And of course when he got ill I looked after him – but really it was nothing! Only I'm so sorry I didn't think to write,' said Lady Kilmichael hastily.

'Where *was* all this, Grace – I'm not quite clear,' Sir Walter said with equable coolness. 'And *when* was it? Recently?'

'Just the week before last – oh, here we are! Yes, in under this arch. I'll tell you all about it presently, Walter. Nicholas, rout out Signor Antonio and see if he's got *spini di mare* today.'

'*Spini di mare* are sudden death, I may say,' Nicholas observed, slouching off towards the hovel in the corner of the courtyard, while the party, still in the utmost mental confusion, sat down at the little tables under the great walnut.

'And vermouth at once, Nicholas,' Lady Kilmichael called.

'The vermouth here is very peculiar, but quite delicious, *I* think,' she observed socially to the General. Out of the corner of her eye she saw a sort of controlled gleam of amusement flash for a moment in Linnet's face, as she said this; she realised that Linnet was enjoying her dealings with the General. Little wretch! She was looking very well, and so pretty, the darling thing! As they drank their vermouth Celia observed to her brother – 'We half expected to come on you in Greece, you know; isn't it funny that we should find you here, where we didn't, and not there?'

'Well said, old mole!' was Nicholas's only reply to this. Grace understood – like him she was beginning to feel the subject of Greece as intrusive as Hamlet's father; she saw Linnet glance at Nicholas with that gleam again – she too had caught the point, and was enjoying it.

Over the *spini di mare* Sir Walter began to display that grasp of essentials and capacity for direct action which had made him an international power as well as an intellectual force. Abandoning the unequal contest with the immediate past, he turned to the future. 'This crab, or lobster, or whatever it is,' he observed, 'is simply paradisal. I should like to eat it for a week! Linnet, what do you say to giving Venice a miss – you've seen it before – and staying here for a few days with your Mother? I feel sure Captain Henry could be persuaded to put in for us on his way south again.'

Linnet said that Ragusa was the most rapturous place she had ever seen, and that she would adore to. Clever Poppy!

'I suppose there's a possible hotel?' Sir Walter pursued, looking enquiringly at his wife.

'The Imperial's quite good.'

'Is that where you are?'

'Yes. Do do that, Walter – there's such a lot I'd like you and Linnet to see.'

'Is the food like this?'

'No – there's no other food like this in Ragusa!'

'It was rather brilliant of you to find this place,' Sir Walter said appreciatively – 'I don't think even in Besançon I've met quite this quality in a sauce.'

'The chemist put us on to it,' Nicholas here observed.

'The *chemist*?'

'Yes – he's a yachtsman too!'

Again Linnet's glance rested for a brief moment on Nicholas. To produce a gastronomic yachting chemist in a difficult conversation was a feather in any young man's cap. But what *was* all this about him, and Mums, and his illness? It was all most intriguing. Linnet was dying to know if Celia's brother was staying at the Imperial too. Mums *was* so artless – she felt sure he was.

So after lunch Sir Walter went down to the harbour, to return to the *Mindora Star*, lying off the mole, and make his arrangements with the captain. The rest of the party showed him the way, and then wandered back along the Stradone. The General, having at last been satisfied about Greece and Nicholas's illness, had more or less resigned himself to confusion about everything else, and embarked with Lady Kilmichael on a subject in which he felt himself at home – the defects in his son's character. He developed this theme, while the girls walked with Nicholas.

'And for another thing, the boy's mad on painting,' he presently remarked.

Grace took a breath and plunged. 'Yes, and he is so extraordinarily good at it that he ought never to do anything else,' she said firmly.

He looked at her, surprised by her tone – his eyeglass gave the impression of disliking what it saw, and dropped the length of its cord.

'It's no career for a man,' he pronounced.

'To be brilliantly successful at something is quite a good career for anyone, I should have thought,' Lady Kilmichael returned stoutly. Linnet glanced over her shoulder at her Mother, and glanced away again.

The General shifted his ground. 'There's no money in it,' he said, rather shortly. This Lady Kilmichael looked so soft and gentle, she had the makings of a charming woman; but she was evidently stubborn at heart, like all the rest of them.

'I'm not really so sure of that,' she said in a deceptively gentle voice. 'Emanuel James makes about six thousand a year.'

This time it was Celia who glanced back. 'He's brought up twenty-seven children on it, you know, Daddy!'

'Celia!' 'The boy isn't Emanuel James,' the General said with disapproving finality to Lady Kilmichael. (How did she know how the boy painted? There was something at the back of this.) 'He's only dabbled with it. Celia is taking it up – that's quite another matter. They think well of her at the Slade.'

Lady Kilmichael's expressions of civil gratification at this intelligence were drowned in the sudden outcry raised by the two girls at the sight of M. Kraljic's trays of jewellery. They must look, they must buy something – and while they examined bracelets of silver chain-work, bags of heavy gold embroidery, and long dangling gilt earrings, Nicholas stepped up to Lady Kilmichael.

'You'll do no good,' he muttered. 'You see for yourself now what he's like.' His face had resumed the discouraged and discontented expression which had so struck her at Torcello. 'This is all quite awful,' he went on. 'And what he'll say if he tumbles to the fact that I've been painting solidly for a month goodness knows! Do be careful.'

'Don't worry too much,' Grace returned in the same tone. 'I think perhaps I may—'

'Mums, I *must* have this! It's only five hundred *dinars*,' Linnet interrupted, coming up with a heavy silver bracelet. 'Have you got some money on you?'

'Five hundred *dinars*! But that's fantastic, Linnet. Give it to me!' She advanced through the group and went up to the shopkeeper, who stood smoothing his stomach in his doorway with an air of happy anticipation.

'Good day, M. Kraljic. So you are making fun of my daughter!' she said cheerfully. 'She tells me that you are asking her five hundred *dinars* for this.' She held out the bracelet. 'Or she is mistaken, perhaps?'

M. Kraljic's face at that moment repaid observation. He had thought himself confronted by the safe and wealthy ignorance of *stranci* [foreigners] from a cruise, and here was that Englishwoman, who was becoming a regular and valued, but a very discriminating customer of his, in charge of the party! It was extremely embarrassing. He explained hurriedly that the young lady *was* mistaken – he had meant three hundred *dinars*. Grace bargained a little, and the bracelet passed into Linnet's hands for two hundred and fifty-five.

'It's really better to buy several things at once,' Lady Kilmichael said to the General, whose eyeglass registered modified approval of this transaction – 'one gets much more off if one gets things in a lump.' Celia now invoked her good offices for the purchase of a gold handbag; then the whole party drifted out of the shop again. Mme Amandi's jackets next caught Linnet's eye, and she and Celia darted ahead to look at them, while the others followed.

'Daddy, one of these I simply *must* have,' Celia declared as they came up.

'This looks a very expensive shop – you'd probably get them much cheaper in some side street,' the General protested.

'No – Mme Amandi is the only person who has these; it's a monopoly of hers,' said Grace calmly. 'She isn't frightfully unreasonable, considering what they are, if you bargain with her a bit.'

'*There*, Daddy!'

'Well, if Lady Kilmichael will kindly help you—' the General said, resigned.

Grace, Celia Humphries and Linnet made their way into the shop. It was at all times so crowded with objects that the extreme mobility of Mme Amandi's ample person about her own premises was an unfailing source of wonder to Grace; but today ingress to one half of it was completely blocked by the reverse of a gentleman in a light grey overcoat, who was stooping to examine some object. Grace, waiting to attract Mme Amandi's attention, glanced at him with involuntary curiosity, to see what he was looking at – to her astonishment she saw that he was bending over Nicholas's nearly finished picture of San Salvatore. At that moment Nicholas and the General, entering, bumped into him; the gentleman straightened himself up with a smart French oath, and turned round. It was M. Breuil.

TWENTY-TWO

Sorry, Breuil,' said the General, recoiling. The Frenchman, usually so punctilious, made absolutely no response, but stood looking with starting eyes at Lady Kilmichael. (Really, this was a day for goggling, Linnet thought, observing them – people did nothing but meet and stand transfixed.) Then he pushed his way across to her, crying '*Mademoiselle Stanway! Mais quel plaisir!*' Lady Kilmichael greeted him with equal pleasure; but at once, briskly, he turned back to the canvas. '*C'est de vous, Mademoiselle?*'

'No – it's Mr Humphries'. Nicholas, come here – you must meet Monsieur Breuil.'

Linnet glanced at the young man as he made his way slowly forward – crammed and jammed as they were in the little shop, every movement was slow and involved the displacement of somebody else; but the girl noticed that he walked like a person in a dream, and that his eyes too were, as she put it to herself, absolutely popping.

'*Ah, je ne le croyais guère! Pourtant il y a des ressemblances! Enchanté, Monsieur,*' the Frenchman said, all in a breath. Nicholas said, 'How do you do?' very deliberately, in English – then he turned to Lady Kilmichael. What with the sudden appearance of his father and Celia, the discovery that his new friends were Sir Walter and the much-talked-of 'Linnet,' and the general embroilment, confusion and surprise, the full import of that half-heard conversation in the cloister had escaped him – he had wondered vaguely at these people's knowing Grace Stanway, as one meets with a certain unbelief a personal friend of the Pope's, but that was all. But the Frenchman's exclamation could not be mistaken. 'Are *you* Grace Stanway?' he said slowly, with a sort of appalled incredulity, staring harder than even he had ever stared before.

'Yes, of course,' said Grace, smiling. She was so delighted at this heaven-sent, though wholly inexplicable, apparition of the dealer that she would have smiled at Rose Barum just then.

'Why on earth didn't you tell me?' asked the young man, almost resentfully.

'Because I didn't want you to know!' She was still gay. Linnet's own eyes were worth observation at that moment – fancy Mums talking like that! Oh, this *was* fun. And why had she swindled the wretched boy?

'That explains a lot,' was all he said, rather sourly. But M. Breuil now intervened again, with a spate of questions in rapid French. M. Humph*ress* had been painting long? Was attached to what gallery, had worked with whom? Nicholas replied, now in French, to all of them – not long, no gallery – he had never shown in his life; Ruskin School of Art at Oxford, on his own, '*et quelques mois à Vence avec Zarini.*' Even the unobservant Grace could not fail to notice the different tone in which Zarini's name was now brought out – and as he spoke it, Nicholas threw her an indescribable glance, with half an eyebrow cocked. Her heart melted to him – angel! he was laughing at himself, even then.

M. Breuil, however, was always the man of business. Had M. Humph*ress* any other pictures here that could be seen? Nicholas hesitated, with a rather helpless glance at Lady Kilmichael. '*Mais oui,*' she intervened, firmly – there were several, up at the Imperial Hotel, only a few steps away – would M. Breuil care to come and see them? That was precisely what M. Breuil not only wished but intended – and off they all trooped, past Onofrio's fountain, out by the Porta Pile, and up through the Borgo. The General, whose knowledge of French was limited, had not been able to follow half what passed, and walked in a state of complete bewilderment – today was a crazy day, everyone seemed to be where they weren't expected to be, and know who they weren't expected to know, and to do what they weren't expected to do. One thing was clear – that young scamp Nicholas had been painting again; wasting his time – and money too, canvases cost a pretty penny – after he'd promised to give it up. He must have a word with him! Most awkward, all these people about – and all the time in streets, or shops, or churches; no privacy, not a chance to sit down and have a word quietly! However, he gathered that that Frenchman Kilmichael was always playing Contract with – though why spoil a good game? – Auction was good enough for anyone – was something to do with pictures, from the way he went on; and despairing for the moment of getting his 'word' with his son, who was entrenched as it were between the two girls, he bethought him to bring Celia into notice, and tackled the fellow.

'*C'est ma fille qui, er, peinte vraiment*,' he said, firmly, as they walked up the hill. '*Elle peinte bien. Elle est à l'école du Slade.*' While M. Breuil, civil but mystified, listened to these statements, the young people walked behind. '*Now* the balloon will go up!' Nicholas muttered gloomily to Celia. 'Father's beginning to boil already. Who is the old beaver, anyhow?'

'*I* don't know – I mean, he's on the cruise, so I know him to speak to, but that's all.'

'He's Mums's dealer,' Linnet put in. 'I gather that much. I didn't tumble to it on the boat. I daresay Poppy did, but he wouldn't have mentioned it.'

'But Nicky, have you been painting, after all? I thought—'

'Yes, well you thought wrong – I have!'

'With Lady Kilmichael?' Celia hit with sisterly accuracy on the one point her brother would have wished to leave obscure.

'She's been so very kind as to give me some coaching now and then,' he said, feeling like Judas for the minimising statement.

'I shouldn't have thought Mums was much good at teaching,' put in Linnet. 'She's so vague – she always says she doesn't know herself why she does things.'

'That's because you couldn't understand, no doubt,' he retorted crushingly. 'She's a particularly good teacher, as a matter of fact. Even when I'd no idea who she was, I realised that I was getting far more good from her than I did from Zarini.'

'Oh well, Zarini!' Linnet's tone dismissed the Corsican as summarily as Halther had done. 'He's not in Mums's class at all.' But she did not resume her own point and develop it argumentatively, as her habit was; instead she looked thoughtfully at the young man beside her. That was twice in about two hours that he had rather noticeably championed her mother. Funny. Mums was funny, too; she was so – so definite, somehow; marching them all up here to see this creature's pictures, when anyone could see that the creature himself was terrified, and his appalling Father ready to blow up at any moment. It wasn't *like* Mums, any of it – she was usually so peace-at-any-price.

At the hotel M. Breuil walked quickly round Nicholas's pictures, as he pulled them out from a corner of his room one after another and propped them on and against various pieces of furniture – the buildings and street scenes; the portrait of Grace, and a ludicrous painting of the hall porter at the Imperial, standing in full uniform at his own flamboyant portals, full of the inane and rather swollen dignity of his kind – finally the conversation piece of Dr Halther being 'tongued' by his cook. At this last M. Breuil made his first observation – '*Tiens, c'est le vieux Halther, de Vienne!*'

'You know him?' Lady Kilmichael asked.

'*Mais oui – c'est un de mes meilleurs clients. C'est bien, ça – c'est fort drôle!*' He passed on to the next, while the rest stood round looking on – the General increasingly restless, and evidently aghast at this prodigious display of the forbidden activity, the girls amused and curious, breaking into fits of mirth over the portrait of the hall porter. But Nicholas himself stood, his fingers nervously fiddling with a button of his coat, and on his face the same strained expression which it had worn that first night on the boat, when he showed his sketches to Lady Kilmichael. Having been round once M. Breuil began again at the beginning, more slowly and carefully now – taking one picture at a time and propping it on a chair in front of the French window leading onto the balcony, to get the light. He took off his pince-nez and peered closely at the brushwork, pushing his thin nose almost into the canvas, oblivious of everything and everybody else. But Grace suddenly realised that for Nicholas the whole thing was becoming quite unbearable – all these spectators, the girls, his father, herself. He was looking quite ill with nervous tension – his inside would certainly go wrong again tonight if this went on! M. Breuil stepped back, snapping his pince-nez open and shut; she knew that trick of his – it expressed satisfaction. And with sudden decision – 'We will rejoin you later, for tea; for the moment we will leave you in peace,' she said, and carried the others off to go back and shop at Mme Amandi's. Linnet protested a little. 'Oh Mums, this *is* such fun!' she whispered.

'Miss Humphries wants to buy her jacket – this way, General,' her mother returned, and Linnet, too astonished for further expostulation, followed.

On the way down to Lina Amandi's Lady Kilmichael expanded to the General on the subject of M. Breuil. She mentioned casually some of the great names in modern painting for whom he was the principal agent – but these proving unimpressive, since the names conveyed nothing to the General, she was reduced to the deplorable expedient of praising M. Breuil's skill as a dealer, and instancing the prices which he had recently got her for her work. By this the General was impressed – 'But of course *your* name's made,' he said. (He had gathered, he could not quite have said how, that in her own way Lady Kilmichael was really rather important, and these sums she mentioned – really ridiculous, just for a picture – confirmed the impression.)

'Yes, but M. Breuil made it. He took me up and boomed me – I hardly sold anything before then,' she told him frankly.

He chewed this over. 'Of course Celia paints very well,' he said presently. 'If this dealer fellow's really as good as all that, it seems a pity he shouldn't see some of her things, too.'

'Yes indeed – has she any of her work with her?'

'Oh, she's at it all the time, you know, off and on, when she gets the chance. Mightn't be a bad plan to bring one or two up for him to look at.'

'An excellent plan, I think,' said Lady Kilmichael.

Celia glanced round. 'My dear Daddy, he can perfectly well see mine on the boat,' she put in repressively.

'Ah, but that's not quite the same thing,' replied the General. 'He might as well see them now, alongside your brother's, while he's really going into it.'

'Very much better,' Lady Kilmichael urged. 'Couldn't you bring one or two up? I should so much like to see them myself, too.'

So the General, after some argument with his daughter as to which of her masterpieces should be produced, also set off for the harbour. Under cover of their discussion – 'Mums, her pictures are really tripe; they're not in the least like his.' Linnet murmured. 'He's pretty good, isn't he?'

'I think it would be nice for M. Breuil to see them, all the same,' her mother returned smoothly. 'Yes, I think Nicholas is good, probably.' She turned away to Celia, with 'Now, Miss Humphries, what about your jacket. Do you want a red one or a blue one?' And raising her pretty eyebrows, 'What *has* come over Mums?' Linnet asked herself. If this wasn't a leg-pull, she had never seen one. Celia herself had said, frequently, that her brother 'thought mud' of her pictures, and had mentioned the trouble over his career; he must have told Mums about it all if they'd been drifting about, painting and being ill, all this time. But when had Mums ever been known even to tweak or twitch, let alone pull, anyone's leg?

They all reassembled for tea on the terrace at the Imperial. Lady Kilmichael and the two girls got back first, shortly followed by Sir Walter, who had successfully made his arrangements with the steamer. (Sir Walter was of that order of beings whom railway and steamship companies are delighted to honour, even to the point of slightly modifying the arrangements of a cruise.)

'What about rooms, Grace? Have you got them for us?' he enquired, sitting down next to his wife, who was deep in a conversation with M. Breuil.

'No, Walter – I've been shopping with the children.'

'Hadn't we better do something about it?' he asked, a little surprised. Usually when asked if she had done anything which she hadn't, his wife said, 'Oh, I'm *so* sorry,' and hastened to repair her omission forthwith.

'Yes, do. Let Linnet go with you and look at them. Try to get them in front, Walter – the view is so lovely,' she replied tranquilly.

'What is your number?' he said, rising. It was clear that she had no intention of coming herself, which surprised him still more.

'Sixty-five – second floor. Linnet knows where it is; she's been up.'

'Not to yours, Mums.'

'No, but it's next to Nicholas's.' She turned back to the Frenchman. '*Évidemment, il manque de technique encore*,' she said, '*mais*—' There wasn't much time, half the party would be going back to the *Mindora Star* at dinner time; she must get in her talk to M. Breuil now, while she had the chance. Walter and Linnet were quite capable of getting their own rooms, bless them. Breuil thought well of the pictures, but he must be made to realise the position. And while Sir Walter and the girls went off, the two Kilmichaels in a state of suppressed astonishment at being allowed, indeed encouraged, to choose their rooms for themselves without the usual maternal supervision – because *that* was the sort of thing Mums always thought no one but she could do properly, Linnet reflected – Lady Kilmichael, in confidence, told the dealer a good deal about Nicholas and his relations to his family, the General's preoccupation with money, and the plan to make the young man an architect.

'*Mais c'est rigolo! Il est formidable comme talent! C'est une bêtise inouïe!*' the Frenchman protested, scandalised beyond measure. There was a future before this young man – his draughtsmanship was *inconcevable à son age*, and with so little work behind him. He continued to analyse Nicholas's technique, with intervals of frowning and drumming on the table; Lady Kilmichael recognised the symptoms of intense mental calculation. She had seen M. Breuil reckoning with new talent before – but she had never before seen him display such reckless appreciation. Her heart rose. She had not been wrong about Nicholas's gift, and Breuil had said emphatically that he had gained a lot from her. If only they could make the General see reason!

That gentleman was presently seen coming up the hill, burdened with a couple of canvases. At the same moment Sir Walter, Linnet and Celia reappeared and gathered round the table under the palms. Grace began to pour out, while she enquired after their success in the matter of rooms. Yes, they had got good ones, same floor, a little further along, and the bus was going down to the harbour to fetch their kit before dinner. Sir Walter had packed while he was on board – Linnet must nip down and put her things together the moment she had done her tea. And then the General, with a 'There you are, Monsieur,' put down two smallish canvases, one after another, on two small white chairs, and stood back, mopping his brow, to watch the effect.

There ensued a rather appalling pause. Nicholas looked as if he were going to be sick. Sir Walter preserved an appearance of civil indifference. Linnet looked at the sky – and then at Nicholas; and finally at her mother, with a familiar expression – a 'Now-you-see-what-you've-been-and-done' look. Celia looked at her shoes. Lady Kilmichael glanced with curiosity at the two pictures. They were the usual uninspired, not very competent, purely derivative effort of the ungifted amateur with 'a feeling for colour' – or a feeling for something; they were, alas, as Linnet had said, tripe. They were much, much worse than she had anticipated; she had expected that they would be comfortably bad, but not as bad as that. And with mounting horror she watched to see how M. Breuil would deal with this situation of her own reckless creating.

M. Breuil dealt with it, as he dealt with everything, deliberately, blandly and quite finally. He rose, teacup in hand, and stood politely before first one canvas and then the other. '*Très-joli*,' he said at length, nodding at one; '*Très-joli*,' he repeated, nodding at the other; then with a little bow to Celia – '*Mademoiselle s'occupe dehors – c'est charmant!*' he said. And that was all. Without an instant's pause he turned away to Nicholas, and began talking to him rapidly in French. Lady Kilmichael, pouring out tea for the General, who had only understood the words *très-joli*, and in his innocence still regarded them as praise, listened with half an ear, and indeed presently was drawn into their conversation. M. Breuil, it soon appeared, was offering to buy from Nicholas, there and then, six pictures – the Halther, the hall porter, the portrait of Grace, the Franciscan cloister, the Piazza scene, and the San Salvatore when finished – it would be done by the time the boat called for the Kilmichaels on its return from Venice. And he was offering to pay for them, now, by cheque, a sum in francs which fairly staggered Grace, a sum on which any young man could live in perfect comfort for a year and a half at least; a sum which would make him totally independent of his Father or anyone else for the time being. The condition, of course, was that he should sign a contract to sell only to Breuil for a term of years. Miss Stanway had a similar contract; she would explain it to him. And in eighteen months' or two years' time, M. Breuil again had a plan – a one-man show in his gallery, to *lancer* the new artist definitely. M. Humph*ress* would in the interval work, paint, produce – but there it was, his offer. And while Grace glowed, and Linnet and Celia gasped with unutterable astonishment, and Sir Walter pulled out a notebook and began to scribble in it, the dealer leant back in his chair, with a satisfied expression, to receive the young man's delighted acceptance.

It didn't come. Nicholas, with a stubborn mouth, said – 'The portrait of Madame is not for sale.'

'*Comment? Mais c'est le clou!*' Breuil expostulated. He looked as astonished as a man could. He must have that – it was exceptional, by much the best; why could he not have it?

'It isn't for sale,' Nicholas repeated. Apart from that, M. Breuil's offer was everything that was acceptable; he was most grateful, he thanked him warmly. He could have anything else instead, of course. But though his mouth was stubborn, his eyes for one moment turned in a sort of helpless appeal to Lady Kilmichael.

'*Mais par exemple!*' M. Breuil was beginning, with rising irritation, when Grace intervened, in her soft, rather appealing voice. She ought to have explained at once, she said, that the portrait was hers; it was so stupid of her not to mention it. She was so terribly sorry; it was entirely her fault.

'It is a commission?' Breuil snapped.

'*Mais évidemment!*' she answered quietly. But Linnet, catching sight of the expression of – well, really, worship was the only word – in the young man's eyes at that moment, realised in a flash that her mother was, for some reason, lying; and apparently very well. And again, What *has* happened to Mums? she asked herself.

M. Breuil perforce subsided. He was not going to have *une histoire* with Miss Stanway on any account, but the rapidity and relative good grace of his subsidence, more than anything else, gave Lady Kilmichael the measure of his opinion of Nicholas's work. Meanwhile there was the General to be dealt with. This was being an extraordinary day, she reflected; one person after another to be dealt with, and never a moment to think. One just had to go from one thing to the next, taking the most urgent first – and some extraordinary force seemed to be bearing her on, enabling her to see, to make cool choices in a hurry, to put aside the less important things, like getting rooms for Walter and Linnet, in a way she had never done before. She was of course putting off one of the more important things, the most important of all – dealing with Walter; but there would be lots of time for that later. She hadn't even tried to explain this to him, by so much as a look; but he would realise that for himself, she felt sure. (It was only later that the thought came to her that it was years and years since she had relied on Walter to understand anything! She had always hurried to do, hastened to explain, for fear of his reproaches. How much simpler just to rely, which really merely meant having a little faith in his good sense and his good feeling.)

Now, however, she braced herself to the task of dealing with the General. She translated the dealer's offer for him. To her surprise – and it aroused her warm admiration, after the appalling snub the girl's own work had just received – Celia came vigorously to her aid, pointing out the advantages of accepting the offer. 'It really means, Daddy, that he will be completely off your hands from now on, if he takes this,' she ended stoutly.

'Does he want to buy yours, too?' her father asked.

'*No*, darling. I'm not nearly good enough yet. Nicky's a bit of a genius, you know. But really, Daddy, it's a terribly good plan, don't you think?'

Before he could really express his views of the plan, Sir Walter weighed in, notebook in hand. He had worked out the sum offered, at the current rate of the franc, in sterling. 'I was *not* making that amount a year, General, at his age,' he said. 'Were you?'

The General had not been making half that sum. He had been a subaltern, heavily subsidised by his parents. It was all very confusing: Celia's pictures overlooked and the boy's, which didn't seem to him nearly so pretty, being worth, apparently, such extraordinary sums. He could not in the least understand it, or why the Frenchman – and all the rest, it seemed – thought so highly of the boy's things. Still, as an architect he was certainly going to have been an expense for years to come – Celia was right about that; and if he could support himself in this peculiar way, perhaps he'd better do it, at least till he got sick of it. It was – again – so awkward; no privacy, no chance for a quiet talk with them all standing round, it was really extremely difficult to say anything but 'yes.' And under the pressure of hurry, uncertainty and public opinion, the General succumbed.

'Very well, Nicholas,' he said, rather grudgingly. 'If your Mother makes no objection to this, *I* shan't.' He failed to observe, though Grace did not, the very neat little wink with which Celia greeted the reference to her Mother.

'Thank you, Father.'

So the bargain was concluded, the cheque signed; the canvases were packed as carefully as might be in the time, and sent down to the harbour on the hotel bus, escorted by Linnet, who was going back to the ship 'to garner a few effects' as she said, for her three days' stay in Ragusa. The General and Celia were despatched to the Dance, the little chapel of the paupers' graveyard, to see the other Nicolo Ragusanos; M. Breuil, at his own earnest request, went up to see what pictures Miss Stanway had been doing since last they met. He bought the Stradone and the one of the irises out of hand, writing her another fantastic cheque for them; he adjured her to complete the one of the reed bed and the Ombla, and that of the Franciscan cloister, and to do more work generally. *Ce jeune homme*, he said, had much more energy than she; look, he beseeched her, at the work he had done in the time! She should remember what Flaubert said – '*Le génie, c'est travailler tous les jours!*' And then as they went back to the garden, with an earnestness unusual with him he thanked her – 'in the name of Art' – for what she had done for Nicholas, setting his feet again on the only path he could follow with satisfaction, and rescuing him from a wasteful and uncongenial career.

'It's you who have done that, Monsieur,' she protested, happily.

'*Disons que nous l'avons fait ensemble!*' the Frenchman said, kissing her hand. '*Au revoir, Madame!*' And he went off with Nicholas to see the other picture at the barber's shop, on his way back to the steamer; while Lady Kilmichael, left alone, walked over to where Sir Walter, also alone, sat under a palm. He rose as she approached, and glanced round him – the hotel garden was fairly well filled with groups of people. 'What do you say to going for a short walk before dinner?' he said as she came up.

'Yes, let's, Walter – I should like to,' she answered. And a little breathless – for now it was upon her, the important thing – she set off beside her husband.

TWENTY-THREE

The immediate problem which occupied Grace Kilmichael was where to walk to. Ragusa is not a large place, nor is the choice of directions great. If they went up the road towards Gruz and out onto the open down-like slopes above the sea they would probably meet the General and Celia coming back from the Dance; if they walked down through the Borgo and along the coast road, they were liable to encounter Linnet returning from the ship; while the town itself was full of Nicholas and Breuil, walking about looking at the half-finished canvases, so casually scattered all over it. There really seemed nothing for it but to climb one of the flights of steps up to the Acquedotto promenade, and potter along that, above the town; the view was lovely, and presumably up there they would be safe from interruption. So turning to the right, to avoid the actual flight up which she and Nicholas had toiled the evening before, she said – 'Do you mind a bit of a climb, Walter? There's a level walk and a lovely view at the top' – and led him up the first set of steps beyond the hotel.

No one can talk much while they are walking upstairs, and long before they reached the Acquedotto promenade Grace began to regret her choice. This climb put off the beginning; and the longer they walked in silence, the harder it would be to begin. By the time they reached the promenade and turned along it towards Gruz she was completely out of breath, as much from nervousness as from all those steps. But it was not as difficult as she expected. As soon as they gained the level Walter paused, took out a cigarette, offered her one, lit both, and throwing away the match said very pleasantly – 'You seem to have unearthed a genius. Where did you pick him up?'

'At Torcello, actually. Only it was an accident my meeting him again.' And she told him of their first and second encounters, and how Nicholas had turned out to be Lady Roseneath's nephew. Walter laughed at the story of the stone she couldn't draw, and she was encouraged by that to tell him also of Lady Roseneath's two abortive confidences. 'And what *has* he got, and lost?' Walter asked, laughing again.

'Do you know, I *still* don't know,' she said.

'Haven't you asked him? How unenterprising of you.' But somehow Walter was being very *nice* about Nicholas; he was taking him absolutely for granted; his questions were only the sort of friendly interest one liked to have taken in one's new friends – and her confidence returning, she found it easy to tell him what she had told Breuil, only in far more detail – her discovery of the boy's passion for painting, his trouble with his Father, and her impulsive decision to let him show what he could do. 'That was very subversive of you, wasn't it?' Walter asked, amused – 'Yes, it was,' she answered frankly. 'But hasn't it been worth it?'

'Apparently it has – only it's something quite new for you to start doing evil that good may come!'

'Oh Walter, no, it wasn't really evil' – and she explained how she had made Nicholas write to his Mother (only the letter was never sent) before she would really undertake to coach him. But she explained undefensively; the old earlier habit, so long lost, of talking freely to Walter, without fear of reproof, was slipping back, somehow, in the most extraordinary way, and she found herself going on to tell him, quite simply and in fact rather enjoyably, the main story of the past few weeks – their sojourns at Spalato and Ragusa, her finding the Tete Mare at Komolac and going there, Nicholas's escapade at the Professor's villa, the advent of the Professor himself, and its happy ending; Nicholas's illness, and their return to Ragusa. There were certain elisions;

she said nothing about herself and Nicholas. But – how curious that was! – it was not in the least from fear of how Walter would take it, now, only out of a sort of loyalty to her dear, her darling child; she had a curious conviction, which grew while she talked, that this too was one of the things which Walter could be trusted to understand, and even perhaps to realise without being told. Because he never asked why, when she was so diligently teaching and helping him, she hadn't somehow managed to take Nicholas *with* her to Komolac, and equally, he never queried the naturalness of Nicholas's stratagems to install himself at the villa. He just laughed over them, loudly. Oh, how lovely was the strange ease of these preciously ready assumptions on Walter's part, by contrast to the icy cross-examinations which had been her lot of late years! What had happened to him? The fact of his not asking made her really want to tell him – sometime she would, but somehow not now, not yet. Anyhow it didn't matter. Then he began to ask, quite seriously, it seemed, about her painting, and how she had got on with that – and she confessed to having been rather idle, what with coaching Nicholas, and the contract.

'I hadn't heard about the contract,' Walter said.

'No – that was fixed up while you were in America,' she replied, blushing a little. 'But I've just sold Breuil two little pictures for thirty-five thousand francs, so I'm quite up on the trip.'

Walter laughed. 'I hope you told the General! Poor wretched man, what a mentality to carry round through life!'

Then she enquired about Walter's health, and now he told her in detail what Sir John had said; and with each question and reply the strange link which *is* wedlock established itself more and more between them. When they came in sight of Gruz and the harbour, with the black toad-like promontory of Lapad lying dark and wooded beyond – 'Dubrovnik means "the woody" ' she told him inconsequently. They turned then, and walked back towards Ragusa – the walls, golden-white, stood out into the sea in their evening splendour, and she pointed out various landmarks – the Torre Menze, the Monte Sergio, the Monte Peline. 'And *Pelin* is the Serbo-Croat word for salvia – they grow wild here everywhere. Isn't it fun to think that once that slope of roofs was blue with salvias?'

'You know a lot about it – how did you pick all this up?'

'Oh, the Professor – Doctor Halther – you must meet him, Walter.'

'I should like to.'

But Walter had a question or two to ask after all. The first surprised her.

'Why didn't you let Nicholas know that you were really Grace Stanway?'

She blushed again. 'Oh, because I was afraid that if he knew *that*, he might think it worth mentioning to Lucia or to his Mother, and that – that it might get round to you or Gina, Walter, and you might try to make me come home. If you knew where I was, I mean. Mother had just sent me on your letter, to Venice, and that frightened me rather.' She spoke hurriedly – here they were, now, at it! – but she spoke the truth.

He listened, and walked beside her in silence. At last – 'And when *do* you think of coming home?' he asked. His tone was almost humble. Startled, she glanced at him – now he was being ironical, and after the confident ease of the last half-hour she felt slightly chilled. But – how very strange! – his face, his very splendid intellectual face, wore an expression both serious and sincere. He *wasn't* being ironical. Grace was ready to faint with astonishment – Walter speaking humbly to her!

'I am nearly ready to come,' she said, not choosing her words at all.

'What else do you want to do?' he asked, still with that surprising seriousness – 'Go to Greece?'

That made her feel slightly hysterical. 'No, Walter, not Greece! Anything but Greece!'

'What's wrong with Greece?' he asked, surprised at her tone.

'Oh nothing, really – only it's become a sort of bogey, a mirage; Greece is like the end of the rainbow! I'll tell you about that some other time. No, but Walter, I do want to come home – very soon.'

'Well, what are you waiting for – besides Greece?' he said, smiling now.

'I think – just till I'm sure I'm quite free,' she said, slowly.

'Free?'

'Yes. From myself and my *amour propre*. I don't want to make a mess of it all a second time, you see. I'd rather like to tell you, Walter – I do see now *what* a mess I've made of everything – especially Linnet. But rather of you, too.'

'How do you think you've made a mess of me and Linnet?' he asked, very quietly.

'By being afraid of you both,' she answered promptly. 'But that was because I wasn't content with myself, and to be what I was – rather stupid, and all that. I wanted to be appreciated. When I wasn't appreciated I was hurt – and then I was afraid of being hurt, and of the people who hurt me.' She paused. 'I seem to be getting rather tied up.'

'No, I think I understand. Go on.'

'You see I was always spreading out all the things I did for you and the children, like goods on a tray in a shop window – only you didn't want any of them! Nobody would buy. That's what was so silly, and must have been so maddening of me. Of course no one wants to pay with gratitude for those things – one must just give them, and leave it at that. They don't entitle you to anything. But I couldn't see that then.' She drew a long breath. 'Now I do. And of course as soon as one stops wanting gratitude and' – she checked a moment – 'affection – one *is* free. And then one is quite all right.'

'How have you found all this out?' Walter asked, when she stopped. He neither affirmed nor denied, but she had a sense, so long forgotten that it was almost new, of a current of sympathetic understanding in him.

'Partly by *being* appreciated, funnily enough,' she said, turning to him. 'But not only that. I began to get onto it alone, and then Nicholas helped a lot. He talked to me about himself, and about Celia and her Mother, just as if I were a young person too; and so I began to see myself from Linnet's end. It's fearfully hard to do that just *as* a parent, because one's own children never explain what it is that irritates them – they just *are* irritated, and leave it at that. But Nicholas did explain about his Mother, and that made me see – oh, no end of things where I'd gone wrong too.'

'But Nicholas didn't tell you about your *amour propre*, did he?' Walter asked, in a curious tone.

'Oh dear no! I don't suppose he realises that a bit,' she said candidly. 'No – that was the Professor. Nicholas showed me the symptoms, as it were, and then the Professor diagnosed the disease.'

'As *amour propre*?'

'Yes – and more than that.' She paused – this really was rather difficult. 'He made me see,' she said, getting the words out slowly, as if she were counting them one by one, 'that it was because I wouldn't accept *inevitable* things, like you and the children getting less fond of me, and needing me less, that I felt a failure and was hurt. And that if I could learn to accept that, I should be free. And then I should be able to carry on all right. And I think I have nearly learnt it. At least I see that I should be able to cope with Linnet much better if instead of giving way to her because – well really because I love her so, and want her so terribly to love me' – her voice was a little unsteady – 'I were to let that take care of itself, and just stick to what's right.'

'I see,' said Walter gravely, and for some time he said nothing more. They walked in silence, now back above the town; now and then Grace glanced at her husband, and wondered what he was thinking. She had put it all so confusedly and badly; though even so, it was a relief to have got it out. But Walter Kilmichael was walking in silence because he was making some almost violent mental adjustments. Though his wife had not expressed herself well, her meaning was clear, and even clearer than her meaning were her fearlessness and sincerity, which took him completely by surprise. This was a new Grace! He had begun already to miss the old one, rather badly; the absence of her unassuming personality had affected his comfort in a way which he had not expected, altered the background of his life most disconcertingly. But life with this person now beside him might, he felt, be more than comfortable; it might even be rather delightful; given such a measure of honesty on her part, there were things they could share which they had never shared, after the delirious and almost unconscious fusion of the first months of marriage. He was startled and moved; and because he was moved, when he first began to speak it was rather formally and generally.

'People are very slow to realise the truth about freedom,' he said. 'Of course it consists in the recognition of one's limitations, primarily, and we are all reluctant to admit those, let alone to accept them. I am glad you have seen all this.'

'Yes, Walter,' said Grace meekly. But amusement began to stir in her, perhaps from the relief of having got her confession over. Walter was talking like a lecture on economics! He *was* so funny when he did that. And she knew him well enough to know why it was. Something stirred in her beside amusement – something warm and glad and curiously inspiriting.

'But one has got to go on accepting them,' he went on. 'It's a great thing to recognise the fact, but the job isn't over and done once and for all, just by recognition. One must adapt and express that in terms of one's circumstances.'

Grace began to smile. 'Yes, yes, Walter – how true!' He turned and stared at her, incredulous. 'Walter darling, I'm not the Central Hall, Westminster,' she said, suddenly bursting into laughter – he looked so funny, with his solemn formality still like a garment on his face, and astonishment looking out of his eyes. She couldn't help it. 'Must you say it so preachily?' she said, made incorrigibly gay by that warm inner happiness.

Walter stood stock still, and stared at her for a moment. Then he too laughed. Suddenly he took her arm. 'Amongst other things you've evidently acquired a superiority complex,' he said, almost as gay as she. She stood so, facing him, smiling – one of those moments of reassurance which glow in the face like a pharos at sea. And then, slowly, her face changed. The light somehow went out of it.

'What is it?' Walter asked.

'Rose! I'd forgotten all about her!'

'What about Rose?' he asked, in a tone of almost honest wonder.

'That's just it, Walter; what about Rose?' Her eyes searched his face.

Walter said, very stiffly – 'I think you were always exceedingly foolish and unjust about poor Rose; you—'

She interrupted, with a hand on his arm – 'Walter, don't *please* say that I worked myself up!'

For the second time in two minutes he first stared, and then laughed. 'Very well – you didn't work yourself up! I didn't know that was a phobia of yours, that phrase.'

'Oh, such a phobia! You can't think how I hate it. It always seemed the most unjust thing of all.'

Something in the fall of her voice on those last words opened all sorts of doors and windows in Walter Kilmichael's mind. Though he had missed his wife, more than he would admit even to himself, though he had wanted her back and worried over her disappearance, he had always thought her departure entirely without reason or justification, one of those mad emotional caprices of women which, to do her justice, had startled him in his Grace. But he was a person of sufficient sensibility to recognise freely that pain beyond a certain point is a reason, if not a justification, for almost anything. In this conversation which they had just had Grace had said nothing at all, save by implication, about the reasons for her leaving home – she had gone straight and fearlessly to a recognition of her own past faults and failures, and their causes; there had not been a single syllable either of complaint or justification. It was only now that those last words slipped out, on the heels of a bit of gay teasing, and the tone in which they were spoken suddenly revealed to him depths of pain and distress which explained almost anything. Unreasonable, mistaken this pain might have been, but of its reality he could not doubt – and it gave him a shock, the more so from the casual manner of the revelation. She had certainly not been working herself up this time! Seen in the light of that pain, her letter about Rose, which he had thought so uncalled-for and silly, looked quite different – and his own aloof and ignoring answer looked different too. He had thought that all artificial, a sham – 'worked up', in fact; and he hated shams. He saw now that it had at least been completely sincere. And having gone off goaded by that degree of pain, his heart commended her for having nevertheless seen what she had seen and got where she had got – and still more, in these moments of explanation, for her silence on the subject till now.

But Englishmen whose hearts commend their wives are apt to give that commendation expression in rather singular ways. Walter's way on this occasion was first to address to his wife a little sermon about Mrs Barum. His sense of dignity would not allow him initially either to admit an error of taste or judgement on his own part, or to suggest anything so crude as jealousy on hers. He just explained, in civilised and lucid phrases, how useful a person of Mrs Barum's equipment could be and had been to him, especially in the preparation of his new book, which was appearing in a fortnight. He emphasised Rose's generosity about giving her time and trouble, 'without any sort of return,' and her disinterested love of the work and the subject for its own sake. As he spoke Grace had a curious feeling that he was being a little bit more than fair to Rose, in the way one is overfair to people when one has an impulse to be slightly unfair or unkind to them. It was an oddly reassuring feeling. But now the book was done, Walter went on, and Rose and her Nathaniel were presently going off to South America for a year to study the effect of Latin racial psychology on the economic aspects of modern life; he was sure that they would make a remarkably fine thing of it. (Was it her fancy, or did his tone express something like relief – so that's the end of that!) At last, speaking more stiffly than ever – 'If I had in the least realised,' Walter said, 'that our really purely professional association might give rise to any talk or ideas which could cause you distress, I imagine I should have done something about it. But such a notion never occurred to me, till later.'

Her generosity sprang to meet him. 'Yes, I am sure of that. It was just my silliness, Walter. No one else would have been so stupid. I apologise, my dear.'

But that generosity turned a last key in the many locked doors of his reserve.

'No,' he said. 'Gina had the same idea.'

'*Gina?*' She was as much vexed as astonished. 'But how could she? I never said a word to her – or to anyone. What *can* she have been thinking of?'

'Like a good many other people, she was thinking about why you had left home,' he answered, rather drily. 'But she considered that I had given you some cause. She gave me a most tremendous dressing-down one day.' He smiled rather wryly at the recollection.

'But Walter, it wasn't only – that – that made me feel I must go away. It was quite as much Linnet as Rose – more, really.'

Generosity and candour can almost overreach themselves sometimes. Told thus plainly that his daughter mattered as much or more to his wife than he did himself, Walter Kilmichael again smiled a little wryly. He knew it was true. But whose fault was that? It did not alter his heart's commendation, nor his new unformulated sense of hope and assurance – it was just Grace all over to say it like that.

'I know,' he said. And then he moved briskly away from the subject that had now been liquidated. 'I say, where are we? Oughtn't we to be getting back?'

They had wandered far along, among the villas and gardens, and were above the harbour. Grace agreed, with a glance at her watch. 'But do you mind if we drop down here and go back through the town, Walter? I never brought my picture back from the cloister, with all these doings. I don't think I'd better leave it there all night.'

So they found their way down and went in through the Porta Ploce and along the Stradone, talking quite easily now. Passing M. Kraljic's shop, Walter's eye was caught by his treasures. 'This fellow has some nice stuff,' he said, pausing.

'Yes. He talks English,' she warned him, in a lowered tone. 'Look – you stay and look at them if you want to, while I slip across to the cloister. It's just there. But don't get Linnet a bracelet,' she added, 'because I got her one this afternoon. Get her earrings, or one of those gold bags.' It never occurred to her that Walter would be buying a present for anyone but Linnet. Happy and relieved, she went over and into the cloister. There was no picture there – stool, easel and all were gone. Nicholas had probably fetched them for her – kind child. She went back to M. Kraljic's.

Within, chests had been opened – articles of superior virtue, not usually disclosed, lay spread about; M. Kraljic's singular English was flowing in an appealing torrent. Walter looked round as she came in; he had in his hands a very wonderful garniture in wrought-silver chain-work – a heavy necklace, a great brooch three inches across, earrings and bracelets to match, all taking the shape of venetian windows, with their fine fretted points. It was the most beautiful example of its kind that Grace had ever seen. 'Oh, what a lovely thing!' she exclaimed. 'M. Kraljic, you never showed me that!'

'Expensif! Madame,' M. Kraljic bowed. 'Gentleman not mind.'

'You're not to ruin the gentleman – he's my husband,' said Grace firmly.

'Do you like it?' Walter asked.

'Oh yes, Walter, it's a beautiful thing. But isn't it a little heavy, perhaps, for her?'

'For whom?'

'Linnet. She's so slight. I don't know – she could keep it for later.'

'This is for *you*,' he said. 'Very well – I'll take that. Do it up, will you?' he said to M. Kraljic. 'I'll come and settle with you tomorrow – I'm at the Imperial.'

'Yes, sir! Very well, sir! Perfectly good, sir! No hurry, sir! This lady's gentleman quite all right, sir!' said M. Kraljic, hurrying to envelop the jewellery in his green and white flowered paper.

'But Walter *dear*! For *me*?' She was almost too astonished to speak.

'Is there any special reason why I shouldn't give you a present?' he asked, rather formally.

So his heart's commendation found its second and to him perfectly satisfactory expression in an expensive present – which is also a very English way of doing things.

TWENTY-FOUR

As Grace and Sir Walter entered the garden of the Imperial they encountered Linnet and Nicholas, coming in from the opposite direction.

'Hullo, darling, have you and Nicholas been for a walk?'

'Yes – somewhere. Mums, this is a divine place; such incredible plants and things.'

'We went to the Dance,' said Nicholas. 'I found her rather straying when I got back from embarking the family.'

'Straying! Mums, do they have cocktails here?'

'Yes, pet – but come and dress first and have one when you're ready, if there's time. The Grk is better than the cocktails – it's like the most lovely sherry. Do you want a bath?'

Nicholas and Linnet had had a rather mutually instructive walk. Returning from the re-embarkation of Celia and the General, he had found the girl sitting under the palms, swinging her small white shoes over the edge of a *chaise longue*. On seeing him she at once asked if she couldn't be shown something.

'What?' Nicholas asked rather heavily. He felt singularly reduced by the events of the day, and really only wanted two things – to lie flat on his bed, and to talk to Lady K. about it all. In the ordinary way he could have combined these; she often sat with him while he rested before dinner – it was a convalescent habit which had clung. However, on being told 'Anything!' he led the girl up the hill and out towards the Dance, where he presently insisted on sitting down on one of the frequent seats overlooking the fortress of San Lorenzo and the sea. 'Sorry, but I'm dropping!' he excused himself.

'Are you? Why?'

'Been ill, for one thing – and all these doings are enough to exhaust a cow.'

'Didn't you know your Father was on this cruise?'

'I knew he was cruising somewhere, but I didn't know he'd be coming here.'

'But why didn't they know you were here?' asked Linnet, who was seething with suppressed curiosity.

'Because you see I told Mother I was going on to Greece; but then I got stuck at Komolac with this complaint. And Lady Kilmichael wrote to my Mamma from there. I don't suppose that letter would have given time to catch Father anywhere. But it did give me a shock to see him come walking into that cloister!'

'Nothing like the shock it gave Poppy and me to see Mums come walking in!'

'Why, didn't you know she was here either?'

'Not a notion. She came abroad to paint, and simply sank without trace. That utterly unreliable Lady Roseneath said she'd gone to Greece. Where did *you* meet her?'

'I was introduced to her in Venice by the said Lady Roseneath, who happens to be my Aunt,' said Nicholas. He applied this good stout *suppressio veri* and *suggestio falsi* in the repressive manner which people usually employ for such a purpose.

'Oh, sorry. So she is – I forgot. And then you and Mums just joined forces and painted?'

'That was about it. Lady Kilmichael was extraordinarily kind about helping me. But then she's an extraordinarily kind person.'

Linnet was a little intimidated by his manner. She had expected this comparing notes to be more fruitful – the young could generally get on very well discussing the peculiarities of the old, however tolerantly. But the yellow-headed young man had a curious knack of infusing a touch of dignity into his replies which made further questions unexpectedly difficult, and clearly he was going to leave 'Lady Kilmichael' to tell anything there was to be told, in her own way. Linnet gave it up, and shifted her ground.

'Yes, Mums is quite a lamb,' she said, very airily, because she was a little nettled. 'For a person of her generation she's really rather good.'

'Have you found many people of your own generation with half her equipment?' the young man asked, caustically.

Linnet stared at him. 'Her equipment? Oh, you mean her painting?'

'I wasn't thinking of her painting – though that's incredibly good.'

'What do you mean, then?' She wasn't nettled now – she was most genuinely astonished. Mums's *equipment*? What could he mean?

'Her intelligence – and all the things she knows. You hardly ever come across anyone with so many interests, or so well-informed. I think she's probably the wisest and the most interesting person I've ever known.' He shot a glance at her, sideways, and seeing her astonished face said, with a rather sour touch of amusement – 'Has it never struck you that your Mother is rather a remarkable person?'

'I never thought of her as particularly *intelligent*,' said Linnet, startled into complete candour. 'Of course she's terribly attractive, and has a wonderful gift for clothes – I give you her being fearfully good-looking.' And she in her turn glanced at him sideways, with considerable interest. But –

'I wasn't thinking of that,' said this extraordinary young man. 'I suppose she is – or at least I suppose she was when she was younger. But I meant—'

'But what nonsense!' Linnet interrupted, roused now herself to her Mother's defence, on more familiar ground. 'Mums is frightfully decorative – surely you must see that? After all, you've painted her!'

'I daresay – I honestly never thought about it,' he said. 'She has a wonderful face to paint, because – well, because of what she is, and because she has good bones.' He stood up. 'Hadn't we better be getting back?'

But all the way back to the hotel Linnet was as it were staring at a new picture of her Mother. Mums intelligent, well-informed, wise, wonderful! And thought so, not by some mouldering elder, who would be carried away by her charm – of course Mums had tons of charm – but by this really rather entertaining young man, who had never even noticed that she was good-looking! Idiot! Mums was really almost lovely, sometimes, although she did practically nothing about it, bar dressing so well. It really was most extraordinary. And she continued, with deepened interest, to study the young man, who was beguiling the way with a rather amusing account of some peasants they had visited in the interior somewhere. He was really quite witty at times. H'm. Well. And that night before she went to bed Linnet began a last letter to her best friend.

> Mums is here! We cannoned into her, entirely without warning, in a cloister today. Poppy nearly had a heart attack! Here and hereabouts is where she's been all the time, painting and teaching a young man to paint. Poppy and I are skipping Venice and staying here for two or three days, really to allow time for a leisurely reconciliation, I suppose – we shall be picked up again when the *Star* dips southward once more. The parents are being very parental, but they've had one walk and seem pretty serene. The final touch is that Mums *has* got a boyfriend! Very much so – twenty-three-ish; the one she's been teaching to paint. Really rather a charmer – definitely one of the nicest seen for ages. He's completely *toqué* about Mums, but whether she spots it or not I'm not *quite* sure. I can't begin to describe the flap that has raged here today, because the young man is

the General's son (I always said heredity was tripe) and *they* didn't know he was here either! It was *coup de théâtre* after *coup de théâtre*, as we all kept meeting long-lost relatives all over the town, and trying to explain. Final sensation occurred when Daddy's Frenchman off the boat, who's Mums's Paris dealer, spotted one of the boy's pictures and raved about it. Mums seems to have coached him to some purpose; anyhow the old fish instantly cornered the whole visible supply for vast sums in cash and Nicholas is now a made man and can snap the fingers at his parents! All *too* unreal. It has been fun to watch.

Something has come over Mums. She's got very definite, all of a sudden – *handling* everything and everyone in the most unwonted way. You should have seen her with the General! I hope it won't go too far. At present she's rather sweet – *une femme magistrale*, but gentle.

But in the interval before dinner Linnet wasted no time on letter-writing, but applied all her attention to her appearance. This might seem a singular perversity and waste of effort on her part, since the only immediate young man had just shown himself so markedly unappreciative of female looks; but even very intelligent people of nineteen do not always think out the things which affect themselves with quite the devastating clearness which they apply to their elders' affairs, and indeed the instinct which governs feminine dressing lies almost below the threshold of consciousness. When Linnet Kilmichael went back to the ship to 'garner her effects' she had, in all her competent haste, garnered two or three of those dresses which in London had proved most efficacious. Into one of these she now inserted herself, and with hair shining subtly along the waves, perfectly arranged complexion, and lips and fingertips matching in carmine brilliance, she went down to dinner.

Lady Kilmichael, however, had also made a special effort in

the matter of a toilette that night. She did so quite deliberately, with the businesslike thoroughness of the woman who dresses for occasions rather than for persons. This was an occasion, in a mild way – Walter liked occasions to be dressed for, and he would expect his present to be worn. Lady Kilmichael was one of those happy women who go on into middle life looking well in white – by good luck, she had a white evening dress with her which would show off the silver jewellery to perfection. So to please Walter – dear Walter! and he seemed altogether in a mood to be pleased – she very much did her best with herself; she was happy too, tonight, and presently came trailing down to dinner clothed in a singular radiance. Walter fairly stared at her – he had forgotten that Grace ever looked like that. Linnet exclaimed over the garniture, which did indeed give the last touch – its barbaric splendour heightening and emphasising that quiet civilised grace. But Nicholas first stood, and afterwards at table sat, entirely unable to take his eyes off her. What with working late, with evening walks, and frequently dining out in little restaurants, he had seen very little of Lady Kilmichael in evening dress – and it may be that Linnet's indignant remarks about her Mother's looks had opened his eyes to other aspects of her appearance than those he knew and loved – her smile, the sweetness and candour by which her eyes were made beautiful, the transparent changefulness of expression which made watching her face almost as good as talking to her. Beauty he had never looked for in her, beyond the beauty of 'good bones' and supple muscles, which he had appreciated with professional detachment; beauty now he found, and it left him dumb.

Altogether, to Nicholas, that dinner was a discouraging meal. Though they were all very nice to him, they so evidently belonged together; they had so much to hear and tell of matters in which he had no real part or interest – what the twins were doing, Nigel's last discoveries at the end of the Easter vac, details of the cruise. They all tried to bring him in, and when Grace's discoveries of the West Highland stones were being canvassed, for instance, he had a brief place. But it meant trying; he wasn't really in. Lady Kilmichael had been so much *his* Lady K. these last weeks – her sympathy, her interest all for him; now she was theirs, and that man, so witty and so distinguished, was her husband. There *was* a prick in that – a prick which he shied away from. And he kept on remembering also that she was really Grace Stanway, the painter with an international reputation – and he had once told her that she couldn't draw! Yes – although she had worked all these miracles for him today, with his Father and that old Frenchman, miracles which even now he could hardly realise or believe in – he, Nicholas, a man of independent means, and free forever to be a painter, with his parents' sanction! – he remained unexhilarated; he felt diminished, unhappy, forlorn. It was senseless and ungrateful, but it was so. And when Sir Walter made them drink to his health and his future success, though he laughed and made some mild witticism in response, his eyes were curiously unhappy when he turned them again to Lady Kilmichael.

All this was not lost on Grace. She realised that something must be done about Nicholas. She would rather have put it off till the next day, but she couldn't let him go to bed with eyes like that! And this new power that had come to her, of seeing which were the important things and going for them first, made it almost easy for her to break up this first evening with her family, a thing that normally she would have found embarrassing and difficult to a degree. When they had drunk their coffee, sitting out under the illuminated palms in the garden, she said with a sort of airy decision – 'Walter, I'm going to take Nicholas to show him a view of San Lorenzo that I think he might do in this light – moonlight and lamplight.' She rose as she spoke, and pulled a fur round her shoulders.

'Oh yes – a walk would be heavenly. Do let's all go!' Linnet said eagerly – her energy and vivacity quite undimmed. Very serenely her Mother turned to her. 'Yes, do, darling – take your Father to see the Porta Ploce; it's quite marvellous in this light. We've often seen it.' And quietly, graciously, but with unmistakeable decision she led Nicholas out of the garden, leaving Linnet almost staring after her. Mums so high hat! The odd thing, Linnet later noted, was that though she had wanted to go for a walk and was done out of it, because Poppy was tired and wouldn't, for some mysterious reason she harboured no irritation against her Mother this time. She had been told exactly where she got off, she freely admitted, but done like that, it didn't seem so tiresome. And presently she went in and wrote her letter.

Nicholas and Lady Kilmichael strolled down the hill, through the warm southern dark splashed richly with the light from the street lamps, and out onto the little promenade below the Forte Bocar. A restaurant stands at one side of this promenade, and they went and sat down at one of the little tables nearest the sea, ordering vermouth as an excuse. It was late, and there were very few people about; such as there were were congregated in the brightly lit space immediately in front of the restaurant, playing cards or gossiping – but out where they sat it was quiet and empty; in the shadows the water lapped gently on the stonework within a few feet of them. Opposite and above them loomed the great bulk of San Lorenzo, rather masked by the nearer buildings in front of it; but its summit, rising clear from the patchwork of light and shadow which flecked these lesser buildings, shone white and splendid in the moonlight.

'You *don't* see it so frightfully well from here, Lady K.,' Nicholas observed, with his grin.

'No, it's not as good as I expected. But I really suggested it because I thought you wanted to talk,' she said, without any embarrassment.

'What a sensitive person you are!' he said. 'Of course I did – frightfully; only I didn't see how it could be managed.'

'Almost anything can really be managed,' she said easily.

'By you, it seems it can. You've managed enough today!' he responded. Then they went on to talk about M. Breuil and the arrangements with him, and the future, and whether Nicholas should try to put in some time with Moru, or spend a year working by himself first, to 'settle down into his own ideas,' as she said. Nicholas was astounded, glad, and abundantly grateful; but rather to her surprise she found that a sort of nervous reaction had already set in – he doubted if he would really be able to do as much as Breuil wanted. 'I realise that he's only bought these things of mine as a spec,' he ended up – 'and suppose I prove a bad spec?'

'That's his lookout,' she told him. 'Breuil can look after himself very, very well, I assure you! But I'm not in the least afraid of your not coming up to his expectations.'

'It's the expectations that give me nerves. And if I get nerves I simply *can't* work. *What* an unfortunate temperament to possess!' he said gloomily. 'I feel that I could have got on so much better for the next two years with nobody but you thinking I was any good at all.'

'Yes, but then you'd have been architecting all the time and made very little headway. No, don't *fuss*, Nicholas – just go quietly ahead doing your best in your own way.' She paused, and then said – 'Breuil believes that one of these days you'll be far better than me.'

His answer surprised her. 'I think that perhaps I shall be, one day, in painting,' he said, with that odd honesty of his. 'You see I shall be a whole-timer and a whole-hogger, and you can't be ever either.' He looked at her. 'Is it loathsome of me to say that?' She shook her head. 'You needn't grudge it me, though I know you could never grudge anyone anything,' he continued, 'because in everything else I shall never come near you.'

She found it hard to answer that, and before she could manage it he went on again.

'*You*'ve done all this for me today,' he said, 'and it's quite a bit; got round my Father, and fixed up with the old beaver – oh yes, I know quite well that *you* really worked that! You've changed my whole life in a few hours. But even that isn't the main thing you've done for me – and nor is all you've done for my painting, though that's enormous too, and I'm not near the end of it yet; what I shall get out of it, I mean.'

'You know I've enjoyed whatever I did – but especially the painting; the rest really sort of happened,' said Grace gently.

'Yes, I believe you do really enjoy doing things for people,' he said; 'that's just the point.' He paused, and then went on in a sort of burst, as if he were afraid that unless he said it quickly he would never get it out at all – 'You see you've made me realise that there's a way of living that I didn't know about – it's like seeing a view one's painted oneself over and over again, treated by someone else, in an entirely new way.'

'Have I?' she said. 'What sort of way of living, dear child?' She was honestly interested and surprised about this.

'I can't say those things – but generously, without fear; and with such perfect honesty.'

The tears came into her eyes then – it was so incredible of him to make the effort to get that out, to say these things that the young find it so impossible to say. This was a very rare offering that he was laying before her, who was so conscious of her own cowardices and failings.

'It's darling of you to say that, dear Nicholas,' she said softly and steadily – 'but really I'm not like what you think. And I've not done anything in particular for you that I can see, except nursing you, and a little coaching. All the rest has been such fun, and so happy.' She paused. 'Keeping it light' wasn't perfectly easy just now. And for once Nicholas was not to be put off – his hour was on him, and he would not be denied.

'You're like those people in the New Testament, who'd no idea they'd ever been in the least good,' he said, with an indescribable inflection of amusement in his voice, even then. 'Do you remember? 'When did *we* ever feed the hungry or tend the sick or visit the prisoners? We've not done a thing.' But they were called blessed, all the same.'

And to that really portentous compliment Grace Kilmichael found no answer at all. She sat in silence, her tears falling onto the white dress that she had put on to please Walter. This kind of devotion – what was there like it, and where would she ever find it again? What had she given, what had she to give, that this did not outweigh? She turned her head away, seawards, and felt in her bag for a handkerchief. The next moment he spoke again, in a different tone.

'I want you to understand that I don't *want* anything,' he said. 'I shall be perfectly content to go on all my life thinking you the most wonderful person in the world. You don't mind that, do you?'

'No,' she said. 'I shall value it.' There was so much she could have said, but better not – so much better not. She had withheld, withdrawn, kept herself in so long – it would be foolish to fail at the last. 'You have made me very happy, my darling child,' she said, 'all the time, and now. And you've taught me a lot, too.' (Here was a ladder to climb out on.)

'*I* have?'

'Yes – all about people of your age. You see I never was *friends* with anyone young before – only a parent or an Aunt or something. But you've let me in – into your mind – and I'm sure that's going to help me no end with Linnet.' (They were well up the ladder now.)

'I'm very glad of that,' he said. They were silent for some time.

At last he said, in quite a matter-of-fact voice – 'Linnet's very pretty – you never told me she was as pretty as that.'

'No – I think it's so unfair to praise them too much – it makes people hate them,' she answered. (Now they were right at the top of the ladder.)

'She's not really like you,' he said, his eyes searching her shadowed face.

'No, she isn't – she's Walter's child.' Then – 'What do you make of her?' she said. She did so much want Nicholas to appreciate Linnet.

'She's sweet,' Nicholas said unhesitatingly. 'But rather silly, don't you think? I suppose it's because she's so young.'

'Silly? Linnet? Nicholas, what *can* you mean?'

'I'm sorry,' he said. 'But I do think she's silly. She's awfully unperceptive. I think it's just her age – I daresay she'll grow out of it.'

Grace smiled in the dark at the severe patronage extended by twenty-two to the shortcomings of nineteen. 'You're quite wrong about her being unperceptive,' she said. 'She's appallingly sharp. Why do you say that?'

He ignored the question.

'I hate all that make-up too,' he pursued. 'Why must she?'

'Well, try and stop her if you can. I shall bless you if you succeed!' she said gaily.

'I'd like you to bless me,' he said. He fell silent then – Grace thought he was thinking about Linnet's nails, and his next words were utterly unexpected.

'Lady K., shall I ever see you again?'

Something that was really near to desolation in his tone took her completely by surprise, shook her almost out of her self-control. She wanted, as she had hardly ever wanted anything in her life, to put her arms round him and say, 'My darling! my darling! Yes, always – whenever you want to!' She waited rather a long time before she said, 'But of *course*, my dearest child! Whenever you're in London I shall always expect you to stop with us, unless you want to be elsewhere. And I want you to come down to Netherstoke this very summer – we're always there all July, till we go to Scotland. There's rather a lot to paint in the Cotswolds – and perhaps if you're there I shall do more work.' She rose – this really must come to an end. 'Come on! We ought to go back. Aren't you dead?'

'Pretty well,' he said. And as they walked back across the little promenade – 'What a happy day!' said Nicholas.

Walter was still on the terrace when they got back to the Imperial, smoking a cigar in a long chair. Nicholas went off to bed, but Grace sat down with her husband. 'Well, did you have a nice talk?' Walter asked.

'Yes, very nice. I had to go, Walter – he needed it,' she said, with her usual simplicity in the choice of words.

'Of course he needed it,' Walter said, 'poor little beast!' This was one of Walter's terms of appreciation; his application of it to Nicholas made her turn and look at him curiously. So he *had* understood without being told. 'I suppose it was his illness that did it?' Walter went on.

'No, it began before that,' she said very simply. 'I don't think the illness had much to do with it, except that he couldn't get away. I went away first; but he came after me, because he didn't understand then – and then he meant to go away, and got ill that very night. So there we were, stuck.'

Walter burst out laughing. 'I like your way of describing your romance,' he said. His laughter was so reassuring that Grace laughed too.

'It isn't a romance, Walter – don't be so silly. It isn't anything very much.'

'No, but it seems a whole heap while it's going on, especially at his age,' he said. 'I like him, Grace – he's very good class.'

This phrase of Walter's had a purely moral and intellectual connotation, and was one of his highest terms of approbation. She was absurdly pleased. 'Yes, he is,' she said. 'I'm so glad you see the point of him, Walter.' She got up. 'I think I shall go to bed,' she said. 'I'm rather tired tonight.'

'Yes, do go – I'm sure you'd better,' said Walter equably. 'Emotional crises are very exhausting.'

TWENTY-FIVE

Lady Kilmichael spent most of the next day finishing off her two pictures, while Linnet and Sir Walter saw sights, driving in the most powerful car which Ragusa afforded to Cavtat and Cannosa. If Walter wondered whether this haste betokened a decision to return with them, he kept his speculations to himself, and Grace said nothing. Once more she and Nicholas lunched together in the restaurant in the Via del Levante, on the little terrace close up under the green pattern of the walnut leaves. She was pleased to find Nicholas in a singularly easy and unembarrassed mood, chattering away as he had not done since his illness. It was as if his talk with her the night before had relieved him of some burden, freed him from some weight of repression; watching him and laughing back at him, she wondered if the Professor had after all been right, and if she had made a mistake not to afford him an opportunity of speaking much sooner. No, she thought, probably not; it might all have been different if it had come sooner. The fact of Walter and Linnet being there, the visible presence of a husband and a grown-up daughter, had almost certainly had its effect on him; modified the quality of his avowal, bringing it within the limits of the actual and, so to speak, the possible. He had given his feelings expression – and to her how more than adequately! – but he had said nothing that either of them need ever be embarrassed to remember. To her frugal and practical mind this was the great thing. Look how unembarrassed he was even now! Whereas if it had all been more like that night in the villa garden – well, for one thing she herself might not have managed to keep her own feelings out of it as much as she had done. It was very well as it was.

In the afternoon she finished her picture of the Duomo. Nicholas came to carry it back to the hotel for her just as she was fastening it up. 'I say, let me look!' he protested. In silence she did so. He peered at it curiously. On the steps of the Duomo there was now a figure, dwarfed by distance and by the heavy rococo architectural masses behind it; very solitary, very small; a tiny flake of yellow for its head. The young man gave her an odd look – 'Is that me?' he said, with the ghost of a grin.

'It's a vision I had of you!' she said, blushing a little.

'Oh well, I like being a vision – it's not my usual idea of myself!' he said, grinning broadly now. 'Lady K., you are rather a duck!'

Next day after lunch Grace took Walter out to Komolac to see the Professor. Linnet and Nicholas were going to Lapad to bathe, and they dropped them at Gruz, where the roads fork at the end of the harbour. Walter had got the large car again – the quickest and simplest (and therefore usually also the most expensive) modes of locomotion were those which he preferred. As they bowled along the river road they overtook the Komolac bus; Walter watched its bouncings and lurchings ahead of them with a fixed and censorious eye, and when they were safely past observed – 'That looks an incredibly dangerous concern.'

'I sat on a monk's lap in that once,' Grace said cheerfully.

'Oh? For how long?' Walter asked, turning an eye now as sardonic as Halther's on his wife. There was a little surprise in Walter's eye too – Grace had lost a lot of her primness, shyness, whatever it was that used to make her so timid about what people thought of her, since she came on this trip. It really had made her a much more amusing companion.

'For miles! All the way from Gruz to opposite Rožat – I'll show you.'

'Is this another boyfriend of yours? And am I to meet him too?' Walter enquired.

Grace gave a gurgling laugh – he hadn't heard her laugh like that for he didn't know how long, except sometimes with the boys.

'No – he was just a pick-up! One sits on everyone in the morning bus, because it's so full, and I happened to sit on him. He held me round the waist to keep me from falling off,' she added complacently, 'and talked to me in French all the time. He was really very civil.'

'*Very!*' was Walter's comment. 'And did nothing more come of this promising opening?'

'No. He did ask me to go to tea and see the cloister – look, that's it, Walter, across the river – that hill with the pines and the campanile – but then Nicholas got ill, and I couldn't.'

As they entered Komolac Grace made the driver slow down, so that she could show Walter the Restauracija Tete Mare, standing up square and white in the sunshine at the water's edge. The Signor Antonio, coming back from his siesta to Pavlé Burié's office, paused as usual to gaze with interest at the strange car, and recognised her – he came up with a flourish of his hat and loud exclamations of pleasure. There were introductions, enquiries for Nicholas; and Lady Kilmichael had to promise to go and call on the Signora presently. While this conversation was in progress the bus arrived, and pulled up at its usual halting-place; the conductor also recognised Lady Kilmichael, and hurried over to ask after the Signorino. When at last they moved on, the car had gathered very little speed before they came to the inn; the innkeeper, seated among the oleanders before his door, instantly recognised the Gospodja, and rose with loud cries. The car stopped again, and this time they were forced to get out and drink a glass of Grk. 'Really, Grace, if these are your and your friends' habits! Drinks at half-past three!' said Walter, scandalised.

'Nonsense!' Grace replied, gurgling again – 'this is a special occasion. We never came here before six as a rule.'

'Who were 'we'?'

'Me and Nicholas – and generally the Signor Antonio too. You see this inn is practically a 'tied house' of Pavlé Burié,' she explained, 'and of course he never gave the Signor Antonio anything but the best – nor us either, after a bit. Sometimes we had something at the cellars up the road, but generally we came here. It *was* fun.'

'So I should think!' said Walter drily. But there was nothing desiccating in his dryness, and when the innkeeper brought out some special Grk, eight years old, and he heard his wife comparing its merits with that of the wonderful five-year-old vintage, now 'coming on,' and telling him, Walter, to look out for the special aromatic quality of the wine in his glass – 'rosemary is the nearest thing to compare it to, Walter – just a breath of rosemary' – he could hardly have said if he was more astonished or pleased. If Grace was going to start taking an interest in wine! And she was right about the rosemary.

'Well, have we got to call on any more of your boyfriends, or can we go to the Professor now?' he asked as they got into the car again.

'No – there aren't any more. *A destra!*' she called to the driver, and they turned into the lane and stopped at the villa gate.

Dr Halther, roused by Maria's nasal and joyful screams of welcome and announcement, emerged onto the veranda. '*Also endlich!* (So at last!) he said, as he bowed over Lady Kilmichael's hand and kissed it – 'And this is your husband?' And he bowed, heels together, to Sir Walter, who raised his hat and bowed in return.

'Yes – but how did you know? You weren't expecting us?'

'Already yesterday I was hoping that you might remember how much I admire Sir Walter's books, and bring him to see me,' he said, smiling broadly at her mystification. 'I am delighted to meet you,' he said courteously to Walter.

'But how *could* you know that he was here?' said Grace, still bewildered, as he led them across the garden to the chairs under the ilex.

'It was the old Breuil,' he said, waving them into seats. 'He has seen this very impertinent picture which young Humphries makes of me, abject before Maria's tongue! – and finding thus that I am here, he has telephoned. I drove in and dined with him before he went back to the ship. He told me that your husband is here, and also the Herr General.'

'Then I suppose he told you about Nicholas too?' said Grace.

'He tells me first of all, and with great triumph, that he has discovered the talent of the century,' Halther said, with his peculiar combination of the benign and the sardonic in his expression, 'and that he has made a contract with him. I ask him how the difficulties with the Herr Papa are overcome, and he says that he ignores this altogether – '*Je paye, moi; pour le reste, Madame s'en charge!*' He reproduced M. Breuil's accent of incisive indifference so exactly that Grace and Walter both laughed.

'Poor Madame had rather a tough time with the General,' said Walter, 'but she brought it off.'

'Madame can, I think, bring anything off if she applies herself to it,' Halther replied. 'But, *gnädige Frau*, how you have deceived me!' he added, turning to her.

'Deceived you? I?'

'For over a fortnight I meet, for over a week I have under my roof one of the two modern artists whose work I most admire, but which, because of the cupidity of the old Breuil, I can never afford to buy!' he said, shaking his forefinger at her accusingly.

'I was incognito,' said Grace gaily. 'That isn't deceit!'

'You hide your pictures,' he went on – 'I do not see one stroke of your brush but the under-painting of a single *toile*, this day by the river. If I had seen a picture I should have known. Is not this deceit?' he asked, turning to Sir Walter.

'Odious deceit,' agreed Walter. He was beginning to like the Professor, and it amused him to hear him ragging Grace.

'That wasn't deliberate,' said Grace, also amused.

The Professor looked from her to Walter and back again, as if weighing something in his mind, before he spoke next.

'And this lady who is not clever, whose lack of intelligence so troubles her, is famous throughout Europe and America! For all this lack of intelligence, she is an artist whose work only millionaires can afford!'

Walter glanced with raised eyebrows at the Professor at this speech, and then at Grace. She blushed a little, but answered readily enough.

'I don't think intelligence and painting have really much to do with one another,' she said. 'People can paint fearfully well and yet be very stupid about living; in fact I think the better they are at painting the stupider they are about all the rest. Look at Emanuel James! He's quite good in any simple straightforward crisis, like people dying, or a motor smash, but he's almost idiotic about daily life and human beings.'

Walter listened to this interchange with considerable curiosity. Grace and the Professor had evidently got onto what he called very rational terms; but that wasn't a thing Grace usually did with anyone. And though she might have recognised that she was stupid, since when had she learned to talk about it in this easy way? For she went on, the next moment, since the Professor merely grinned at her – '*That* certainly wasn't deceiving you – to tell you I wasn't clever. You can ask my husband. He'll bear me out.' And she glanced, with a very serene little smile, at Walter.

'My dear Grace!' Walter protested. 'Have I ever said you weren't intelligent?'

'Oh, Walter *darling*! Where *do* you expect to go?' She turned to the Professor. 'Doctor Halther, I promised that I would go and see the Signora – will you excuse me if I go now and then come back for tea? We want to stay for tea!'

'That you must! Do this, *gnädige Frau*!'

'And you can cross-examine him while I'm away!' she said, nodding at her husband. 'No, don't get up! I'll come back as quickly as I can.' And she went off, leaving the two men under the ilex.

It is not easy to pay a surprise visit in Komolac. Lady Kilmichael found the whole establishment at the Tete Mare hoping expectantly for her appearance; the Signora in her best black sprigged dress, Teta setting out coffee cups in the garden. She answered the enquiries about Nicholas, described the sudden arrival of her husband and her daughter, and heard such local news as there was.

'And now with your *famiglia* you return home, back to *Inghilterra*?' the Signora asked at length.

Grace answered – '*Si, domani, probabilmente*' before she thought what she was saying. She laughed then. The Signora smiled too – she thought the English lady was laughing with happiness at the idea of going home. And Grace was in fact happy as well as amused to find that her decision to go back with the others next day had taken itself so easily that she had never noticed it.

Before she left she asked the Signora to let her go up to her old room. She stood looking out through the window to the cypresses on the island, whose shadows were beginning to slant through air which looked almost as solid as clear gold, so thick all through it lay the afternoon sunshine. As she stood there, the flock of pigeons wheeled out over the river, circled round those grey-green spires, and returned; she watched them, remembering how in her first days at Komolac their flight had seemed to her an image of her own freedom. Now she was going back to her old life, to the prison-house, as she had thought it then, from which she had escaped; but she was going gladly and without dismay.

A sound roused her, shattering the afternoon stillness outside – the grinding rattle of the bus, setting off on its return journey to Gruz. She watched it, from the other window, pass in its cloud of white dust along the road. The last time she had heard the bus set off, in this room, was the morning of Nicholas's illness, when she believed that he was on it – and she remembered how she had lain in bed, startled almost to indignation at the unexpected pain of parting from him. Well, she was going to part from him tomorrow – and no one was going to Greece this time! But somehow the pain was much less sharp. She would miss him; she would love him – not always, but probably for a long time, she thought, with her inveterate honesty and moderation – but there were all the other people she loved so much too, Linnet and the boys and Walter. Remembering the sharpness of that past pain, she had a sense of having emerged from a dream into waking reality, where familiar figures stood all about her, instead of just one face of dream-enchantment. Nicholas wasn't a dream, of course, and she recognised honestly the depth of her feeling for him; but somehow that feeling was now *manageable* – she need not feel indignant at its tyranny. 'Perhaps this is freedom, too,' she thought, as she went downstairs.

Tea was already laid, out by the fountain, when she got back to the villa, and Walter and the Professor were discussing the relation of philosophy to the higher mathematics with every appearance of satisfaction. She poured out for them, without joining in the conversation – it gave her immense pleasure to watch them together, to note the interest in each face, the quick response of one mind to the other which their tones of voice, more than anything else, betrayed. But they reached a conclusion of some sort, presently, and when tea was over Walter did a thing for which her heart applauded him. While he was here, he said, he ought really to see the source of the Ombla; if Dr Halther would permit, he would go and look at it, and come back and pick up his wife. And he went off, leaving Grace and the Professor together.

When the gate in the hedge had given its familiar click behind Walter, Dr Halther looked across at Lady Kilmichael and said '*Na?*'

She smiled at him, but did not answer at once. She liked the comfortable intimacy of that little monosyllable of interrogation. It was nice to be back here again in the garden, talking to him by herself. How odd it was she thought, that she should want to talk to him by herself; that there should be things she could speak of to him that she did not speak of to Walter. It wasn't exactly having secrets from Walter, it was just that these things belonged to a relationship which was independent of him, which was all her own. It struck her suddenly that this had never happened before; in all her married life, except with women, she had never had a relationship of her own like this. Walter talked to the men; she listened, or went away. Now there were two men, Nicholas and the Professor, with whom it was desirable that she should talk alone, because she had her own relationship with them. And oddest of all was the fact that in spite of the novelty of this situation, Walter should instantly recognise it and sanction it, first with Nicholas, now with the Professor. That was very clever of Walter, and very nice.

'*Na?*' Dr Halther repeated, as she still did not speak.

'I'm very happy,' she said, smiling at him.

'That is good,' he said. 'You have reason, I think. You are fortunate in your husband. I like him extremely. As an intellect I admired him always, but as a man he is also *höchst sympathisch.* I know you deserve your good fortune, but people do not always get what they deserve.'

'No, I know. I'm glad you like him,' she said simply.

They talked for some time then of the Humphries family, of Breuil and his plans for Nicholas, and of her return to England, a move which Dr Halther applauded. At length – 'And the little Nicholas – what does he think of it all?' he asked.

'He's really glad about his work, I think; he was a little bewildered at first.'

'And what does he think about that which is not his work?' he asked, with his remorseless glance.

She laughed. 'I wasn't hedging – I was coming to that! I think that is all right too. We had a talk – after the others had come.'

'Well, and did he open his heart at last, *der arme Junge*?'

She looked ahead of her. 'It was more his spirit,' she said at last. 'He did it – very beautifully, really,' she said, turning to him.

'That I believe. He has great quality. And now?'

She hesitated for a moment. 'I think now' she said, with a slight effort, 'that probably he will very soon fall in love with somebody else, somebody of his own age, which is exactly what he ought to do!'

He gave her a long keen look from under his bushy brows. '*Brava!*' he said at length, significantly.

She widened her eyes at him, at that – and then blushed. 'You are quite right,' she said, with a funny little smile – 'you always know everything! When did you guess?'

'With a person of your honesty and simplicity, this is not so difficult, to know things!' he answered, rather more gravely than she expected. 'When I guessed I am not sure – perhaps from the first. But not from any lack of discretion on your part. It is only that, as you know, I use for others these categories into which we do not care to put ourselves! – and when one sees a woman who is not happy with her family, who feels defeated and a failure, greatly loved and admired by someone else, one shall expect that her heart will make some response!' He paused – his cheroot had gone out, and he threw it away. 'But one thing I saw which I had not expected to see,' he said.

'What was that?'

'Something outside all my categories, *gnädige Frau* – a self-restraint so perfect that it made tenderness unafraid. This cannot have been so easy.'

She blushed deeply at the unexpected praise. 'Thank you,' was all she said.

The latch of the gate clicked again. Dr Halther rose, came over to her, and kissed her hand. 'Your husband also loves you very much!' he said, as Walter came in at the gate.

TWENTY-SIX

Linnet and Nicholas had not returned when the others got back to the Imperial, and when they had bathed and changed, and came down for dinner, there was still no sign of them. 'It's no good waiting,' said Walter, as the clock struck eight – 'Linnet's probably dragged him off to do something quite mad. Let's begin.' They went into the dining room, where the rather good small orchestra was playing at one end, and sat down. But before they were halfway through their soup the pair appeared, newly browned with the sun, sandy, dishevelled, and in tearing spirits. They had had the brilliant idea of chartering the *vecchio piroscafo's* boat and sailing round the Lapad promontory to the bathing beach on the seaward side; and coming back, with the wind against them, they had had to row, and got late. 'So sorry, Mums,' said Linnet nicely, at the end of this recital.

'Well, sit down now, and have some dinner – don't bother to change,' said her father.

'No, I won't change, but I must just tidy up,' she said, rising from the chair into which she had dropped.

'Why? You look perfectly nice as you are,' said Nicholas. 'You won't better yourself!'

'Oh, very well!' she said, sketching the very slightest *moue* at the young man, as she reseated herself and began to look at the menu. Grace noticed that the girl's lips were much less red than usual, and that there was nothing but a touch of powder on her face; she had evidently refrained from making up afresh after her bathe. She smiled to herself – Nicholas was making a beginning with his proposed reforms, it seemed. The pair of them had evidently got onto quite different terms in the course of the day –

they were 'Linnet' and 'Nicholas,' they were teasing and at ease. And she remembered the idea she had had weeks before, of how well they would 'do' for one another. That gave her a small pang, now – and seeing them together, so gay and equal, she thought suddenly 'He doesn't need to forget *her* age!' It was surprising how sharply that hurt. Talking, listening to their adventures, smiling and responding, she fought down this irrational pain. It wasn't what she had gone for, his love and admiration; she hadn't sought it for herself, she had tried honestly to put it aside, to 'let him off his own feelings lightly.' Then what could be better than that he should like Linnet? Why should she mind if it should be taken away, his immediate personal love of her? But though her mind and will obeyed her reason, the place inside still hurt, like the place whence a thorn has been withdrawn. Let it hurt, then, she told herself stoutly, as they passed out onto the terrace for coffee; and it continued to do so, obediently, when Nicholas, having given her her cup as she liked it, sat down on the further side of the little table to pursue some argument with Linnet. She talked quietly with Walter, but the effort was fantastically severe; it actually made her head ache. And then the orchestra began to play 'Morgen', with a clarinet solo.

Lady Kilmichael pushed her chair a little further back, into the shadow of a palm. She heard Nicholas interrupt Linnet with 'Half-a-minute – do you mind? I want to listen to this.' As the secretive melody was gradually unfolded and released, and the clarinet came in, carrying the part of the voice, she remembered the fortress of Clissa, standing up insubstantial as a shadow thrown on a wall against the paleness of Mount Mossor; remembered how darkly the river broadened to the sea as they came drifting round the bend of the Ombla, and she sang to please Nicholas; remembered that scrawled and panic-stricken postscript to his note of farewell. But these things, she thought, pulling her mind away from the intruding images, were not what the song meant –

they were just its pilgrims, a train of rather pitiful disciples, attached to it only by her remembering heart. The music meant something different. And suddenly, as happens sometimes to thoroughly unmusical people who listen with the heart, at the bidding of the unfolded harmonies a picture sprang out in her mind, as clear and unexpected as that picture of the town which sprang out under the ship's searchlights the night she and Nicholas came down the coast – a picture so lovely that she closed her eyes against quick tears. It was of Linnet and Nicholas, those two so terribly dear to her, coming up hand in hand from some shore, bounded by a wide-flung blue horizon, in their faces that grave look of absolute security and rapture which is the song's meaning. How strange this was – though the real pair were sitting just opposite to her, only hidden by her lowered eyelids, this picture had far more intensity, as if seen under a brighter light, than their living faces only a few seconds before. And it was lovely, this vision, and peaceable – so lovely and so peaceable that it was taking all that desperate and humiliating pain away. She breathed deeply, testing herself for loss of pain, as one does when morphia begins to take effect. No – it was gone. The music was sealing up its secret again, at the close; but now she held the core of the secret within her. She opened her eyes, as it came to an end. Nicholas came over and took her cup. 'More coffee, Lady K.?' he asked.

'No, thank you, Nicholas.'

'How awful the coffee was at Clissa,' he said, sitting down beside her. 'Do you remember?'

The words and tone were like a hand held out. (One must take a hand held out, but neither cling to it, nor press it.)

'Yes – simply frightful. Nicholas, do show Linnet the sketch you did of the pink flowers at Clissa – she'd love to see it.'

'Your sketches were better, and they give more of an idea of the whole place.'

'Well, fetch mine down too, and show her the whole lot.' And for the rest of the evening she watched the two heads, the yellow and the dark, bent together over the sketchbooks. She could do this now with a sort of satisfied calm. To her surprise she found herself once remembering the sickroom at Komolac, with the monkey tree outside the window, and Nicholas playing feebly with her unresisting hand. That was odd, because this was not really in the least the same; except – yes, that once more she had fought her way into freedom from the tyranny of her own feelings. And she smiled then, so that Walter asked what the joke was. 'I was thinking of the way Teddy talks,' was all she said. She had been thinking that Teddy's way of expressing her thought just then would undoubtedly have been 'Freedom is the ticket!'

At bedtime Linnet followed her Mother into her room and gave her that very unwonted thing, an uninvited kiss, as she said good night. Having said good night, however, she did not go to bed – she hung about, fiddling with her Mother's toilet things and the new silver jewellery, and chattering. 'Lapad *was* lovely, Mums,' she observed presently; 'this is a lovely place. I wish that old steamer wasn't coming back tomorrow night – I should have liked to stay here another week. There's such masses to see.' Grace agreed. Linnet, still dangling the silver necklace, pouring it from one hand to the other, seemed unable to leave the room – presently she came over to her Mother, and draped the splendid ornament across her breast, from shoulder to shoulder, like an alderman's chain. 'You look like the Lord Mayor!' she said, with a soft giggle, and went on, without any pause – 'Mums, Nicholas is rather a pearl, you know.'

'I know he is, rabbit,' said Grace, amused, startled and touched at this *démarche.*

'Is he coming to Netherstoke this summer, or are we too afraid of being involved in the General?' Linnet went on.

'Oh, I've told him he must come to Netherstoke – I don't think we need worry about the General.'

Linnet continued to drape and re-drape the necklace across her Mother's figure – Grace waited for what was to come next; she had never seen the child as shy as this. At last, in a sort of burst – 'He says you've made him the man he is!' she said, laughing.

Grace respected that laugh, a shield to cover embarrassment – she laughed too as she said 'Nicholas talks a great deal of nonsense, as you'll find out in time!'

The girl gave her a quick look, half-questioning, half-startled; she seemed to find some reassurance in her Mother's face, for –

'Yes, but not *all* the time, you funny Mums!' she said. And with that she gave Grace a quick hug and ran off, letting the door slam in her haste to be gone. The next second she put her head in again – 'So sorry – it was a accidents!' she said, quoting an old baby phrase of Teddy's – and was off again.

Grace went out onto her balcony – the bedroom, large as it was, seemed too small to contain her happiness just then. What a heaven on earth it was when the child treated her like that! This was like the old Linnet, the Linnet of a year ago, with whom all was happiness and ease, whose little silly sentences and jokes spelt love and tenderness, however carefully disguised. She leant on the rail of the balcony, looking across at San Lorenzo, immense and white in the moon, and remembering the astounding things that Nicholas had said to her two nights ago, when they looked at it together from the little promenade, she thought – 'Nicholas has done this for me, the dear child. *My* dear child!' What a complete, an overwhelming return this was for anything she had ever done or tried to do for him – to give her back Linnet's love and approbation. For she was sure he had done it, somehow. Dear, darling boy!

She was still out on the balcony when she heard her door open. 'Grace?' Walter's voice said.

'Yes – come in. I'm mooning out here.' She turned back into the room to meet him. How splendid he was to look at, Walter, with his distinguished face under his grizzled hair, and that curious combination of lordliness and sensitiveness in his expression. She gave him a cigarette – he lit it, and wandered about looking at her paintings, asking which were the two Breuil had just bought. 'How long did that take you?' he asked, indicating the one of the irises.

'About three days – no, four.'

'I call that easy money – a hundred and fifty pounds for four days' work.'

'You're talking like the General!' she told him.

Walter put the picture back in its place.

'Linnet seems to be getting on rather well with that nice boy of yours,' he next observed.

'Yes, I know – I mean I think so too. But don't *watch* them, Walter, even in your mind; let them be. It would be so lovely if anything were to come of it.'

Walter looked rather oddly and doubtfully at her, at that. She saw his face, and realised what he was thinking. 'Yes, *lovely*,' she repeated, going over to him as she spoke, and nodding her head at him. He threw his cigarette out through the doors onto the balcony and took her by the shoulders, studying her face; she faced him with such clear sincerity and security that he knew that she spoke the truth, though the tears gathered in her eyes. She nodded her head again, instead of speaking, and the tears fell. 'He's such a darling, Walter – that's why I'm so silly,' she said, still looking at him steadily. 'Give me your hanky.'

He gave it her. 'I think you've done both those children rather well,' he said gravely, and putting his arm round her shoulders, he kissed her. The grave tone of approbation, the kiss – the first he had given her since they met again, the first real kiss for so, so long – moved her to an extraordinary depth of happiness.

'You must have managed the boy rather cleverly to leave him so unscathed,' Walter went on.

'Oh Walter, I was so worried. I didn't know what to do about him, and I'd no one to ask but the Professor, and he had such very foreign ideas. But I think it has worked all right.'

'I think it's worked all right, too,' he said, and kissed her again. Then he looked amused. 'Poor old Professor!'

'What's wrong with the Professor?'

'The same trouble as Nicholas, my dear.'

'Walter, what *utter* rubbish! No, how can you say such things?' She was quite vexed. 'It's completely absurd.'

But Walter merely looked naughty. 'You've had a thoroughly devastating journey,' he said impenitently, his whole face sparkling with mischief, as it used to do – 'it's high time I took you home.' In spite of her vexation the old teasing was music in her ears. Walter went on, in an altered tone – 'He's very good value, your Professor – he's perfectly first-class. And he'll be all right; he's a philosopher by trade. You've done him nothing but good – he said so.'

'*Said* so?' She looked her astonishment.

'Yes – he said you'd taught him quite a lot.'

'Walter, that's nonsense too – he was teaching me all the time.' But she remembered the Professor's words to her about Walter; they must have talked about her – the Professor and Walter being what they were, they had probably said everything in the world! He's done *us* rather well, too! she thought – he's shown me how to get freedom, and now I suppose he's converted Walter as well. 'Dear Professor,' she said aloud.

'Yes, he's rather a discerning person,' Walter said. Then he put his arm round her again and gave her another kiss – the kiss of strong abiding affection, such a kiss as *anciens amants* exchange through the completing years.

'All the same, one wouldn't really have expected *you* to be the person to ensnare a philosopher, would one, Miss Stanway?' said Walter.